THE HAUNTING OF ABNEY HEIGHTS

CAT THOMAS

Gwillion Press

For Paul, with love

CONTENTS

PROLOGUE

I've been hunting down the dead for a long time now. They can be evasive. They can seem out of reach. Yet, nearly always, when you've been chasing them for so long you despair of catching them, something happens. They suddenly stop, turn around and look at you.

In that instant, you know you've got them; you see who they are.

This time was different. I got them, oh, I really got them; it wasn't that. It was – that they got me; and they wouldn't let me go. Still haven't.

Maybe they never will.

You have ways of protecting yourself in this job. Otherwise the dead will take you over. They get into your dreams and fill up the crevices in your day. Make you their advocate. Haunt you. That's a rookie problem – a bit of experience, and you learn ways of distancing yourself.

But this time that didn't work. It all went horribly, spectacularly, wrong.

. . .

So I have to try to make sense of what happened. I'm gathering it all together – the diaries, letters, newspaper cuttings, journal articles, emails and surviving text exchanges – everything that matters. I've changed the texts to intelligible English and I've laid it all out in order.

I'm trying to force some meaning out of it. Then maybe I can escape from them.

Maybe.

Meghan Morgan, 10 December 2019.

CHAPTER 1

REVENANT AT THE ASYLUM

A fizzing sound and the overhead light stutters out, leaving me in the dark. Shadows on the window move, re-group and re-align themselves. From the cemetery comes the lone hooting of a tawny owl, with no mate to answer him. I shiver; feel a familiar absence.

With a flash, the light hiccups on again, so I carry on with my work.

I'm finishing the day's archiving in the cubbyhole that the developers, Monarch, put aside for me. It's off the foyer and intended for a caretaker once they've got everything up and running at Abney Heights. As it's now called.

Abney Heights is a 'Stunning Italianate building, housing a high-end complex of luxury apartments. Built around beautiful community gardens, it reflects our collaborative and green values.' According to Monarch's brochure.

According to me and anyone else round here, it's the old madhouse. Hackney's finest Victorian lunatic asylum, hidden up in the borough's northern corner of Stoke Newington.

Eccentricity's always been part of our local charm, but nowadays you don't usually get locked up for it.

Not that I'm a local any more. Unlike Monarch's development I'm not 'situated in vibrant East London, with its trendy bars and restaurants, rich history and off-beat charm.' I'm situated in rural South Wales, and all the better for it I am too.

Monarch tell me the flats in their gated community are mostly finished, some are sold and some are even occupied. I've seen the odd builder, disappearing round a corner, but I've spotted no tenants yet. The whole place feels like a film set without actors. Splendid, creepy and unconvincing.

The electrics have been on and off all day. Very high-end. It's a major pain, as sunlight barely makes it through the dusty little window of my workroom and I need the overhead light to make sense of the asylum (or psychiatric hospital, as it was later re-christened) records. Some of them are barely legible and they're all muddled up together in their boxes. They were abandoned in a damp health authority basement until recently, and it shows.

By half-five I'm plunged back into darkness; my cue to call it a day. I start packing up by the eerie glow of my laptop.

It's gloomier than ever this evening, with inky clouds blocking the feeble autumn light. The owl calls again, fainter this time, as if he's running out of hope. I pull myself and my belongings together, navigating my way out of the room by the sinister torchlight of my phone.

The massive oak front doors are electronic so they haven't worked since yesterday afternoon. I leave the dark foyer through the tradesman's entrance again, down the shadowy stairs to the basement and out the back of the building. What did the tradesmen bring in when it was an asylum, I wonder? Dirty washing to keep the lunatics busy in the laundry? Coal for the feeble fires?

Out in the cold and the pissing rain, I pull my hood up and scuttle round to the front. I look up at the gates. Big, robust wrought-iron barriers, to keep out people who lack the developers' collaborative and green values. I wave my key fob over the control panel.

The gates stay stubbornly in place.

They're electronic.

I try again and again. Swear a lot. Call Monarch, get their perky answerphone, swear some more. Jesus. I had so many misgivings about work dragging me back down to Hackney; the last place on earth I want to be. But even my worst imaginings didn't include getting locked in an asylum on my second day here. I'm about to retreat to my cubbyhole, where at least it's dry, when a figure appears on the other side of the gates. Tallish, casually dressed, messenger bag slung crossways over broad shoulders. Even through the waterfall he's vaguely familiar.

When his key fob fails, he looks at the ten-foot-high gates thoughtfully, then jumps up and climbs over them with enviable ease.

'Third time I've had to do that this month.' He stands there looking at me through the downpour. Humorous dark eyes, light-brown face, close-shaved head. Much as he looked twenty years ago. A few life lessons about the mouth, maybe.

'You need some help to get out?'

I gaze up at the gates I've no chance of scaling, even with help, and my hood falls back from my face.

A whoop of surprise. 'No! Meghan Morgan. What you doing here, Mogs?'

Antoine Byrne. Still impossibly cool. Still irritatingly likeable, despite that. Only rich as well now, if he's living here. Even Antoine's been gentrified.

So, proper hugs all round, although I'm not naturally huggy

and it's a bit wet for that sort of thing. Haven't seen him since school – so, you know, bit of a thing. Or at least, I haven't seen him since my mother's funeral, but that doesn't count because I barely spoke to anyone. Let alone hugged them.

When he finds out I'm working at Abney Heights and trying to escape round the corner to my digs, he invites me back to get dry, eat something. Tell him what I've been up to all this time.

'The electricity'll be working again soon. It's just moody.' That's Antoine, ever the optimist.

We re-enter by the door I painstakingly secured with all five locks, minutes ago. Back up the narrow basement stairs.

Naturally the lift's out. 'Tell me you're not in the penthouse,' I say, as we cross the gloomy marble foyer and head for the broad sweep of the grand main staircase.

'Sorry, mate,' Antoine's laugh echoes creepily around the dark entrance hall. 'It's only five flights.'

I stop for a moment and look up the shadowy stairwell before we ascend. Abney Asylum had specialised in the treatment of the young. Did those poor child lunatics patter up and down these stairs, maybe even slide down the inviting mahogany banisters? I feel them watching us from darkness, whispering to each other. Listening.

MONARCH'S BROCHURE goes on about the 'wow factor' of their apartments, so I'm careful not to say 'wow' when we step through the door to Antoine's living room.

'You've come up in the world.' We grew up on the same estate, the Edgar Allen Poe, so the only way is up, really. Still, this place is a big leap on the ladder. Even in the grey evening light it looks swish. When he fires up the candles, still dotted round the room since the last power cut (or romantic evening), it looks sensational.

Soft candlelight reflects back from gleaming metal and wood surfaces. It's sumptuous, beguiling. Huge sofas promise comfort. A wall of glass transforms us both into golden ghosts, hovering above the trees of the woodland cemetery behind the building.

'We were the first ones in, six months ago. Wasn't exactly my idea ...' He looks pleased with himself, but a bit sheepish. Gestures to one of the squishy sofas. I take up his offer and discover it's as comfy as it looks.

'Posh girl?' I ask, from my luxurious perch.

He nods as he heads for the kitchen area. Posh girls have always been Antoine's weakness. Even at infant school.

'Still around?'

He shakes his head. Mournful. Embarrassed. 'Didn't stay long after we moved in. Mum reckons the place is cursed. Wants me to get Father Dom round to chase out the evil.' He opens the enormous American fridge. 'Drink?'

'Ooooh, re-fillable microbrewery bottles. Get you.'

He deposits beer and glasses on his upcycled coffee table, which appears to be a piece of old railway truck complete with wheels. 'So you working for Monarch? Thought you were an academic, researcher or something?'

I grapple with a flip-top ceramic stopper which opens with a satisfying pop. 'Long time ago. Now I'm your local community archivist. For the next three months anyway. Sorting out the old psychiatric hospital records, so Monarch can put them online. It's their sop to local history, creating an asylum archive. Council made them do it, part of the planning deal.'

He brightens. 'Heard about that. Any good stories?'

'Still a Hackney hack then? *Comet*?'

'Editor though. So are there? Any good stories?'

He's got that keen look he used to have when he ran the school paper at St Expiditus. I'm back to being fourteen, trying to impress him with my article about the Newbury Bypass protests, only to have him edit down my careful truths and make them flashy. Reporting isn't a soapbox, Meg, he'd say. There has to be a story.

'Hard to say. I'm a genealogist by trade, and one of my clients had a great-aunt in the asylum during the early twentieth century. That's the lead I'm following. The archiving work kind of happened to me when I contacted the health authority to look at the records.'

'She interesting then, this great-aunt? Is she our story?'

Our story. Realising I'm flattered by that, I pull myself up. I'm not awkward Mogs Morgan now, trailing after my cool mate, in my Niko trainers from Ridley Road market. I'm not tragic Meg, either, with her 'difficult' home background. I don't need the reflected glamour of Antoine's friendship to save me from the social dustbin any more. I'm grown up, independent, happily divorced Dr Morgan, with my own micro-business, house, and garden, complete with organic veg patch. I am *so* not reverting to being Antoine's swotty sidekick just because I'm back in Stokey.

'We—ll. She died mysteriously. Broke her neck. Fell, jumped or was pushed ... from your roof terrace, probably.'

He doesn't flinch.

'Let's see your source, then.'

HACKNEY COMET

25 JUNE 1907

Report of Coroner's Inquest

Our coroner, Mr P. Oswald, held an inquest at Abney Lunatic Asylum on Monday evening. Mr J. Perkins was chosen foreman of the jury. The inquest concerned the death of Emmanuella Hope Murray, spinster, aged twenty-nine years, who died at the asylum last Thursday.

Being seated at the front, your faithful *Comet* reporter was able to observe that all the witnesses appeared saddened and uneasy about this tragic death.

Martha Siskins, the Asylum Matron, spoke first. She deposed that on Thursday evening, twentieth June, an attendant, Nell Smith, ran to tell her that Miss Murray had not appeared for dinner. Matron Siskins went to the gentlewoman inmates' dining room, where she found two ladies present, Miss Englethorpe and Mrs Fitzherbert. Miss Englethorpe said she had not seen Miss Murray since luncheon, when the deceased had complained of a headache and repaired to her room after the meal. Mrs Fitzherbert claimed that last time she had seen the deceased, Miss Murray had been cavorting with Satan in the graveyard.

There was whispering and some laughter at this point. This led the coroner to remind the public of the serious and tragic nature of the proceedings and to order quiet.

Matron Siskins told us she then went to Miss Martin's bedroom, sending Nell Smith to look for her in the airing court where the inmates took their exercise. The deceased was not found in either place. Thinking Miss Murray had escaped, Matron Siskins then sounded the alarm. Doctor Charles Wood, the superintendent, quickly appeared, followed by more attendants. They mounted a thorough search of the asylum itself and of the grounds.

Matron Siskins and Nell Smith were searching the gardens at the back of the building when they discovered Miss Murray's body lying in a shrubbery, close to the asylum wall. The deceased lay on her front with her head to one side. Her limbs appeared twisted. Matron Siskins sent for Dr Wood.

Next to take the witness stand was Nell Smith, appearing nervous and scared. Miss Smith deposed that when Miss Murray did not appear for dinner, she had a premonition that something terrible had happened. She ran as fast as she could to find Matron. Miss Smith asserted that when she searched the airing court it was empty, yet echoed with a ghostly whispering. When pressed by the coroner she admitted that this could have been the wind in the trees. Mr Oswald asked her to relate only the facts of the case.

Miss Smith then claimed that she knew the alarm bell to be a death knell as soon as she heard it ring. She said as much to Matron at the time and Matron told her not to be a fool. But she was not a fool because the lady *had* died, she asserted. What is more, Miss Smith had been drawn to the shrubbery at the back of the asylum during the search, in a way that she could not explain and that is how they had discovered the body. Mr Oswald again entreated her to cover only the facts. He instructed the clerk not to record Miss Smith's account of her own psychic powers and the jury to disregard them.

There was muttering and a little laughter at this intervention. Miss Smith continued that when she approached the laurel bushes, she saw the deceased's hand and arm stretched out from under the shrubs. 'It was like she was pleading with me to come and find her, your honour,' Miss Smith said. She added that the deceased's wrist bore two small puncture marks, which resembled the bite of a savage foreign animal, like the ones in Mr Bostock's menagerie. She ended her colourful statement by saying that, in death 'Miss Murray's face was white as curdled milk and blood trickled from the corner of her mouth.'

Dr Wood attested that on arrival at this scene, he found Miss Murray to be dead. He judged she had been so for less than one hour. He attributed her death to impact injuries cause by her fall from the building. A thorn bush in the shrubbery was the most likely cause of the puncture wounds Miss Smith mentioned.

Dr Wood recounted that he had been treating the deceased for severe agitation, hypermanic episodes and persecution fantasies for four months. Miss Murray had made significant progress in that time. She was a British lady, of good character, who had lived for some years in the United States of America.

Dr Wood stated that the building's roof terrace was occasionally used by himself and his guests. Its door was always locked and the key hung in his study. This key was found to be missing and was discovered in the keyhole of the door itself.

The coroner asked if Miss Murray was ever on the roof terrace. Dr Wood replied that as a gentlewoman inmate, Miss

Murray regularly attended tea parties in the parlour adjoining the terrace. Mixing socially with others of her class from outside the institution, under Dr Wood's professional guidance, was a modern form of treatment for her illness, he said. In good weather they had tea on the terrace. Miss Murray had been taken with the views over the Abney Park woodland. She felt close to God there, she told the alienist.

Mr Oswald asked if Miss Murray knew where the key to the terrace was kept. Dr Wood replied that he did not know how she could have found that out. The foreman of the jury interjected that the key did not seem to him sufficiently protected from the patient. Dr Wood responded that the Commissioners in Lunacy inspection had considered all the asylum security procedures acceptable. He added that, in any case, only his four gentlewoman patients could access the fourth floor, where his study was situated, and none were severe cases.

Mr Oswald asked Dr Wood if he thought Miss Murray had jumped from the roof terrace on purpose. He replied that although she had been disturbed, and even aggressive at times, she had never shown any suicidal tendencies.

The jury returned a verdict of 'Accidental Death'.

DR WOOD'S DIARY
17 FEBRUARY 1907

Now that I am embarking on a new project, I resolve to keep a research diary concerning the patients involved. This will differ markedly from my standard clinical case notes, being more personal, subjective and experimental. I am intrigued by the work of Professor Freud in Vienna, and wish to explore an approach influenced by some of his ideas. I have tried to use the talking cure with my young parish inmates, but they are not articulate and inclined to keep secrets. Perhaps I will have more success in this area with my new private patients, who are all adult women. In documenting their treatment, I will retell the accounts they give of themselves and their pasts. I will also examine my own response, as the new discipline of psychoanalysis suggests we should. As a scientist, I will attempt to be as accurate as possible, but naturally I shall employ some degree of discretion. Parts of this diary may one day be published, like the journals of other scientific innovators.

Miss Emmanuella Murray, the first patient in this project, arrived at our asylum yesterday. I shall be admitting three other gentlewoman inmates in the coming weeks. They are to be accommodated on the fourth floor, two storeys up from my parish patients. As well as having private bedchambers, the ladies will have their own drawing room and dining room, where I shall sometimes join them. To further re-acquaint them with the normal manners and behaviour of society, I shall invite them to take tea with my friends, in my quarters. I am pleased to note that the Asylum Board has supported this exciting new private patient project with enthusiasm. All the refurbishment of the ladies' rooms has been generously carried out by three board members, who own construction and furnishing companies. Others have volunteered their personal assistance in the socialisation of my patients.

My first patient, Miss Murray, is twenty-eight years old, of good family and has been a resident of California, in the United States of America, since her father moved the family there twenty years ago. Mr Murray is a lawmaker in his adopted land and a gentleman of some importance. A fellow dissenter, he supports the moral values which underpin my work at Abney Asylum and, as a forward-looking gentleman, he approves of my modern approach. He also feels the change of climate and situation afforded by the London suburbs might prove beneficial for his daughter.

From what Mr Murray tells me, my patient has suffered with persecution mania, which has made her angry, argumentative and given to episodes of violence. This aggressive behaviour renders her unable to take part in polite society. Mrs Murray despairs of ever being able to make a suitable match for her daughter and fears she will never marry.

Miss Murray's problems began some years ago, shortly after she left college. She received conventional treatment from an American alienist and her family saw some improvement. Last year, however, the terrible earthquake in San Francisco brought about a sudden and profound relapse in her mental state.

Today I undertook my first talking session with Miss Murray. She is an energetic young lady and was quite recovered from her long and arduous journey. A handsome woman, she is tall and appears physically robust, but is far too emphatic and unfeminine in her movements and stance. This may be attributed to her condition. Despite her manner, there is something pleasingly frank in the directness of her gaze. Her clothing is a little odd, even allowing for American tastes, being rather plain and unadorned, albeit well-cut and expensive.

She tells me she is pleased to be back in London. She is curious about my asylum and the area around it. I asked if she missed California and she looked immediately unhappy and haunted. She said she was sad to leave her family, particularly her little niece, of whom she is very fond, but not to leave her home. She has not been happy there, of late.

Miss Murray then became agitated and began to pace around the room, muttering to herself and shaking her head. Her excess energies would make her an ideal candidate for an innovative treatment I wish to trial, which involves restoring health by channelling patients' restlessness into spiritual communication. Yet I fear she lacks the sensitivity this new method requires, despite being a woman of strong faith.

I asked her to sit down and talked to her about our asylum Sunday service, led sometimes by a lay minister and sometimes by members of the board. Would she like to contribute? She was intrigued by this idea and gradually grew a little calmer. Whatever she may have suffered in the New World, I am confident I will be able to offer her some cure at Abney.

CHAPTER 2

GHOSTS IN MY HEAD

While Antoine reads the two accounts of Emmanuella Murray's life and death, I press my nose against the glass doors leading to his rooftop garden. The place where Emmanuella crossed the border between said life and death. Behind his rainswept terrace, the trees of Abney Park form sinister black outlines against a grey sky. They sway slightly. They watch.

'Did Monarch mention its deathly history when they sold you the place?'

His reflection looks slightly uncomfortable. 'Might have been next door's terrace.'

'Fifty per cent chance then. Your flat was probably the parlour where Wood had his therapeutic tea parties.' I turn back from the terrace. 'Entertaining posh ladies. How times change.'

'Yeah, now I'm entertaining you.' He sits up, squares his shoulders. 'You can't rattle me, Meg. Wood might have been into "spiritual communication", but you know I don't buy all that stuff.'

Neither of us did. Never had. Not like our mums, off to their spiritualist meetings together, to raise the dead. That had provoked much superior youthful eye-rolling on our part.

'Question is,' there's a newshound glint in his eye, now, 'did she jump or was she pushed?'

I sensibly point out that it was more likely to be an accident. She could have had a panic attack, got confused. Passed out.

'Or she might have been murdered.' He was beginning to like the idea that his home was a homicide site. As long as there was a story in it. 'What else do you know about her?'

I tell him I'm just starting out, so not much more, yet, apart from what's on her birth and death certificates. She kept a journal, which I'll get from my client, Betty, any day now and there'll be more case reports in the asylum papers. He perks up at the idea of an Edwardian lady's diary, hoping for secrets and dreams. I haven't the heart to tell him that Betty can't make any sense of it, so it's probably just an engagement diary. Tea with J, pay the M, P's bday.

He wants to know if she's buried in London

'Ho yes. In your backyard. Abney Park Cemetery.'

Antoine looks a tiny bit creeped out, then the excitement of a news story takes over again. 'Even better. There's our photo, atmospheric tumble-down grave, lots of ivy, *Edwardian Murder Mystery* headline.'

Again, I don't like to tell him that her grave's a bland, tidy marble affair. Anyway, aren't there enough crime stories round here? Why does he want to dig up – or invent – old murders?

'Ah, y'know. Hackney's more pop-up than drive-by nowadays. There's only so much mileage you can squeeze out of another microbrewery or artisan patisserie. But juicy local history, everyone loves that.'

I try not to be pleased that Antoine wants to make a story out of my humble research. I imagine Betty would be delighted to have her great-aunt immortalised in the *Hackney Comet*, judging by her first email.

To: Meghan Morgan
From: Betty Gardiner
Subject: Tracing Emmanuella Murray
Date: September 8, 2019

Hey Meghan
Greetings from foggy old San Francisco!
I wonder if you might help me? I'm looking for a British genealogist and you come recommended.

I need background information for a book I'm working on about the women in my family. My forefathers were prominent lawyers and local politicians, so they're well documented, but no one in the family knows much about the wives and daughters. It's time to set that record straight; these women deserve to have their story told.

This will be my third book. My first, on the history of San Francisco's women's movement, is still on the university Women's Studies reading list; my second, documenting the lives of sex workers during the gold rush, taught me the benefits of outsourcing background research. So I'm reaching out to you.

I'm looking for someone who can find out more about my great-aunt, Emmanuella Murray, who died in 1907. She was an inmate in Abney Asylum, in Stoke Newington, London, UK. My late mother, Violet Gardiner, told me her aunt Ella had a tragic life and I always got the impression the family thought there was something shameful about her. So, lots of fascinating content for my book there, I expect. Maybe even some family scandal if I'm lucky!

It's too far for me to travel to go through the asylum archives, so I wonder if you could take a look for me? Maybe there's more you could find out, locally, being on the ground? I also have Ella's journal, which I can't make any sense of myself. Perhaps you'll have more luck with it.

The terms you set out on your website sound reasonable and I'd be prepared to pay a little more if you can start straight away.

Looking forward to hearing from you
Warm wishes
Betty

ANTOINE'S PREPARING FOOD NOW, in his shiny metal kitchen, by the unnatural blue light of the gas hob. I watch from the sofa, like a TV audience, while he chops veg with professional flair. When did he get so capable at that stuff?

I'm pouring a second bottle of designer beer when a vision appears in a dazzling light. It has three heads, stripy legs and is furry. The vision resolves itself into a girl, who's somehow wearing a torch and carrying two enormous fluffy cats, one grey, one black. The grey one looks like he's smiling.

'Mulder and Scully want their dinner.' She speaks quickly, with a slight Eastern European inflection, her voice resonant for someone so small. Antoine introduces her as Uzi.

In a dizzying whirl of light and speed, Uzi puts down the creatures and dims her torch. Long purple hair, short puffy dress, striped tights and Docs; tiny without added cat. She looks like a Gothic Pippi Longstocking.

She turns to stare at me. 'You like cats?' she's stopped her perpetual motion and her manner is focussed and intense. Which feels slightly eerie if you're on the receiving end of it.

I tell her I'm single and knocking forty so I try not to like them too much. She carries on staring, as if a sufficiently hard look will make my top layer peel away and allow her to see my secret self. The grey cat jumps onto my knee, puts his paws on my shoulders, grins up at me. Tries to rub noses. Fishy breath.

'Mulder likes you,' says Uzi, with kindly sadism.

She whirls off to feed the creatures something smelly and turns down Antoine's offer of food. She's going out. Antoine warns her the gates aren't working, but she just shrugs. I imagine her scurrying over them like Spiderman, but she's so slight she can probably just slip through the bars.

After she leaves I let the silence thicken until he feels compelled to explain himself.

'My lodger.'

'She looks about fourteen.'

'And she's my *lodger*, Meg.' He runs a hand over his stubbled head. 'What do you think I am?'

'Her name's really Uzi?'

Ursana Ursica, he tells me. She's Romanian, describes herself as herself Transylvanian, but mainly to freak British people out. She's a postgrad student, over on some prestigious international art scholarship. He points to one of her paintings, on the wall.

I take a candle over to the canvas. In it, a human figure, whose outstretched hands are full of white flowers, is attempting to run towards me. Spectral forms clutch at the figure with clawed hands, holding them back. Nobody has a face and most of it is greenish and shadowy, apart from the flowers. Which are just creepy. It's like Chagall performed by Alice Cooper.'

'That's – not at all disturbing.'

He laughs. She's okay, he tells me. Applies herself, because life is short but art is long, apparently. Uzi and her mates are better people than we ever were at that age. They want the world to be fairer and kinder. Her partner works in the veggie café I used to drag him to, the Happy Cat.

So Mulder and Scully are from the café's cat re-homing sideline?

He shakes his head. 'They were Felicity's.'

'You got to choose the names, though.' Massive X-files fan, Antoine. Loves a good conspiracy theory.

'Felicity called them Cassiopeia and Andromeda. The banker she went off with had a Weimaraner; so I was able to reveal their true identities to them.'

'Sure they're grateful for that. Shall we fill the bottomless pit of your grief and pain with more of that fancy beer, then?'

So we try. Fortified by Antoine's exceptionally good stir-fry and designer ale, we spend an evening remembering stories about school, and crafting taller stories about our lives since. His are taller than mine. Obviously.

He tells me how he landed a job on a big daily tabloid and was there for thirteen years. Good money, prestige, but in the end the pointlessness began to weigh him down. He was offered the editorship back at the *Comet* and decided that was what he really wanted. Felicity wasn't impressed by his early mid-life crisis, however cool Hackney was nowadays. Eventually the banker became more appealing to her and she went Up West. As we don't say round here.

'So you're reduced to renting out your spare room to students to pay the mortgage?'

He shrugs. He bought his first wreck of a place back in the day, did it up, so he's not mortgaged to death, he tells me. He can afford to work somewhere he's happier.

'The *Comet* might be a local, but stuff happens here; we're the voice of Hackney all over the socials. We've got integrity, too, y'know – we've won awards. I don't have to churn out celebrity gossip or put up with the usual crap. I'm the boss, I can make it what I want. Felicity didn't get that.'

I tell him I'm happy, too, in my little witch's cottage, beside a babbling brook. I lived for a few years in a shiny new executive apartment in Cardiff Bay, but Hugo bought me out. It was never really me, anyway.

'You married someone called Hugo?' Antoine laughs so much he gets hiccups. Fair cop after all the grief I've given him about his choice of girlfriends, but still. He deserves the hiccups.

'Least Hugo didn't abandon cats,' I mutter.

He wants the story, so I tell him Hugo liked me because I was different from him: gritty urban origins, principles, all that. But then he wanted me to fit in with his dinner-party world, where you sit round talking about nothing all evening and no one ever disagrees.

Antoine laughs. 'Yeah, I got some of that with Felicity's mates. You mention something real and it's like you're being vulgar.'

'Exactly. Thing is, Antoine, you know how to disagree with people charmingly, whereas I just wade in and eviscerate their assumptions. Apparently, that's offensive. But, y'know I was an academic, that's what I'm trained to do.'

He laughs. 'Meg the dinner-party destroyer. Love it. I heard you did a degree in fairy tales somewhere up a Welsh Mountain.'

PhD in fairy tales, in fact, not just a common or garden

degree, I tell him. I stayed at St Cadog's to do post-doc work, but couldn't hack the university politics. That's when genealogy took over my life; it's research without the departmental pressures. Been doing it fifteen years now, clients all over the world. Work at home a lot, travel here and there to poke around in local records and skulk around cemeteries. Suits me.

'Get you. Doctor of all the fairies and witch of all the dinner parties. Turned dead-people detective.'

We laugh and clink glasses. I'm partly enjoying being round at Antoine's again; the other part I push away for now, aware that it will come back to haunt me. But I have good memories of being round at his place as a kid; his mum, Claudette, felt sorry for me, tried to feed me. His dad, Terry, told me hilarious stories. They were so proud when me and Antoine took First Communion together at Our Lady of the Sorrows.

Claudette knew my mum from church, tried to befriend her once we moved to the Poe. Kathleen wasn't easy to befriend, by then. She'd retreated into her romantic novels, her tranquilliser haze and her aloneness. Almost like she enjoyed it. Her only contact with the outside world was through going to mass at Our Lady with her cousin Breda, or to spiritualist meetings with Claudette.

Both church and seances were social events for most of the faithful. For Kathleen they were acts of desperation. The only way I take after my mother is that the dead are central to my life.

Despite their shared interest in saints and spirits, Claudette was a different proposition to Kathleen entirely. For a start, she was from New Orleans. How glamorous is that? Her accent turned everyday words into gold. She was lively where my mum was still, she was funny whereas my mum seldom laughed, or even smiled. She was a presence, whereas Kathleen just radiated absence. My mum called herself Irish, although she was born in London. Claudette still loved New Orleans, still felt American, but she was proud to be British too, and to be a Black Londoner. She even tried to like tea.

They both went to the same church, heard the same sermons and sang the same hymns, full of dungeon, fire and sword. But, for my mum, religion was a series of traps, of ways to be wrong; for Claudette, it was the mystery and the beauty that held her. My mum was all about the dungeon whereas Claudette was more fire and sword.

Not that Claudette was perfect. She was mega-strict and had a fierce temper when Antoine broke her rules. Which he did quite a lot, so he took shelter from the fiery fallout at my place. He envied me my autonomy. I envied him pretty much everything about his home.

As we sit in his fancy flat, we 'do you remember' the times when Antoine's charm just wasn't enough and I covered for him with Claudette, our teachers, or his girlfriend-of-the-moment. We 'do you remember' the (very few) near misses I had when working and the (not so few) times I got far too wasted in my leisure time; when he stopped things going pear-shaped for me. We were a great team, back in the day. No one suspected me of wrong-doing because I was so earnest and uncool, and everyone trusted him because he could do that innocent boyish charm thing, like his dad. Between us, we could get away with anything.

We don't 'do you remember' about Michael, even though Antoine's one of the few people who knew him.

We certainly don't 'do you remember' about Sophie.

Then, because the electricity's still off, I sleep on the sofa with Scully, despite Antoine's gallant attempt to loan me his bed. At three in the morning the lights blaze on, waking me with a sickening lurch. In the horrible brightness, I see someone at the window, pursued by people who are devouring them. But it's just the creepy picture, the beer and the evening of stories putting ghosts into my head.

UZI'S MESSAGES
17 SEPTEMBER 2019

Zana: Antoine brought a woman back

FairyGirl21: He is courting? What kind of woman?

Zana: Like a Waterhouse model, dressed to go hiking

FairyGirl21: Statuesque and red-haired?

Zana: Flaming. Childhood sweetheart

FairyGirl21: How romantic

Zana: How's your BF?

FairyGirl21: He wants me to be different.

Zana: Babe! If he loved you he wouldn't wanna to change you.

FairyGirl21: I have to be a nice, normal girl for him

Zana: Dump him

FairyGirl21: You know I can't. Don't tell anyone, but I've met someone. I like him, he listens. Only...

Zana: Only?

FairyGirl21: He wants something too. I don't know what. Something ... unwholesome

Zana: These guys of yours! Be careful hun, they're just gonna drain you

FairyGirl21: They're coming, I have to go. Love to Mulder and Scully. Love you x

Zana: You too babe x 🖤

CHAPTER 3

WHEN LUCY CEASED TO BE

Antoine calls this morning when I'm in my cubbyhole. This is getting too much like the old days, I only left his place a couple of hours ago. I've just finished an awkward call from my cousin Eileen who wants me to pick up my mother's old trunk from her parents. Up to here with work, I tell her. Monarch breathing down my neck, I tell her. Soon, I promise, soon.

So, after that, Antoine's news is light relief.

'I've found another body,' he says.

'Where?'

'Abney Park Cemetery.'

'Hold the front page.'

'No, listen, unburied. Another asylum patient. And, get this: she died in the same way and around the same time as your girl. Suspicious, huh?'

HACKNEY COMET

27 JUNE 1907

A body is discovered

Our beautiful and orderly necropolis has this week been witness to tragedy, when the recently deceased body of a young lady was discovered in Abney Park chapel.

Cemetery employee, Frederick Sydenham, discovered her body when entering the building to prepare it for a funeral on 26th June. Mr Sydenham thought he saw someone in the nave, slumped against the back row of pews. Thinking a vagrant was using this sacred place to sleep off the excesses of the gin bottle, Mr Sydenham moved forward to accost the man. He realised quickly that the figure was that of a well-dressed young lady and was, sadly, lifeless.

The deceased has been identified as Miss Lucy Patience Northaway, twenty-one years old and from Manchester. Miss Northaway's family own several mills in the north of England and she was shortly to be married to the Hon. Alfred Homeward, son of Lord Godmansworth of Suffolk.

From the medical evidence, it appears that she either fell

backward from the chapel balcony, or was cast down from it by an unknown hand. Tragically, Miss Northaway landed upon one of the sharp iron decorations on the back of the pews, which punctured her heart. This occurred some days prior to the discovery of her body.

It is not known how Miss Northaway came to be in the burial chapel, and suspicions are abroad that she was abducted and taken thence by rogues. Police investigations have been rendered difficult and unpromising, due to a lack of witnesses. The public are asked to come forward if they saw a slight, fair-haired young lady, wearing a pale-grey costume and broad-brimmed hat, in the vicinity of Abney Park, between Thursday 20th June and Monday 24th June.

She was being treated for nervous exhaustion by Dr Charles Wood, of Abney Asylum. Dr Wood told our reporter that Miss Northaway had left the asylum after a full cure, on the morning of 20th June.

CHAPTER 4

THE ANGEL OF THE ASYLUM

I read the *Comet* article twice, then sit back in my chair and stare up at the weak sunlight trickling through my dusty window. I think of Lucy Northaway leaving this building, in the midsummer sunshine, with high hopes for her future.

Or did she leave with the intention of taking her own life?

I call Antoine back. 'They must have known each other well, being locked up together like that.'

His imagination takes him straight to his headline story. 'They were both killed by the same person.'

'You don't know they were killed at all,' I reason. 'It could be suicide, or an accident.'

'Too much of a coincidence. Maybe they found something out. Had to be silenced.'

'What dangerous information are two women shut in an asylum going to uncover? Matron short-changing the laundry clients?'

'People in those places didn't have any rights back in 1907. Perhaps bad stuff was happening to them.'

I roll my eyes and see dust motes evading each other in the pale golden rays of the sun.

'Wood wasn't one of those old Victorian superintendents who chained people up and treated them as subhuman,' I say. 'He was Mr Twentieth Century. This isn't Dickens's world, this is more like E. M. Forster. It's very nearly Virginia Woolf.'

'Just because he's Mr Modern doesn't mean he's squeaky clean.'

'We've got no evidence he did anything wrong.'

'We've got two mysterious deaths.'

'It's much more likely to be suicide.'

'Who throws themselves backwards off a balcony?'

I sigh. 'Fair point, but life's just not that sensational, Antoine. People trip and fall.'

'Two friends dying like this within days of each other is beyond suspicious, you have to admit. It's your job to find out what happened.'

He's right about that.

It is my job.

'The good news,' he adds, as if presenting me with a gift, 'is that you've got me to help you.'

DR WOOD'S DIARY
5 MARCH 1907

Miss Lucy Northaway has been recently been admitted to my care by her father, a prominent northern industrialist. Her fiancé, my good friend Alfred Homeward, is also taking an interest in her welfare and is contributing to her asylum fees. This arrangement has been agreed between Homeward and Mr Northaway. It has also been approved by Homeward's aunt Ernestine, Lady Barnum, who is one of our leading board members and benefactors.

These irregular financial arrangements for Miss North-away's treatment cause me no concern as I am confident of Homeward's absolute integrity and respectability. We have been friends since Oxford, where he was a cricket blue, known for exemplary sportsmanship and absolute Christian decency. A modest chap, he is always at pains to point out to my acquaintances that he was never a 'clever blighter like Wood here' in our university days.

Homeward's family are prominent in the non-Conformist community and, although on the more conservative wing of our movement, have long been supporters of my project. Indeed, it was Lady Barnum's idea that we should admit Miss Northaway. Lady Barnum has no children, so her considerable estate will go to her nephew; consequently, she takes a close interest in his affairs.

Homeward wishes to marry his fiancée as soon as I am able to effect a cure. Now I have met the lady, I understand his haste.

Miss Northaway is a truly lovely young woman of some twenty-one years of age. In appearance she is petite and delicate, with a fair complexion and yellow hair. She dresses in a manner that is both modest and feminine. Although her condition renders her fearful and enervated, it is, on meeting her, the unaffected sweetness of her disposition that impresses one most.

Her manner is innocent and somewhat childlike; she clearly has girlish concerns about the importance of appearing proper and ladylike, which can make her appear a little prim. This I attribute to her family's manufacturing background and her imminent elevation to the aristocracy. One day she will be Lady Godmansworth and she desires to do the title justice and be a credit to her future husband. These are welcome sentiments in a female, particularly in this day and age. They also suggest she is sufficiently pliable and will follow my direction. This will prove important in our therapeutic process.

Miss Northaway suffers primarily from hysteria. In the daytime, she lacks vitality and is pale and languid. Although she has been able to perform simple teaching duties with the children, she is physically weak and cannot walk far without becoming breathless. Her appetite is poor and she is given to fainting fits. Her family are concerned about how slender she has grown.

The patient is haunted by fear and anxiety. She has difficulty sleeping, and awakes racked with terror in the early hours, believing that an evil creature has come for her in the night. Her parents report episodes of sleepwalking although, like most somnambulants, she has no recollection of this. They have consulted doctors in Manchester but none have been able to improve her physical health or appetite, or quiet her night-time horrors. She has no underlying physical ailments and it is clear to me that the origins of her problems are psychic rather than somatic.

Miss Northaway may be the ideal patient for my new spiritual communication treatment. Her unconscious energies, which present as these night-time horrors, may benefit from being siphoned off by this new method, even though she does not show an excess of vigour in the daytime. I will discuss the matter with Professor Von Helson, who has created the machine I will use in this branch of my therapeutic work.

There is more I will be able to persuade Miss Northaway to tell me about her fears, but in our first talking session I could see she was uncomfortable speaking of herself at length. She clearly felt such behaviour smacked of vanity and self-importance and feared it was not appropriate for a lady. An admirable sentiment in many ways, yet one I regard as an unconscious blocking strategy. Unchecked, it would prevent the whole process of the talking cure. Yet I am confident I will be able to change her behaviour. Miss Northaway has already come to trust me and I know she will follow my guidance.

Indeed, she is the research subject I have been waiting for. A combination of talking therapy, based on Professor Freud's model, mesmerism, experimental electro-therapy, and my pioneering use of the Spiritual Engine, will be perfect for her symptom pattern. As she is compliant, willing to please and motivated to improve, I anticipate a successful outcome.

Indeed, given the radical combination of therapies I will

use with this patient, I believe I may take forward medical knowledge in the treatment of hysteria. I get ahead of myself, but I already have a title for the case study I will publish if I succeed. It is, in the imaginative manner of Professor Freud, 'The Angel of the Asylum'.

CHAPTER 5

ORIGINAL FEATURES

S hanaz from Monarch peeks round the door of my cubbyhole, dangling keys from her manicured fingers.

'Good news, Meghan,' she beams. 'Your flat's ready. You'll be able to live near your friend now.'

Having Antoine on my team clearly comes with advantages. Shanaz's boss promised me a temporary show flat when he offered me the three-month contract. A live/work space he said, in their more affordable range, so doubtless a converted cupboard, but better than a BnB by night and the caretaker's cubbyhole by day. The office has been making excuses about it all week, but now the Byrne charm's worked with Monarch, too. Or maybe it's the Byrne journalistic ability to affect their reputation.

Although Betty happily agreed to it, I have some misgivings about giving Antoine access to the folder where I upload copies of all the documents about Ella. He seems intent on turning Ella and Lucy's deaths into a murder mystery, and I don't want my research hijacked by sensationalism. Even if he has fast-tracked my flat.

Shanaz enthuses about the many benefits of my new 'apartment', as I follow her obediently out of my office, wondering how she manages to make that long, loose cardie seem so stylish. On me it would look like I needed a pair of comfy slippers and a few cats as accessories.

We walk across the grand foyer. A place of departures and arrivals. I imagine fragile Lucy, putting on her picture hat and stepping out of the door and into the sunshine, cured and ready to start her new life. Ella, striding through the arched entrance in her austere travelling outfit, looking around with interest at the ornate tiled floor and the grand staircase. Original features, Shanaz says.

Now that it's my turn to find a temporary home here, I feel some foreboding. I pull myself together. I'm not being incarcerated. I'm joining an exclusive gated community, according to Shanaz.

Apologising for the tardiness of my inclusion among the gated, she shepherds me toward the lift. 'We've been *sooo* busy lately. Just completed a block sale of all the fourth-floor units.'

I look suitably impressed.

'Overseas investors,' she confides. When she presses the down button, I realise why magnificent views over Abney Park weren't in her litany of my new pad's attractions. No loftlets for me. I'm in the servants' quarters.

The lift judders slightly as we're lowered to the basement. In its shiny chrome doors, I notice how Shanaz's flowing cardigan contrasts subtly with her bright top and tones perfectly with her hijab. Next to her I hover murkily, an ungainly ghost. How do people achieve that casual elegance? Hugo could do it, he'd make a much better woman than me. We'd go shopping and he'd put together outfits for me. Long dresses and skirts in vibrant colours suited me, he'd say, why be so low key when I could look sensational? But unlike Shanaz, you could see I wasn't comfortable in my elegant clothes. I looked like a contestant on a dating show, dressed by the studio. So I'd wear Hugo's gear for special occasions, but for everyday I went back to dusty black.

For an ominous few moments, the lift shudders to a stop, the light flickers and Shanaz presses the button, slightly desperately. 'Just a few teething problems with the electricity.'

The doors open reluctantly and she sweeps me along to my flatlet. The front door is right opposite the entrance to the pool and gym, so I can feel guilty every time I come home with a pizza.

The flat itself is actually really nice, if small. Its front door opens straight into the pristine lounge and immaculate little open kitchen. A couple of white sofas face each other across an Ercol-effect coffee table. Textured throws adorn the sofas and a neutral fake-fur rug decorates the wooden floor. It's a tad short on natural light, but long on fashionable lampware, with stylised Edison-bulb creations perch on the side tables. A couple of big mirrors reflect what light there is. It's all tastefully uncluttered, but it won't take me long to put a stop to that. Under the window there's a little table, which will serve me nicely as a desk. Once I've conquered the flat's slightly bleak minimalism, I might even manage to feel cosy, cwtched up on a sofa with a mug of tea and a packet of Hobnobs. I remind myself I'll be home in twelve weeks; I can handle being back here until then. It'll be fine.

Black-and-white photos line the walls. Fauxtos in fact, as they're of ethereal 'Victorian' maids in white muslin, operating mangles and dolly tubs; they patently don't have the heft for such activity.

'An authentic touch,' Shanaz says. 'This was part of the laundry. The windows are original.'

I look out of the multipaned metal windows onto the

gloomy area steps. Above, I see a small pair of feet in purple Docs, speeding past on the building's forecourt.

'Listen, Meghan, any chance you can move your archive stuff down here today?' Shanaz asks as we leave the flat. 'They want to start fitting out your office for a concierge. I might be able to get someone to help you with it,' she adds, doubtfully.

I tell her I can manage the boxes myself and she looks relieved. She buzzes open the massive oak front doors, now functional. They open slowly and creepily, as if operated by an invisible doorkeeper who is reluctant to let us go. Outside is Uzi, whose feet I spied from my new basement. She's looking up at the building. Shanaz asks her how the course is going.

'I am doing good work in this place,' she replies. 'I give voice to the suffering of its past.'

'Lovely,' Shanaz beams.

Shanaz reminds me I'm due to come in and sort out the archive data categories with their intern, who needs to get on with creating the database. The council are pressurising them to get the asylum website up by Christmas; it was meant to be ready months ago. They should have employed me months ago, then, I don't say, and make dazzling promises about data structures and – lo! – even content by tomorrow. Satisfied, she bounces off back to Monarch central and I resign myself to working till midnight.

I tell Uzi I'm joining them as a resident of the madhouse. She nods, continuing to stare up at the brooding bulk of Abney Heights, with the focussed intensity she has when she pauses.

'You know it is haunted?' she says, conversationally.

I look up at it, too. Silhouetted against the grey November sky, its extravagant arches and towers certainly look sinister.

I tell her I don't believe in ghosts.

'Antoine says you are a folklore scholar. Wizards and magic.'

'I *studied* it. I didn't take it literally.'

She looks disbelieving; Uzi's the sort who can spot haunted people. I ask her what else Antoine said.

'You live in a witch's cottage and you turn men into toads.'

'That bit's true.'

Her laugh is small and sharp. 'I go for lunch at the Happy Cat. You want to come?'

Reluctant as I am to revisit a place from my past, I'm starving and I've got a long day ahead. I follow Uzi as she bleeps her way out of the big gates. She hurries across the cobbles, and through the bollards, which are meant to discourage outsiders from congregating in the gateway for nefarious purposes. Defensible space, the planners call it. We walk briskly down Manor Road towards the anarchist café. I used to go there as a teenager, I tell Uzi, when I manage to catch my breath.

'Your family still live here?' she asks.

'They died a long time ago.'

'All of them?' Uzi's even less capable of small talk than me. Or maybe she just rejects it as inauthentic.

'My brother then my father, when I was small; my mother when I was eighteen. I don't remember my grandparents.'

She doesn't flinch. 'That is sad.'

'It's all a long time ago. Plenty of kids I grew up with didn't have dads. I still have cousins round here to remind me that family isn't all it's cracked up to be.'

'Families are difficult. Mine have never accepted my choice of lovers.'

'Your partner works at the Cat?' I ask, as we approach the red and black facade.

'Rowan is my lover and friend. Not my partner. I do not believe in partners.'

'Like I don't believe in ghosts?'

Another quick, unsettling laugh. 'It is not for me.'

'Rowan okay with that?'

Uzi shrugs. 'They accept me as I am.'

Antoine didn't mention Rowan's non-binary. Probably thought it uncool to say. The pillock.

We eat vegan comfort food in the packed café. I've just finished a Mexican novel so I order tacos. I'm massively influenced by what people eat in books, I tell Uzi. Those lady stories where all the action takes place over afternoon tea are a disaster for my five-a-day.

'You drink blood when you read vampire novels?' she asks and I tell her I stick to cranberry juice.

I eye the punters as I eat, realising the place has become fashionable in my absence. Quite a few twenty-something creatives, having lunch with their Macs, and visitors to London who've found it on restaurant apps. All the crusties have disappeared, although there's still a sprinkling of the café's traditional Rasta clientele, tucking into their ital. There's a display of craft objects and plant-based chocolate, instead of the anarchist bookshelf; pictures for sale on the wall by local artists, instead of animal rights posters. On the table behind me, two girls hold an intense conversation about food and self-care.

Rowan turns out to be a calm, serious sort of person, possibly even younger than Uzi, but with a certain kind of hippyish gravitas. Can't imagine Rowan would be a polyamory sort of person, but maybe I'm a romantic antique. With a mass of earrings, shaved head and fatigues, Rowan would have looked at home in the Cat of my teens. Most importantly, I detect a South Wales accent.

'I'm visiting from Monmouthshire,' I say.

Rowan brightens. 'I'm from Abergavenny.'

'You miss it?' I ask.

'My life's here at the moment.' Level grey eyes flick towards Uzi. 'I miss the countryside, mind. One day I'll go back.'

'Rowan is involved in nature politics. Extinction Rebellion,' Uzi tells me, as Rowan disappears to get our coffees. 'Mostly Animal Rebellion. That is how we met.'

'You do eco politics?' Uzi's nothing like the Greens round my way; can't see her hoeing a row of organic parsnips.

'I do resistance through my work. Sometimes I join protests about the rights of animals.'

Rowan appears again and puts mugs of oat latte in front of us. 'Have you seen Uzi's work? She's really talented.' Taking out a phone, they click and scroll with long-fingered, capable-looking hands. All their movements are calm, careful, economical. Big contrast to Uzi's dizzying speed and disturbing pauses. Rowan's built on a much larger scale than Uzi too.

As I flick, Rowan says, 'You have to see the originals to get the full impact, that screen isn't big enough.'

I peer at intense paintings, often collaged with photos. Humanoid figures, animals, plants and landscapes tumble together. They all have the eerie, unsettling atmosphere of the picture on Antoine's wall. Rowan's right, Uzi definitely has something; I can see why she's been awarded a fancy scholarship. Not sure I'd want her artwork lurking in my home, though.

'How are your murder investigations going then?' Rowan asks, after I've praised the images sufficiently. 'Antoine was talking about it,' they add, carefully, seeing my surprise. 'He read us some of Dr Wood's diary and stuff.'

Antoine should have bleeding well asked me before he broadcast my work. Inaccurately, too. 'He's jumping to conclusions,' I tell them. 'Their deaths could have been accidental.'

'Then Abney Heights would not be so haunted,' Uzi insists. 'Dr Wood was responsible, I think. He wanted to use Lucy's illness to help his career; he exploited her. He is a misogynist, also.'

'Not for the time,' I say. 'His ideas about how to cure people with mental health problems were radical.'

Rowan considers this, nodding slowly. 'Lucy was colluding with him, mind. All that obedient, compliant stuff.'

Uzi frowns. 'This is according to Wood.'

'Fair points,' I say. Maybe Antoine was right to tell Uzi and Rowan. Good to get other perspectives, and they're nearer in age to Lucy and Ella than we are. They're thinking about it properly, too, and taking it all much more seriously than Antoine. I'll see if Betty's okay with their involvement.

I buy a supply of soya wax candles because I can see I'm going to need them in my new flatlet, and a few bars of vegan chocolate because it would be rude not to. Coming for lunch here has been less disturbing than I expected because it's all changed so much.

Which is disturbing in itself.

Uzi and I make our way back along Manor Road, where a woman is shouting at cars. Murderers! Their fumes are killing us, she tells us. We agree and continue along the road. Hatted and overcoated Haredi teenagers hurry by us; while adolescent corner boys – low-slung pants, carefully styled hair – flick their eyes over us and return to talking, observing and posturing. Uzi exchanges greetings with a wiry, eighty-something bloke called Henry, in a daffodil-yellow zoot suit and fedora. A jazz musician, she tells me.

Things have changed round here, but it's stayed the same in its multi-layered eccentricity. Radically different parallel realities still coincide in the same space. It's a place with no centre ground; the opposite of Middle England. The comfortable, familiar oddness draws me back in. *This is your home*, it whispers. Yet I feel a fragmenting sensation that's anything but comforting. Being back in this place makes me feel like I'm still the unfinished, damaged girl who was formed here; shaped by absence and loss. The person I am now, I've created since I left. She might not be polished or particularly normal, but she's a fully functioning human being. A cold wind blows down the street; I pull my jacket tightly around me. *This is not my home*, I tell myself. *I've moved on.*

Uzi's talking about Ella and Lucy. What had it been like for them to have been imprisoned in Abney Heights, albeit in a genteel way?

'Not having your freedom must have been suffocating,' I say. 'I'm not sure about the electro-therapy and Wood's 'Spiritual Engine', but otherwise the asylum regime sounds fairly benign. Whatever you think of Wood, he did cure Lucy. Maybe Ella, as well.'

'I think they helped each other to become well. Wood just locked them up and did his experiments on them.'

As we enter our defensible space and she bleeps open the security gates to the building, I feel uneasy. Is locking the world out of this place any different to locking people in it? How are the excluded supposed to feel about it? And how does it affect the gated? Do they all end up watching the world fearfully from their luxury flats, feeling anxious and besieged?

I'm shaken from my dark thoughts by the excitement of a parcel with a San Francisco postmark in my mailbox. I tear it open to find a battered brown notebook. Ella's journal. Now we can begin to find out what really happened all those years ago.

DR WOOD'S DIARY

10 MARCH 1907

Miss Murray, or Ella, as she has asked me to call her, has now been with us for a month and is much improved. She is calmer, able to converse normally, and has fewer episodes of agitation and anger. Whilst under my care she has had none of the violent episodes her father mentioned. She is still quick to imagine conspiracies against her, but has gained some awareness that these may not be real.

Her mood has particularly shifted since the arrival of a fellow patient, the charming and beautiful Miss Lucy Northaway. They quickly became close friends, and the sweetness of Lucy's disposition has a soothing effect on Ella – as it has on everyone around her. Myself included.

Ella has been giving readings at our prayer meetings for some weeks and has now begun to take part in other useful activities. Lucy and one of our other lady patients, Miss Englethorpe, have taken over some of the children's teaching, which was previously carried out by church volunteers. Miss Murray has now joined her friend in this proper endeavour.

With my supervision, she has begun to instruct the children in drill.

In her classes she teaches calisthenics and an American version of rounders. Ella has some knowledge of botany, so she also takes the children on nature walks around the grounds. Although she has less patience with them than Lucy, her enthusiasm for sport and nature is infectious and they are benefitting from her tuition.

It is no easy task to teach children whose behaviour is so little governed by reason; they can be a chaotic, unruly rabble. Yet under Ella's guidance, they have become less rowdy and more biddable. Such is the calming effect of physical activity on the mind. They are also learning to cooperate with one other and follow simple rules. One of our most troublesome girls, Florence Azikiwe, has made herself Ella's second-in-command. The orphaned daughter of an Irish washerwoman and an African seaman, she is a delusional child, unable to distinguish truth from lies. For example, although she was found roaming the streets of Whitechapel, she claims her grandfather was a prince. Yet even Florence's mental state and behaviour has begun to improve since she started drill classes. Her aggressive behaviour has become more moderate and she demands less attention. Ella, too, is benefitting from this useful work by learning the Christian values of self-control and patience.

I am pleased with Ella's efforts yet have had to rein her in, in some regards. I found that on her nature walks she was encouraging the children to climb trees. This is dangerous for all of them and completely unsuitable for girls. What's more, it may encourage them to try to escape over the asylum wall. Naturally, I stopped her at once. This episode has led me to observe the extent to which Ella is inclined toward risk-taking and is unable to govern her impulses in a manner proper for a lady. We will work on this.

We have spoken of her ambition to spend time on the Continent when she recovers. Her family would permit this, she thinks, if she can find a suitable travelling companion. She is taken with the idea of Paris, a city she has read much about and one she would dearly love to explore. Her great hope is that her niece may be allowed to join her, to learn French, if she settles in Paris for a while.

Today, because of her improved condition, I asked Ella more about California. Previously, she became too disturbed whenever I mentioned her life there, so in the talking sessions we have concentrated more on her current feelings and on her dreams, which have sometimes been violent and distressing.

It was when she was describing a dream she had last night, that the subject of her American home arose. In this dream she was in her parents' house in San Francisco, where they lived before the earthquake. Her family were absent, and the house was shadowy and full of menace. Servants flitted in and out, but they had become odd creatures with hostile faces and she could not call on them for aid. She ran from room to room, trying to escape from the house, her fear and anxiety increasing. She gradually came to realise the horrible truth: all the doors to the outside world had disappeared. She banged on the windows, but passers-by either ignored her, or smiled and waved, which made her desperation worse. As she ran through the rooms, she repeatedly thought she had found an external door. Hurrying toward it, she was again confronted with an image of herself; it was another one of the huge looking-glasses that decorated the walls. Yet she continued to believe that each new mirror might provide her with escape, and was continually bitterly disappointed.

I asked her if she had ever felt imprisoned in her parents'

house in real life. She replied that she thought she had more freedom there than ladies have in England. She received a good education and on leaving college had mixed socially with other educated ladies and gentlemen. Among these friends she had been able to speak her mind without censure, and they enjoyed lively discussions. Although her mother did not wholly approve of Ella's friends, thinking them too unconventional, she was not prevented from spending time with them. She also joined them in many energetic activities, enjoying horse riding, bicycling and long hikes.

I asked her more about her parents' house and it became apparent that her dream house was in some ways unlike the family home. It was grander, she said. There were fewer books and far more mirrors. When I asked her who might be in this house she became agitated and in the end required sedation.

I am intrigued by this house of mirrors. I believe it may hold the key to Ella's troubles, if only she can find the courage to return to it in her mind and face the horror which lurks within.

CHAPTER 6

SECRETS AND CODES

I trace the writing on the cover with my finger. *The Journal of Ella Murray*. Her script is bold and firm, the ink still dark. This book hasn't seen much sun.

With mounting excitement, I open it. Ella's first entry is dated March 11, 1907, in the same resolute hand, so it's definitely a record of her time at the asylum. After that, well. Betty was being literal when she said it made no sense to her. The first line reads:

c vh jkr rbe fcjl kt wkhvj wbk feemq v dkspjvg. c lk jkr wcqb rk wpcre viksr rbe

My disappointment is bitter. I'm puzzled too; Ella came here to have the darkest recesses of her thoughts and dreams revealed. Why would she write in code?

Uzi just shrugs. 'Perhaps it is better that some secrets are hidden,' she says, and hurries off back to her work.

Back in my cubbyhole, I throw the useless journal onto my desk. On top of my frustration, I'm annoyed at what Betty's expecting of me. Code-cracking isn't an obvious part of a genealogist's job description, but this isn't the first time I'd been asked to decrypt ancestors' private papers. It's not the sort of thing that comes naturally to me and my success rate hasn't been great. Some years back, my geeky librarian friend, Charlie, taught me how simple ciphers work, but even she hasn't been able to help with some of my tougher ones. They're actually impossible if you don't know the key.

I'll certainly make a stab at Ella's code, rather than just giving up and expecting someone else to sort it out, like Betty's done. Like rich people do. But first, I've got an office move to deal with. Sighing, I pick up the first box.

My new flatlet disapproves of me as soon as I walk through the door, breathless, sweating and carrying clutter that will ruin its beautiful minimalism. Its displeasure deepens every time I come back with another box. When I slip out and retrieve my suitcase from my BnB, the flat positively frowns at me.

I decide I'll have a go at Ella's journal now and finish the data structure stuff for Monarch later, maybe even in the morning before I head out to their office. It's easy and Ella's code probably isn't. I fire up the designer kettle, switch on the industrial-effect Edison lamps and throw myself on a sofa with Ella's journal, paper and pencil.

The good news is that the diary is written in irregular-length groups of letters, like normal English. It has punctuation and paragraphs. Pro encrypters do devilish things, like writing everything in one long string with no gaps, so you aren't helped by standalone or double letters. The bad news is that there's no capitalisation, so I can't decipher anything from the familiar names that will crop up.

I try a classic substitution cipher where you reverse the alphabet so that A is Z, B is Y and so on. The first three words translate as *x e iyv*, so that isn't going to work. I take another tack and, laboriously, I try one where the letters of the alphabet are offset one place from their usual position. This time I get *d wi kls*.

Fuelled by my chocolate bars, I continue in this vein until mid evening, leaving the sofa only to re-up with more tea, or pollute the unfeasibly clean bathroom with my bodily processes.

DR WOOD'S DIARY

13 MARCH 1907

I am finding this research diary useful, but on reading back over previous entries I feel I need to include more of the my patients' words in my account. This will remove some of my own bias, and also permit me to read back over their utterances in future.

I shall attempt this now in my record of today's talking session with Miss Northaway. She has now fully settled in and we have spoken at some length, both in our private sessions and in the company of the other three ladies. I have also observed her in the schoolroom.

The patient is trusting and childlike in our interactions. She acquiesces to me as her alienist, but also exhibits signs of tender feelings towards me, although she has not yet articulated the latter. Such transference of affect is an expected and important stage in her talking cure. I am alert for emotions of counter-transference in myself, but do not think I am more attracted to her than any man would be. She is a highly appealing creature.

When Miss Northaway is with the other inmates, she

encourages them to speak and gives them her full attention, gently asking questions about their lives and making them feel their words and stories are valued. This is more than just polite drawing room manners. Miss Northaway – Lucy, as I now call her – seems genuinely interested in others and appears to care about their happiness.

I mentioned this in our session today.

'Is that not proper, doctor?'

I reassured her that such kindness and care for others is an ideal trait in a woman and will make her a good wife and mother. Had she been this way as a child? Perhaps her mother had encouraged it?

'Mama was an invalid and often indisposed, so I relied on Miss Symonds, my governess, for guidance. Miss Symonds said it is a Christian duty to put others first. I have practised this for so long I have come to find other people fascinating. Do you not find this so, too, Doctor Wood? You must, in your profession?'

Noting her evasive tack, I observed that she seemed to have a marked warmth of feeling for her fellow humans.

'If those around me are unhappy, then I, too, am sad,' she replied. 'That is normal, is it not? This could be a place of despair, but because of your approach, it is a refuge of peace and calm. I wish to be calm and peaceful too.'

I remarked that her nights were far from peaceful. The patient then appeared nervous and haunted. She evaded my questions on the subject and was disinclined to speak of it further, so I judged this an ideal moment to employ my mesmeric technique.

I took a scalpel from my bag and, holding it up, told her to focus on the blade. Within a minute or so, her pupils had begun to dilate and I could see she was in a state of light hypnosis. I asked her how she felt at night.

'I cannot get over the fear.' My patient's voice was slower and less guarded. The voice of the unconscious. 'It comes to me in the night. I sense that there is something or someone evil, out there. They threaten to enter my room. I feel such terror, I cannot sleep.'

I asked if she connected this with the injury to her neck. I noticed these marks yesterday when I conducted a full physical examination of the patient, but elected to wait until a more suitable time to quiz her about them. They are two small, red puncture wounds, about an inch apart, on the right-hand side of her neck.

'I do not understand. My neck is not marked.'

I bade her stand in front of the mirror and undo the high neck of her blouse. Lucy reddened and appeared self-conscious at this instruction, even in her hypnotic state. Yet she obediently did as I told her, fumbling the buttons. Keeping eye contact with her in the mirror, I pulled the lace at her throat aside to show her the marks.

I observed her staring at the wounds with astonishment, as though she had never seen them before. As I watched, the astonishment changed to revulsion. She tried to cover them up with her collar, but I intervened and stopped her hand.

'Observe this wound, Miss Northaway. Do you know how these marks came about?'

She shook her head, putting a hand up to shield her neck. I pulled it away.

'Miss Northaway. Lucy. Look at these marks. How did you come by them?'

Her dilated eyes fixed on my gaze in the mirror. 'Is it ... am I like the other Lucy? In Mr Stoker's novel? Is this what has happened to me, doctor? Am I now infected, like her? Tainted.' She began to sob and clutched at my hand. 'Can you help me, Doctor Wood? Can you cure me of this thing?'

CHAPTER 7

I WILL BE FAITH

A ntoine looks intrigued, Uzi disgusted, and Rowan thoughtful, as I finish reading them Wood's account of the treatment session. Even Mulder and Scully look round for a moment before turning their attention back to the birds in the treetops.

We're having Sunday lunch on Antoine's roof garden. It's a bright, clear September day and, despite the dark history of the terrace, we're enjoying the last of the sun. There's just enough room for our table and chairs in between the planters of lavender, sage and little olive trees which border the left and right edges of the terrace. At the end of the roof, a Perspex parapet gives us a clear view over the cemetery. It feels slightly godlike to be so high up, looking down on the autumnal trees and tiny graves, far below. I can see why Ella was so taken with it; before it killed her. Uzi's adamant that she fell from Antoine's terrace, not his neighbour's. She can sense it, she says.

Uzi and Rowan disappear to the kitchen and return with an aromatic vegetable and lentil stew. Her grandmother's recipe,

Uzi tells us, adapted to plant-based cuisine by Rowan. Cooked by Rowan, too, I assume, although Uzi makes much of her role as creative director.

'And I've seldom seen such beautifully sprinkled dill,' Antoine says.

I've accepted Uzi and Rowan as part of our Scooby Gang now and Betty's happy to extend the team of investigators. I like both of them, particularly Rowan, who's the more grounded of the pair. Uzi has her own quick, quirky charms; she's clever and makes me laugh, but I don't envy Antoine being around someone who embodies such a mix of speed, passion and intensity. I definitely couldn't live with someone so permanently artistic.

Still, sitting down to eat with the three of them today feels effortlessly comfy. I can just be myself here and so can everyone else. No chance of a dinner-party destroyer situation. None of the awkwardness I'd get with relatives, either; I've had two texts from Eileen already today about that sodding trunk. Told her I'm working all weekend, which is pretty much true, but really I'm hoping she'll just give up. Then I won't have to deal with it. Or them.

'Does Wood think he's writing a novel?' Antoine asks, as we tuck into the food. 'All that dramatic stuff.'

'It was normal for psychoanalytic case studies,' I tell him. 'Freud is full of literary flourishes. They *are* writing about patients' stories, and it *is* usually disturbing material, so not surprising, really.'

'Not complaining here,' Antoine says. 'The vampire of Abney Asylum, how brilliant is that?'

I can hear the headline in his voice.

'What Lucy's doing, it's self-harm, isn't it?' Rowan says. 'The puncture marks. She reads *Dracula* and wants to be like the other Lucy. Then people will care about her, instead of her having to do all the caring.'

I nod. Insightful, I say, through a mouthful of Grandmother Ursica's hotpot. It's delicious; food from a novel I haven't yet read.

The big grey cat, Mulder, starts trying to get through the lavender hedge onto the dog-owning neighbour's roof. Not the sharpest cat in the world. As I scoop him up and plonk him on my lap, I ask if anyone else found Wood's account creepy.

Uzi nods. 'That way he forces her to uncover her neck while he watches? Even though it will upset her?'

It's the way he makes her watch while he pulls her blouse open that got me, I tell her. Verges on coercive, slightly sadistic?

'This man is a voyeur,' Uzi says, firmly. 'He makes Lucy witness his power over her.'

'He fancies her too,' Antoine adds.

'I get all that,' Rowan says. 'Wood's dodgy in lots of ways, but he has to make her face up to what she's doing. She won't recover otherwise. He did cure her in the end.'

Uzi thinks maybe Lucy isn't self-harming. Wood might have inflicted the wounds with his scalpel, after he hypnotised her. Antoine's enthusiastic about the idea that Wood's gaslighting her and making her think there are supernatural forces who've got it in for her. That's all too fanciful for me and Rowan.

'Nah, come on.' Antoine says. 'There's something about Wood's asylum and vampirism. Lucy has puncture wounds on her neck. Ella's body had them on the wrist, remember? Wood's got them both locked up and he's manipulating their minds. Something smells sinister.'

Uzi says Wood wants to use Lucy for his published case study, to further his career and prove his project works. He feeds on her for his success, like a vampire. But Rowan believes the wounds are a way to get Wood's attention; she's playing at being Dracula's Lucy and you can't be a victim if you haven't got a vampire.

Uzi looks out over the cemetery with narrowed eyes. 'Poor Lucy has more than one of those.'

I suppose it's the artistic thing that's making her feel so deeply for Lucy, but I'm bothered that she's taking all this completely seriously. She doesn't realise Antoine's default setting's irony.

I try to lighten the atmosphere. 'So we start off trying to find out how Ella and Lucy died and now we're vampire hunters? Fine, as long as I don't have to be Buffy.'

Antoine opens another bottle of wine. I brought along a couple of bottles of Malbec, feeling I need to contribute more to the party than horror stories.

'You can be Giles.' He tops up my glass. 'Specially as you're busy cracking the cipher in an ancient book.'

I stroke the lavender-scented Mulder, who sits purring in my lap. Tell them I'm still struggling with that. That I'm pretty sure it's a simple substitution cipher, but one that uses a keyword. The key's probably six letters long, could be more, and it might begin with C or V. Not much to go on, but it took a lot of sweat to work that out.

'What sort of word do people use as a key?' Rowan puts a hand over their glass. The youngsters disapprove of any meaningful drinking. 'Is it like a password?'

Similar sort of thing, only all letters, I tell them. They shouldn't get their hopes up, I don't know if I can work it out; we might never hear Ella's story in her own words. Antoine points out that people use rubbish passwords; his dad used WestHam before he made him change it. Rowan laughs, tells us their sister uses her baby's name.

With a familiar stab of aloneness, I realise it's news to me that people are hopeless with security, because I've never known anyone else's password. You have to have a family for that sort of thing. A father. A sister. Or a brother.

On cue, the owl hoots again and I shiver. We should go inside soon, Antoine says, it's getting cold, but I shake my head.

Mulder rolls over luxuriantly on his back and I have to stop him falling off my lap. Antoine's black cat, Scully, looks on with jealousy and mild contempt.

'People use place names and pet names, too,' Antoine bends to stroke Scully, who's now tapping his leg. 'Anything that's important to them.'

Uzi looks a bit sheepish, so I suspect her password is Mulder or Scully. I can't imagine someone like Ella being so careless with her secrets though. Reluctantly I promise to give this newfound information a go.

'Passwords from the heart, Meg, not the head,' Antoine laughs at my disbelief. 'You're definitely Giles.'

'Stereotyping. I'd rather be a vengeance demon.'

Bored with our fandom fantasies, Rowan disappears to get dessert.

'Obviously I'm Spike.' Antoine lifts the disgruntled Scully onto his lap. She definitely thinks she should be the chosen one. 'Or Angel.'

Rowan returns bearing a plate of flaky apple pastries, so I ask if either of our new recruits is volunteering to be Buffy. Uzi shakes her purple locks, which are decorated with snakes and lace today.

'I will be Faith,' she announces.

CHAPTER 8

CIPHERS FROM THE HEART

It's early in the morning, but I'm wide awake, so I get up, make a robust coffee. Horrible night. Everything I've been trying not to think about since I returned came back to haunt me in my dreams. My mum, and that last night in our flat. Michael. What happened with Sophie. Even my dad, whom I barely remember. Thing is, since I left, I've concreted over that particular howling pit of absence and loss, and built my life on top of it. I really don't need it opened again.

I nurse my coffee and wonder if I can handle this. Being back where I grew up, with the ghosts of the past whispering around me every day. And every night. Was it a crazy decision to take the contract? A week here and I'm jumpy, sleeping badly. Drinking a bit too much. Maybe I should cut my losses and go.

Except I can't turn down the kind of money Monarch's paying me. Or let a client down.

I pour another coffee, pull myself together. I'll focus on the job, that always works. It'll be fine. I'll be fine. Yesterday's insight has given me a lead on Ella's diary, so maybe I can get somewhere with that.

I sit and brainstorm keywords that might come from Ella's heart. Maybe something that begins with C or V because those are the two single letters scattered through the text, so one of them's probably going to be represent 'A'. It's not England where she was born, or Paris, where she wanted to go. California?

Probably too long, but worth a go.

I write it all out.

```
A B C D E F G H I J K L M N O P Q R S T U V W X Y Z
C A L I F O R N B D E G H J K M P Q S T U V W X Y Z
```

Using this, the first three words come out as *a vm nog*. Not California. How about family? That comes from the heart, apparently. I look up her parents' first names. Her father's is Zachariah; wonderful name but no use to me. Her mother, on the other hand, is plain old Claire. Fantastic.

```
A B C D E F G H I J K L M N O P Q R S T U V W X Y Z
C L A I R E B D F G H J K M N O P Q S T U V W X Y Z
```

This time the first three words come out as *a vk lme*. I'm losing hope. Antoine and co were wrong, after all. Ella wouldn't use anything so soppy or obvious as someone's name.

Sighing, I get up to pour myself another coffee. Watch several pairs of builders' boots walk past my window, plus the familiar pedigree paws and immaculate designer trainers of Antoine's next-door neighbours. Turning, I think I see movement on the far side of the lounge. I stop and stare. Nothing there. Must be a trick of the light reflecting in the mirror, but it's happened a couple of times lately. I don't know whether it's the destabilising effect of being back in Stokey that's confusing my senses and my sanity, or if it's something about this odd film set of a place. The strange way the old and new exist together is somehow unsettling; it's as if the building's standing back and laughing, ironically, at what's been done to it.

Then again, being shut up in here all day, I'm probably becoming one of the unbalanced gated. I push all these thoughts out of my head, look back at the journal. Work is always the cure. I'll give it one last try this morning. Ella's middle name is Hope and her sister's name is Fanny – neither of them any use. I wonder if Betty has any idea what the family pets were called? I drop her a quick text.

Then there was the niece Dr Wood says she missed? What was she called? She's Betty's mother so I've got her name, though I haven't done the tree yet. I rummage in my notes. Violet. Brilliant. Hurray for Violet.

I write it all out again, with Violet as the key. This time when I painstakingly transcribe the first three words they make sense. *I am not.*

Bingo!

It's fantastic to have cracked the code, but this is going to be a slow, painstaking translation. It will take me weeks, given that I've got to fit it round the asylum archive work. No way I'm going to farm it out, though, I want to be the first to know what Ella has to say. I'll spend some time on it today, catch up with the archiving tonight.

Ella's journal starts with the words 'I am not the kind of woman' and I bet she isn't. Although she is the sort of woman who uses a hopeless, sentimental keyword, but I'll let that go for now. It means I get to hear her story, after all.

ELLA'S JOURNAL
MARCH 4, 1907

I am not the kind of woman who keeps a journal. I do not wish to write about the minutiae of the drawing room, or document my hopes and fears regarding beaus and balls. I have little interest in gowns or hats, or, indeed, in any of the trivia ladies are meant to record in their private diaries.

I am embarking on this task on the instruction of Dr Wood. It will be beneficial to write down whatever comes into my head, he tells me. This will be quite private, although I may wish to discuss some of the thoughts that surface with him. It will help me to get better.

And I mean to get better.

I believe I can become a woman deserving of freedom again. I cannot change what I have done, or what that has made me, but I intend to regain my strength of mind.

So here I am, a lady journal keeper, scribbling down the fluttery, feminine secrets of a young gentlewoman's breast. Yet not so young, as my mother is at pains to remind me, for an unmarried woman.

I wish to ensure the degree of privacy that the doctor

suggests. I am not entirely sure I trust him not to pry, and I certainly would not trust the attendants, if any of them know their letters. Thus I am writing this record in my secret code. I know this almost off by heart by now, having used it back home, to correspond with a beloved friend. I find now, as I found then, the practice of writing in code to be calming. It slows down the tumult of my thoughts.

So, if I am not to write about the marriage market or my wardrobe, what then shall I set down? I go nowhere and do nothing. I must record something, so I will emulate the writings of lady travellers and capture my impressions of this place and its people, and say a little about how I come to be here.

I arrived here two weeks ago from my family home in California. We have lived in our country place in Hillsborough since last year, when the terrible earthquake made it impossible to return to our house in San Francisco. I was pleased to come back to London, a city where I spent a happy childhood, before my father moved us to America. We left England because Papa felt he could put his excellent legal mind, and his zeal for justice, to greater use in the New World. Indeed, he has done much good in our adopted country.

My family likes to do good.

London is so much older and more stable than my home, which seemed to me full of cracks and rough edges, even before last year's horror. This is true even of well-mannered Hillsborough. It is more obvious in the city of San Francisco, where Papa works. I always preferred San Francisco, before the earthquake. Manners are more rough and ready there, but people are genuine.

I feel polite society is a thin papering over of something more visceral in my Californian world. At the same time, London lacks the energy and individualism of America. Here, one must be more ladylike, one must never speak out of turn.

Ladies have less freedom here, for all the culture and civility of the place.

Or maybe because of it.

I am in a quiet, respectable suburb of London, called Stoke Newington. From the carriage on the way here, I observed that the leafy streets do not have the hustle and bustle of town, something I welcome at present. For the most part, the middling classes live here, although the poor are everywhere in this world. I saw one or two smarter carriages on the road, and Dr Wood tells me numerous wealthy non-conformists also make their home here, particularly those of a more radical stripe.

This sounds promising.

Although I like London, when I recover I wish to travel to Europe, in particular to Paris, but also to Rome and Berlin. God willing. I have read much about these cities and talked to others who have journeyed there. How wonderful it would be to walk around Paris, now. Yet at present I know I need the predictable solidity of England and the calm of Abney Asylum.

An insane asylum. I sometimes wonder how I have come to this. I am a strong person, a resourceful person, not some dizzy, feeble-minded little chick. How can my mind have broken? Is the Lord punishing me for my sins?

Although, in truth, being here is a relief from having to pass for normal.

I was the first of Dr Wood's private patients to arrive. When I first came here, all the other inmates (for that is what I am. An inmate. At any rate, it is preferable to being called a lunatic) were parish patients. They are poor children up to the age of twelve or thirteen. The boys grow vegetables for the asylum table, under the eye of the head gardener and they also learn woodwork. The girls labour in the asylum laundry, which takes in washing for local households. Matron Siskins, who is a fierce, pious woman, but not unkind, also trains the older and more able ones in service. Thus, our servants here are a little unpredictable, being inmates, but they are keen to please.

Abney Asylum is a spacious building, very like an English stately home in appearance. It is built of yellow brick, in the Italian style, with great oaken doors and huge windows. Our private patients' quarters are light and airy, and are plainly but pleasantly furnished, in the modern style.

The asylum was built over eighty years ago, as a private hospital. It must have been a fine place for the recuperation of sick Londoners, away from the busy life of the capital. The large gardens would have been ideal for the physically infirm to sit and take the air.

I, too, am grateful for the gardens. Walking there produces in me a sense of optimism, as the plants emerge from winter bleakness and put out green shoots and bright flowers. I am intrigued by the different specimens that grow in England and have learned their names from the gardeners. I have learned to identify the British birds too, who are showing off their spring plumage. I love to watch them squabble and preen as they hop around the lawns and alight on the shrubs. I do not know how I should manage without the small freedom this green space gives me.

When Abney Park Cemetery was constructed to the rear of these grounds, perhaps that was disconcerting for the hospital patients? At any rate, the building changed its use a few years after the cemetery was opened, becoming an old-fashioned Victorian lunatic asylum, where the parishes sent their insane. My new friend Lucy says she still feels the unhappiness of the poor souls who were incarcerated here, in those cruel, unenlightened times. It makes her shudder to see the rivets, still set in the walls, where some unfortunates were chained.

The asylum is quite different now. Since Dr Wood took over five years ago, he has modernised the place completely. He has provided us with hot and cold running water, and has even installed electric lighting, which fascinates Lucy, who is used only to gaslight. She says the brightness of the illumination cheers her, as it keeps shadows at bay.

Our youngsters believe the glow of the electric light to be a form of alchemy. They have lived most of their miserable lives in poverty and such markers of civilisation are wholly new to them. Under Dr Wood's regime, their lot is improved in many ways. They have sufficient food and warm clothing, as well as a secure place to sleep every night. They are educated, obliged to be clean, expected to be polite and civil, and must carry out the useful activities I mentioned earlier. It is not surprising that for most of them, those changes have brought about a marked improvement in their behaviour.

Their lives may be better in some ways, but they are still imprisoned. I try not to dwell on this, but cannot help doing so. We are all caged birds here.

Perhaps I am not sufficiently busy and that is why I dwell on my lack of freedom. To be useful and occupied improves us all, in Dr Wood's view. At home I helped Papa with his work, when I was well. Here I have little to do. I swim in the basement pool every day, I walk in the airing courts frequently, and the grounds when I have permission, but I still find myself restless. I have my books, but find it difficult to read. Looking out of my window I try to see into the woodland cemetery, but my view of this is obscured by a great plane tree, as well as by the bars, which are on all our windows here. I watch the birds fly among the garden trees and soar off into the cemetery; I cannot settle.

Although I know I must be here, the sense of confinement seeps into my every waking minute. I cannot go horse riding or drive to the other side of town to visit a friend. Those freedoms now seem like extravagant fantasies. I try to write this journal, but concentration is hard to come by when my mind flies out of the window and explores a world where my body may not go.

ELLA'S JOURNAL

MARCH 12, 1907

Wind howls around the asylum tonight and rain beats a tattoo on the window. The storm outside gives me a sense of release. I part the curtain and look out from my window. Beyond the bars, trees dance and wave to me. My ghostly reflection waves back. How I would love to be out in the wood, getting wet and muddy, like a naughty child.

Wanting to go out walking in a storm is exactly Matron's idea of madness, so I keep those desires to myself. Like so many others. Instead, I concentrate on my role as a secret explorer, examining this closed world of the insane, and chronicling it in this journal. This evening I shall try to capture the inhabitants of the asylum in my secret code.

Until the other private patients arrived, I saw little of the other inmates, apart from the servants. They were present at morning prayers and I sometimes caught sight of them in the airing court, a walled garden to the side of the building, where we may exercise. The children were nervous of me then, perhaps because I sometimes give the reading at morning worship. Recently I began to help Lucy and Miss Englethorpe with their education, so now I have much to do with the little ragamuffins and they have lost some of their fear. Teaching the children is the sort of thing Lucy would think of doing and I would not. I confess I am not naturally inclined to good works, despite being a Murray. Or maybe because of it.

Lucy teaches them their letters and I teach them drill (mainly baseball, thus far) and woodcraft. Miss Englethorpe instructs them in Bible Studies. The children are a rabble, but we all have fun in my lessons. Some of them are quite disturbed or slow in their understanding, which must be difficult in the classroom. Yet, like all children, they enjoy running around and hitting a ball, and are delighted by nature. Dr Wood has tried to put a damper on some of our more energetic activities, taking the view that they are dangerous and inappropriate for the girls. I do not know what sort of lives he thinks girls of this class have had. Since his intervention, I make sure we do nothing too boisterous when he is watching. Florrie, a quick little coloured girl, has elected to be my lookout. A resourceful child, she is turning out to be a sharp-eyed helper who helps me organise the other youngsters.

Lucy was the second lady to arrive here. What can I say of dear Lucy? She is the beauty of our little world, an exquisite creature, fairy-like and very much the English rose. Despite her enchanting appearance, her porcelain cheek is too pale and her swan-like throat too slender. She cannot sleep for terrible nightmares and is often fatigued. She confided in me that, at home, her sleepwalking obliged her parents to lock her in her bedchamber at night.

We are all locked up in our rooms at night here.

Despite her problems, Lucy is no languid lady invalid. As well as teaching the children, she helps everyone in a hundred different ways. Whether it is giving one of the servant girls an encouraging word, or listening to the ramblings of poor Mrs

Fitzherbert, the third lady inmate, or helping old Miss Englethorpe, the other gentlewoman, with her sewing, she is always busy. Everyone seems to want so much from her and she is happy to give it. Or, at least, she sees it as her duty.

I am delighted to have found an intimate friend in Lucy. Although we are so different, there was a spark of understanding between us from the moment we met. I was setting out for a walk around the grounds when she arrived at the asylum. As she nervously descended from her carriage, her blue eyes wide with apprehension, I went up to her, introduced myself and escorted her into the building. She relaxed a little as I did so. Nell, one of the more foolish attendants, came hurtling up to us in the foyer, in a panic. It had been her job meet the carriage and the idiot girl was brusque with me for usurping her. Clearly transported by the vision Lucy presented, in her pretty gown and picture hat, she led her up the staircase as if she were royalty. Lucy paused on the stairs and looked back at me; I could see she would far rather have remained in my company. When I gave her an encouraging wave and she smiled back, I knew a bond had already been forged between us. The next time we met we were on first name terms.

Lucy is intrigued by my experience of a world outside England and I find her charming and sympathetic company. We talk together for hours and are completely at ease with each other. I am only concerned that all the demands placed on her by others are too much for her frail health. Only I see how tired it makes the poor angel.

I should describe the two other gentlewoman inmates. Mrs Fitzherbert is a lady of thirty-five, who became confused after her son was born and has never regained her senses. She claims her husband has locked her in here so that he may spend her (considerable) fortune, cavorting with chorus girls. This may be true, but the poor lady is still significantly deranged and sees conspiracies, spies and double-dealing everywhere she looks. The wide stare of her protuberant eyes and her shrill, alarmed way of speaking add to the impression of her instability. Dr Wood is good with her, but I doubt even his modern methods of healing the mind will work with someone so unhinged.

Miss Englethorpe is not likely to be healed by Dr Wood either. In her case this is because there is nothing the matter with her. She is an elderly lady, who, since her brother died, has had no home. Her nephews do not want her living with them and she has not the funds to set up an independent establishment. Miss Englethorpe is a deeply religious woman and an ardent Congregationalist. Her nephews are Church of England and are affronted by her frequent references to religious matters. They say she has religious mania. An old-fashioned person, very much the Victorian, she is rather stern and serious and has not time for worldly fripperies. Yet she gets along perfectly well in this dissenting establishment and if she lectures the servant girls on sin, it is probably no more than they get from Matron Siskins.

All the ladies here are from non-conformist families. Dr Wood is passionate in his Christian mission to help the suffering through innovative treatment. He is quite a personality. A tall, thin man, he has intense dark eyes. When he concentrates his gaze upon one in the talking sessions, they are like beams of energy. He is tremendously intelligent, forward thinking and has boundless vigour. Yet I cannot get over the feeling that he sees us all as creatures on which he can experiment and that this asylum is one big laboratory, where he tries out his new methods. I have told him as much in my sessions. He labels this viewpoint my 'laboratory fantasy'.

Dr Wood wishes to introduce us lady lunatics to some of his social circle, who are reformers and freethinkers, as he is.

He sees this, too, as part of our cure. To this end, he has invited the four of us to tea on Thursday. My impression is that while his friends are of the same religious persuasion as my family, their ideas of reform may go beyond what Papa would consider wise and what Mama would consider proper. Although a tea party is not the sort of thing I would normally welcome, I am very much looking forward meeting these people.

CHAPTER 9

RAISING SPIRITS

Now I've translated Ella's first two entries I'm so delighted, I have to tell a live person. Texts won't do. Antoine's busy at work but I know Rowan's working in the former kitchen garden next door to Abney Heights. As one of my jobs today is comparing the map of the old asylum to the current building for the archive website, I can go and boast about my success while completing a work task. Double whammy.

My success with the journal has lifted me out of my early morning doubts about being back here. At least, for a while. I push away the thought that such a dramatic mood swing isn't particularly healthy either, as I make my way to the garden gate. I'm fully intending to be supercool about my triumph, but as soon as Rowan opens the gate I shout 'I've done it! I've cracked Ella's code.'

'Oaoh, that's fabulous, Meg,' Rowan's calm face cracks into a big grin.

Uzi's sitting sketching the laden apple trees and swelling

pumpkins in the chilly sunshine. She pauses to congratulate me and demands I read them Ella's story.

I park myself in an old garden chair next to her and look around with interest. It's a big plot for London, and well kept. Council-owned now, it's run by an eco social enterprise, Local Roots, that feeds people for free. Rowan volunteers there.

I read out Ella's account of the asylum to the companionable backdrop of Uzi's pencil scratching away at her sketchpad and Rowan's spade chomping its way through the soil. When I finish, we smile round at each other. Rowan's as excited as I am to hear Ella's voice. We like her strong-mindedness, her restless energy and her engagement with the natural world. Uzi's interested to hear the diary entries but is less impressed by Ella herself. She thinks she sounds patronising about Lucy and snobbish about the children. A kind of bossy PE teacher. Rowan and I protest that the kids obviously like her, and she teaches them to love nature.

Rowan looks round the plot and says, nodding. 'Good that the asylum kids learned to grow veg here too. It'd help their mental health. Grounding. Working with the earth gives you a sense of connection to the planet.'

This is verging on the hippy dippy for me (although, technically, I sort of agree with Rowan about the mental health bit, and that's partly why I have a veg patch of my own, back home). So I can't help but smile when Uzi points out that Wood was using child labour to supply his kitchens. As well as to cook, clean his asylum, and labour in his laundry business. I tell her it's a fair point but you have to look at the context. The children were from desperately poor backgrounds, some of them were street kids like Florrie, who'd been living on their wits. They were sent there by East End parishes, who paid him to get them off their hands. Educating them and training them to earn their own living was radical in 1907.

Uzi just mutters about social control, while Rowan looks thoughtful. Seeing the two of them together now without the distractions of other people, I can see what they've got in common. They're both intense and serious, in their different ways. The contrast between them is much more marked, too; Rowan's a bit taller than my five nine and their strength is clear from the way they're slicing through the waterlogged clay like it's nothing. Uzi is almost elf-like, curled up on her chair with her sketch pad. A magic art-elf. The most significant difference, though, is velocity not mass. Uzi is in permanent motion, except when she pauses to focus intently on something that interests her. Like when she's sketching. Rowan's movements are slow, steady and purposeful. They never speak without considering what they're going to say first. Rowan definitely strikes me as someone who get things done, despite the woo-woo hippy stuff.

'Rowan's going to start an ecology degree next year,' Uzi says.

Rowan looks uncertain. 'Maybe having qualifications would help me to convince people. Don't know if I can spare three years, mind, we're running out of time, and even ecologists don't always see the bigger picture. Not many people completely get our psychological and spiritual dependence on the planet.'

Uzi's already told me Rowan's interested in Paganism, so I'm more surprised by the personal urgency than the spiritual stuff. Looks like Rowan's in even more of a hurry than Uzi, despite that laidback manner; art may be long, but the planet's future might not be.

I take a few photos of the allotment for the archive website, under Uzi's supervision. The ones with the pumpkins in the foreground look suitably creepy and artistic. Then we look at my floorplans and trace what's where.

'I'm in the laundry, here and you're in Dr Wood's parlour. The walled garden next to the building is part of the airing courts.'

'Not much of the grounds left,' Rowan says.

'It was mostly sold off and Monarch built out over some what was left,' I reply. 'We've got a bit, and a few of Ella's trees are left, near the cemetery wall.'

'The interior floor plan's totally different,' Rowan says. I agree and tell them that although the front of the asylum looks the same, inside it's hard to recognise the old building in the new.

'You have photos of inside the asylum?' Uzi asks. I tell her I haven't found any yet.

'That is what you need,' she asserts. 'It will reveal the place to you as much as Ella's journal and Wood's writings. Then you will see the old through the new.'

DR WOOD'S DIARY
14 MARCH 1907

Today I began my new social experiment. My four lady inmates took tea with myself, Von Helson, Mrs Kerr and Mrs De Morgan. I have selected a little-used parlour for this purpose, near my private apartments on the fifth floor. Should our group move on to the other activity I have in mind, we will be able to keep our apparatus safely in here, away from prying eyes and fingers.

I chose my outside influences carefully. My first guest was Professor Von Helson, my old friend and scientific contact who is a gifted engineer and inventor. He resides in Vienna but often stays in London with a member of my church community, a widowed lady named Harriet Kerr.

Harriet, as I have come to call her (we use Christian names at the Church of the United Souls), is an energetic reformer. She uses her significant wealth to support many worthwhile projects, including mine. Harriet is something of a blue-stocking and a keen suffragist, but a devout woman, unlike many of her sisters. As the United Souls is a modern dissenting church, it encompasses many different viewpoints; since I have known Harriet, she has taken an interest in Theosophy, vegetarianism and Christian Anarchism. This puts her on the radical wing of our congregation, most of whom adopt more moderate and scientific perspectives, as I do.

My third guest was a friend of Harriet's, Evelyn De Morgan, the wife of the renowned writer and ceramicist, William De Morgan. Mrs De Morgan is also a painter of some repute. Like her husband, Mrs De Morgan is an advocate of the Arts and Crafts movement, believing in the dignity of the craftsman and the fulfilling nature of such labour. This stately old lady has advised me in Arts and Crafts training for my young inmates. Based on her suggestions, two of our board members who run construction companies, William Finleigh and Ezekial Chamberlain, have lent some of their workmen to teach carpentry and decorative crafts, and a third, Barnabus Grimthorpe, a manufacturer of furnishings and garments, is providing sewing instructors for the girls.

All three of my tea party guests are fellow members of the League for Psychic Studies. Like myself, they are open to the possibility that the mentally disturbed may have greater sensitivity to the spirit world than the sane. My guests are also interested in my theory that communion with the afterlife may be therapeutic for some disturbed individuals.

Once we were seated and supplied with refreshments, Von Helson entertained us with an enthusiastic account of his new machine, the Telepathic Transfer Engine, for which we both have such high hopes. I found that observing my patients in a social setting provided me with useful insight into their conditions. Their response to the idea of the Engine was also illuminating.

Von Helson beamed round at the group. 'My electrical machine is the next step forward for technology, following the invention of the telephone and telegraph. Now we can contact not just those separated from us by earthly distance, but those who have moved to another plane, also. My Engine will record their messages.'

'Can that be godly, professor?' asked Miss Englethorpe.

Despite the patient's sharp, disapproving manner of asking, this is a reasonable question. I have, as yet, seen little evidence of any religious mania in her. It is not a question for Von Helson, however, who sadly has many doubts about religious matters.

Harriet fielded this theological query, telling Miss Englethorpe the Engine was the most spiritual of machines. 'It is heart-breaking for the living to lose those who have moved beyond the veil,' Harriet said. 'Our Lord would not wish it. The professor's machine is a re-uniter of souls.'

'How does your machine record these messages from the dead, Professor Von Helson?' Ella asked.

Von Helson explained that the electrical vibrations from the other side are drawn in from the aether by a succession of coils and transformers, which are fed by wires into a gauntlet. When a suitably sensitive person places their hand inside this glove, the circuit is activated. The machine will then transcribe the words of the departed through automatic writing.

'This sensitive person must become part of your machine, professor?' Ella asked.

Von Helson gave one of his loud roars of laughter, which made my patients jump. He told them his machine would have a therapeutic effect on the person by siphoning off their excess energies.

Ella's face stiffened, but she did not respond. I suspect this idea awakened her paranoid laboratory fantasy. I will address this with her in our next talking session.

Harriet was quick to reassure my patients, telling them that both she and Mrs De Morgan both tried to animate the machine. Sadly, the spirits had not spoken, although Mrs De Morgan has so much past success with automatic writing.

'I have, but I'm afraid my sensitivities do not work with the Telepathic Transfer Engine,' said Mrs De Morgan. 'Perhaps, for me, spirit writing is more an art than a science.'

'It will be *so* exciting when we find the right person,' Harriet said. 'For humanity, this is the beginning of full and reliable community with the spirit world.'

Mrs Fitzherbert looked horrified. 'You forget there are evil souls in the afterlife, too, Mrs Kerr,' she shrilled. 'They might possess the sensitive and be unleashed on humanity!' She began to rock backwards and forwards, becoming quite agitated. Neither Von Helson's laughing rebuttal, nor my attempt to reason with her, nor Harriet's sympathetic reassurance could calm her. I thought I should have to sedate her until Lucy intervened. She grasped the lady's hand and looked into her eyes.

'I believe the departed souls of our friends can mean us nothing but good, Mrs Fitzherbert. They are in a place of light and beauty and will bring us only peace and joy. The evil you speak of would not be permitted to hurt us, in God's ordering of things. I am not a strong creature, but I trust that the professor's invention will do no harm. I would certainly be prepared to try this myself, if I were to be of any use.'

Mrs Fitzherbert stopped rocking and relaxed a little. My social experiment may even be helping her, my most challenging gentlewoman patient.

Harriet turned to Lucy. 'You do strike me as a sensitive, my dear.'

'Indeed, Miss Northaway,' said Mrs De Morgan. 'You have a most ethereal quality. Otherworldly, one might say. It is a rare characteristic in these modern times.'

'If the good doctor is happy,' said Von Helson, 'I would be

delighted to have such a beautiful lady to activate the Telepathic Transfer Engine. How could the spirits resist?'

Lucy blushed at these compliments.

Ella, however, bridled. 'If this machine draws energy from the person connected to it, I cannot think that will be a good thing for you, Lucy. All the other demands on you leave you so fatigued.' Ella looked over to me, with a slight challenge. This is more evidence of her paranoia, displaced onto her friend in this case. I told her that for Miss Northaway, the Engine may well draw off harmful energy, thus acting as a tonic.

Lucy smiled at me apologetically, then took Ella's hand in both of hers. 'Ella, you are so good, thinking of my health like this. My dear, I truly believe the Lord will protect me if I try to provide this comfort to the bereaved. We must be brave and have faith.'

Thus the angel of my asylum may also become the catalyst who sparks Von Helson's Telepathic Transfer Engine. How precious her presence is becoming to us all.

ELLA'S JOURNAL
MARCH 15, 1907

I am concerned about Dr Wood's plans for Lucy and this is making me agitated. So I will write down the events that brought it on and describe how they have left me feeling, as Dr Wood has encouraged me to do. Yet I have some doubts about the doctor at present and am glad that my thoughts are locked up in a code he cannot read.

It all began at Dr Wood's tea party yesterday. I was pleased to be invited, as I was eager to meet his suffragist friend, Mrs Kerr, and the British artist, Mrs Evelyn De Morgan, whose work I admire. Disappointingly, I was unable to converse much with these ladies. Dr Wood had other plans for the event.

We met in a parlour on the top floor of the building. I was immediately struck by the fine views we had over the woodland cemetery and the beauty and variety of the trees, which are just coming into leaf. Abney Park holds a fascination for me, partly because the view of it from my room is obscured, which makes me feel that it is a place of mystery. The other reason for my interest is that it was inspired by the famous Père Lachaise, in Paris, a place I would dearly love to see.

Despite the felicitous setting, our tea party did not turn out as I had expected.

I was immediately impressed by Mrs Kerr and Mrs De Morgan. I am used to the elegant society ladies who adorn my mother's charity events at home, but Dr Wood's guests are very different.

Mrs Kerr I know to be a wealthy woman, active in local charitable causes, and a patroness of the asylum. This is not obvious from her appearance. She wears round spectacles and has a refreshing disdain for fashionable grooming, wearing her (expensive) clothing loosely and inattentively. Indeed, she reminds me of the White Queen in Mr Carroll's novel, for she always seems to be losing her hair pins or shawl. Her boundless enthusiasm for ideas and projects can make her almost ecstatic about them at times, but that is no bad thing.

Mrs De Morgan is also of unusual appearance. An older lady, she dresses in what I believe to be a European artistic style. Her clothing is richly coloured and flowing, hinting a little at the gowns worn by the subjects of her paintings. A slender woman, I suspect she has done away with wearing a corset altogether; indeed, Mrs Kerr may have joined her in this act of liberation. Perhaps all the ladies in their circle have abandoned this restriction? I would dearly love to emulate them, a move my mother would consider utterly unthinkable.

Mrs De Morgan's artistic eye – and she has tremendously artistic-looking eyes, heavy-lidded and soulful – was taken with Lucy, whom she described as ethereal. Lucy was looking particularly lovely yesterday, in a blue tea gown made especially for the occasion. I suspect Mrs De Morgan will wish to paint her. What artist wouldn't?

Mrs Kerr was intrigued by my interest in women's suffrage.

She urged me to come for tea at her house, should Dr Wood permit such an activity, as she would love to hear about the American movement. We had little chance for such discussion at *this* tea party, as the doctor's third guest, the Viennese engineer, Professor Von Helson, held court all through the event. We could to do little but respond to his description of his new invention, an aid to automatic writing which he calls the Telepathic Transfer Engine.

Dr Wood has known the professor for some time and they have an easy way with each other. Like Mrs Kerr, he is of middling years. He has a bushy, unkempt, greying beard and hair; indeed he is rather bear-like in appearance. The doctor clearly trusts him implicitly, but I am unsure whether this is wise.

Both Miss Englethorpe and Mrs Fitzherbert were horrified at the idea of the professor's new machine, feeling that it might permit demonic possession. As he intends to use it for raising the dead, who can blame them? Their views were made light of by the professor. When I asked him a question on this matter he roared like a bear, which I gather is his way of laughing. But surely, the point of this Engine is that the spirits should take over the living? A person is strapped into it entirely for that purpose.

All three visitors and Dr Wood were enthusiastic about the possibility of communing with 'our brothers in the afterlife'. I believe the doctor and professor have planned a dangerous scientific experiment together, which the two visiting ladies are only attracted to by high-minded social motives.

'How wonderful it would be to unite all humankind,' Mrs Kerr said. 'Not merely across divides of nation and wealth, but to bring together the living and those who have passed. That would be a true brotherhood of man.'

Yet as poor Mrs Fitzherbert pointed out, all souls are not

good souls. What devils might they awaken with this machine? Although Dr Wood is convinced that this 'modern technology' will help to calm 'his' lunatics, who is to say that it won't drive us to new heights of madness? Are we to be convenient, helpless subjects for his experimentation?

When the idea emerged that they should use Lucy to operate the machine, I became even more concerned. I cannot think that being part of this experiment will do her good. It may steal what little energy she has.

In fact, I begin to wonder if we were taken there yesterday just so that Lucy would agree to be possessed by the dead. Dr Wood says this is a paranoid fantasy, but I remain suspicious of his motives.

Lucy says I make too much of it and that she wishes to do what is right. This new Engine of Dr Wood's may cure the disturbed and comfort the bereaved, so it is her duty to help in any way she can. She admits to being a little scared, but says as long as I am there to hold her hand, that will give her strength.

I feel less agitated now I have written all this down, but I see clearly that my misgivings are correct. I want nothing to do with the business, but I will not deny Lucy the comfort of having someone there who cares for her. I fear I may be the only person present who values her well-being above the lure of psychic research.

CHAPTER 10

BREATHING LIFE INTO
THE DEAD

Betty's delighted by the last entry in Ella's journal. She read the transcript as soon as I uploaded it last night. So did Antoine. I look at their texts over my morning coffee.

Betty: What a magnificent woman Ella is and so solicitous of Lucy.

Antoine: Loving the sound of this Telepathic Transfer Engine. Steampunk spiritualism.

Betty: I wonder if these seances had anything to do with their deaths? Sounds pretty creepy.

Antoine: Sinister. Any pics of the Engine?

I smile at their predictability. As I'm replying, another text slyly materialises.

Eileen: Your trunk Meg???

Also predictable, but not amusing. The trunk key's stuffed in a kitchen drawer, where it ambushes me at every possible opportunity. Much like my cousin's texts.

I ignore Eileen's message, and the shadow it brings, and focus on my other news. Antoine's researcher at the *Comet*, Sam, has been through the various legal and press reports of Ella and Lucy's deaths and delved into the local police archives. Great to have someone else do the work for me. Lucy was last seen on the day she left the asylum when she took a cab from the hotel she'd checked into, back to Abney Park Cemetery. It's a reasonable assumption that they died on the same day. Their deaths were both declared accidental, so no further enquiries were made.

By mid morning I have a much better find than Sam's. I'm virtuously doing my archiving work, far less interesting than finding out why Ella died, but it is meant to take up more of my time. Inspired by Uzi's comment yesterday about old photos of the asylum giving me a context for understanding it, I search through the boxes. My reward is a tin of pictures, not so much of the asylum interiors, but, even better, of the inmates and staff. Great for the online archive, obviously, but potentially a chance to see some pictures of Ella's world and hopefully of her and her friends.

Many of the photos are dated on the back and most are much later than Ella's period. I organise them into the different years, creating small piles of pictures all over the floor. Then, exercising enormous self control, I put each pile into an envelope and mark it with a year, before stowing it in a box to take to Monarch central later, so the intern can upload them to the archive database.

Duty done, I transfer the 1907 pile to my table and gloat

over them for a few seconds. It's gratifyingly larger than any of the other years. Then with mounting excitement, I go through them methodically. They're all dated in the same careful hand. Some are portraits of adults in normal Edwardian clothes, other pictures of children in fancy dress. Lots of pirates and fairies.

I spread them out and gaze at them, fascinated. Who are they and what can they tell me? My concentration is broken when Scully, Antoine's black cat, jumps up on the table to demand my attention. My flat's become a feline day-care centre, as Antoine and Uzi are out most weekdays. Scully's Oreo-sized paws pad over the photos, so I pick her up and hold her fluffy, purring warmth.

'Do not compromise the archive.' I look into her whiskery face. 'Or walk on the dead. First rules of genealogy.'

I put her on my lap, where she chirrups happily, and go back to staring into the long-dead faces. I'm checking my phone to find the photo of Ella that Betty sent me, for comparison, when it rings. Benedict.

'I'm in a dreadfully featureless hotel in Bloomsbury,' he says. 'They seem to have discovered Ikea since last I was here. Frankly I preferred the chintz and disreputable carpet stains.'

'I'm staring into the eyes of the dead,' I tell him. 'How's the conference?'

'Oh, quite similar.'

Benedict was my tutor at university. He helped me pick up the pieces when I was an undergraduate, after my mum died. Because of him I stayed sane and stayed at university. The dead have always held a special place in our conversation.

'When someone dies,' I remember saying to him, when I was beginning to come out of those nightmare times, 'it's like the part of you that knew them dies too. It doesn't have a purpose any more, and there's no one else to remember it, so it just – disappears.'

'Are you sure?' he'd asked. 'It's still a narrative, even if the person it's about isn't alive any more.' Benedict's a Celtic mythology specialist. He's all about narrative, especially stories of the dead.

'OK,' I said, 'it's still narrative, but it's, sort of, archived. It's not live data any more.'

'In a sense, but it changes,' he replied. 'Every time you remember them – every time you access your archive – you alter it a little, because you've changed. You breathe life into it.'

That's what I do for a living, now. I access the archives and breathe life into the dead. The archives of strangers, mind. I've no interest in my own family history. Other people's dead are a fascinating story; your own are a tragic burden.

Everyone thinks Benedict and his husband, David, are my surrogate parents because they're a generation or so older than me and he was my doctoral supervisor, but it's not like that. They're my friends. They live near me. David designs gardens so we've got stuff in common, too, even though he's less interested in narrative, death and dragons.

Benedict's giving the opening keynote speech at his conference but he's free this evening, so we arrange to meet for dinner. He's intrigued by my haunted asylum and steampunk machine for summoning ghosts. A sucker for magic tales, our Benedict.

My doorbell rings. I rise to answer it, depositing Scully on the smaller sofa. She performs a look of such forlorn incomprehension that I pick her up again immediately. Because I am a mug.

Uzi and Mulder greet us.

Perfect, because I want to show her the photos. Although I

can tell they're professional quality – and whilst I can read some visual cues, like the period of the clothing and interiors – I want someone with a more professional sense of visual literacy to look at them.

'I have, perhaps, ten minutes.' Uzi is more careful with her time than anyone her age I've ever known. Her art is the voice of youth and in a few years it won't be, apparently. She's definitely a girl in a hurry.

Uzi deposits her fluffy grey bundle on the sofa cushions and his sister demands to join him. They're so massive, they take up the whole sofa.

'I read about the seances. Antoine is not pleased the dead were contacted in his flat. He does not appreciate this is why it supports creativity.'

'Tell him it will improve its value,' I say. 'He can do tours.'

She gives one of her disturbing laughs and turns quickly to look at the pictures.

'They are good,' she says, examining them with the laser-like focus she reserves for creative matters. 'All are taken by the same person, I think. It is probably the same camera, also.' She picks up the rather dashing portrait I'd been looking at and examines it closely.

'I think that's Ella,' I say. 'It has EM written on the back next to the date and it looks a bit like the one Betty sent me, taken a few years before in California.' I hold out my phone to show her the shot of a young woman, posing stiffly with a bicycle.

In the new photo, a handsome woman in a long, loose, coat and narrow skirt stands looking directly at the camera. Her pose is theatrical, her booted right foot on a low step, right hand resting on her thigh and left fist on hip. There's something intimate about the way the camera catches her ironic gaze and the confident angle of her head. She looks every inch the forceful, impatient writer of the journal.

'A modern photo, for the time, yes,' says Uzi. 'It is a parody of a Victorian gentleman portrait, made less formal. The photographer sees who she is, not just how she looks. It is art.'

'I wonder who took them? Perhaps Wood hired a professional.' I pick up the picture I think might be Wood. It has CW written on the back and shows a spare, saturnine man in his thirties, looking up from his desk as if the photographer had just entered his office. His stance radiates energy and his gaze is, as Ella documented, intense.

'Predatory,' Uzi says.

'Maybe he's just keen and alert?'

'Ha. Alert for prey. A perceptive, skilful portrait.'

We look in vain for a photograph of Lucy, but there are none that fit her description or are labelled LW.

'It is because Wood keeps them for himself,' Uzi picks up her bag, which is decorated with Gothic Hello Kitties. 'To wank over.'

After Uzi dashes off, I examine the other prints.

Von Helson is easy to spot because of his bushy beard. A burly man, he does indeed, look like a clever, good-humoured bear. He's been caught in a stance that looks like he's giving a speech, one arm held out, palm upraised full of zeal about his subject. I can't share Ella's antipathy for the man at all, but then he isn't trying to get the dead to possess someone I care for.

His friend, Harriet Kerr, also radiates good-natured enthusiasm from her eager, bespectacled face. She is pictured reading a book; her clothing is unstructured for the time and she looks more rumpled and relaxed than most rich Edwardian women. Here is Wood's bluestocking, and I thoroughly approve.

These people are intriguing.

I come to a portrait of AH, which might be Lucy's fiancé, Alfred Homeward. An athletic man of about Wood's age, he stands half-turned from the camera, his arms folded. The most remarkable thing about him is his enormous, droopy moustache, which lends his face a puzzled look. Or perhaps it's being around all these 'clever blighters' that gives him that bemused expression.

There's also a photo of 'Lady B', a stout older woman in late Victorian finery, who must be Alfred's aunt, Lady Barnum. She looks haughtily down her nose at the viewer through a pair of lorgnettes. I don't envy Alfred that connection.

I also find a picture of the other three asylum board members, Finleigh, Grimthorpe and Chamberlain sitting around a small table. Finleigh is little and round with bulging eyes, Grimthorpe is perched stiff and straight on his chair, both hands on his ornate walking cane, while Chamberlain looks completely relaxed, smiling merrily at the camera, as if sharing a joke with the photographer. I wonder if the joke is the other two board members?

The last five pictures had a background of slightly fussy late Victorian furniture. Wood's parlour maybe? The next one has a different setting, with clean-limbed chairs and tables and lighter walls. It's more pleasing to my twenty-first century eyes, but probably seemed a little austere at the time. I'd guess it's the private inmates' living room. Two upper class ladies, JE and HF sit embroidering in front of an Art Deco fireplace. The older one is bony and stern, presumably the hyper-religious Miss Englethorpe. The younger is plain, distracted Mrs Fitzherbert, she of the shrill voice, post-partum condition and gold-digging husband.

There are other photos of adults, but not of anyone who has been mentioned by Ella or Wood, other than Matron

Siskins, who looked like a particularly capable all-in wrestler, and is photographed flanked by a couple of her attendants. One of these is a dough-faced girl with the initials NS. Nell Smith, perhaps; the one who found Ella's body and Matron called a fool? This photo is taken in a plain walled garden, possibly the airing court.

Among the pictures of the mischievous little pirates and winsome fairies, there's also a portrait of a little mixed-race girl, FA, also wearing a long dress that looks like a nightie. Ella's resourceful drill deputy, Florrie Azikiwe? She stands with her head high. Calm, self-possessed. Maybe a little resigned? She isn't giving much away.

Definitely no Lucy. No Evelyn De Morgan, either; maybe artists don't like being someone else's subject. I've already Googled her and found only a couple of images of her looking patrician and rather bohemian, in a bobbly smock.

I sit back and stare at all the faces of the dead. Forceful and clever. Self-assured. Perplexed and distracted. Funny. Naughty. Haunted.

Are any of them murderers? Mulder comes over and pats my knee, so I pick him up. He's a satisfyingly heavy animal, half cat, half bear.

'Who's your money on, mate?' I ask him. 'Who killed Lucy and Ella?'

He swats a photo of a sweet-faced fairy with his massive paw. An unlikely choice. I should have asked Scully, she's the clever one. Anyway, I still think their deaths were probably accidents or suicide. They *had* both been mentally ill, after all.

I'm staring out of my laundry-room window at anonymous feet, a view lady inmates like Lucy and Ella would never have seen, but one that would have been familiar to Florrie and her friends, when my phone goes again. Antoine this time.

'I've found photos of everyone from Ella's journal.' I tell him

'Good ones of Lucy and Ella?'

'None of Lucy yet.'

'Keep looking. Find the name of the photography studio. I can't run my Edwardian murder mystery article until I've got a photo of both of the vics.'

'They were people, Antoine, not vics.'

'Ahh. That's why my mother always liked you so much; your worthy tendencies. And that's why she's invited you round for lunch today. Meet you there at half twelve.'

ELLA'S JOURNAL

MARCH 16, 1907

Today Lucy and I had a visitor when we were sitting out in the airing court with the children.

Two of the bigger girls, my Florrie and her friend Annie, were looking after a few of the littler ones. Florrie and Annie think themselves too old for the fairy stories Lucy was telling the little mites who clustered round her, but I could tell they were as engrossed as the others. They all looked up at her with shining eyes as she wove her tale. Naturally, all the children adore Lucy. Indeed, as she sat there with the sunlight glinting on her golden curls and caressing her delicate cheek and rosy lips, she could have stepped straight out of a fairy story herself.

'Once the wicked queen had enchanted the children, she banished them to the dark forest.' Lucy was saying, when Dr Wood appeared. With him was a lady whose imperious demeanour was certainly queenly, but perhaps not wicked. She embraced Lucy warmly and was introduced to me as Lady Barnum, Mr Homeward's aunt.

Once the children were banished, Lady Barnum bade us sit. She announced that as a member of the asylum governing board, she wished to ask me about my experience here, and began to question me closely about my day-to-day life. I railed at her arrogant assumption that this was her right, but pushed down my anger for Lucy's sake. It was clear from Lucy's anxious expression that she wished my interrogation to go well. As, indeed, did Dr Wood, but I am less concerned about his sensibilities.

Lady Barnum is certainly a formidable woman. She has a habit of tilting her head back and looking down her Roman nose, which make one feel as if one is being judged and found wanting. Given the doctor's obsequious manner towards her, I suspect she is not only an influential board member, but also supports his charitable venture financially. She has power over our enclosed world.

'I disapprove of American laxity in general,' she announced, after she had quizzed me for some time. 'Yet you seem to be a decent, sensible young woman and a credit to the doctor's methods. You will be a suitable companion for Lucy.'

Lucy told me after she left that this was high praise indeed. 'Aunt Ernestine' as she is encouraged to call her, disapproves of so much that Lucy was vastly relieved I had passed her test. In truth I would not have relinquished my friendship with Lucy had I failed Lady Barnum's interview. I am not that easily intimidated and do not need my elders' consent to love a dear friend.

Yet despite her overbearing personality, Lady Barnum is clearly fond of her future niece and is concerned for her well-being. So, although I find her interference offensive, I cannot actively dislike her, as I feel she is the only other person I have met who truly puts Lucy's interests first.

DR WOOD'S DIARY

16 MARCH 1907

Today I consulted Homeward about our use of the Spiritual Machine to treat his fiancée. Lady Barnum is happy for us to go ahead, and although I have no formal need of Homeward's assent, he is an old friend and deserving of this courtesy. Additionally, I find the perspective of my patients' families significant, as it can sometimes shed additional light on their condition.

Homeward said he trusts me implicitly and was prepared to approve the treatment, with one stipulation. He wished to be with us for the experiment.

'Not my cup of tea, Wood, spirits and all that, but I'd be failing in my duty if I didn't show.'

Naturally, I agreed. I told him she was improving every day.

'I'm grateful to you for helping her,' he replied. 'A girl like Lucy, she's so pure and innocent. There's a threat to that, in this permissive age and I want to protect her from it. You know the sort of thing I mean, all this "new woman" business, with the marching and whatnot.'

I said I didn't see Lucy as a suffragist or a bluestocking.

Was he concerned about Ella's influence? I have a slight, and perhaps misplaced (or projected?) concern that Ella may be harbouring romantic feelings towards Lucy, but naturally I didn't mention this to Homeward.

'Oh, Miss Murray's not a bad stick, we've had some good chats about horses. Some funny ideas, maybe, but she's a decent type and Lucy dotes on her. No, it's not just this suffrage nonsense, Wood, it's that sometimes I feel − I don't know how to put these things—' He tugged on his moustache in frustration. 'I sound old-fashioned, but we live in morally corrupt times. This kind of laxity of principles we see all around us? It might affect a sensitive little thing like Lucy. Could this be the reason for her illness, d'you think?'

I told him I didn't think it was the dissolution of our age that was producing her night terrors.

'I meant more that when the moral fabric of society is crumbling, well, women need the traditional ways, don't they? Much more than we do. It helps keep them stable.'

'It's possible that uncertainty and instability might frighten her. Yet she is your fiancée and the life she is embarking on with you continues the traditions of centuries. It's hard to imagine anything more secure and enduring. I believe it is not the outer world of the present that haunts her, Homeward, but her inner world of the past.'

ELLA'S JOURNAL
MARCH 20, 1907

In my sessions with the doctor we talk about my home, my family, what makes me happy, and what makes me anxious or angry. I disclose much about my life, but we dance round certain events: those ones I have been charged not to speak of. I cannot tell him what happened to me, or what I became as a result. Only God can know of my guilt and shame and only he can forgive me.

Dr Wood wishes to know how I feel about my parents, so I tell him I know my duty to them, but that Mama exasperates me. In the eyes of the world my mother is a charming, elegant, philanthropic woman. Although she is sincere in her wish to help those less fortunate, it is also true that she loves to have prominence and reputation in her well-connected social world. By organising fundraising events for worthy causes, she can enjoy her role as a leading society hostess, whilst appearing virtuous.

I sound cynical. Perhaps I should be less critical of her, but Dr Wood encourages me to say what I really feel and this is welcome to me. At home I must never say what I think. The only conversation acceptable to my mother and sister is light chit-chat, or sentimental homilies about the poor.

I would be less judgemental of Mama if she were not so exercised about the world's opinion. 'Should we not be more concerned with our own views of ourselves and our family?' I ask her. She says my question is yet another example of my wayward behaviour.

Papa, in general, judges me less harshly. He works hard to bring about legal and political change in our adopted country. When I could assist him, I had his respect. He appreciated my energy and thought me clear-sighted and capable. I was profoundly disappointed when he followed my mother's lead over the terrible event and its aftermath. I could tell he had doubts, but he allowed my mother to persuade him it was all further proof of my ungoverned ways.

My sister Fanny is not at all ungoverned. Everyone speaks of her virtue.

Fanny is three years older than me. Her husband was carefully selected for her by Mama; they and little Violet live with our parents. Fanny manages our houses and servants for my mother, who is too busy charming the world to concern herself with the mundane tasks of running a home. In truth, my mother does not actually organise most of her fundraising socials, but delegates the humdrum work to Fanny. This arrangement suits them both. Fanny, who is a worthy woman, but lacks both my mother's beauty and her ability to shine socially, can make herself indispensable. Mama gains a reputation as a successful hostess and homemaker, as well as a prominent fundraiser.

Fanny, however, is competent at the social arts of never saying what you think, and being nice to people you despise. Unlike me, she does not ride or swim or walk for miles. She regards bicycling as a common form of transport, fit only for people who cannot afford horses or a carriage. 'What might people think, Ella, when they see you out on a bicycle?' she asks.

I have made Fanny sound dull, but, in truth, there is a sisterly bond between us. For the last five years our love for Violet has strengthened this immeasurably. Violet is a delightful child, clever and sweet-natured, with such gentle, affectionate ways. How dreadfully I miss our time together. I miss her serious, absorbed little face looking up at me when I read her stories. Lucy reminds me of Violet, a little, except that Violet has a definite mischievous streak. Fanny and my mother put this down to my influence and I sincerely hope they are right. I also hope that Violet has not become a wholly good little girl in the time I have been away from her. I hope, too, that she misses me, but not too much. I would never wish her to be sad.

Today I am apprehensive, as it is Dr Wood's first experiment with Professor Von Helson's Telepathic Transfer Engine, using Lucy as the object of their vivisection. Dr Wood tells me I am too protective. He says Lucy is not Violet, she is a grown woman who has offered freely to take part in the automatic writing exercise. I, of all people, should respect her right to do that. I can see that perhaps I should acknowledge Lucy's freedom to do as she chooses. Yet the doctor encourages us to consult our feelings as well as our logic, and to me this situation feels sinister and dangerous.

CHAPTER 11

FLOWERS AND SPECTRES

I haven't been to the Edgar Allen Poe estate since I cleared my mother's flat, over twenty years ago. As I walk there on this grey day, I observe that although my old patch is now fashionable enough to appear in edgy TV dramas and William Gibson novels, it hasn't yet been gentrified to a state of blandness. Everything might be cleaner and better maintained now, but the place I knew hasn't gone away, even if chichi coffee shops have begun to creep up Stamford Hill. That battered laundrette and the ramshackle little roti takeaway are definitely old Hackney. The Haredi clothing and provisions shops look exactly the same; their retro shopfronts have suddenly become cool, as hip urban documentation sites 'discover' them. Images of their faded 1940s shop signs have been materialising on my newsfeeds for a while, like insistent ghosts. It makes me feel obscurely resentful, like a displaced, unwilling subject of someone else's anthropology project.

Guess there's more than one kind of vampirism.

Feels like there's more people around the streets than when I lived here and they're younger and more fashionable. Maybe that's because I'm older and more provincial. A pair of pony-tailed twenty-something girls in big cashmere scarves clutch takeaway coffees and talk loudly about their consultancy work. What can they be consulting on at their age, I wonder? Hopscotch?

My twisted nostalgia for the old familiar places is bitter-sweet anyway, with the emphasis on the bitter. Living here was difficult and leaving was an escape. And get real, I tell myself, I'm more coffee shop than laundrette nowadays. Who wants to live in scratty places? It's depressing. I half convince myself and then feel like a traitor.

This is not my home, I repeat to myself. Another ten weeks and I'm out of here. Getting sucked in is dangerous, I can't give this place any power over me. I take the familiar turning into the Poe, my stomach churning. Uzi thinks there's ghosts at Abney Heights, but that's nothing to the ones waiting for me here.

It's always been an okay estate, the Poe. Better than the Daniel Defoe, anyway. I mean, if you live in London, you're on your guard all the time anyway, aren't you? Unless you're stupid. I stand and stare at the tower block where we lived. Stark against the slate clouds, it glowers down at the more desirable low-rise buildings surrounding it. Do single-mum-on-benefit families like ours still get offered flats here, now it's cleaner and smarter? Or do they get shipped off to damp, smelly seaside BnBs?

One or two people cross through the estate, stabbing at their phones while listening to secret music on their head-phones. *Asking for trouble*, I think. Are they mad, or am I just out of date?

I scan the buildings, the kid's playground, the basketball court. A flood of memories rush towards me, an entire army of insistent spectres that threaten to overwhelm me. I steady myself. Breathe. Block them and turn towards Claudette's.

Her cherished front garden is bright with rudbeckias, crimson flag lilies and autumn berries. I hesitate in front of the familiar polished front door. Much as I love her, I'm dreading all her questions. Why haven't I kept in touch? Why do Breda and the others never see me?

As if summoned by that thought, my phone rings. Eileen. Perfectly reasonable to decline her call, mustn't be late.

When the door flies open and Claudette engulfs me in a massive hug, I feel like crying. Bite it back. Obviously.

She's smaller than me now — she has to reach up. Maybe she was before; Claudette has a tall personality. Her neatly chignoned hair is grey, but she's still trim and elegant. She has the same wide cheekbones and easy smile as her son; Antoine's always been her male mini-me. The main thing Antoine's inherited from Terry, apart from the charm, is his superpower: the ability to do a convincing wide-eyed innocent look, when he most certainly isn't. An essential survival tactic for life with Claudette.

She pats my shoulder as she ushers me in. 'Antoine, why didn't you tell me Meg had grown so handsome?'

Antoine appears from the kitchen looking a little surprised. Claudette's eyes narrow. 'You been eating that food?'

Antoine considers using the superpower, but instead laughs and put his arm round his mother's waist. 'Guilty as charged; you know I miss your cooking. I'll bring it through, shall I?'

Once Claudette has pocketed Antoine's phone to stop him glancing at it every few minutes ('it's work, Mom'), we sit around the table in the living room and eat Claudette's tofu jambalaya. I miss her cooking too. She's been a chef for years, way before it got fashionable. She can cook anything, *and* she could always make it vegetarian when I showed up. Everything she makes is stellar. Most of all, I used to love her veggie versions of Louisiana classics: hoppin' John, cornmeal pot pie, collard greens, cornbread, black eyed peas and the rest. Food I'd only ever heard about in Alice Walker novels (although Claudette reckoned her creole cooking was *way* more sophisticated than southern country food. Alice Walker with a hint of Paris – even better). That was when I first realised there's something special about eating food from novels. You feel like you're accessing a more valid reality.

'Terry's off flogging dodgy phones down Whitechapel market,' Antoine tells me.

Claudette flicks him with a tea towel. 'Have some respect for your father when you're under his roof.'

She hands me the rice. 'It's good to have you back in this house, honey. We've missed you these years. *He's* missed you.' She nudges Antoine, who's busy heaping food on his plate.

'Didn't get chance to talk to you at your momma's funeral,' she continues. 'A sad time.'

Although I stare fixedly at my plate, I can sense Antoine shooting his mum a look. She sails right on.

'Poor Kathleen, what a troubled life. Her momma running off like that, then losing her poppa so young, in that tragic way. When I first met her at Our Lady, she was starting to overcome all that sorrow. Such a beautiful woman, with a husband who adored her.'

'Mom,' Antoine says, 'that's ancient history. Me and Meg weren't even born then.'

'You don't remember? I used to take you round their house in Dalston to play with Meg and Michael. Kathleen was so happy and light-hearted then, with her beautiful twin babies, then just a few years later—' she shakes her head.

I push a piece of okra round my plate.

'Meg lost her brother, too, Mom.' Antoine always has my

back. Always. What's more, he doesn't go 'Oh, Mom, Meg lost her twin when she was three, imagine how alone that would make you feel. Like, forever,' because he knows that would crush me more than Claudette's tactlessness. That's why I care about him, even though he's so infuriating.

'Listen to me running my mouth off like this,' Claudette puts her hand on mine. 'All the misfortune you've had and here you are, Doctor Morgan, with your own business and everything. Don't know where you got such strength.'

'School,' I say, ruefully.

'True,' Antoine grins. 'You were always a swot.'

I smile back. Good memories. As soon as I went to school, I realised the teachers possessed a special ability. They controlled their worlds, imposing structure on time, space and knowledge, instead of letting life buffet them one way and the other. Organisation. Method. Planning. I watched, learned and copied. I knew it was this that would save me from ending up like my mother. And it did.

Mind you, Kathleen's non-interventionary approach to parenting did make me pretty autonomous. I was, in a manner of speaking, running my own business when I was a teenager.

'You were always a clever girl. Round here helping him with his homework.'

In truth I was no cleverer than Antoine, just more focussed. By the time he was thirteen he was more interested in writing for the school paper and chasing girls than he was in *Sense and Sensibility*.

'You two were always together. Then there was that girl Sophie too, the three of you thick as thieves.'

The okra I'm chewing goes slimy in my mouth.

'Nice manners, that girl. Plenty of airs and graces too. Where did she go?' Claudette asks.

Antoine darts me a cautious look. 'Off to university.

Bristol.'

'Off to university and left my boy. Like they all do.'

There was almost an awkward pause, but Antoine laughs. 'It wasn't like that, Mom. Sophie met someone at Bristol. Got married, big house in Clifton, kids, ponies, the whole shebang.'

I nod, genuinely interested. We didn't have social media back then, so you weren't chained to schoolfriends forever, watching their glittering lives laid out for you in pictures.

'She work?' I ask. Sophie had never exactly been a grafter. She turned up when we were seventeen, halfway through A-levels. Sent to our school because her parents divorced and couldn't afford private fees any more. Hackney, in the nineties – she would have got *so* bullied and she did at first, girls mocked her accent and manners, called her Bony Beauvoir Bitch. I felt sorry for her and started helping her with the work she'd missed. Because she was my mate, she became Antoine's, too. Once she had his approval, the other kids started to see her social polish and her coltish tangle of limbs as glamorous, not freakish.

It never occurred to me, as Sophie rose to become the beauty of St Expiditus, that her appeal came from her upbringing. People who grow up with the impression they're special hold themselves differently. They expect people to think they're fabulous. True, they might have that kind of clean-limbed grace that comes from childhood ballet lessons and pony riding, but they don't actually look better than the rest of us. I worked that out once I met more people like that at university. Teaches you a lot, higher education.

Antoine gives me another uncertain look. 'PR consultant.'

Of course she was. Sophie called me an 'auburn intellectual', when everyone else thought I was a ginga swot. My home life was 'marked by tragedy' instead of being sad, shabby and hopeless. My mum was a woman who 'suffered too deeply to speak of her pain' rather than a ghost who lived in a Valium haze.

Better at spin than hard work, that was our Sophie. I'd had to drill her and Antoine hard at our A-level revision sessions, round at her place.

'Do you remember Sophie's house?' I ask him.

'Ah, man. All those polished floors and handmade rugs.'

We'd never seen anywhere like that before. It was a huge house down in the leafy de Beauvoir neighbourhood. Almost Islington. A comedown for Sophie's mother, but exciting luxury for me and Antoine. Proper art on the walls and groceries from Waitrose.

'What about those homemade chocolate brownies her mum used to give us?' I asked. 'And quiche. With things like broccoli and asparagus in it?'

Claudette sniffs derisively. 'Not as good as your food, Mrs Byrne,' I add, quickly.

Yet it was delicious in a different way, more Alice Thomas Ellis than Alice Walker. I was eating my way through the literary canon. The difference was that Antoine's mum fed me because she liked me, whereas Sophie's mum fed me so I'd help her daughter pass her exams.

'High time you called me Claudette, honey. Now, how long you staying at that asylum of Antoine's?'

Until December, I tell her.

She looks pleased. 'Then we'll expect you for Christmas, just like the old days. But you tell me, what's this about those poor dead girls and the vampire bites? And all that spirit writing? In a mental hospital? That's no place to worry the dead or scare the living, no wonder trouble came knocking at the door. So maybe Father Dom should visit?'

We're trying to persuade Claudette that Antoine's flat doesn't need exorcising, although the whole place could do with the services of a decent electrician, when Terry turns up, just in time for the peach cobbler. He's always been Terry to everyone, I can't imagine anyone calling him Mr Byrne.

'You early, honey?' A note of suspicion in Claudette's voice.

'Shorter working day than anticipated, my love.' Terry takes her hand in a courtly manner and kisses her on the cheek. I can see her thawing.

'Trouble from the feds, Pop?'

'Those young coppers down Whitechapel got some rigid ideas. Round here, they understand an honest businessman might not always have the paperwork on him. A more flexible approach to policing.'

'Would that be because they're your drinking buddies?' Antoine asks.

Terry does the wronged innocent look. It's even more convincing now his wide blue eyes are faded. 'Don't know what they're teaching those youngsters at Hendon nowadays, son, I really don't. Form-filling and box-ticking, not proper community policing.' Terry shakes his snowy head. 'Now, about those electrical problems you're having. I'm expecting a consignment of surge protectors soon. Maybe Monarch would be interested in them?'

Antoine shakes his head. 'You never going to retire?'

I'm amused to see Antoine's still embarrassed by his father. Personally, I've always been impressed by Terry's initiative, not to mention his brass neck. More front than Selfridges, Terry Byrne.

'I'm semi-retired. We go to Spain, don't we my angel, get a bit of sun.'

'See your mates,' Antoine mutters.

'A true businessman can never fully retire.' Terry leans back in his chair, opens his hands. 'There's always new opportunities in our evolving economy. I'm thinking of getting an app.'

ELLA'S JOURNAL
MARCH 21, 1907

I have been pleased with my progress toward sanity. As has Dr Wood. In general, I am calmer and the world around me has seemed less threatening and hostile. Until today.

Yesterday Lucy performed her spirit writing with great success. Although, as I had feared, it caused her to faint, once she recovered she was energised and happy. I concluded that perhaps my disquiet about this whole exercise was unfounded, which gave me cheer.

After the session, the doctor promised that Lucy and I might soon take a walk outside the grounds of the asylum. At this prospect of a little liberty, albeit bought by Lucy's spiritual labour, I was flooded by delight and hope for the future.

So, yesterday, I was buoyed up by relief about Lucy and the happy anticipation of a little freedom. Yet today I have had a terrible setback, which has caused my happiness to evaporate. I am trying to contain myself, although my reaction is a mixture of horror, dread and anger. At least I am able to reflect on these emotions and put names to them, which is progress of a kind.

I will calmly outline what has happened, in the hope that it will make me less agitated. In truth, it is a triumph that I can sit still and hold a pen. That I can achieve this is partly down to the calming effect of translating my turbulent thoughts into code.

This morning I received an anonymous letter. In rough and uneducated tones, it accuses me of something for which society would judge me harshly. It then goes on to demand a sum of money. The letter was posted locally and instructs me to send the monies to a London post office.

One of my family's servants must have betrayed me. Perhaps they gossiped about my secret to their relatives when they wrote home.

How dare the writer of this letter speak to me, Emmanuella Murray, in these terms? How dare he judge and threaten me! He deserves the full force of my anger and scorn. What a loathsome, cowardly, blackmailing excuse for a human being he is!

Yet I cannot tell him this. I do not want everyone here to know of my shame; that would be intrusive and unbearable. So I must meekly pay this vile man the sum he asks. In truth, rather than paying him, I would prefer to set about him with my baseball bat. That, I recognise, would not be progress, so I shall refrain from such an activity.

CHAPTER 12

FENELLA AMONG THE
DREAMCATCHERS

F ollowing in Terry's footsteps, I set off for
Whitechapel after lunch. Unlike Terry, I'm not
heading for the market. I'm visiting the English
Occult Society, whose base is near the London hospital. Given
the ghosts my visit to Poe raised, an occult society feels pretty
harmless to me.

I'm on the trail of this League for Psychic Studies that
Wood and his cronies belonged to. In particular, I need to find
out more about Von Helson's Telepathic Transfer Engine and
what they got up to with it. Neither Ella nor Wood seem interested in providing detailed accounts of its use, as far as I can
tell. When I've run searches on Von Helson I've found stuff
about his engineering research, but no trace of the magical
Engine. He never even registered the patent. Outside the
immediate circle of his spirit-seeking friends, it seems to have
been a secret.

So, after a lot of phone calls and emails, I've finally tracked
down what's left of the League for Psychic Studies archives
and made an appointment with a spaced-out posh lady, Fenella,

to look at them. I'm really hoping I get something here, because my search for the Engine has run into brick walls everywhere else.

The Occult Society isn't the oddest place I've visited in search of the dead. There have been many stranger. It's down a tatty side alleyway, away from the high-street busyness of the coriander-and-diesel scented market. There you can buy whole boxes of ripe papayas, cheap cigarettes, or bracelets glittering with acrylic jewels, all at knock-down prices. As well as dodgy phones. I spot an old-fashioned oil lamp that'll be handy next time the lights fail at Abney Heights. Mulder keeps trying to stick his tail in the candle flames. While I'm at it, I buy a five-quid box of mangoes. I have no use for them at all, but what a bargain.

The society's premises are up dark, wonky stairs above a printer's shop. Pretty much on the site of the seventeenth-century Stepney Mount plague pit, as it happens. That's the sort of thing you know about in my job. Where the bodies are buried.

Fenella greets me at the door. She's draped in swathes of floaty scarves and wears so much silver jewellery that she tinkles when she moves. She ushers me into a room where the windows are festooned with dreamcatchers, and the walls with esoteric pictures.

After admiring my new lamp, which blends in perfectly here, Fenella shows me into the room next to hers. It's crammed with dusty shelves, laden with books and files. To the left of the table, a glass-fronted case contains arcane equipment. Crystal balls, a tarot pack and a Ouija board jostle for place with animal skulls and ceremonial daggers. Everything in the cabinet is carefully polished and looks well used. Maybe Fenella unlocks it after hours and raises the souls of the thousands of dead, unceremoniously bundled into the earth deep below us.

On a table, Fenella has placed a few tattered old box files, *The League for Psychic Studies* written on their marbled covers in faded ink. I know better than to ask whether any of the League's records have been computerised.

She taps the files with a long purple fingernail. 'This is all there is on the League. Small organisation. Didn't last long. Know much about them, do you?'

I indicate I know virtually nothing.

'They thought they could create a brotherhood of the living and the dead. Particularly committed to the technique of spirit writing, one gathers.' She pauses for dramatic effect and lowers her voice reverently. 'That is what we call it when the dead write through the hand of the living.'

'Like – possession?'

'Now *that* is largely the stuff of Hollywood movies. The spirits are rarely hostile, you know. You'll find many examples of automatic writing during the early twentieth century. Henry James wrote at length through his former secretary, Theodora Bosanquet, after his death. And William and Evelyn De Morgan, both League members, were sensitives. Many artists were and still are. I have had some success at it myself.'

'So that's all they did? The League?'

'Their ideas were a little different to some of the other groups. They were socialists, suffragists, vegetarians, that type of thing.' Fenella waves her be-ringed hand in airy dismissal of that type of thing. 'Non-conformists of various kinds, some of them connected to a radical chapel, the Church of United Souls. Their church held a doctrinaire belief that everyone should be equal. The League expanded on that, wanting the living and the dead to be part of the same communistic brotherhood.'

'Do you know anything about the League's Telepathic Transfer Engine?' I ask.

'Machine to aid automatic writing, wasn't it? I don't believe it took off. Technology rarely holds the answer when it comes to the spirit world.'

She picks up the top box file. 'There are some newspaper clippings from the psychic press in this one. Do be careful with them, they're old and rather fragile.'

I produce a pair of the white cotton gloves. This mollifies Fenella to the extent that she offers me tea and tells me I can stay as long as I need. She'll be here all evening; there's a séance tonight.

'Ah, just one last thing, Fenella?' She turns in the doorway, her scarves fluttering. 'You've never heard of a connection between the League and, umm, vampirism?' I ask, sheepishly.

Fenella's laugh is surprisingly hearty. Vampires, too, are the stuff of Hollywood films, it seems. She leaves me to my enquiries into the equality between the living and the dead, returning only to present me with a cup of exquisite China tea, served in a cup and saucer so delicate it could have been woven by fairies.

You can say what you like about the genetically posh, but they do take their hot beverages seriously, an approach I wholeheartedly commend.

PAPER GIVEN AT THE LEAGUE
FOR PSYCHIC STUDIES

An Experiment in Spirit Writing

This automatic writing trial took place at Abney Asylum, Stoke Newington, in the drawing room of the superintendent, Dr Charles Wood, on 20 March 1907. Those present were two gentlewoman inmates, Miss N___, who was to perform the spirit writing and her friend Miss M___; Miss N's fiancé, the Hon Mr H___; Mrs Evelyn De Morgan, the prominent artist; Professor Gunther Von Helson, the inventor of the machine used in this session, the Telepathic Transfer Engine; Dr Wood; and your humble recorder of this momentous event, Mrs Harriet R. Kerr.

Along with the doctor, Mrs De Morgan and myself, the professor had previously experimented with the Engine, but we had failed to find the ideal sensitive to make it function. We remained confident that the machine would succeed, once the right person was discovered. I am delighted to say that the following account proves our faith as 'Spiritual Machinists' was not misplaced.

Professor Von Helson's invention consists, to the non-engineering eye, of a large rosewood box on wheels. Two doors covering the top surface open to display a great many brass pistons and cogs, and numerous glass tubes. These are connected to each other with belts and cables; at the front of the box is a series of glass-fronted brass dials. The machine is attached, by wires, both to a brass helmet with spokes radiating from it, and to a soft leather gauntlet.

We formed a circle around the Engine. Miss N___ was placed in a chair behind it, with leather restraints attached to the arms, back and seat. A wooden flap on the rear of the machine was pulled down to form a desk for her and she was provided with a notepad and pencil.

Mr H___ sat to her right and Miss M___ to her left. Both appeared anxious and concerned for her well-being, as Professor Von Helson strapped her into the chair and set the helmet apparatus on her head. Standing behind her, he then inserted her hand into the long glove and showed her how best to grasp the pencil. Miss N___ herself appeared nervous, as she clutched Miss M___'s hand. Yet she courageously acquiesced to her part in the event.

The professor moved a lever on the machine and looked at it intently, adjusting some controls at the back. It began to hum quietly. He took his seat and the seven of us joined hands, Mr H___ placing his left hand on Miss N___'s shoulder, as instructed by the professor, in order not to obstruct the writing process. He whispered something in her ear as he did so, but she smiled at him bravely and shook her head a little.

We closed our eyes and I invoked the spirits in the usual way, although nothing about that afternoon felt at all usual. We had high hopes for Miss N___'s abilities as a sensitive. Everything about her suggests it. She has a gentle, luminous, type of psychic energy. We felt the spirits would find her biddable.

Both Mrs De Morgan and I are sensitives, although our powers have not been of the sort to serve Von Helson's Engine. As the vibrations in the room grew, she and I both felt the magnetic aura and cried out with one voice, 'They are here.' To be part of the Engine's first successful use was tremendously exciting. We knew we were making history.

We all kept our eyes closed and waited. There was no sound but the scratching of Miss N___'s pencil on the writing pad. This continued, on and off, for about ten minutes, then Miss N___ gave a little cry. Miss M___, who sat to my right, immediately (and highly inadvisably, but it was the lady's first experience with the spirits) broke the circle and jumped up to help her. Once our circle was disturbed, the spirit presence vanished and we all opened our eyes. It transpired that Miss N___ had fainted, although her body was held up by the chair's straps.

Mr H___ helped Dr Wood move Miss M___, who was somewhat agitated, out of the way so the doctor could administer sal volatile to Miss N___. She came to immediately and looked around with shining eyes. As the professor released her from the machine she asked:

'Has it worked? Has anything been written?'

She appeared fully recovered, perhaps even energised by her experience. Dr Wood was pleased with this outcome, as he hopes to use the Engine therapeutically. After he performed some checks on his patient, he declared her fit to remain with us while I read out the spirit messages.

I record the messages below. Miss N___'s questions intersperse the spirit's answers, as we instructed her prior to the experiment. For clarity, I have indicated which utterances are from the spirit and which are from an earthly source.

Miss N___: Are you here?

Spirit: Yes, but I am not from here.

Miss N___: Where are you from, spirit?

Spirit: Many miles away. Another country. A beautiful place, full of light, where many flowers bloom.

Miss N___: What is it like where you are?

Spirit: There is no want. We have art, music and dancing. We may love whoever we choose.

Miss N___: What is your name?

Spirit: You may call me Countess Zana.

Miss N___: Do you have something to tell me, Countess?

Spirit: I want to tell you that you must be careful, my golden beauty. There are those in your world who would cause you harm. They may drain your life force.

Miss N___: Who are these people?

Spirit: They are many.

Miss N___: Do you have messages for anyone else?

Spirit: Tell him he should not try to change that which he most loves.

Miss N___: Who is this message for?

Spirit: He knows.

Miss N___: Are there other messages?

Spirit: This will be your greatest work of art. Art is the most important thing. It is greater than love, greater than life, even.

Miss N___: Is that message for Mrs De Morgan?

Spirit: I must go now.

CHAPTER 13

HOUSE OF THE SPIRITS

I take a photo of Harriet Kerr's spirit writing report. It's fascinating to hear her voice, which sounds more breathless and excited than I expected. I guess messages from beyond the veil were a big deal for them.

Great to get a physical description of the machinic reuniter of soul at last. Antoine'll be pleased, although sadly there's no pics of the Engine. So still nothing to illustrate the steampunk séance murder article he'll no doubt want to write.

The two contemporaneous excerpts from the 'psychic press' (why did they even need a press?) don't add much. One is equally thrilled, the other a little snarky. The snarky account refers to the group as 'the self-styled Spiritual Machinists' with their 'communistic views'. Both articles clearly had nothing more to go on than Harriet's report. One used a photo of Professor Von Helson, a stiffer, more sober-looking image than the one I found in the asylum archives this morning.

I sift through the League's archives for the few months after the Engine's success, which was reported at their April meeting, and discover Fenella was right. There's nothing more about the machine. What's more, I can find no reference to Harriet's merry gang after June 1907, although there are plenty of incidental mentions them attending meetings and events in the years before this.

Finally, after much searching, I find a later trace of them. It's in the minutes of the October 1907 meeting of the League.

Dr Charles Wood, Professor Gunther Von Helson, Mrs Harriet R. Kerr and Mrs Evelyn De Morgan tendered written resignations to the League for Psychic Studies as at the date of this meeting.

There's no explanation or discussion of their exit. What could have happened?

I scan through the minutes for the following couple of years. The only later allusion I find to them, or to the Engine, is in 1908, in a discussion of whether typewriters can be used for spirit writing. One member says that the League would not wish to turn themselves into Spiritual Machinists and everyone agrees that this would be an undesirable and potentially hazardous path.

Had there been a schism? A political difference, maybe? Their radicalism might be considered 'hazardous' at such a turbulent political time. There was unrest all over Europe in 1907, the Russian revolution was brewing, and an actual peasant's revolt was going on in Romania while they were contacting the spirits in London. My thoughts are interrupted by my phone. Antoine. He wants us to meet up later so I can show him what I've found. I'm seeing Benedict tonight, I tell him, pleased I can demonstrate that I have a life.

'Bring him round for dinner,' he suggests.

Despite misgivings about mixing my past with my present, I agree to see if Benedict fancies dinner with the Scooby Gang. Given that it will involve good food, a chance to meet my childhood friend, and an exciting narrative mystery, I'm pretty confident he will.

Eating at Antoine's for the third time this week, though? Like being back at school, except that he can cook now, and pretty impressively. Claudette's obviously passed on some of her skills. My mum lived on Pop Tarts, so the only way I learned to boil an egg was to teach myself and I'm still pretty rubbish at it – another way I fail the femininity test. I'll really have to invite Antoine back for a takeaway now I'm grown-up though.

MULDER AND SCULLY REGARD BENEDICT with interest, as we settle ourselves on their sofas before dinner. Scully, always on the lookout for new acolytes, takes over his lap and Mulder settles in between him and Uzi, demanding attention from them both, while we bring him up to speed on our mystery.

I'm surprised at what a massive relief it is to see Benedict. It makes me feel that I have a real existence outside here, where I'm relatively normal. It brings home to me how subtly destabilising it's been for me to be back in Hackney, hanging out with Antoine, like I'm still a teenager and the intervening twenty years never happened.

University was a big deal to me. For the first time, I was with people who only saw me as the girl in front of them. Unlike everyone I'd grown up with, they couldn't see the part of me that had disappeared. I stopped being the twin who wasn't, the one with the dead family and the crazy mother. I became a presence, rather than a being built round absence. Instead of being a spooky Polo mint, I was a Refresher. Maybe even a Love Heart? Anything was possible. Even Kathleen's death, after my first term, was a thing that happened to me, not a thing that was me.

So I definitely feel more relaxed having Benedict here, despite the strange collision of worlds his presence creates.

We abandon the cats (their view, not mine) to sit round Antoine's dining table and tuck into Thai curry and corn fritters. What about Wood's idea that Ella might have romantic feelings for Lucy? Antoine wants to know.

'He's far from definite about it, and he thinks he might be projecting,' I protest.

Antoine admits that, yeah, fair enough, Wood does have the hots for Lucy; Uzi thinks we can't let a misogynist like Wood define a woman's sexuality; perhaps we should wait until Ella tells us her feelings herself, Benedict suggests.

Antoine's keen to tell us his news: Sam's uncovered a story about William Finleigh, one of the local worthies on the asylum board. Finleigh's mother died when he was a young man and the circumstances were thought suspicious by the police. He was questioned, but not arrested. As he inherited money in her will, which he used to launch his business empire, the rumours about his role in her death never completely went away.

A potential matricidal killer is all the encouragement Antoine needs for his unlikely theories. 'Finleigh tries to assault Lucy,' he suggests. 'She fights back, there's a struggle and she falls. Or he pushes her.'

'And Ella?' I ask.

'She saw him.'

Antoine can't come up with a plausible reason why Lucy and Finleigh were in the cemetery chapel that day and why Ella was watching them, so none of us are exactly convinced.

After we've finished my mangoes, served up with some of Claudette's exquisite lemongrass sorbet, I read out Harriet's account of the automatic writing session and explain how the Engine and our spirit-chasers vanished from the League's archives after its first successful outing.

'How mysterious.' Benedict's light-blue eyes glow in his pale face. Everything about Benedict is light and somehow non-corporeal. If Harriet saw him she'd have him strapped to the Engine before you could say magnetic resonance. He's not biddable, though, he's an academic. 'And you've been unable to find any record of their endeavours after that?'

'Not in spiritualism. Wood has a profile as psychiatrist, Von Helson as an engineer, De Morgan as an artist and Harriet Kerr as a philanthropist and activist. I can't find any later mentions of the Engine or their Spiritual Machinist project.'

'These people cover their tracks,' Uzi mutters. She's looking tired. She's always verging on hyperactive, but today she's kind of jumpy with it. That's new – she's usually so self-possessed. I notice she hasn't invited Rowan.

'Why would they?' I ask, as she slips quickly away from the table to calm the two cats, who are clearly influenced by all the psychic talk. They're both standing, gazing with rapt attention at the same spot on the wall in front of them, as if it's a hole some evil mouse vanished into. They do a lot of that, mind, being cats.

'Because Von Helson wanted to keep his invention secret until they proved how successful it was,' Benedict says. 'He wouldn't have wanted anyone duplicating his work in the early stages of research.'

'Plus they wanted to be in control of their own PR,' suggests Antoine. 'So they could get maximum impact when they released the story. Then something went wrong, so they buried it.'

Uzi shakes her head, her eyes on the two cats she's stroking. Their gaze is still on the invisible mousehole, but their fur's no longer standing on end. 'It is worse than this. These two men and Harriet are exploiting Lucy. They are all her vampires, who make her do their bidding. The men use her to help their careers, and Harriet to speak with the dead. Here, in this room.' She gestures dramatically at Antoine's lounge. Benedict looks around with interest.

'This damages her eventually,' Uzi continues, 'so they kill her to cover up what they have done.' She seems unduly upset; she's really taking all this to heart. Is that what being an artist is like, I wonder? Having that level of emotional permeability?

'Evelyn wasn't part of their dastardly plot?' Antoine asks her.

'Evelyn De Morgan is different,' Uzi asserts. 'She is a talented artist. She painted one of her best works in here, that is what drew me to live in this place.'

Antoine's expression suggests this is news to him.

'How exciting, which of her works is that, my dear?' Benedict asks.

'"The House of Spirits",' says Uzi.

DR WOOD'S DIARY

20 MARCH 1907

I'm pleased to report that our automatic writing experiment has been successful, not just in a spiritual sense, but also in a medical one. After her treatment, Lucy showed every sign of being galvanised by the whole experience. Indeed, she exhibited interest in the Engine itself, asking the professor questions about its operations. I interpret this curiosity as evidence of the machine's enlivening effect upon the patient. I have great hopes for its use as a therapy.

After the séance, Homeward wanted reassurance about Lucy's health, which I was pleased to give him. He then asked me, rather awkwardly, if I thought the message from Countess Zana about not trying to 'change that which he most loves' had been for him.

I told him he mustn't take spirit words literally; the point of Lucy undergoing treatment was to bring about a change for the better.

'But, look here, the Countess said someone wanted to harm her. What kind of bounder would hurt an angel like Lucy?'

I told him it might be metaphorical. On seeing his puzzled expression, I explained that it may refer to the blood-sucking monsters of her troubled dreams.

'These spirits see into our dreams?' He looked shaken at the idea.

I tried to allay his fears. The modern world is a trial for a chap like Homeward. In truth, I am not even sure the message was for him.

ELLA'S JOURNAL

MARCH 26, 1907

My intention to write my journal as the field notes of a lady explorer has rather fallen by the wayside. Perhaps this is a good thing; I am living life instead of observing it. My friendship with Lucy has deepened into something rare and beautiful.

I now use this journal mainly when I must confide in someone other than my darling Lucy, or, indeed, than Dr Wood, in my talking sessions.

Today Dr Wood asked me if I was envious of Fanny. Perhaps I am, I admitted. Not only does she have Violet, but she also possesses a capacity for action I appear to have lost.

After the earthquake, Mama raised funds for the relief effort and Fanny travelled into town to administer the running of soup kitchens. I went with her. I was much recovered then from my earlier difficulties and even my family thought I would cope.

Yet when we arrived at the desolate city, it was a terrible shock to me. I saw a ruined place where people had lost everything and were camping in the rubble. Fanny rolled up her sleeves and set to ladling out food for them. I was meant to join her, but I could not. The lines of dusty, homeless ghosts filled me with horror. I had to leave that place.

In great agitation, I walked away. I wandered, lost around the city I knew so well, recognising nothing. Its buildings were shattered, its people bowed and hopeless. I picked up my pace, moving faster and faster through the never-ending nightmare. Turning a corner, I came to a quiet street. Half the houses were still standing, although some were smashed into rubble. No one was around; the respite from encountering those desperate people began to calm me. My heartbeat slowed and I walked a little way down the silent street, wondering at two sticks poking out oddly from a pile of rubble. As I came nearer, I realised they were not sticks.

They were limbs.

The unburied dead.

I could not move. I could not stop looking at the arm and the leg. A man's arm, in a shirt made grey by dust. His leg, in brown tweed trousers. An arm, a leg, they seemed so ordinary. Yet so horrific.

I recall sinking down onto the ground. I was shaking violently. Perhaps I was screaming. I do not know. I remember little more until I awoke, back in my bedroom. After that I was not well for some months and eventually was sent here.

So, yes, I envy Fanny. When tested, I folded completely, collapsing like a feeble woman, while she was able to dole out stew to the homeless and somehow find me and take me home. She was resilient and capable.

Like I used to be.

All this I relate to Dr Wood. Is it making me better? I do not know. I am calmer, certainly, but that might be down to Lucy's gentle influence. Or, indeed, to the water therapy.

Every day I swim for an hour in the silent basement pool. Each splash echoes around the dimly lit, blue-tiled walls. An attendant sits, impassive, bored, watching me glide up and down, up and down, cutting my way through the blue water. I love this time. Here I feel I am most myself whilst being able to forget myself and my problems. There is nothing in the world but my movement through the water. My thoughts are still and my mind becomes that of an aquatic creature, focussing only on my movement, as I dive under and see nothing but my watery world, slow-moving and silent. For an hour, I am master of my element.

Sometimes the movement back and forth, as I swim lap after lap, becomes hypnotic and I enter a trance-like state. Then I sense another presence. A benign being, someone who accepts me as I am and does not think I need to be less wayward. Someone who sees that my passion and my anger is part of who I am and not something to be cured. Perhaps it is the presence of a friend I feel, in the flickering light of the pool; a visit from one of Harriet Kerr's benign spirits. Or perhaps it is the presence of God.

Dr Wood's water cure also includes hot baths and cold baths. Bracing treatments, not the cruel Victorian water torture which both froze and half drowned the poor patients. It is not so long ago that this happened here, although it seems like another age. Lucy says she can feel the anguish of those previous inmates in the bathing basement and that is why she does not like to go there. Dr Wood gives her modern electro-therapy instead, in his study. She says it hurts a little, but that the doctor thinks it is helping her to recover.

UZI'S MESSAGES

2 OCTOBER 2019

Zana: Hey babe

FairyGirl21: Hello sweetheart

Zana: Listen, that thing you asked me? About those guys?

FairyGirl21: Did you discover anything? It's hard for me, I cannot get out much and they are always watching

Zana: That's not good

FairyGirl21: What did you learn my sweet?

Zana: They're mostly ok, except William

FairyGirl21: Why?

Zana: Secret, right? 🌕

FairyGirl21: Of course

Zana: I hear he killed someone

FairyGirl21: No!

Zana: It's worse. His own mother

FairyGirl21: But that's terrible. Was he not apprehended?

Zana: Not him. But you can't tell BF. Or anyone

FairyGirl21: Oh I won't. You can trust me

Zana: I totally trust you babe

ELLA'S JOURNAL
APRIL 1, 1907

Something delightful has occurred. We have been outside the grounds of the asylum. Not once, but twice!

I feel such a sense of liberty from these small experiences. They change the way I am – indeed, they change *who* I am – once I am back inside these four walls. I feel so much more alive, more like the woman I used to be; yet improved by Lucy's influence.

The first delicious taste of freedom was some days ago, when Lucy and I were invited to tea by Mrs Kerr, or Harriet as I now call her.

She sent her carriage for us. During the journey I looked excitedly out of the window, eager to see the world beyond the asylum. It was a sunny spring afternoon and the gardens were bright with golden daffodils. These sent Lucy into raptures; she felt they were God's sunlight, made into flowers. I laughed and explained how botany teaches us that God's sunlight is quite literally transformed into flowers, which delighted her. Our journey took us down a wide, leafy avenue of handsome terraced houses. Gaily dressed servant girls stepped lightly to assignations in the tearooms or park on their afternoon off. Tradesmen's carts trundled past, and starched nannies pushed perambulators along the sidewalk.

All this I drank in, greedily. Only Dr Wood's presence reminded me this was not merely a jolly drive to attend a social occasion; it was also another of his experiments. He was on hand to observe how his subjects behaved.

As we turned into a smaller road, Dr Wood pointed out a building which looked a little like a warehouse. He told us it was a giraffe house. When we expressed amazement and disbelief, he suggested we ask Harriet about it, which we later did.

It was a short journey to Harriet's home in Church Row. We passed several fine dwellings on this street, set back from the road and partly obscured by plane trees. When the carriage stopped outside the gates of Carfax House, Lucy said she felt we'd been transported into one of the novels of Miss Austen, for the house is a secluded Georgian dwelling almost hidden by an informal riot of spring flowers. It made her think of a particularly fine country vicarage.

There is nothing old-fashioned about the interior of Harriet's home, which is light and spacious, with beautifully decorated wallpapers and fabrics, and elegant wooden furnishings, all in the modern Arts and Crafts style. Everything is neat, clean and polished. I know Harriet has more important things to think about than the running of her home, so I had expected it to be rather more haphazard. Apparently, she has an old and faithful housekeeper who keeps everything in order for her.

Harriet was a welcoming hostess and we did justice to the treats she provided, which were all vegetarian but nevertheless delicious. They were brought in by a neat little maid whom Dr Wood greeted as one of his former patients. I offered to pour when I saw Harriet's inattentiveness around practical matters was likely to result in calamity. I got a nod of approval from the doctor at that.

It was enjoyable to talk with Harriet on an occasion when we were not attempting to raise the dead. Her ideas are more radical and far ranging than any I have come across. She is, for example, an enthusiastic anti-vivisectionist, as well as a committed vegetarian. I admire this. Horses and dogs have much more sense than people, I have always thought. She told us the giraffes imprisoned in the warehouse were captured in Africa by an evil man named Frank Bostock, who also enslaved lions. All these poor wild animals he treated with great cruelty in order to cow them and force them do his bidding in his circus acts.

A horrifying tale, and the only point when I feared our outing might go awry. Lucy became anxious at the idea that lions might be roaming around in the woodland behind the asylum and began to shake a little. I could see Dr Wood becoming concerned, but when I put my arm around Lucy and spoke to her softly, she became calmer.

'Such a sensitive soul,' Harriet murmured. 'That is why you have these special powers.'

Much as I like and respect Harriet, I am concerned that the success of this Telepathic Transfer Engine is turning her enthusiasm for contacting the dead into an obsession. And all of it depends on Lucy.

There have now been three spiritualist sessions and I remain uneasy about them, despite their positive effects on dear Lucy. At each event her Countess sent messages for those present. Harriet heard from her late husband, Peter, another keen reformer. She was particularly pleased to be told that their dog, Carlo, is with him.

The make-up of these seances has varied a little. Dr Wood, the professor and Harriet have always been there, but Mr

Homeward has had to attend to his family affairs in the country and Mrs De Morgan has her work, so they are both sometimes absent. To make up the numbers, two members of the Asylum Board have joined us. They are a Mr William Finleigh and a Mr Ezekial Chamberlain.

Mr Finleigh, a confident little man, received messages from his late mother, which threw him entirely out of countenance. Mr Chamberlain is a friendly and good-humoured young gentleman, who treated the whole affair as a parlour game. Perhaps because he wasn't visited by ghosts.

Am I afraid of hearing from the ghost I dread? Could this be part of the reason why I dislike these sessions? Dr Wood encourages me to interrogate my motives when I feel hostile or angry. Anger is often a manifestation of fear, he tells me, and it is this fear which we must uncover. Yet I believe that anger is sometimes righteous. There is much in this world to be angry about.

There was nothing to spark such feeling at our Church Row tea party, so it was not only enjoyed by us all, but was deemed a success by the doctor, who was pleased with our ability to act like normal ladies in a drawing room. We will be permitted to return, a prospect which pleases me enormously. Lucy is a little less enthusiastic.

'I cannot take part in the clever conversations you and Harriet have,' she said. 'It makes me feel I can never be the friend to you that she is.'

I reassured Lucy that my friendship with her is deeper and more intimate than any I have ever had. She need not be jealous of Harriet. Yet a small, unworthy, part of me was secretly pleased that she cares enough to feel that way.

Today we were allowed to go for a walk outside the grounds, accompanied only by an attendant. It was a short stroll as Lucy, though improving, is not yet strong enough for anything strenuous. Our outing took us back down the grand parade of Manor Road, then along some streets where the middling classes live. We made sure to keep away from the giraffes of Yoakley Road, as Lucy is upset by the idea of their imprisonment. I do not like it either. I have some fellow feeling for the beasts; at least we are prisoners who are allowed to see the sun and breathe the fresh air. Our attendant, Nell, was happy to avoid the street, telling us that the smell of the creatures was enough to keep a Christian away. She believes Bostock secretly keeps lions locally, too, and swears she has heard them roaring when the moon is full.

CHAPTER 14

AGITATORS AND AESTHETES

P ainstaking though it is to translate Ella's journal, I'm enjoying it; letters and diaries have always been my favourite way of bringing the dead to life. I'm getting quite fond of Betty's great-aunt, despite her autocratic tendencies. I like her wry observations, such as her account of William Finleigh being contacted by his mother's ghost. I want to know whose ghost is haunting *her* and why she's being blackmailed.

Benedict's still in London but he's been busy with his conference. We're meeting up with the others tomorrow to see the 'House of the Spirits' at the De Morgan Centre, before he returns to St Cadog's. Uzi's insisting we have to trek down to Wandsworth to see the original painting. Website reproductions just aren't good enough.

I've spent the last few days, and half the nights, pushing on with the asylum archive. Lots of pressure from Monarch. Today I took a massive pile of categorised papers round for the intern to copy into our database, that'll keep them quiet for a bit. Plus the intern's just created a decent-looking web interface, capable lad, which gives them something to show the council.

So I'm coping. I haven't fallen apart. Yet. Mostly I'm alright, I just don't think about the past unless I get a text or call from Eileen. Then it all comes flooding back. So I avoid her, concentrate on my two jobs, and ignore anything lurking in the shadows.

Managing Betty's been occupying too much of my time recently. She's pretty chatty for such a busy woman. When I let slip that I'm originally from Hackney, she started asking about my background. It's other people's family stories that interest me, not my own, I told her. Clients aren't usually so nosy, but that's Betty for you. Our initial exchange included her grilling me about my domestic circumstances; presumably to make sure I could drop everything and take off to London at a moment's notice.

Betty's happy that our merry band of vampire hunters has expanded again to include Benedict (who could definitely play Giles). The six of us even have a text group. Betty's okay, really, just demanding. I'm pretty sure she thinks she's Buffy.

My phone bleeps. Yet another text from Betty (but better than being from Eileen).

Betty: Sifting through some family letters has given me an idea about Ella. Can we talk about it? Maybe a video call this time?

Normally I'd make a client wait a couple of days for a meeting, expectation management and all that, but I'm too eager to know what she's found. I agree to talk later.

As our appointed meeting time approaches, I glance at the mirror, release my haywire corkscrew hair from its scrunchie, rake my fingers through it and tie it back again, trying to change the effect from 'unkempt' to 'artfully dishevelled.' It's our first video call, so I want to make the right impression. I smooth down my rumpled hoodie and pick off the bigger bits of cat fluff off my T-shirt. Try on a smart professional smile and abandon it when it looks more like mania.

Why is normal so hard to achieve?

Feet trot past my windows stepping daintily in a pair of buttoned boots, topped by the hem of a lace petticoat. I blink and realise they're actually ordinary chelsea boots, worn by one of the rarely seen tenants. With jeans. I've done this a few times lately and it's beginning to bother me. It's partly lack of sleep, partly that I'm obsessing about the past and seeing it in the present.

Pushing away the thought that my job is all about obsessing over the past, yet this has never happened to me before, I take my laptop out into the walled garden. I won't get distracted by ghostly feet here and, more importantly, I can avoid tidying up. It's a pretty little place, this surviving part of the asylum airing courts, where the children clustered round Lucy to hear fairy stories, and Ella got interviewed by Lady Barnum for the post of Lucy's friend. The stairs up to it are near my flat, so I can still get a decent signal. I often have my working lunch out here.

BETTY PACKS in a lot of presence from my laptop. A spare woman with a grey bob and TV-screen glasses; bright clothing and statement jewellery.

'Hey, so good to see you, Meghan.' She looks out at me with a hungry intensity. Like a carnivorous Uzi. I'll use my phone next time, she might feel more manageable smaller.

She's delighted to hear that I'm sitting in Ella's airing court and insists that I show her what it looks like.

'Did you find out anything about the picture of Ella?' I ask, when I've finished the tour of the little courtyard.

Betty had offered to circulate the asylum photo to her cousins. They're the offspring of Fanny's younger daughter, Rosemary, whom Ella didn't live long enough to meet. Apparently, they'd been closer to grandmother Fanny than Betty ever had, so it was worth a go.

She shakes her head. 'It was new to all of us, Meghan. What a good portrait, though; my aunt certainly was a dashing lady. It kind of backs up what I found in the letters. As do some of the hints she drops in her diary, and the fact that she was being blackmailed.'

Betty knows Ella's secret. I sit up eagerly on the patio chair.

'The letters I mentioned are mainly between Ella's mother and father, when he was away on business,' she continues. 'Her mother wasn't happy about the company Ella was keeping here. She calls them "Young women with outlandish ideas about suffrage, and communistic young men". She felt it was affecting Ella, giving her attitudes that would damage her ability to make a good marriage.'

'Interesting,' I say. 'When she says in her journal that her mother thinks she's wayward, I assumed that was mainly about her mental illness. As well as all the feminism and bicycling.'

'Her mother starts complaining about it way before her first breakdown. She really doesn't like Ella's friends. She refers to the young men as "either agitators or aesthetes".'

'I'm assuming neither was good in those rugged gold-mining days?'

'Not as far as Ella's mom was concerned. Aesthete is a curious word to use as a slight, isn't it?'

Like the way people talked about Oscar Wilde at the end of the nineteenth century, I wonder?

'Exactly,' Betty replies. 'A coded slur about gay men. So, I'm wondering, is that her main concern about Ella? Not only that she's interested in women's rights, but that she's also interested in women?'

ELLA'S JOURNAL

APRIL 9, 1907

It seems I have not become a frequent journaler. Indeed, nowadays I prefer to talk to my darling Lucy, rather than scribble out my thoughts in a book. Although I now write my code with relative fluency, when I look back at my earlier accounts I find it slower to decode. Deciphering it makes my entries feel as if they have been written by a stranger, perhaps by a lady in a nineteenth-century novel writing of her confined world, her hopes and fears, and the disallowed yearnings of her heart.

This afternoon Lucy and I had the wonderful good fortune to visit the woodland cemetery behind the asylum, which I have looked out at longingly during these two months of incarceration. Seeing it through the barred windows of the asylum, or, at a greater and unobstructed height, from Dr Wood's drawing room, has made it into an exciting, forbidden place in my mind.

I say we have had good fortune, but in truth we have earned this reward. It is well deserved, as yesterday we had our fourth session with the Telepathic Transfer Engine. I shall not dwell on it, as I still do not find these events comfortable and neither, I believe, does Mr Homeward. He has not the wit to express his concerns and merely goes along with the wishes of his clever friend Dr Wood. Yet, only today, when I was helping Lucy pin on her hat before we ventured out, I noticed that under the lace at her neck there are red marks, which I can only think are caused by the Engine. This cannot be good.

Dr Wood is certain that the improvement in Lucy's health is partly from the spirit writing, but who can tell? Sometimes I still feel the doctor is treating us as creatures in his laboratory. My disgust at that is as strong as my horror of the animal vivisection Harriet campaigns against.

Whatever the reason for her improvement, Lucy is now rosy-cheeked and much less languid. She is not as tired by all the demands made on her and is excited to go out walking. Apart from today's delightful outing, we have previously had other short excursions along the local streets since the last I recorded. On one occasion we went up the grand parade of Stamford Hill, the new electric trams clanging past us. Lucy managed the uphill walk admirably and took much interest in some elegant ladies' boots in a shop at the top of the hill.

Today's visit to Abney Park Cemetery was so much better than our other walks. The park was conceived as an arboretum, as well as a resting place for the dead, and has many fine trees from all over the world.

We were accompanied by Nell, as ever. After our earlier excursion, I warned her that she must not say anything to upset Miss Northaway. No more lions, I told her. She was surly about it, but Lucy is a favourite of hers, so Nell will keep a check on her tall stories if she thinks they might cause Lucy any distress. In truth, Nell is a witless, insolent workhouse girl who dislikes me and often tells me that she is my keeper, not my servant. She does not dislike my money, however, and today

I was able to bribe her to keep her distance from us. She may have done it without bribery, if Lucy had asked, but I feel it is better to put these matters on a business footing.

Approaching the cemetery is exciting in itself, as the grand entrance is on the high street. We have not previously walked this way, although I recall glimpsing it from the carriage when I was first brought to the asylum. I had other preoccupations then. Now I can think more clearly, I was able to observe the hustle and bustle of suburban traffic and commerce. Although far more muted than the noise of a city, it still seemed busy to my unaccustomed senses. Women milled around the shopfronts, where Lucy was distracted by a milliner's. I promised we should visit there on our next outing.

We entered through imposing Egyptianate gates. Carvings of lotus flowers decorate the pillars, and the gatehouses are adorned with hieroglyphs. Yet it is tasteful and restrained, in keeping with this dissenters' burial ground. Less so is the advertisement for Dunkley's monumental masons which loomed above us as we passed through the gates, being opportunistically painted on the side of their premises next door.

Once inside, we promenaded along the wooded avenues, like fashionable Parisian ladies taking a turn around Père Lachaise in the April sunshine. Blackbirds I once envied, when I saw them from the barred windows of my room, sang to us from the treetops. The first butterflies of spring flitted around us.

Seen from the ground, it is an impressive, elegant park, with such a wide range of trees that even I do not know the names of some of them. I resolve to look them up. Lucy, bless her, was excited even to learn the difference between an elm and an oak tree. I would love to show my little urchins these exotic specimens in their woodcraft lessons, but that would never be permitted.

In the middle of the park stands a charming little brick-built funeral chapel, turreted and crenellated as if it has fallen from a fairy tale and into the woodland. Ivy covers the front of the chapel, lending it a most mysterious air. It is ornate for a dissenters' cemetery, but Lucy was very taken with it. Nell told us it was known to be a place where spirits walk and that it was bad luck to enter. Naturally, we ignored her and found the interior to be charming. It is furnished with plain oaken pews, the back row being ornamented with a line of wrought-iron fleur-de-lis, which again made me think of Paris. I felt they were a sign. Although the chapel altar is pleasingly simple, the windows are arched Gothic affairs, rich with stained glass. Lucy loved it all so much, I forgave the architect his unseemly excesses. She was particularly delighted with the internal balcony, which is lit by a sapphire-and-gold rose window. She skipped up its spiral staircase and struck a dramatic posture at the front of the balcony, as if on a stage. How lovely she looked there, illuminated by the jewel-coloured light. She called down to me that she was a princess locked in a tower and I must climb up and save her. We were still laughing when we re-joined Nell, who was standing guard outside.

It is fortunate Nell is so superstitious, as it means we now have somewhere private to go when we are in the outside world. This is precious, and we will certainly return to the chapel on our future walks.

We had another wonderful moment later on, in a sunny glade, when an electric-blue dragonfly came swooping down and hovered in front of us, as if watching to see what kind of creatures we were. Lucy was scared at first and clung to me for support. 'My governess called them devil's darning needles.'

Once I assured her the dragonfly would not sting her, she began to appreciate the creature's elegance and agility. 'I learn so much from you, my darling,' she said. 'You help me to have courage.'

She is a dear girl, indeed, and I believe her to have courage of her own, for she is able to participate so bravely in this project of communing with the spirits. Everyone at these events demands too much from her. Even Mrs De Morgan wishes to paint her, which is an honour, of course; but must she be an artistic muse as well as a psychic and scientific one? Then there are the demands Mr Homeward makes of her. It is little wonder he adores her and wishes to marry her as soon as possible, but it is for his sake that she feels the pressure to transform herself so quickly into a capable and composed wife. So many people want so much from the poor soul and she is such a frail creature. Sometimes I think of her as a fairy surrounded by mortals who all insist she grant their wishes.

In addition to the work she already does with the children, there has been talk about her helping them put on a play. The scenery and props would be made in the boys' craft sessions, and the costumes in the girls'. As Lucy teaches them their letters, she would help them to learn their lines and oversee their acting.

Everyone is excited about the idea, particularly the little ragamuffins themselves, but I cannot help feel her new project is too demanding. She already gives so much to the children. She is forever buying them little gifts of sweets and is always there to dry their eyes and listen to their childish fears, when they are distressed. Naturally, this is quite often, as some of them are confused, others overwrought and some just slow, simple and inclined to be bullied.

I resolve to help her with this play in any way I can. She must not take too great a burden on her delicate shoulders.

Lucy and I now spend much of our free in each other's company. She tells me of her home, of her hopes for the future and of her fears. She loves to hear my stories of California and wants to know all about my darling Violet. When I tell her tales I have read about other countries and talk of my wish to travel she is enchanted. She has never been outside of England.

Lucy says she has never been able to talk to anyone this way before; our friendship is a special one. Indeed, I cannot help but think that part of the reason for her improved health is because she finds my companionship soothing. I know I feel so much better for spending time in her company.

It pains me when I hear her cry out at night in fear and there is no one but the half-witted attendants to go to her. They are not bad women, not vicious as in some institutions, but they are one of Harriet's many social projects. All are from the workhouse. They have not the education or refinement to understand the fears of a lady like Lucy. I sound like my mother there, but sadly it is true. They are not what she needs when she awakes in terror, and it tears at me to hear her, knowing my door is locked and I am not free to give her the comfort that would surely calm her.

CHAPTER 15

MONSTERS AND BLOSSOMS

E ntering the De Morgan Centre on Saturday morning, we're greeted by throngs of fantastical beasts and exotic flowers. They crawl over jugs, tiles and plates; William De Morgan's ceramics hold pride of place in this small, tightly packed gallery dedicated to the two pre-Raphaelite artists.

Antoine stops before an ornate set of turquoise and blue tiles. 'Looks like the mosque at Dalston.'

'He is influenced by the Turkish ceramic tradition,' Uzi answers.

'Ripped it off, you mean,' says Antoine.

Uzi shrugs. 'All art is re-imagining.'

'Maybe, but there's still a sort of colonial thing going on,' Rowan says and we all start squabbling about art and cultural imperialism, with Benedict refereeing, until his eye lights upon a tiled fireplace surround.

'Oh, my goodness, they have the Jabberwocky work.'

A medieval galleon sails across the top of a fireplace, while lustrous red dodos and jabberwocks gambol down its sides.

'It's the one De Morgan made for his friend Charles Dodgson,' Benedict says. 'Lewis Carroll, that is.'

I gaze at the eerie creation, fascinated. The Alice books have always had a special place in my heart.

'Wasn't he the one who took dodgy photos of little girls?' Antoine asks.

I huff. 'Common belief, no evidence to support it.'

'I've seen the photos he took of that Alice kid. They looked pretty suspicious to me.'

'I believe one of Dodgson's biographers took that perspective.' Benedict hasn't put up with Antoine's lurid conclusions as long as I have. 'However most take the view that his photographic work was similar to that of other Victorian artists. They depicted children in a state of innocence.'

'Interesting that the De Morgans had a possibly dodgy friend, though,' Antoine says.

'Dodgson was a prominent writer and photographic artist,' Benedict replies, mildly. 'So he was friends with a number of the pre-Raphaelites – Rossetti, Holman Hunt, Millais. They all shared an interest in spiritualism.'

Antoine narrowed his eyes. 'Curiouser and curiouser. Maybe he was the asylum photographer.'

'That would be really creepy,' I say. 'Seeing as he'd been dead for years by then.'

'This is a beautiful piece of work.' Uzi stares at the fireplace. 'Superbly executed. But come see the "House of the Spirits". It has more power.'

We follow Uzi through all the monsters and blossoms to a separate room containing Evelyn's pictures. Uzi halts suddenly in front of an enormous gilt-framed painting.

It depicts a very young woman seated on a throne. She's tied down by wisps of ectoplasm, while bolts of lightning strike the chair from above. All around her, the sketchy forms of devilish creatures hover, stretching out their hands to clutch at her. They looked carnivorous and hungry. I shiver. I can see why Uzi is so attracted to this picture.

The striking thing about the painting isn't the rapacious ghosts, alarming though they are. It's the seated girl. Her head is tilted slightly back and her unfocussed, heavy-lidded eyes hold an ecstatic, yet terrified, expression. Her body glows eerily as she stretches back in the chair, her neck exposed, as if being sacrificed to a bloodthirsty deity.

She doesn't have the strong, goddess-like beauty that you get in a lot of pre-Raphaelite art. She's gentle, delicate and otherworldly. Rather childlike. Despite her obvious fear in the face of the invading spirits, everything about her face and the arch of her body suggest a kind of panicky, electrified pleasure. If she *is* a sacrifice, she's a willing one.

It's then I realise. Ella says De Morgan wants to paint Lucy and this picture was painted in the asylum, according to Uzi.

'Uzi, is this Lucy?' I ask. The thought had never occurred to me when I'd looked at a little reproduction of the picture on my phone.

'Of course.' She stares up at it, transfixed.

Why has she only just told us? We've been chasing Lucy and Ella's ghosts together for over a fortnight.

'Fascinating,' Benedict peers at the image. 'Would I be right in saying this is a little untypical of her work, Uzi?'

'It is her best.' Uzi is still gazing raptly up at the painting.

So, now we have it. A portrait of Lucy, the woman everyone wants so much from.

'What you said last week about Lucy choosing victimhood?' I say, quietly, to Rowan. 'She does kind of look like she's colluding with those demons. Unless that's just how Evelyn De Morgan wanted to see it.'

Rowan nods, slowly.

I look round for Antoine, who's already back at the entrance desk, getting details of who to contact about reproducing the painting. He looks delighted, in a way that's particularly aggravating. It's just the sort of picture an editor would want for a murder story.

The painting is wonderful, but it makes me uncomfortable, under the circumstances. The others continue to take it in – Benedict thoughtfully, Uzi greedily and Rowan impassively.

'The angel of the asylum,' Rowan says.

I HAVEN'T FOUND much about the Church of United Souls in my searches, other than that their biggest congregation was in Hackney. In 1907 they were based at a chapel in Clapton, which must have been the one Wood and his mates frequented. So, on my detour to Paddington to see Benedict off, I ask if he knows anything about the group. Benedict's a devout Methodist, in fact he was a Methodist monk for a few years in his twenties, until he met David. Given how much he knows about pretty much everything, I thought he might have heard of the United Souls. And I was right.

'Hmm, one of those radical groups from the first half of the twentieth century, I believe. They've probably mutated into something else now.'

'They were into spiritualism?'

'Well, of course, everyone was at the time. Mark Twain, Sir Arthur Conan Doyle. Messages being sent between the living and dead, telepathy between the living, it was all the rage. Von Helson wasn't alone in thinking it was the next step for technology.'

'Nothing sinister about the United Souls?'

'I've never heard of anything dubious. They were keen on

communal living, so I seem to recall they had a resurgence in the late sixties, but I never had any direct contact with them. I'll ask around for you, shall I ?'

'That would be great, thanks. Listen, I haven't told the others yet, but Betty has this idea, based on some hints Ella's mother dropped in letters, that Ella was gay. Which backs up what Wood says earlier. Although we haven't explicitly heard from Ella on the matter...'

'... she does seem rather fond of Lucy, I agree.'

'How would the United Souls respond to that?'

'Interesting question. Some of them would have been accepting, as long as discretion was observed. Her psychiatrist wouldn't be one of them, I'm afraid, even though there were probably lesbians and gay men in his social circle. Like most of his profession at the time, Wood viewed "inversion" as something he could cure.'

CHAPTER 16

ALL ABOUT LUCY

Sitting down to make an early start on the archiving, I unearth an email in my junk folder from the cemetery office. I ordered a grave search for Northaway, on the unlikely off-chance that Lucy's buried next door too. Surprisingly, she is and they've sent me the location. Excellent.

Mid morning, Antoine calls. I resist his invitation to come out and play.

'Still doing your homework on Sundays?' he says and I point out I'm still working two jobs. He insists that his job is always on, which it is, but that he can still find time to relax, which he can. So, in the interests of work-death balance, I agree to take him to Abney Park later this afternoon, show him Ella and Lucy's graves.

'I'll bring Uzi,' he says. 'She can take atmospheric pics.'

IT'S AN OVERCAST, blustery day and there are few people around when we pass through the massive Egyptian-themed gates which so impressed Ella. They're still pretty magnificent, despite the graffiti.

I've always loved the cemetery. It's a wild, uncanny place, built by the Victorians as one of their famous 'Magnificent Seven' necropoli, intended to house dead Londoners out in the suburbs. Now the grand gates are a portal from the inner city to thirty acres of enchanted forest full of dilapidated graves and secret, overgrown footpaths. It's a peaceful coexistence of dog walkers, goths, street drinkers, birdwatchers and guys looking for quick, masculine liaisons in the woodland of the dead. At night it belongs to foxes, owls and bats. Not to mention the dead themselves, drifting down the moonlit pathways. They don't feel especially absent in the daytime.

Angels with broken wings watch us from their ivy-covered pillars, as we walk down the path where Ella and Lucy promenaded. There's an autumnal smell of damp earth and faded flowers. It feels strange to be in the place Ella and Lucy discovered together on that spring day, over a hundred years ago. No dragonflies for us on this chilly afternoon, but we're seeing some of the same trees and graves, and walking the paths they trod. I feel the intimacy of our two realities overlaying each other, separated only by time. It echoes all the other unlikely coexistences that lurk among the marble and the brambles.

I take them to see Ella first, despite Uzi's impatience; it's Lucy's grave she's interested in. I've visited Ella before, it was one of the first things I did when I got here. She's easy to find. On the broad avenue of imposing monuments where Ella's buried, snooty angels look down their noses at us from their elevated height, and massive obelisks thrust their way into the cloudy heavens. Dunkley's monumental masons did a cracking trade down this ghostly street.

Ella's tidy grave is fashioned from smart black marble, topped with a big draped urn and surrounded by a spiky wrought-iron border. In the symbolism of funerary architecture, metal spikes are supposed to protect graves from demons. Personally, I think they were used to keep the Victorian poor from sleeping on the graves of the rich. Defensible space for the dead.

On Ella's defended tomb it says:

Emmanuella Hope Murray
1 May 1878 – 20 June 1907
Beloved daughter of Zachariah and Claire Murray

In my father's house there are many mansions

Antoine looks disappointed. It's nothing like the atmospheric ivy-covered decay he's hoping for. It's conventional, free from demons and completely lacking in personality.

Nothing like Ella either.

'Pretty impersonal,' he complains. 'She died young, in suspicious circumstances and that's the best they could do?'

Uzi unsheathes her camera. 'What does this mean?' she asks, gesturing at the tomb. 'These mansions?'

'Probably that heaven is open to everyone,' I reply. 'Even someone as wayward and troubled as Ella. In her family's view.'

'Harsh,' says Antoine, while Uzi takes deft photos from unlikely angles.

'Listen,' I say, 'if I tell you this, Antoine, you have to promise you'll use it sensitively in your story.'

He does the innocent look and crosses himself.

'Betty thinks Ella was gay. So that could be what the blackmail was about.'

Uzi looks up from her photographic work. 'That is why they committed her.'

'Partly, but she did have a breakdown and other mental health issues, too,' I say.

'Not to be accepted for herself, this would cause mental illness, yes,' Uzi says. 'It is still the same.'

'Fair point,' I reply. 'It's not the whole story though. She hints at something else, in her journal, remember. Something in her past.'

'The question is,' Antoine goes straight for the human interest story, 'Was there anything between her and Lucy? It gets pretty romantic when they come here for their walk. All that princess in the tower stuff.'

I think so too, but I'm not giving Antoine's imagination any encouragement. 'Women described their friendships with other women like that,' I say. 'Remember how Mina talks about the other Lucy, in *Dracula*? It doesn't have to signify romance.'

'Homeward found out,' Antoine continues. 'That's why he murdered them both. In a jealous rage.'

I sigh. 'We don't know that they were murdered, Antoine.' I know I sound like a stuck record, but I've already had enough of Betty's theories about a murderous Homeward. She loves the idea of a moustache-twirling, amoral British aristocrat.

'Lucy would not like Ella, anyway.' Uzi turns away from the grave. 'She is too bossy and patronising.' She flounces off to take photos of the angels.

'Uzi's taking all this to heart,' I say, quietly. 'Is she okay?'

He looks over but she's moved out of our sightline. Uzi doesn't hang around.

'Yeah, no, she's just not that into Ella. So she doesn't want her to be Lucy's girlfriend. I am concerned about her, though. She has been weird lately; Rowan's noticed it, too.'

'She does look tired. What's she been up to the ficing artichokes at the full moon?'

'That would be normal. Nah, like you said, she's taking this mega-seriously. Getting too preoccupied and emotionally involved with it. And she's speeded up; she's getting kind of manic. She comes out with funny things too.'

'Like what?'

'Like – last night she asked if me and you were walking out together.'

I feel myself blushing and turn away, pretending to examine the metalwork surrounding Ella's tomb.

'I hope you put her straight,' I chortle. Since my return I've been uncomfortably aware that Antoine might have misunderstood why I dropped contact.

It wasn't about the romance thing; there'd never been any romance thing, not between us. It was about something far more important.

It went back to that day, three months after our A levels. Me, Antoine and Sophie had become a tight unit. We supported each other through the exams and celebrated together afterwards. We went everywhere together; the three musketeers, Claudette called us.

That sunny day in September, I went to meet them on Stoke Newington Common. They didn't see me at first. They sat still on the grass, staring into each other's eyes. Not touching, or giggling. That wouldn't have been so bad.

The moment I walked in on their silence, I realised it was over. They meant far more to each other than I meant to either of them, now. My two best friends were together and I was a spare part. They hadn't even noticed me standing a few feet away from them. I stood looking at them for what felt like hours, but was probably seconds, while my whole world disintegrated around me.

ophie were everything to me. When I
to them, I had nothing to fall back on. I
of meaningful family. No other friends. I
irrelevant.

away. Left London, went to university, re-
built myself. Never looked back. My reluctant return that
Christmas was just to check on Kathleen. Despite what
happened then, I was gone in a fortnight and managed to
avoid pretty much everyone.

So ... Uzi asking if we were an item? Shaming in a way that
brought back old ghosts.

'No,' he said, 'it's not that she asked that. It's her saying
"walking out". It's weird. Rowan's concerned that she never
relaxes, she's kind of preoccupied and frantic about her work.
Apparently she just blew up when Rowan tried to talk to her
about it.'

'Well Rowan does see mental health issues everywhere, to
be fair.'

'Mmm. Look, I don't know if it's connected, but apparently
Uzi's seeing someone else. Virtually, at least.'

'When did all this start?'

'Since you showed up.'

'I am the harbinger of strangeness,' I say. Uzi's nowhere to
be seen, so I consult my map and we take a shortcut through
the bushes towards Lucy's grave. We'll call her from there.

We plunge down a fox-scented track and turn right at a
child-sized tomb ornamented with a marble dove. With the
manic laughter of the woodpeckers and squawking of para-
keets, it feels like we're navigating through a jungle. We skirt
around dense undergrowth, punctuated by alarmingly wonky
graves. They look like their inhabitants rose up and broke
them open. I shiver. It's a creepy thought in the failing light,
although I know it's just natural subsidence. And I've got

Antoine with me. If the undead rose up in front of us, he'd demand an exclusive interview.

We soon spot Uzi, who's standing quite still on a narrow path in front of a grave. It has a life-size white marble angel on it: collapsed, weeping, face hidden by her arms, wings drooping. Uzi's shoulders are bowed too, and her face sorrowful. The white stone figure in front of her glows eerily in the dimming light. Ivy insinuates its way up the tomb and sneaks around the angel of grief's neck and shoulders, moving subtly in the chilling breeze.

Lucy's tomb is everything Antoine wanted Ella's to be. I approach it and brush away a tendril of ivy to see the inscription.

Lucy Patience Northaway

19 January 1886 – 20 June 1907
Beloved daughter of Endeavour and Agnes

They can no longer die; for they are like the angels. They are God's children, since they are children of the resurrection.
Luke 20:36

'You must have a good memory, Uzi,' I say. She only glanced at the map when I showed it to her earlier.

She ignores me. Antoine gives me a 'see what I mean,' look.

Uzi suddenly comes to life and starts photographing the grieving angel, with practised expertise, while we stand there looking at it. Even Antoine goes quiet. It feels sadder than Ella's grave, tucked away in the overgrown woodland and forgotten by everyone. It's one of those places where even an old cemetery trooper like me gets swept up by the bittersweet poignancy of the grave. Yet why is it even here? Why isn't she in Manchester in some flashy Northaway family vault?

Eventually I tell Uzi we'll have to get a move on if she wants to visit the Bostock stone lion before the cemetery closes. She separates herself from Lucy with some difficulty.

When we get to the menagerist's grave, she's delighted with the life-size lion, as everyone is. Yet she's fully alive to the irony of the memorial. 'This man was not brave, he was cruel and cowardly,' she says. 'He did not tame the animals, he enslaved them. The lions will tear his heart out in Hell.'

'You don't believe in Hell,' Antoine points out. Bravely.

She stops snapping pictures and narrows her eyes at him. 'Nature will have revenge.'

Antoine looks puzzled. 'How's it going to manage that?'

'Oh, you know, like mad cow disease, or bird flu.' I say. 'We mess with nature, it messes with us, it's—'

I'm interrupted by the car horn that heralds the locking of the gates.

We manage a quick detour to the chapel before we leave. It was gutted by fire some years back and it's still quite dilapidated; nothing like the fairy-tale castle Ella writes about. Still, you can see the remnants of an exquisite building, in the dissenting Gothic style, even if you can't go inside. We peer through the wrought-iron gate that serves as a front door into the dark, empty space of the nave. No pews or altar now and no stained glass to offend dissenting sensibilities. It's shadowy and poignant. Full of loss. The lone owl hoots again. We're all full of loss here.

Well maybe not Antoine and Uzi, I think, looking round at them. But Uzi's frozen to the spot, staring into the darkness, her expression desolate. She takes no photos, turns away. Antoine gives me another meaningful look.

. . .

WE HEAD towards the Church Street exit and an early dinner in the Keralan restaurant that I've definitely missed.

'If Ella was in love with Lucy,' Antoine muses, as we reach the gate, 'then she wants something from her too. Love. Attention. She's another kind of vampire.'

'Everyone wants something from Lucy,' Uzi says. 'Even the two of you. You want your newspaper mystery and your historical story.'

'But,' I protest, 'my story's about Ella, not Lucy.'

Uzi looks up from where she's kneeling to photograph a crow that's sitting hunched on Eric the Punk's memorial stone.

'You are wrong,' she says. 'It is all about Lucy.'

ELLA'S JOURNAL

APRIL 19, 1907

In the last two days, Lucy and I have become closer and she has confided in me that she has some misgivings about her future plans. Now I am not sure quite what to think and am left feeling more than a little confused.

Yesterday Lucy was excited about taking tea with Lady Barnum, yet she returned from Belgrade Square looking downcast. I asked her if she had not enjoyed her outing with Mr Homeward and his aunt. She told me she had felt composed at first, but became uncomfortable once they were in the noise and bustle of London. Then Annie became almost breathless with the excitement of travelling through town in a private carriage and Lucy had to calm her. Annie Lee is a silly girl, vague and slapdash, but Lucy is training her as a lady's maid and has patience with her. Annie, of course, adores Lucy, who is kind to her in so many ways, giving the girl her cast-off trinkets and fripperies, which naturally delights the child. Lucy is so sweet to the children. Annie's friend, my little Florrie, gets such raw hands from her work in the laundry (for Florrie is always in trouble with Matron and is given extra chores) that

Lucy insisted on giving her a bottle of her own hand lotion. She is so thoughtful.

'Annie was meant to be looking after you, my dear,' I told her, 'not getting into a flutter at the opulence of Lady Barnum's landau. You should have made her sit on the box with the driver.'

Lucy looked a little shocked. She could not be alone inside a carriage with a gentleman, she told me, not even with her fiancé. I smiled at her old-fashioned correctness. I could imagine the three of them sitting there, Annie over-excited, Lucy trying to quiet her, and Mr Homeward tugging on his moustaches in helpless confusion.

'How was your tea party with his aunt?'

It was Lady Barnum's idea that Lucy should be treated here, so I am grateful to the terrifying aunt on that count. I am also amused by the fact that Lady Barnum's visits to our asylum scare the attendants out of the little wits they possess; even Matron Siskins is less herself in Lady Barnum's presence. Although I have been conditionally approved by Lucy's future aunt as a suitable companion (despite my American laxity), Lucy is the only person in the entire world of whom Lady Barnum fully approves. As Lady Barnum intends to leave Mr Homeward her considerable fortune, her affection for his fiancée is an important matter.

Lucy told me that Aunt Ernestine had been pleased to see she was improving.

She was pleased to be proved right about your treatment, I thought.

'She wished to talk about the wedding. Aunt Ernestine thinks it should be a simple ceremony, so that it does not worry me, nor inconvenience Mama. I will be content with whatever she wants, except...'

'What, my dear?'

'She ... she wishes us to name a date.'

I asked her if that could not wait until she was quite better. Lady Barnum thought it would encourage her to become better, she told me. Alfred agreed with her.

Naturally he did.

Yet poor Lucy looked far from encouraged. I told her that Lady Barnum and Mr Homeward had her best interests at heart, but were mistaken. It would make her feel under pressure to improve quickly and so she would feel anxious.

'Oh, Ella, you describe my state of mind perfectly. How well you know me. Am I wrong to feel this way? Alfred is such a good, kind man and has been so patient with my weakness.'

I told her Alfred knew he was lucky to have her and would be patient a while longer. I took her hand in mine and asked if he knew about her nightmares. She looked startled.

'I hear you, you know. I am only next door,' I said.

She felt so ashamed about it, she told me. Dr Wood had suggested Annie sleep in her room, so she would not feel so alone. This had not worked, as during the night Lucy arose from her bed; Annie heard her rattling the door handle and woke her. It was dreadfully confusing to find herself standing there, shivering in her nightgown. She had felt embarrassed in front of Annie. She should be setting the child an example of ladylike behaviour, not night-walking or wailing like a banshee.

'Even when you wail it is a musical, genteel sound.' I squeezed her hand. 'My sweet, I have an idea.'

She looked at me eagerly.

'Would it help if I slept in your room?'

'Oh, Ella, that would be wonderful. I am sure I would feel more secure if you were there.'

Dr Wood approved our scheme and last night we were like two little girls on holiday, whispering and giggling to each other until far too late. Lucy did awaken, sobbing piteously, but I held her and she returned to sleep like an infant. She did not sleepwalk while I was with her.

I was able to ask her about the red marks on her neck, but she was vague about their origin. She thought they might have been caused by her electro-therapy, or perhaps she had hurt herself by accident when sleepwalking. It was not the Engine, she said, but I am not so sure.

She is so dear to me. It is cruel that she will be snatched away from me so soon by marriage, a marriage both to ineffectual Mr Homeward and to his bullying aunt, who will run their lives. I fear for her happiness in this future situation.

This morning the following passed between us, which has compounded my feelings of uncertainty.

Lucy was sitting at her dressing table while I re-styled her beautiful hair after the mess Annie had made of it. I asked what her family would think of an early wedding date. She said her papa thought it a good marriage and wanted it to happen as soon as possible. He was afraid her weakness would scare Alfred away and ruin the chance of an advantageous connection for the family.

I paused from my pleasant task, concerned to see her sad expression in the mirror. 'Your father must have some concern for your happiness?'

Her reflection looked resigned. Her papa was a practical man, she told me, who thought security would make her happy. He was much concerned with the mills at present and she did not want to bother him with her problems. Her mama was an invalid whose health had recently worsened. Lucy could not burden her with these worries.

She must speak with Dr Wood, I told her. He would certainly agree with us, and even Lady Barnum could be swayed by medical opinion.

I finished pinning up her golden tresses. 'There. How well you look, my lady.'

She smiled at me from the mirror, as I stood, my hands on her shoulders. We looked as if we were posing for a family photograph. 'How easy you make everything, my sweet,' she said. 'I'm sure I would not mind marrying Alfred tomorrow, if you were to come with me.'

UZI'S MESSAGES

8 OCTOBER 2019

Zana: Great to see you the other day

FairyGirl21: You were so sympathetic. You understand so much

Zana: Aww

FairyGirl21: I have news. A secret!

Zana: About the new guy?

FairyGirl21: I'm unsure about him. He listens, but sometimes I feel he wants too much

Zana: Sounds like he's using you, babe

FairyGirl21: You're not the only one saying that. Listen, my news. There is someone else

Zana: Another guy?

FairyGirl21: A girl

Zana: Good choice

FairyGirl21: I don't want to choose, it is too hard

Zana: No, me too

FairyGirl21: Is Rowan trying to make you choose?

Zana: Not actually saying, but wants me to be exclusive

FairyGirl21: You must love whom you wish. Especially me x

Zana: Specially you, babe x

ELLA'S JOURNAL

APRIL 21, 1907

Today Lucy and I passed another important staging post on our journey back to normal life. We went to worship at Dr Wood's church. I am pleased the doctor judges us fit to mix with his wider circle of acquaintance. Presumably we are living, breathing, evidence of how successful his radical methods can be.

The Church of United Souls is a modest building, housed a little way back from an imposing street, behind a peaceful mossy graveyard. Inside it is plain, like most non-conforming chapels, but unlike my church at home, it is old and has a stately air. We arrived early and were able to see the local ladies and gentlemen as they turned up in their finery, as well as the working people in their Sunday best.

We both felt nervous and I was deeply touched when Lucy slipped her hand in mine as we sat. I held it tightly. It was comforting also, in the midst of all this newness, to encounter Harriet and Professor Von Helson, who came and sat with us, and to see some regular visitors to the asylum. Strutting little Mr Finleigh and solemn, be-whiskered Mr Grimthorpe nodded to us, politely, while jolly young Mr Chamberlain gave us a cheery wave.

It was a simple service. The minister delivered a sermon about poverty in the East End of London and about how Christians must try to alleviate this. There was much support in the congregation for this view; I know many of the asylum supporters carry out such charitable works. We sang hymns about love for one's fellow man, and Dr Wood gave the reading, a familiar passage from Emerson about God and nature. 'There are new lands, new men, new thoughts,' he read. There are new women, too, I thought; the sun shines for us also.

I found the service uplifting. Was this because of my communion with the Lord, or because I felt Lucy and I had once more joined civilised society? Afterwards, as everyone milled around outside, I was able to converse with Harriet as though we were both normal women, despite the hovering presence of Nell. Mr Chamberlain talked pleasantly enough with Lucy, but I did not like the way his eyes lingered on her face and form. I doubt he would look at a lady that way were she not an asylum inmate. I managed to stem the rising tide of anger inside, by telling myself that Chamberlain's clumsiness was typical of a nouveau riche. Indeed, what young man would *not* wish to look upon a creature as beautiful as Lucy? I was pleased that I could calm myself thus and so make a success of Dr Wood's experiment.

Now that we have passed his test, he may allow more inmates to attend church. This can only be good for their sanity, as well as their souls.

CHAPTER 17

ANOTHER LONE OWL

I've arranged another video call with Betty. I want to revisit what her mother, Violet, told her about her aunt Ella, in the light of what we've learned recently. Clients don't always realise, or recall, the important stuff about family stories until I unearth some new information. Then they say, 'Funny you should mention that, a tear always came into Grandad's eye when anyone talked about Scunthorpe.' Or whatever.

Annoyingly, the electricity in the building has failed again, so I'm doing it without lights or Wi-Fi this evening. I don't mind using my phone, Betty's less forceful on a smaller screen; it's just that the dim yellow light from my oil lamp makes everything look spooky. As if I'm about to tell a ghost story. Which I suppose I am.

Betty loves the lamplight though. She thinks there's something pleasingly creepy about the power problems, given the history of the place. I had her down as more rational than that, but you never know. Anyway, she jumps straight from her theories about supernatural electrical meddling into Ella's unproven relationship with Lucy.

'I'm so pleased that my great-aunt found someone who loved her in her last months.'

'I know it sounds that way from the last journal entry, but we don't absolutely know that she and Lucy were lovers—' I begin.

'Oh, Meghan, it's clear as day.'

'Even if they were, it's a pretty ill-starred relationship. Lucy was about to get married.'

'And her fiancé found out. If Lucy left him he might not have got Aunt Ernestine's fortune. We've got a man with a motive there.'

I protest feebly that he could just have broken off the engagement. It would have been a dishonourable act, but it was easier than actually killing Lucy, risking prosecution, and living with the guilt for the rest of his life. My logic gets drowned in the tide of Betty's unreason. There have already been texts from Antoine and the others this morning, following the news about Ella and Lucy's sleeping arrangements.

Antoine: Wood finds out they're lovers. Kills them both. Crazy jealous and protecting reputation of asylum.

Uzi: How Ella feels not Lucy

Benedict: Indeed. Ella may not be a reliable narrator.

Rowan: Lucy might be attracting Ella for her own reasons? Doesn't definitely mean they became lovers.

'About your mother,' I say to Betty. 'Is there anything else she said about her aunt Ella? However small?'

I want to trust Ella's account. Wood doesn't see her as a fantasist, but maybe Violet gave Betty more ideas about her aunt's reliability.

'Like I said before, my mother always looked a little nervous when I asked her about her aunt Ella. She'd try to change the subject or say she couldn't remember much. If the family thought Ella was gay, that might be the reason. I do recall now that Mom mentioned Ella played ballgames with her and showed her how to climb trees. Her mother, Fanny, tried to stop her doing it, said it was unladylike. Ella read her stories about faraway countries, Mom said, which she loved. No one told her when Ella died. She kept hoping her aunt would come back.'

I try another tack. 'What was Violet like?'

'Mom was a correct, conventional woman. A rule follower. Her younger sister Rosemary was the same; they took after their mother, Fanny. My grandmom. Mom didn't much like having a wayward daughter.' Betty laughed. 'She wouldn't have chosen a wayward aunt. That reminds me, when I left college at eighteen my family weren't happy and Grandmom said something about Ella dropping out too, after all the cost of her education. She'd gone to Bryn Mawr, a Quaker college in Pennsylvania, but left a few months before she graduated.'

'Did Fanny say why?'

'I got the impression she was thrown out. It's a residential women's college, maybe she had a relationship with a fellow student.'

I make a note to follow that up. 'Did Violet or anyone inherit Ella's belongings? Photos or anything. Letters.'

'Only the journal and maybe a few pieces of jewellery. I have a nice art deco dragonfly brooch that I believe was hers.'

'Is there anyone else in your family who remembers Ella? Might Rosemary have told her children family tales?'

'No, I knew, even as a child, that Ella was a taboo topic both with my whole family. That's why I've always been interested in her. I'm her spiritual inheritor.'

Clients love to talk about how their forebears have influenced them. With some difficulty I steer Betty away from her spiritual inheritance and bring the call to an end. Lively and likeable though Betty is, I can't help but feel it's her financial inheritance that's her most important ancestral influence. Freedom and confidence can be bought.

I think of Sophie. Until recently I've pretty much buried any memory of her. Now she re-appears in my thoughts, large as life and twice as entitled. I remember how teachers always valued Sophie's classroom contributions and looked puzzled when she did so badly in tests. I didn't realise at the time that an expensive accent and confidence makes people seem intelligent. The opposite was true for me, schoolteachers were always a bit suspicious of how good my grades were, compared to my muttered comments in class. At university it was the same, until Benedict encouraged me and my confidence grew. Once I understood how the con-trick worked, I ditched my accent overnight. Shameless and treacherous, I know. Duplicitous too, but I don't care about that part; if middle-class people can't spot a fake that's really not my problem.

None of this is the fault of the posh, individually, they can be perfectly nice people. Sophie had a lovely generous spirit, and actually I really like Betty. I find her funny combination of bossiness and vulnerability oddly touching. It suggests to me that, despite her privilege, life has given her a thorough kicking at some point.

It's something you get to recognise in other people. A kind of loss that isn't simple bereavement. As someone who's been trailing their ghost twin after them since they were three, I major on complicated loss. I wasn't really supposed to grieve for Michael after the first shock. Grief was Kathleen's province and everyone thinks little children are adaptable. But I was defined by him. By what I wasn't. Betty, I sense is marked by something similar. Somehow, she's another lone owl.

CHAPTER 18

OFFBRAND

'You promise I won't end up buying this, Terry?' I look up from the app and catch Rowan and Uzi exchanging an indulgent 'ahh, old people don't trust the tech', glance. They don't know Terry like I do.

He's enticed us all down to Ridley Road market with the promise of meeting his stallholder friend, Birdie, who might have information about our mystery. It's early morning and the stallholders are still setting up in the chilly autumn mist. Whilst we're waiting, munching bagels at tables outside the bakery, Terry's got us beta testing his app. Buying pretend phones, laptops and tablets, plus various accessories, such as the famous circuit breakers that he hasn't managed to flog to Monarch wholesale. Yet.

'Seems to be working okay, Pop.' Antoine doesn't sound convinced. 'I've had the right texts and email confirmation for all the things I'm supposed to have bought.'

'It is good.' Generous praise from Uzi. 'The photos could be made better.'

She and Terry have a surprisingly technical conversation about optimising the photo quality, while I surreptitiously check my bank account to make sure I haven't actually bought anything.

'Good prices,' says Rowan.

'It's not bad gear,' Antoine says. 'All my family use it. I would if I didn't have work kit.'

'You? Use an offbrand phone?' I chortle. 'That'll be the day. You're as snobby about tech as Ella is about social class.'

'Ooooh, glass houses, Morgan.'

'I am so not a snob. How can you even say that?'

'Aunt Breda, Eileen and the rest? You're not that enthusiastic about your working-class roots nowadays. You haven't even seen them yet.'

'It's all very well for you, your family like who you've become. They're more...' I glance at Terry, 'flexible. Mine think I'm weird; everything about me offends them.'

'They're always asking after you at church, according to Mom.'

'I'm a divorced, over-educated atheist with no kids. I'm incomprehensible to them, so they pity and resent me.'

He points out that, being a dinner-party destroyer, I could end up cutting myself off from both worlds if I'm not careful. I tell him that's what education does to people like us. It leaves you marooned between the place you came from and the one where you'll never really fit in.

'Because rich people think you are offbrand,' Uzi says, and I laugh.

'Exactly. That look they give you when you use the wrong knife?' I say.

'It's different for me,' Antoine says. 'No one expects me to get the cutlery right,'

'Ironic, eh?' I say. Antoine could set a banqueting table like a pro by the time he was ten. With a mum like Claudette, you don't have much choice. He had a supporting role in her work for years.

'Child labour is underrated as a pathway to social mobility,' Terry says. 'Lad next door who built this app, he's only fourteen. He'll be a millionaire by the time he can vote.'

'Were Ella's family millionaires?' Ever-practical Rowan brings us back to our project.

'Her father's family were just upper-middle-class professionals,' I say. 'Claire's folks were more upmarket. I expect that's the source of her patrician attitudes. That's where their money came from originally, though her dad increased the family fortunes.'

'Claire?' Antoine asks.

'Her mother,' I say

'Her mother is not called Fanny?' says Uzi.

'Fanny's her sister. Look.' I sketch out a rudimentary family tree on a paper napkin.

Zachariah = Claire
Martins
  ┌──────┴──────┐
William = Fanny   Ella
Standhope
       ┌────┴────┐
Victor = Violet
Gardiner │
       Betty

Uzi takes a photo and uploads it to our folder.

'I've got a proper one,' I protest. 'With dates and wider family and everything.'

'We don't need that kind of detail, Meg,' Antoine says. 'Just focus on the story.'

A WIRY BLOKE in camo gear comes up, looks over Terry's shoulder at his app.

'No flies on you, Tel,' he says. 'You gonna start calling your stall a pop-up project?'

'Good to see you, mate,' Antoine pushes a coffee and a paper bag towards Birdie.

'Bribing your sources, eh, Antoine?' He opens the bag and takes a bite of the bagel. 'Tell you what, you need to do an article on those reed warblers nesting down by the Lee. Need proper protection, they do, people letting their dogs run around there, total liability.'

Antoine makes a note and tells Birdie someone will call him. Nature stories are always popular, and if Birdie's got any good pics? Which of course he has.

Once we've looked at enough photos of mega-cute warblers, Birdie takes his phone back and swipes us to the picture we're really interested in.

In it, an older gentleman, very much the Victorian, stands tall in a stovepipe hat, surrounded by his household of half a dozen servants. Young maids in starched white aprons and caps, a formidable housekeeper in black silk, a capable cook sitting with the kitchen cat on her ample lap, a couple of boyish manservants.

'1905 that was taken. That's my gran there.' Birdie points at a thin-faced girl on the edge of the group looking doubtfully at the camera, as if seeking a way out. 'And that,' he stabbed his finger at the man in the middle of the picture, 'is your Mr Grimthorpe.'

Barnabus Grimthorpe still looks stiff and formal in this picture, but he appears more at ease than in the photo with his colleagues. He's the master here.

'What did your gran tell you about him?' Antoine asks.

'Wasn't a bad employer in general, strict like, but pretty fair and paid decently. The only thing was, him being a bachelor, all the maids knew you had to make sure you were never on your own with him. They'd try and look out for each other, but it didn't always work. My gran managed to keep away from him, she hid in the dumbwaiter once, and behind the bins another time, but the other two weren't so lucky.'

'How old are these girls?' Uzi looks at the picture, with focussed intensity.

'Gran was twelve when she started there, luv. The others'd be about the same.'

We're silent for a moment as we stare into the blank faces of the child maids.

'She said they all knew he must be getting up to the same sort of thing in his charity work. One of his big things was a religious place that saved fallen women. Don't bear thinking about does it? Then there was your asylum.'

I'M BACK in my flatlet, building the archive of the dead, when Eileen calls me, again. I don't want to deal with that damned trunk today. It can wait. I decline the call (yet again) and read a new text from Benedict. He's found someone who might know about the Church of United Souls. The Reverend Antrobus, a distant acquaintance of his from the old days. She's the minister of the United Souls' Upper Clapton HQ, though it's now been returned to mainstream non-conformity and re-branded Bethesda Chapel. He's up again in a couple of weeks and has arranged to have a chat with her. Would I like to join them?

UZI'S MESSAGES

20 OCTOBER 2019

Zana: Tough day 😔

FairyGirl21: Rowan is still seeking to control you?

Zana: Not so much. Heard stuff about Barney, worried for you 😟

FairyGirl21: You're so sweet. He is no danger to me, do not be concerned

Zana: Good. Getting confused. Am I seeing too much of you?

FairyGirl21: You wish to break contact?

Zana: No

FairyGirl21: That is a relief. You are the only one I can be honest with

Zana: How's GF?

FairyGirl21: I do love her

Zana: Aw, that's great. How about her?

FairyGirl21: She feels the same. But she wants me to herself

Zana: Another one of them

FairyGirl21: Also there's a younger girl she's close to. I believe this girl will always be more important to her than me

Zana: I've heard about that girl. Sounds like she wouldn't want you in the picture

FairyGirl21: That is what I believe. How wise you are

Zana: GF would be crazy not to put you first

FairyGirl21: You are so kind, my sweet

Zana: You're my muse, FairyGirl

FairyGirl21: I wish to inspire you. Love you

Zana: Love you more

ELLA'S JOURNAL
MAY 1, 1907

Today is my birthday; I am twenty-nine years old. This year my mother is not present to add 'and not yet married' to that statement.

To celebrate, Lucy and I were allowed to roam a little farther afield to a public park. Matron calls it Paradise Gardens, but I believe it is more properly known as Clissold Park.

How ordinary I would have thought the practice of taking these walks, only last year. How sweet and precious these small experiences of liberty are to me now. We have called on Harriet twice, almost like normal ladies. Harriet is such an interesting woman; she has travelled much herself and has lent me a fascinating book about Miss Kingsley's adventures abroad. She sees no reason why I should not explore Europe, when I am better.

Lucy has commissioned Harriet's dressmaker to make her two new summer costumes. She has such an appetite for pretty things, bless her. Naturally, they are styled rather differently to Harriet's clothing and I imagine she will wear them rather differently too! Harriet's carelessness with her expensive clothing is something dear Lucy finds *quite* inexplicable.

Our favourite walks of late have been in the cemetery; we have both grown to love its shady avenues. I have learned the names of all the trees, many of which are native to far-flung countries. There are Bhutan pines and swamp cypress, but my favourite is the service tree of Fontainebleau. Even Lucy remembers this one, because of its exquisite clusters of creamy little flowers. One day I will see it in its native woodland outside Paris and when my beloved Violet joins me there, I will show her how to climb in its branches. How wonderful it would be if Lucy were there with us.

Today I was immediately pleased by Paradise Gardens, which is landscaped with ponds, mature trees and sweeping walks. They were once the grounds of Paradise House, a beautiful old mansion which sits on a little hill at one side of the park, overlooking the river. Its grand symmetrical frontage has six white pillars, in the classical style, and it makes me think of the ancient buildings I shall see in Rome one day. When I am free.

Perhaps, if Matron permits, next time we venture this way we can pass through the majestic entrance of Paradise House, to take refreshments, as it is now an elegant tearoom. Always we must seek permission for even smallest thing, because we remain captives, for all our promenades and tea parties.

Yet to stroll in these gardens with Lucy today was delightful, even though we were accompanied by the ever-present Nell.

At least she keeps the beggars away.

As we stopped to look at Paradise House, I noticed a governess with a little girl in a sailor suit standing next to us. The child reminded me so much of Violet that it hurt. I told Lucy this and she said *she* would have little daughters just like that and I would be their dearest, most beloved Aunt Ella. I looked up at the stately portico and down at its flickering reflection in the water, our images, and that of the little girl, caught between them. Two alternative entrances to two possible futures. The solid material one that might be taken; and, shifting and sparkling in the spring sunshine, the one that did not quite have a form. The other one.

We walked on, arm in arm, pausing by a pond to admire a regal swan as she sailed past, with her sweet cargo of gawky cygnets.

'How proud she is of her little family.' Lucy smiled and her pink cheeks dimpled. She looks so well now and is often free from those terrible nightmares. When she does have them, I am able to quiet her.

I told her that although the young swans all had the king's protection, I believed a mother's love was far more beneficial to them. Lucy smiled at me warmly and said that a friend's love was beneficial too. Being with me was making her a better person. My heart leapt at this and I glanced over to where Nell was standing, a few feet away. Happily, she was making eyes at a young man on the other side of the pond and paid us no heed.

I told Lucy I believed being with her was making me calmer. She was healing me. At that, she put her little hand on mine, where it rested on the railing surrounding the pond. Pressing it tenderly she looked into my eyes. She wanted to make my birthday special for me, she told me. Then, with a triumphant little smile, she presented me with a small jewellery box.

Inside was a delightful dragonfly pin. It was to remind me of the day I opened her eyes to the beauty of the dragonfly in the cemetery, she explained. I replaced her fear with wonder. She pinned it to my lapel, where it clung delicately, its body glowing electric-blue and its huge lapis lazuli eyes seeing all.

She looked up at me, eager for me to like her gift, and saw I was close to tears at her thoughtfulness. I would wear it always, I told her, in a choked voice, and she put her hand on my shoulder to comfort me.

It is an exquisite present, yet to be there in the sunshine with Lucy was a greater gift.

Paradise indeed.

Nell glanced over at us and Lucy quickly took a step back. We began to speak, in louder voices, about the Peter Pan play. I told her she must not organise it all by herself, it would make her ill. In truth I will be delighted to assist with her theatricals. As well as helping my beloved Lucy, I will be proving to myself that my organisational skills are returning.

'I could not do it without you, Ella,' she said more quietly, glancing at Nell, who was still peering over at us. In a jollier voice Lucy added 'I would not know how to manage Mr Chamberlain and Mr Finleigh's men, when they show the boys how to make scenery and props. Or Mr Grimthorpe's seamstresses, in instructing the girls. I am a little scared of Mr Grimthorpe.'

Mr Grimthorpe may be a stiff, old-fashioned Victorian gentleman, but he is a kindly old man, very devout and most helpful. He keeps his friend Mr Finleigh in check, and makes Mr Chamberlain take the production seriously. 'Mr Grimthorpe dotes on you, my darling, you know he does,' I said.

'Perhaps that is why he frightens me. When he comes into my classes and sits at the back, I feel like a pupil, myself.'

I told her it was their prerogative to come and observe us poor lunatics whenever they chose. Cheerful young Mr Chamberlain had joined in my drill sessions once or twice and proved a great favourite with the children, particularly as he always has pockets full of sweets. 'Mr Finleigh has not yet visited us,' I added.

Our eyes met and we laughed, wickedly. Mr Finleigh does many good works and is certainly generous, but he is small and round and somewhat pompous. It was amusing to imagine him jumping rope with my unbalanced little urchins.

Nell obviously disapproved of our levity. She told us it was time to return, else Matron would have her 'guts for garters', which sounds medieval, even for Matron Siskins.

CHAPTER 19

BOX OF DEMONS

By the time I uploaded Ella's most recent entry, Betty and Benedict had heard about Grimthorpe. The texts flew in:

Betty: Ew, he was in the classroom!

Uzi: Stalking Lucy

Rowan: Or the children

Antoine: Possibly both. Lucy looked young for her age, remember? Ella says he took a shine to her

Benedict: How appalling. Could he have played a role in Lucy and Ella's death?

We agree he could have killed Ella because she knew about him and was going to tell Wood. The same might be true for Lucy, or he might have tried to assault her, then ended up killing her when she fought back. We wonder if Finleigh, the possible matricide, was involved? But we have no evidence that he was a paedophile like Grimthorpe. We also can't think of a sensible reason why Lucy would have met Grimthorpe in the chapel, although Antoine comes up with numerous imaginative possibilities.

I PARK THE TEXT DISCUSSION. I've got a mass of papers to finish categorising before I take them over to Monarch, on the way to the task I can't put off any longer. Today I have my own unappealing past to revisit. I'm obliged to give in to Eileen's increasingly irate requests. I need to pick up my trunk, remember? Her parents are moving to their Southend retirement flat tomorrow, so if I don't come and get it, it's going out with the rubbish. *She's* got nowhere to put it, we don't all live in bleedin' cottages in the countryside.

I understand her irritation. It was good of Breda and Jack to store the thing in their loft when I cleared mum's flat. They forgot all about it, in the intervening years. I tried to, but failed. I hid the key from myself, but never managed to lose it.

Truth is, the trunk's the last point of contact I have with my mother and that distant past. That continent I sailed away from years ago. It's an archive I'd prefer to keep sealed.

GOING to fetch it is as much fun as I anticipated. My 'aunt' (not my aunt, my first cousin, once removed, as I consistently pointed out to my mum throughout my childhood) Breda plies me with tea, cake and inappropriately invasive questions. My actual (second) cousin Eileen sits poking her phone, catching up with local gossip. She probably knows more about my movements since I returned than I do. Occasionally she tells her kids, who are using the packing crates as a playground, not to do something. Not-my-uncle Jack watches *Real Deal* from the safety of his armchair. A prudent response to the bedlam around him.

'We haven't seen you since Kelly's wedding,' Breda says. 'Ah, that was a lovely affair, you can't beat a spring wedding. Bridesmaids in lemon silk and Kelly with primroses in her hair. Didn't she look beautiful, Eileen?'

'Blooming. Not surprising seeing as she was three months pregnant.'

'Ah, nonsense, you know Conner was premature, poor little mite. He's walking now Meghan, that's how long it's been.'

Because I'm bad, I'm bad.

'Now, your poor mother's trunk, Jack can have it open in a jiffy if you've mislaid the key.'

I indicate that there's no need, but she's not that easily beaten. 'Sure, it's no trouble. Is it, Jack?'

'Two hundred quid for that old rubbish?' murmurs Jack, his eyes fixed on the screen.

'See, he doesn't mind. Now, do you recall what's in it?'

'I didn't have time to sort it out after ... at the time. I had to get back to college.'

'You always were a terror for the books. We never understood why you had to go so far away to study. "Are there not universities enough in London?" your mother used to say.'

I'm pretty sure Kathleen said nothing of the sort. When I started at university, Breda took over delivery of the Pop Tarts and library romances and managed any bill paying I couldn't automate. Whatever guilt I've lived with since my mother's death, I've never kidded myself I was indispensable.

'She was pleased I got a place at St Cadog's.' If Breda can invent the past, so can I.

'Oh, her children were everything to her. She never got over your brother's passing.'

'We both missed Michael.'

'Sure you did, but you were, what, not three years old? A mother's feeling for her son.' She shakes her head. 'Then losing—'

'I lost my father, too, you know.' I try not to sound hostile, but come on, do you know how many times I've heard this stuff?

In truth, my memories of my dad are limited. I recall him showing me how to put my socks on, and I have a strong sense that he was a stable and constant presence who balanced my mother's capricious excesses. But I might have written that into my memory archive since – four is pretty young.

'I was going to say,' Breda huffs, 'that she lost her beauty. A hard thing for a woman like your mother. She'd been modelling since we were teenagers.'

Before Michael died, Kathleen's looks lived their own glamorous life and earned their own income. They were almost a separate entity. When they left, along with my twin brother, all that remained of my mother was the skeletal grey ghost who haunted our house, weeping.

'Even when we were kids, she had a professional way with make-up,' Breda reminisces. 'And she could make a cheap outfit look like a million dollars.'

'Meg's not interested in that sort of thing, Mam,' Eileen says.

'Kathleen loved dressing you up in pretty frocks when you were little,' says Breda, 'but you always preferred the books.'

Because I'm bad, so bad.

There's a crash, followed by scolding and tears, as one of Eileen's kids falls into a half-packed crate.

'Well, I can see you're busy packing, so—'

'Oh, nonsense, we've nearly finished, you'll have another cup of tea. Now, have you got yourself a new young man, yet?'

'Meg's back with her childhood sweetheart,' Eileen shouts from the kitchen.

'That's grand. Lovely boy Antoine, good Catholic family. Maybe you'll have a proper church wedding in London this time?'

'Antoine's just a friend,' I mumble.

'Ah, sure he is.' Breda nudges me. 'Your mam will be looking down on you when you walk up the aisle at Our Lady's.'

A disturbing thought in so many ways. I make another move towards the trunk. Breda gets there before me, helps one of her grandchildren climb off it.

'Your granda made it for Kathleen, did she ever tell you that?'

Endlessly, Breda, endlessly.

'Ah well, she doted on her father. My favourite uncle, Gerry was. You wouldn't remember him.'

'No, he killed himself before I was born,' I say. Breda and Eileen exchange a look.

'Your grandma running off and leaving him like that, it brought him down. Kathleen couldn't have been more than sixteen, fancy a mother abandoning her only child. She always was a hard woman – more for work than family. "The Harpy" Kathleen used to call her.'

'She told me I took after her.'

'You have a look of her, being so tall. She was a fine figure of a woman, I'll give her that. You get your red hair from our side, though.' She moves to tousle the head of the gingery infant demolishing her packing cases. While she's distracted I grab the trunk and start heaving it towards the door, muttering my farewells as I go. Jack helps me lug the thing outside.

'You'll come and see us in Southend, once we're settled?' Breda follows us out to the cab. 'Do you good, a day by the sea.'

I promise faithfully I will.

Who's bad?

BACK AT ABNEY Heights I'm dragging the trunk across the grand hallway and into the lift when I get a rare sighting of two other occupants. A smartly dressed couple descending the stairs are concerned I'm scratching the tiles. Do I realise they're original? So are the electrics, I tell them, precipitating an avalanche of tutting and sighing. I wonder if they were this brittle before they joined the ranks of the gated?

Happily, once I'm down in the basement Rowan appears, just as I'm wrestling the trunk out of the lift. I'm no weakling, but Rowan lifts the other end like the thing's made of plywood.

'Just been to the pool,' Rowan grins, seeing my expression. 'Keeps you strong.'

I admit that despite having been in my flat for well over a month I've neglected to use any part of the executive fitness centre. I even avoided checking it out when I was comparing floorplans.

'The pool's the original one Ella swam in. Fabulous place. I go whenever I stay here.'

I switch on the light in my flatlet and get a small shock.

'The electrics in this place are even worse than Antoine's,' I say.

Rowan switches the light switch on an off a couple of times with no ill-effect.

'I'm an electrician's daughter,' I say. 'They're trying it on.'

Rowan smiles. 'Come and see the pool.'

It's worth seeing. Housed in a huge, double-height room, it has stained glass windows high up along the wall that forms the back of the building. The light from them makes shapes on the faintly rippling blue water, as a lone swimmer performs elegant lengths. White painted girders support the ceiling, and turquoise tiles reflect the water and stained glass, creating a subtle sense of space and movement.

'Uzi says the place is haunted because the inmates' emotions have become part of the building fabric,' says Rowan.

I think about the things I keep half-seeing, then not seeing. But I know that's down to my own mental state, challenged by returning to my childhood haunts and obsessed with the troubled past of the building's former inmates.

'Is that what you think?' I ask.

Rowan places a capable hand on the wall's cracked glaze, as if to make contact. 'It's similar to the presence I feel in nature, only more like a person. Maybe events can write themselves on a building. I feel something here, in this room. Someone. When I'm in the pool.'

I can see why the pool seems haunted. The shifting light on the water, the eerie silence. The moving shapes of the pool surface, reflected on the ceiling. I think of Ella, gliding effortlessly through the water, temporarily free from her limiting family, social constraints and personal demons. I watch the swimmer's elegant somersaults at the end of each length.

'Uzi thinks it's creative energy, up in the flat,' Rowan says. 'Helps her work. She doesn't like the pool, feels like there's a hostile presence here. She's got a bit weird about it.'

'Uzi's got a bit weird about a lot of things,' I say.

. . .

I RETURN to my flat and my own haunted object. The monstrous thing crouches among the borrowed luxury of my apartment. You wouldn't know from looking at it that it's a box of demons. It's a handsome piece of work, inlaid cedar, exquisite craftsmanship. It held Kathleen's fancy-dress outfits when she was a kid; I imagine it overflowing with pink tulle and taffeta.

I retrieve the key from the kitchen drawer, comforting myself that it will ambush me no longer. It's an ornamental faux-medieval affair, as beautiful as the box. As beautiful as the girl the box was made for. I slip it into the keyhole, then sit in front of the trunk and stare at it. My courage fails me. I shove the whole thing into a corner and chuck a tasteful throw over it.

I'll deal with it one day, but today is not that day.

DR WOOD'S DIARY

1 MAY 1907

I received an unwelcome letter by this morning's post. It is not signed, but I suspect it is from a former gardener, whom I dismissed for theft; this man must still be party to staff gossip.

I admit I am thrown by this development. I hesitate to commit what follows to my research diary but as a scientist I must be truthful in my own records. This letter brings up an issue I have been turning over in my mind for some weeks. In short, it accuses me of being in love with Miss Lucy North-away and carrying on improper relations with her. It demands money in return for silence. Were there no truth in its lewd and badly written suggestions, I would not hesitate to disre-gard it. However, although nothing has passed between us, I am now convinced that my feelings for Lucy go beyond mere counter-transference.

I love her and she, me.

Can this be what Homeward means, when he talks about Lucy's purity being tainted by the immorality around her? He has discussed this matter with me more than once. Homeward is not the most articulate of fellows, so I have struggled to understand exactly what he is getting at. I thought he was either concerned Harriet and Ella might influence Lucy with their 'New Woman' ideas, or that Ella might entice her into sexual inversion. These are fears I have seen no evidence to support; in fact, I am so confident that Lucy is free from Sapphic tendencies that I have permitted them to share a room.

Yet I now wonder if Homeward was accusing *me* all along? Perhaps he senses she has feelings for me?

There is nothing to be done. Homeward offers Lucy an elevated station in life; it is the marriage her family want and she would not disobey them. Nor would I betray my position or Homeward's trust. That would be the act of a cad and a bounder.

I must bear my burden and she hers. It would be better for us both if she leaves here soon to be married. Then we can both come to terms with our loss and move forward with our lives. She is much recovered, sleeps better and eats well and no longer suffers from her vampire fantasy.

And the letter? I know this former employee to be a serial blackmailer. Harriet consulted me in confidence, some weeks ago, about a similar communication she received. It accused her of improper relations with Von Helson. The professor is married, although his wife has been in an untreatable vegetative state for some years. I do not believe there is substance to these allegations and for her part Harriet resents being criticised according to a Victorian moral code, as she sees it. Yet she decided to pay the sum demanded, as she felt any scandal might affect the standing of her charitable activities. She did not wish these causes to suffer because of an amount trifling to her.

To date, she has had no further demands.

I am not a rich man. Every penny I earn goes back into my asylum, so the sum for me is not inconsiderable. Yet now I have written all this down, the action I must take becomes clear. I will pay this scoundrel, for the same reason as Harriet. I cannot risk bringing my life's work into disrepute.

CHAPTER 20

UNITED SOULS

I wake early to a hangover and an unwelcome message from Betty: she can't access the shared files. I opt for a gentle restorative swim before I face my tech problems. She'll be asleep by now, anyway.

I'm glad I listened to Rowan about the pool. First thing in the morning it's not busy and you do get a feeling of serenity as you swim back and forth in the untroubled water. Mind you, I put the atmosphere of tranquillity down to the spatial dynamic created by the arched ceiling and big windows, rather than to the presence of friendly spirits. Churches use the same techniques and plenty of their visitors feel touched by a supernatural presence.

As I don my bathrobe and drip my way back to the flat, Antoine turns up to deliver Scully on his way to work.

'Coffee?' I ask.

'Extra strong.' He puts his furry bundle on the even furrier rug, where she yawns and stretches. He does the same thing on the sofa.

Last night Uzi and Rowan took us, Claudette and Terry, to

a local Halloween drag show. We were marking the launch of Terry's new app. Claudette, Rowan and Uzi were also celebrating the night of the dead. All in slightly different ways.

Although Claudette found the show's compere, Skirts Galore, too potty-mouthed, she enjoyed the party. Terry ended up on stage singing 'Bat out of Hell' with a drag king. Standing ovation, obviously. I was actually persuaded to dance and a good time was had by all. As we parted at the end of the evening, Claudette warned us to take care in 'that haunted place' today. All Souls' Day, when the dead are walking.

I hand Antoine a coffee and sit down. 'Had the pool to myself again. Not even Rowan's friendly ghost showed up. Is no one else ever going to move into this place?'

'Not to the floor below me, it's owned by a foreign bank now. They don't bother with tenants. Some flats on the upper decks are occupied but they don't venture down here to the servants' quarters. Just you and the ghosts for now.'

'Ghosts are less annoying than your neighbours. Listen, I meant to ask last night, what's the verdict on the photography studio?'

Antoine got Sam to track down the names of the local studios in 1907 and to find examples of their work. It's taken weeks, but Sam gave Antoine a folder of samples yesterday.

'I showed Uzi the examples from the studios. She reckons the style's different to any local photographer. That's how it looks to me too.'

'Uzi says our pictures are art. I can't find any reference to Evelyn De Morgan taking photos. Maybe one of her acolytes?'

'Speaking of art, did Uzi tell you she wants to paint you?'

'What? I'm not weird enough for one of Uzi's paintings.' Scully jumps up on my lap. I stroke her soft dark fur.

'Something about re-imagining the "House of the Spirits"?'

I shiver at the thought. Instead I concentrate on Scully,

who is trying to rub noses with me. Her nose is a surprisingly pink among all that black fluff.

'Anyway, hate to harsh your cat therapy and add to your headache, but I can't access any of our shared files. Nor can Uzi. Or, as she put it, in her new level of weirdness, "Meg has closed her library doors to me".'

Not just Betty having tech problems, then. I sigh. 'Can you both get into the folder?'

'Yeah, but neither of us can see the sub-folders.'

Frowning, I check on my phone. Nor can I. The sub-folders, the files, all the records of Abney and Ella are gone. I open my laptop, which is charging on the coffee table. It refuses to start up. I do a soft reboot, but nothing. It's dead.

I swear a lot.

Antoine covers his face and groans. 'Tell me we haven't lost all the records?'

I let him stew for a few seconds, because if it was Antoine that's exactly what would have happened. Then I say, 'This is me, Antoine. I back up to an external hard-drive and to another cloud drive.'

'Whew! Suspicious though. Our cloud folders disappearing the same day your laptop decides to quit. Maybe your cloud account was hacked?'

But none of my other cloud folders have been touched. Probably one of us deleted the folders accidentally last night, jabbing at our phones, taking drunken photos. As for the laptop, it's just bad luck or bad electrics that it's chosen today to expire. Uzi texts that it's because it's All Souls' Day and Antoine, naturally, starts fabricating conspiracy theories about shadowy religious or psychoanalytic organisations trying to shut us up. Being the star that he actually is, though, he produces an old laptop for me to use before he goes.

He has some good news too. He's reviewing a photo exhibition of 'Historic Clissold Park' next week. Do I want to come to the preview? Might give me a sense of what the park was like when Ella and Lucy used to walk in it.

Ignoring my (hangover-created) ghosts, who keep flickering past my window, I spend a whole morning setting up my desktop and changing all my passwords. Time I'll have to make up by working past midnight again tonight. Then I alter all the permissions so only Antoine and I can make changes to our shared folder and put a double security layer on it to stop us doing anything stupid. After that I open Terry's app and buy a few surge protectors. Don't want to fry Antoine's laptop as well as mine.

The texts about Wood's last entry pour in minutes after I sort the tech.

Antoine: Maybe Wood was the murderer after all. Jealousy. Crimes of passion.

Uzi: Exactly

Rowan: Most people don't turn into murderers when their hearts are broken

Benedict: Indeed. Yet it is unprofessional of him to nurture these inappropriate desires.

'The Church of the United Souls?' Philomena 'call-me-Phil, darlin'' Antrobus, shakes back her braids and gazes thoughtfully up at the modern stained glass window. Christ helping out at a foodbank, by the look of it.

She's wearing a dog collar, with a tailored jacket and skinny jeans. The effect is authoritative and very slightly cool. For a vicar.

Phil's pleased to see Benedict, who's up in London attending some high-powered meeting. He does a lot of that stuff now he's Dean. Despite his distracted manner, Benedict's brilliant at university politics, an aspect of academic life I always found totally baffling.

For the first ten minutes, Phil and Benedict catch up on various non-conforming mutual acquaintances. Most of whom seem to be organising things I thought social services ran, like homeless shelters and meals on wheels. I'm obviously behind the times.

While they gossip (I believe it's called networking) I look round at the minimalist interior of the former United Souls HQ. There's no pews, just semi-circles of Ikea chairs arranged in front of the plainest altar imaginable. Energy-efficient-lighting globes hang from the high arched ceiling. My flat's designer would like it here, but it's too austere for my Papish tastes.

'Yeah, they were ahead of their time in many ways, the Church of United Souls,' Phil says, her gaze returning to us, from the one ornamental part of the building. 'They grew from an interfaith abolitionist group and had links with the early Labour movement. Believed in the sort of stuff our faith is all about today: brother and sisterhood, mutual aid, equality. Definitely the kind of local history we need to remember. One of my excluded school students is doing her GCSE project on them, she's the person I wanted you to talk to. Letitia's been combing through all the church records and linking it up with other searches. Got quite a flair for it. Her group'll be here soon.'

'So your church was used for the same sort of things in 1907 as it is today?' I ask, as Phil starts re-arranging some of the chairs around a trestle table and we get up to lend a hand.

'It would have been a social hub for the people you're researching, as well as a place of worship. Not to mention an organisational centre for their welfare projects.'

I imagine Lucy and Ella sitting round uncomfortably on the Ikea chairs, clutching their prayer books. Wood leaning forward over the trestle table to convene a meeting of worthies. He'd fit right in here.

Phil busies herself making coffee and putting out the chocolate brownies we brought. Half a dozen teenagers mooch in, jostling each other and looking at us warily. Some of the boys seem more or less grown up, until they see the cake; then their eyes light up with childish desire.

Letitia is small and wiry. Everything about her is immaculate, from her spotless trainers to the explosion of multi-coloured twists on the top of her head. She takes her stuff out of her rucksack and arranges it neatly on the table before addressing our question.

'Why you want to know about the United Souls?' Her serious black eyes give nothing away. 'You into that spiritualism stuff?'

I explain we're looking into two unsolved deaths of women connected to the church over a hundred years ago. No, not feds, we reassure her. We're acting for the family of one of the women.

Her eyes glow with conspiratorial interest.

'You mean Lucy Northaway, innit? The girl in the painting. The Spiritual Machinists were part of the church and she was, like, their medium? But she was in a mental hospital so they shouldn't have done that. They thought they were doing her good, but they made her worse and she killed herself.'

Phil shakes her head, sadly. 'No proper safeguarding measures.'

'What about Emmanuella Murray?' I ask.

'Yeah, they let her go to the seances and she killed herself, too, so that was bad.' Letitia says. 'So, this League for Psychic Studies they were all in, it kicked the Machinists out. The United Souls thought the mad girls got possessed with demons and it was the Machinists' fault. *They* didn't boot them out, but they made them stop.'

'Do you think it was demons, Letitia?' I asked.

'Nah. Usually people, innit, give girls problems? Demons nothing to that.'

Letitia's delighted to have our pictures of Ella and the Spiritual Machinists for her project. She stares at them hard, trying to decode their faces. I tell her more about what we know and what we're planning to do with it. We can have her reference documents about the Machinists, she says, as long as she gets credited when we publish. Which impresses Benedict.

Promising to send her the other photos and tell her if we get anywhere with the mystery, we leave the group to their studies.

'BRIGHT GIRL,' Benedict says to Phil as she shows us out through the graveyard. 'Why would she be excluded?'

'We don't dwell on the past, here. Everyone deserves a second chance.'

'Is that why the United Souls didn't throw the Machinists out, I wonder?' I say. 'A second chance?'

Phil smiles. 'We're all about forgiveness, here, darlin'. Not exclusion.'

ELLA'S JOURNAL
2 MAY, 1907

Something disturbing has happened. It has shaken me until I
hardly know myself. I am by turns delighted, perplexed and
angry.

Today Dr Wood spoke with Lucy about her impending
marriage. A little while ago Lucy told him she did not feel
ready to leave here by Lady Barnum's proposed date, which is a
mere eight weeks hence. At the time he was sympathetic to
her view.

Yet today he told Lucy that because she has made such
excellent progress, there is now no need to delay the wedding.
He has discussed the matter with Mr Homeward and Lady
Barnum. They have come to the agreement that Dr Wood will
visit Lucy to continue her treatment in her new home.

Arthur's home.

Shocking and deeply disappointing as this idea is, this is
not what has shaken me the most. It is Lucy's reaction to this
news.

The prospect of the marriage itself is making Lucy
nervous. She told me of it while we were working on some

props for her play. Lucy was busy ornamenting Annie's diaphanous fairy costume, which the girls made in their sewing lessons. Annie is to play Tinker Bell and Lucy needs a more theatrical effect than Mr Grimthorpe's needlewomen have taught them to produce. She was occupied with adding azure spangles and diamantes to the garment. She desired to make Annie look as dazzling and captivating as our Abney Park dragonfly, she told me.

I fear Annie will make a hapless Tinker Bell. She is a dreamy, uncoordinated girl who can neither throw nor catch a ball, any more than she can dress a lady's hair. She would have fallen more than once in our tree-climbing activities, had Florrie not been on hand to save her. Let us hope she is not required to fly.

I will attempt to reproduce our exchange below so I can be sure of what Lucy meant. I am tormented by this conversation and wonder if my desires have led me to misunderstood her meaning?

'You see, I worry I do not feel as a bride approaching her wedding day *should* feel.' Lucy looked up from her glittering work. 'Is this normal, or is it because I am still unwell in my mind?'

I applied another papier mâché strip to the parrot I was modelling. Sounding like Dr Wood, I asked her how she *did* feel. She told me Arthur was a good, kind man, whom she respects. He offers her security, a place in society and a comfortable home. She paused and looked up. 'Yet I do not feel for him what a wife should feel for her husband.'

I concentrated hard on my task and did not catch her eye. 'What are those things you think a wife should feel?'

'Tenderness and closeness. An intimate sense of knowing the person so well, that one feels completely happy and at ease with them. A sense of feeling more alive, when one is with them, than one has ever felt before.'

'That intimacy is hard to come by, Lucy.' I still did not look up from my parrot. I had pasted so many strips on it, it was beginning to look like a chicken.

She leaned over and put her hand on my arm. 'It is what we have. You and I.'

I dared to raise my eyes and look at her. There was nothing but love and sincerity in her beautiful face. We sat that way for minutes.

'Then do not marry Mr Homeward,' I said, simply.

She looked away. 'I must. I must marry someone. Alfred loves me, he will indulge me.'

'In what way?'

'You could come and live with me. Alfred would not object.'

Since this conversation, my mind has been in turmoil. I go over and over what Lucy said, but am not sure I fully understand. Can it be possible that my hopes have substance? That she feels the way I do for her, and sees a future for us? This is what I have been longing for and, partly, I am overjoyed. Yet if she feels this way, why would she expect me to share her with Homeward?

This makes no sense. Why must Lucy marry Homeward, if she does not wish to? Her family are wealthy and she obviously has a generous allowance. Her parents may not welcome a broken engagement but neither will they want her to make an unhappy marriage. This is not the nineteenth century. Perhaps, with persuasion, they will permit her to come to Europe with me instead? Mothers often send girls on continental tours to cure their broken hearts or ill-health. It is quite a respectable thing to do. I have met ladies who travelled for years, in suitable company. I am older and of good family; I cannot think that her parents would object to me as a companion.

If the worst happens and they do not permit it, well. I have independent means on which the two of us could live most comfortably.

We will talk more. I must be patient. It is still two months until the wedding.

236

CHAPTER 21

THE OTHER ONE

'Cheers.' I take a sip of the pint Antoine's just bought me. 'Gentrification may be a form of social cleansing, but it definitely improves the beer quality.'

We're off to the Clissold Park exhibition private view, via the pub where we once celebrated our A-level results. Last time I was here I was so happy and relieved I'd got my ticket to a new life. Before what happened happened. Anyway, being here isn't as bad as I expected, because I barely recognise the ghost of the King's Head in the Bell and Raven, as it's now called. Our old pool table has been purged and the sticky carpet ejected, exposing battered floorboards. Artfully tatty plaster walls replace the flock paper and none of the furniture matches. Jean, the matriarch of the King's Head, would be scandalised.

Antoine raises his glass. 'To Ella and Lucy's doomed love. Now it's official.'

'Does it help us with the mystery of their deaths?' I ask.

'Wood's still in the frame. A gay love affair wouldn't reflect well on his asylum project or his reputation, not in 1907. Plus he had the hots for Lucy.'

'Two deaths don't reflect well, either. Think of the scandal Letitia uncovered. The Spiritual Machinists thought they'd found the answer to life and death. Instead they got booted out of their psychic group and were disciplined by their church.'

'What's the spirit writing got to do with their deaths?' Antoine muses. 'What did the church and the League suspect that we don't know about?'

'Like Letitia said. Demonic possession. Or haunting. That stuff was real for them.'

Letitia's source documents had been dry and minimal, but both hinted that the Machinists' use of unstable young women for psychic experimentation was spiritually hazardous, as well as morally questionable.

'So why wasn't there speculation in the press? Demons and ghosts are front-page material.'

'Maybe the Machinists were powerful enough to keep it out. Philanthropists, aristocrats and rich businessmen have plenty of pull.'

Antoine sips his beer. 'You still agree with your new mate Letitia? The seances drove Ella and Lucy mad, so they topped themselves?'

'I still think it was either accident or suicide but like Letitia says, maybe other people were implicated in some way.'

Antoine tries a new tack. 'Maybe the spirit writing sent Wood haywire and he killed them.'

'No evidence in his diary that he was anything other than rational,' I said. 'So far, anyway.'

'So the spirits told him something that made him angry and jealous. Murderous.'

'Like what?'

'Like Lucy and Ella are together.'

'He's a bleedin' psychoanalyst, Antoine. He wouldn't need the dead to point that out to him.'

Antoine points out that he's not mentioned it in his diary and I tell him that's not because he can't see they care for each other, it's because he doesn't take same-sex relationships seriously. Lucy's getting married and Ella's 'inversion' is something he's curing.

ON THE WAY to Clissold House my phone pings.

Betty: So good to hear for definite that Ella had someone to love her!

Betty: I'm sure now that Homeward killed them both.

Antoine grins. 'Likes the murderous English aristocrat angle, your Betty.'

I sigh. 'The aristocracy married for advantage, not love. Homeward wants a pretty, tractable wife with the right kind of manners, who'll provide him with heirs. Lucy's all that, even though she's nouveau riche. He won't care what she does in private as long as she behaves in public. Plenty of wealthy women had female live-in lovers, while their husbands were off huntin' shootin' and chasing village wenches. Or gamekeepers, for that matter.'

'So you think he'd agree to Lucy's plan for a ménage à trois?'

'*He* might, but it's not Ella's style is it?'

We go through the gates of Clissold Park. Paradise Park, as Matron Siskins still called it, even though it changed its name long before. I get where she was coming from. The pub we've just left will always be the King's Head to me.

'I heard back from Ella's college, yesterday,' I tell him, as a dog whizzes past us on a skateboard. I try not to get sucked into missing this place. 'According to their records, she didn't get kicked out, she left for health reasons. Mental health, presumably.'

We carry on past a bloke doing pro Tai Chi, with a fag in his mouth, (still not getting sucked in) towards the Georgian mansion that so impressed Ella. I pause for a moment as we walk up the steep slope to pass under the six white pillars and enter the building. I look down at the stretch of water below, where Ella saw her image reflected and imagined an alternative future for herself and Lucy. The other one.

Antoine's welcomed warmly by the nerdy looking bloke who's responsible for the exhibition. He presses drinks into our hands and tries to show us round personally, although there are plenty more people flowing in.

'Didn't realise you were such a local sleb,' I say, when we've shaken nerd-boy off.

Antoine tries to look modest and fails. We wander around looking at photos of pre-war children in rowing boats on the lake. On their own! Those were the days. We see Victorian people gathered in front of Clissold House for an event. Enormous hats, bustles and moustaches. Antoine points out a photo of the bandstand, dated 1907. I look hungrily at the moustachioed men and bonneted women gathered round it. Are Lucy and Ella in the crowd? What about the kids? Are any of them hapless Annie or resourceful Florrie?

'I found a picture of Annie, this morning,' I tell him. 'The one who played Tinker Bell. You know, the girl Lucy was training to be a lady's maid. At least, it's a portrait of AL dressed in a sparkly fairy costume, so I guess it's her.'

I get my phone out and show him the photo of a sweet-faced fairy with big scared eyes.

'Florrie's mate,' he says. 'Wonder what happened to the two of them.'

I flick to Florrie's picture. Her composure is even more marked compared to Annie.

'Service, all going well,' I say. 'Probably not long after, they were both old enough to work.'

'Hope they managed to keep out of Grimthorpe's way.'

'The kids seemed to be pretty well supervised. There were always other adults around, they wouldn't be as vulnerable as the staff in his own household. It's possible he never got the chance.'

We carry on through the exhibition paying close attention to any of the Edwardian pictures. All those leisurely, happy looking people seem a long way from Lucy and Ella's trials, not to mention Florrie and Annie's lives. Suddenly Antoine, who's a few paces ahead of me, calls me over. He looks triumphant. Gesturing towards the picture he says 'Anyone we know?'

It's a photo of people strolling round a pond. In the foreground a striking dark-haired woman is laughing up into the face of a man, her sparkling eyes lively and mischievous. She's rather ornately dressed for a walk in the park, in an embroidered jacket and ruffles, topped off with a massive cartwheel hat; the man whose arm is around her is less remarkable, apart from his huge moustache.

Before I manage to work it out Antoine says 'It's the Honourable Alfred.' And it really is, although he doesn't look at all bewildered out of doors with this beauty on his arm. He looks in his element.

'So,' says Antoine, gesturing to the date. April 1907. 'He's got another woman too. Puts him squarely in the frame.'

'It could just be a dalliance,' I protest. 'Even if it wasn't, and he changed his mind about Lucy, he could have just broken off the engagement.'

'Aunt Ernestine wouldn't have like that, though, would she? Dishonourable behaviour and all that.'

'Not as dishonourable as being tried for murder.'

'But he wasn't, was he?'

After Antoine's told nerd-boy which pics to send him for the article, and charmed him into letting me use them as local colour for the archive website, we head back to Abney Heights and back to work. First we do a detour round the ponds, retracing the steps of Lucy, Ella and poor old gooseberry Nell.

'See that swan,' I point to a handsome specimen who's eyeing us, hoping for food. 'That's a descendant of the cygnets Ella wrote about.'

'A pint and some warm prosecco and you get sentimental. I expect they ate the swans round here during the depression.'

'Nah, they belonged to the king.'

'King didn't get to Stokey much, Meg.'

Antoine uploaded his snap of Alfred's photo as soon as we saw it. So as we admire the swans, texts start to appear.

Betty: That's definite then. He killed Lucy and married this other woman

Benedict: This lady doesn't really look like marriage material for a young aristocrat.

Rowan: If he didn't love Lucy there's no crime of passion motive

Uzi: He loved Lucy but was seeing someone else. Doesn't mean he wasn't angry when he found out about Ella.

'Does Benedict mean she's too, umm—' Antoine asks.

'Tarty? Probably, and maybe too old, she's about Homeward's age. Not enough child-bearing years left to reliably fill the family nursery.'

Before we leave the park, Antoine tells Sam to find out what happened with Homeward after Lucy died. If I wasn't under so much pressure to get the archiving done I'd have done that as a matter of course. I'm annoyed at myself.

We follow Ella and Lucy's footsteps up Grazebrook Road towards Abney Heights. A row of manicured three-storied Victorian semis set me off on my sentimental journey again.

'Those houses,' I gesture expansively at the upmarket dwellings, 'were built by Messrs Chamberlain and Finleigh.'

Antoine laughs. 'And furnished by nasty old Grimthorpe. Which reminds me, I had Sam dig around some more about those guys. They were pretty wealthy, particularly the builders. Pillars of the non-conformist community, did other charity work, like Birdie said. Grimthorpe was never caught and no mud stuck to them over the Spiritual Machinist stuff, or anything else, except for the mysterious death of Finleigh's ma.'

'Well blood-sucking capitalists have always got away with murder,' I say.

'Booze making you radical as well as sentimental? Local entrepreneurs and job creators we call them round here nowadays. You've been away too long, Meg.'

UZI'S MESSAGES

6 NOVEMBER 2019

Zana: Hey sweetie. How's things with BF?

FairyGirl21: He is so suspicious

Zana: Not good 😿

FairyGirl21: He claims he is true to me, but I believe otherwise

Zana: Sorry to say, I heard you're right

FairyGirl21: I would like him to be honest with me. He thinks me a child

Zana: Is it okay me saying?

FairyGirl21: Oh, yes. I rely on you to tell me the truth. Everyone else treats me like an infant

Zana: What friends are for babe! 😊

PSYCHIATRIC REVIEW

1908

Excerpt from Journal Article, *The Sacrifice,* by Dr C. Wood.

My patient, whom I shall call Lydia, is a young woman of twenty-one, from a respectable family. Her father is a prominent industrialist and she is the youngest of three children.

Lydia presented with fatigue, poor appetite and weight loss. She was weak, pallid and often short of breath. She also had a number of sleep-related issues. Lydia suffered from insomnia, due to an overwhelming fear that she would be attacked while asleep. She also had intermittent somnambulance. Her sleep was haunted by terrifying nightmares, which often awakened her. Although she claimed she could not remember the content of these dreams, they left her in a state of paralysed fear once she awoke. The most curious aspect of her illness was two red puncture wounds on her neck, which she told me appeared one morning and never healed. Because of this she developed the conviction that she was receiving nocturnal visits from the type of vampire she read about in popular fiction.

Lydia is a pretty, delicate young woman. Her temperament is gentle and she has a marked desire to please others. She is engaged to be married, an alliance encouraged by both her parents and her fiancé's family. She wishes to become well enough to fulfil her future role as wife and mother, thus gaining the approval of those around her.

My patient's symptom pattern is clearly that of hysteria. I have been treating her intensively, in a residential facility, using the talking cure and medical electro-therapy, for a period of three months. She has also participated in automatic writing sessions, using a new method pioneered by myself and Professor Von Helson, of Vienna University. In this approach, the effect is amplified by the use of Von Helson's electromagnetic machine, the Telepathic Transfer Engine. We propose that the Engine may have a therapeutic effect on some patients. Lydia is the first subject to benefit from this therapy, so our work is at an early stage.

For the first few weeks of her talking therapy, Lydia spoke of her concern that her condition is a burden to her family and fiancé. This was her main anxiety and all of our sessions led back to it. Her mother has a heart condition and she did not wish to upset her. She also felt that she was letting down her father, by being ill.

'My father would want me to have fortitude and perseverance,' she told me. 'He is a Christian man, a devout man. He lives by his faith and expects others to do the same.'

'To live by his faith?' I asked.

'To have Christian courage,' she replied. Her father had troubles enough to deal with in his work, without having to deal with her silly imaginings, she felt. She should be braver.

For some weeks our discussions revolved around this topic and she was unwilling to move past it. However, after Lydia commenced her automatic writing sessions, not only did she become less fatigued, but she also started to recall the childhood memory outlined below. Although I now relate it as a coherent story, I learned it in fragments, over several weeks.

We were visiting, once again, the topic of her father needing Lydia to show fortitude. I asked what her earliest memory was of this. Over the course of several sessions she recalled numerous examples. One was that, when she was a small child, he had not liked her to cry when she fell over. Another involved the death of Lydia's week-old sister. Her mother was weeping over her loss, while Lydia tried to comfort her, in her babyish way. Her father scolded them both. Satan was tempting them into weakness and despair, he told them. They must be strong in their faith and not give way to dejection of spirits.

She told me she had needed to be brave when her father's mill workers went on strike. She had been a child of five at the time. This reminiscence appeared to cause her much anxiety and at first she said she could remember no more. Over the next few sessions she recalled, with difficulty and with clear signs of psychic pain, the following memory.

One evening, several days into the strike, a large group of mill hands surrounded the family home. They made a great deal of noise, chanting slogans and shouting for her father to come out. Her terrified mother and the three children stayed together in an upper room of the house, along with their governess, Miss S_, while her father went out to reason with the mob. If that proved impossible, he planned to go and get help.

While the family waited nervously for him to return, Miss S_ led the children in singing a hymn together, 'Oh God Our

Help in Ages Past'. Lydia recalled clearly that the woman's confident voice rang out above the noise below and that Lydia's mother joined in, in her quavering soprano. Lydia and her brothers tried to sing up bravely. As they reached the words at the end, 'Be thou our guard while troubles last,' the door crashed open. Her father stood on the threshold, pale with anger, his face cut and bleeding. She felt a sense of dread at the sight of him and it became an enormous effort for her not to cry.

The strikers had not listened to him, he announced, drunken rabble that they were. Then, when he had tried to go for help they had jeered him, accusing him of running away and leaving his family. They had blocked his way. He was concerned that in their state of madness, they would try to burn down the nearby mill. They might even set fire to the house, with the family inside it.

The governess tended to his injury, while he urged Lydia's hysterical mother to calm herself. In the midst of all this, a brick smashed through the window, narrowly missing her two brothers, who had gone to look at the chaos outside. Her mother screamed and pulled the boys close, retreating with them to the corner of the room. Her father rang for the servants, but no one came. He rang again, cursing them for lazy, feckless idlers, but still no one showed. The domestics had either abandoned them, or been prevented from coming.

They were alone.

Her older brother, a stout boy of about eleven years, said that he would go to get help. He could put on old clothes and slip out without being noticed or stopped. Lydia's father told him he was a fine, brave boy, but they could not risk him. The mob were bound to recognise the company heir; even if the adults left the child alone, the mill lads would set upon him.

At this point her father turned his gaze thoughtfully on

little Lydia. Not even the lowest of the band of drunken ruffians would harm his fairy girl, would they? He looked round at his family, but none of them replied. Then he bent down to Lydia. Did she remember the way to the magistrate's house? She had been there only last week, to his daughter's birthday party?

Lydia bit her lip to keep back the tears and shook her head. Miss S_ came over and smoothed Lydia's hair. She recalled going to Annabella's house, did she not? There was a little dog whom Lydia adored and they had all had pink ices to eat.

Lydia knew she must tell the truth. Reluctantly, she had nodded. She saw a look pass between Miss S_ and her father. Miss S_ told her she must go there now. It was not far, just around the corner. Lydia would be safe there and could play with Annabella's puppy.

'I will give you an important letter for Annabella's papa,' her father said. 'You must not tell anyone else you have it and you must give it directly to him. Do you understand?'

They heard another crash, as a brick went through a downstairs window.

Lydia was terrified at the idea of having to go out into the crowd and looked to her mother for help. Her mother would not meet her eye. Instead she looked down at her two sons, hugging them closer.

They made her leave by the servants' entrance. As soon as she stood on the step and saw all the hostile faces in front of her, lit up eerily by the flames of their torches, she thought her heart would give way. Lydia looked back to catch sight of her family one last time; she found nothing behind her but a closed door.

All that was ahead was a sea of dirty, ragged mill hands, who had worked themselves up into a fury at her family. Yet

Lydia had no choice but to go forward. She took a deep breath and with her eyes cast down, walked into the crowd.

The first thing she noticed was the smell of filth and poverty. Then she heard the mocking, jeering and cat-calls as she stumbled through the starving, angry mob. They were ridiculing her father, calling him a coward for sending a child out to do his business. Someone shouted to stop her, she was going to get the constables, but a woman said they should leave her be, the lass was just a infant and anyway the police were already on their way.

Struggling through the crowd, she felt disgusted at the smell, mortified by the name-calling and afraid that they would kill her. She was jostled by children, filthy, scraggy urchins with eyes full of hatred and hunger. They wanted to devour her, she thought. As they pushed her, she fell into the dirty road and they laughed as she tried to scramble to her feet. One girl grabbed the fine muslin skirt of her dress and tore it, then another, laughing gleefully, pulled her sleeve, ripping it off from the shoulder. Her eyes swimming with tears, she managed to right herself and scurried on through the throng. On and on, she went, her head down, until eventually the laughter and jeering was not so loud and the shoving was not so fierce. She looked up to see that she was reaching the edge of the crowd would soon be out of it. With a desperate sense of hope, Lydia picked up her pace.

As she ran down the street, through the remnants of the mob, Lydia felt a sharp pain at her throat. She put her hand to her neck and saw blood on it. Had someone cut her as she tried to escape, or maybe thrown a sharp object at her? She did not know. Bleeding, dirty and dishevelled, with her clothes in tatters, she stumbled onwards to the magistrate's house, where at first the servants took her for a beggar girl. A maid noticed the fine work of her torn clothing and eventually they realised her identity and let her deliver the letter hidden in her underthings.

'I was expected to be brave then,' Lydia told me, 'and I must be brave now.'

When I asked her if it she thought it reasonable to send an infant out into a violent mob, she said that her father had no other alternative. I told her there were three adults in the house, all of whom were alternatives. Her mother might be an invalid, and the workers might have prevented her father leaving, but why could not the governess go for help? Or why could they not wait for the constables, who would, as the workers realised, surely come soon?

She said her father did not want to jeopardise the mill by waiting; Miss S_ was a well-educated woman, whom he valued highly. He would never have sacrificed her.

'Is that what you were, Lydia?' I asked. 'A sacrifice?'

CHAPTER 22

SETTING THE GHOSTS FREE

'I read the paper by Dr Wood,' Uzi says, from behind her easel. At work, she's even more intense than usual. 'The one Benedict found.'

I'm not supposed to speak, but I manage an 'Uh huh,' without moving my mouth.

'Lucy's family hurled her to the wolves.' Uzi's passion is controlled, but palpable. 'Dr Wood found that out and wrote it out like a story. He exploited her abuse to make his name.'

Wood may have made Lucy's history into a compelling narrative, but it's one that's sympathetic to her plight. His journal article goes on to dissect how she felt about what happened that night. Her sense that her parents thought her unimportant and disposable was key to understanding her neurosis, he argues. He also makes links between her neck being cut as she passed through the hostile crowd, and what he calls the 'vampire stigmata' she presented at his asylum.

'Umm, umm,' I say, in gentle disagreement.

Wood also talks in his paper about the transference Lucy experiences. In their sessions she behaves as though strongly attracted to him, he claims. He describes this as displaced emotion, which they will work through in the therapeutic process. A rather different view than he articulates in his private research diary.

Benedict also found out that Sigmund Freud wrote to Wood congratulating him on his 'Sacrifice' paper and inviting him to join his new psychoanalytic organisation. So Uzi's right that Lucy's case study made Wood's career; his use of the Engine can't have left any significant reputational stain.

Not moving is surprisingly hard work. I'm standing in what was a relaxed position when we started, my feet planted apart, hands on hips. As instructed. It's now extremely uncomfortable. Uzi gave me a long, loose shift to wear, and then pinned swathes of scratchy fabric to fall from my shoulders and drape around my bare feet. The cats are now using it for a game of hide and pounce and I fear for my toes. What's worse, Uzi insisted my hair should be loose and it's tickling my face and neck. Purgatorial.

'You may rest.' Gratefully, I move around a little, curtailing the cats' game and stretching my stiff limbs. 'For a moment, only,' she adds.

Mulder sits watching me, grinning his Cheshire cat grin, while Scully stalks off to sharpen her claws on the sofa.

'Wood did cure Lucy, ' I say, through aching face muscles.

'This is what he says.' She narrows her eyes. They still have shadows under them and her pallor has increased. 'He says she is attracted to him and this is not true either.'

'His employees must have thought there was something between them, if someone was blackmailing him about it.'

We hear the sound of the front door and Antoine appears. He stares at me like he's never seen me before.

'I know I look like an idiot,' I mutter, 'but I'm furthering the cause of art.'

'You look – nice. Like that.' He seems confused and bends down to make a fuss of Mulder. His favourite, Scully, glares at them, incensed that her brother's being greeted before her. Treachery!

Uzi ignores Antoine's entrance and continues with our conversation. 'Probably the whole world knew Wood was in love with Lucy.' She barks out a laugh and flicks her eyes towards Antoine. 'Long before he did.'

Uzi motions me back to the middle of the floor, then quickly and deftly arranges all the itchy material around my toes again. Scully comes over to sit on my feet, pointedly ignoring Antoine.

Antoine watches Uzi, still looking obscurely bewildered and not even realising how furious Scully is with him. Idiot, he must be used to Uzi doing arty things in his living room by now. Is everyone going weird on me?

'We will be thirty minutes,' she tells him, moving back to her easel.

'Right. I'll make us some food then.'

He goes and potters in the kitchen, occasionally sneaking puzzled glances in my direction.

'Sam turned up something interesting today,' he says. 'Get this, Homeward's marriage!' He pauses for dramatic effect. Uzi carries on sketching and I'm not allowed to move; he looks disappointed at the audience reaction, but carries on manfully. 'To one Gertie Stubbs, a chorus girl, six months after Lucy's death. His son and heir was born a fortnight later. Aunt Ernestine disinherited him and left her loot to the Church of United Souls.'

Blimey. Even Uzi looks up from her work. 'That is Gertie in the park photo?'

'Looks that way. And before either of you ask, Gertie was

furthering her glittering career on the New York stage when Lucy died, so that puts her out of the picture.'

'But not Homeward,' Uzi says. 'He did not know he would lose the inheritance.'

'Dunno,' Antoine says. 'Pretty obvious Aunt Ernestine wouldn't accept a chorus girl into the family, up the duff or not.'

I nod vigorously. 'He could keep Gertie and the baby in a separate establishment,' I say, without moving my lips, like a ventriloquist, 'Marry Lucy, inherit the cash.' Uzi frowns at me and carries on, working in silence.

'Unless Gertie threatened to tell Aunt Ernestine?' he muses. 'But I s'pose that's more likely to put her in danger than Lucy.'

He then reverts to his pet subject of the Telepathic Transfer Engine, spinning wild theories about what happened to it. 'Maybe it still exists, somewhere. In a cellar in Hoxton, attracting evil spirits and sensitive maidens. Or it was taken to pieces and our task is to find all the bits and re-unite them. Then we can contact the other side and free Abney Heights of all its ghosts.'

Uzi looks round at him. 'That would be a bad thing. It is better haunted.'

As she turns back to her easel Antoine gives me an eloquent look. 'You like the company of ghosts?' he asks her.

'The past is reaching out to me,' she says. 'I feel its power shaping my work. That is how ghosts are freed.'

ELLA'S JOURNAL

MAY 23, 1907

Lucy's production of *Peter Pan* was a resounding success last night. I am so pleased for her. I have pasted our notice into my journal, to remind me of this evening.

We had a good audience. As well as the inmates, most of the staff attended, some in their off-duty clothes. Their watchful expressions suggested they were not really off duty.

Lady Barnum and Mr Homeward were in the front row. It was the first time I've seen Mr Homeward for a while. He was discomforted by a scolding message at one of the spirit writing sessions, from a Mrs Stubbs, and has not attended since. Lady Barnum positively preened herself at Lucy's success, as if she were personally responsible for her recovery. It took a great effort on my part to greet the two of them civilly, given that they are trying to ruin Lucy's life and our chance of happiness together.

Our other board members, including Harriet and Messrs Finleigh, Chamberlain and Grimthorpe also joined us. Additionally, there were families present whom I have seen at church and a number of ladies who have made charity visits to the asylum with clothing for the parish inmates.

ABNEY ASYLUM THEATRICALS
presents
PETER PAN

Directed by Miss L. Northaway

Harry Sedgeworth: **Peter Pan**
Florence Azikiwe: **Wendy Darling**
Annie Lee: **Tinker Bell**
Jim Reilly: **Captain Hook**
Fred Nyes: **John Darling**
Hannah Rose: **Princess Tiger Lily**
John Symms: **Michael Darling**
Edward Jones, Ruben Gold: **The Lost boys**
Henry Mitchens, Jack Murphy: **Pirates**
Eliza Smith, Katie Higgens, Winnie Wright:
Fairies/Mermaids

Stage Manager: Miss E. Murray

Sponsors
Grimthorpe's Soft Furnishings
Finleigh and Chamberlain Construction

I was pleased to see that the De Morgans both attended, with some of their followers. As I surveyed the crowd, I also heard

Professor Von Helson's bear-like roar of laughter cut across the hum of conversation. He and Harriet brought one of their Russian friends with them, a man of about my age with a great shock of dark hair, spectacles like Harriet's and a goatee beard. Harriet's house is full of Russians at present; they are attending a political meeting in a church near here, which they are not permitted to hold in their own country. Harriet says it is most exciting and she believes her friends are making history. She and Von Helson looked like a married couple as they entertained their visitor; the professor always stays at her house when he is in London. Although I do not think him worthy of Harriet, I do not judge; people should live their lives as they wish. Perhaps love should not be confined by marriage.

The children gave an excellent account of Peter Pan and his adventures in Never Never Land. They enjoyed the unaccustomed attention. Little urchins they may be normally, but in the play, they were bold pirates, dangerous mermaids and courageous princesses. Even silly little Annie was transformed into an acceptable fairy. Florrie gave a characterful performance as bossy Wendy, as I hoped she would. She has been a little subdued lately; the prospect of her dramatic debut may have made her nervous.

Watching the transformed little ragamuffins made me think of Violet. I miss her so much. She is the cleverest, most beautiful girl in all the world. I ask my sister for news of her every time I write. She tells me only dull things, such as what dresses Violet likes to wear and whether her hair will keep a curl. I want to hear of my lively, funny little girl, who likes to run around and laugh and play. It makes me sad to think that my sister may turn her into an obedient doll, while I am locked up in here. It is for Violet's sake, as well as for Lucy and for my own chance of happiness, that I try so hard to recover.

During the evening I was busy overseeing all the practical

matters. We used the main classroom as the actors' dressing room and green room, with the smaller one for all my stage equipment. The performance itself was in the main hall, next door to the classrooms. Taken up with props, scenery and lighting and getting the children on stage at the right time, I hardly saw Lucy all night, except in passing. Like me, she had a hundred and one jobs to do. During the play she flitted here and there, reassuring the little actors, prompting them and making sure photographs of the theatricals were taken. She wore an exquisite new gown of shimmery azure that made me think of my dragonfly. At the interval Dr Wood took her to meet all the local benefactors. I could see she was a great success with them. Lucy has a wonderful ability with people; she's so interested in everyone and knows exactly what to say to them. Not like me, I just plough right in and speak my mind, as my sister always tells me. Yet that is another reason why Lucy and I complement each other so well: sometimes it is important to be charming and at other times one must say what one means.

After the play, Lucy was off in the green room organising the cast photographs and presenting the children with their gifts. She is such a thoughtful soul, she spent hours wrapping little presents for each of the young actors and crew, as a reward for their efforts. While she was busy with the over-excited children I was obliged to socialise with our guests, as a poor substitute for Lucy. As soon as the first of them began to leave, I slipped off to supervise the dismantling and packing away of the scenery and props, which I'd left my stage crew working on. I picked up my portly parrot, which was lying on the floor. It had been convincing on Captain Hook's shoulder, but still looked misshapen close up.

'Back to Never Never Land with you,' I said, putting it away in a crate with the crocodile and some clouds.

It was late by the time Lucy had finished all her work and could return to her room. She was drooping with fatigue, but her eyes sparkled and there was a rosy glow to her cheeks. I could see she was still caught up in the excitement of the evening. It was wonderful that we had made this a success, she told me. Our play had been so good for the children and for her own recovery.

I embraced her, and told her she had reaped the rewards of virtue if she had been able to profit by helping others. Smiling up at me happily she said, 'I truly hope that is so, my darling. For I feel this evening has been the making of me.'

LETTER FROM MRS
NORTHAWAY TO DR WOOD

24 MAY 1907

My dear Dr Wood

My husband wishes to extend his sincere thanks for your last communication about our poor daughter. What a triumph her little play must have been for you. When she left here, she was barely capable of attending a dinner party, yet now she can help a group of rowdy children perform a drama. Quite a transformation.

It was heartening for us both to hear she is making so much progress in your care. We are delighted that you have approved a wedding date of the 29th June and we agree that there need be no fuss. Too much excitement would not be good for the girl. Lady Barnum has kindly offered to make the few necessary arrangements for a simple ceremony in her local chapel. This is indeed welcome, as my physician absolutely forbids any such activity on my part. I cannot tell you what a relief it is to us to know that our daughter will soon be married and capable of performing her duties as Mr Homeward's wife.

I must now mention a delicate matter. Mr Homeward may

already have spoken with you about this. He and my husband have agreed that Mr Homeward will now meet the full balance of the fees for Lucy's treatment. As the young couple are to be married so soon and as Mr Homeward is a gentleman of such impeccable character, my husband has no qualms about this arrangement. He is obliged to take this untoward step as business costs have been trying, of late. In any case, we are delighted to welcome Mr Homeward into our family and view his generosity towards our daughter as a demonstration of his respect and regard.

We thank you again for your tolerance and dedication in effecting a cure for Lucy.

I remain
Yours in sincere gratitude
Agnes Northaway

CHAPTER 23

CAT IN THE BOX

'The Northaway empire was going west, then?' Antoine's lounging on my big sofa, reading the latest uploads between work phone calls and messages.

'Interesting isn't it? Explains why her grave's in London, anyway. Homeward must have paid for it.'

I'm sitting on the floor in front of my unappealing family trunk. Antoine offered to come and lend me moral support to face the thing on this rainy Saturday afternoon, and I'm ahead on the archive work, so I've no excuse to ignore it any more. I take a deep breath and click open the medieval key. Then I look round at him. 'After I read that, I ran some searches on the company. They'd been sailing close to the wind for a while and Northaway went bankrupt in 1908.'

'No wonder Lucy's mum was so chuffed she was marrying Homeward,' Antoine says. 'He might have bailed them out. Or improved their credit rating.'

I nod and turn back to face the return of the repressed.

Taking a deep breath, I creak open the lid and sit staring at my unwanted archive, where my dead are waiting for me to breathe life into them.

It doesn't actually look scary. No mummified hands, hangman's rope, not even any dead people's hair made into mourning jewellery. It's just a mass of paper kipple. Maybe it won't be as bad as I've feared? Mulder jumps straight in and curls up in the middle of it, which somehow feels like a good sign.

'What interests me,' I say, 'is how Lucy managed to maintain herself. Being a lady required a lot of expensive upkeep. Ella says Lucy has a generous allowance and talks about her shopping for hats and boots and ordering new dresses. Then there's the gifts she's always giving people. Yet her family couldn't even afford to pay her bill at the asylum.'

Antoine suggests that Homeward gave her money, but as I point out, having your lover pay your medical bills is one thing, but accepting cash is something else entirely. So he speculates that Ella bailed her out. But she'd have said when she talks about Lucy's finances, I protest. It would change her idea about how independent Lucy could be.

'Maybe she accepted presents from someone else,' he surmises. 'From Dr Wood. For services rendered.'

Antoine has a seriously lurid mind, as I point out to him. He grins and expands on his theory: Wood knew her family were broke, so he gaslighted her into a sexual relationship and then paid for her silence.

I can see how Lucy would have been embarrassed, maybe even desperate, about not being able to keep up her appearance. Wood, though? He wasn't even rich. 'I know Wood goes on about how submissive and obliging she is, but he wouldn't risk his reputation,' I protest,

'Not just submissive and obliging but also poor and locked in his asylum.'

'Yuk. But I don't think so.'

Antoine won't let it go. Other men then, he suggests. The local worthies on the asylum board. We know Grimthorpe assaulted his serving maids, Chamberlain leched after Lucy and Finleigh was maybe a murderer. So they're all well dodgy. The three of them work together, he claims, building their web of flattery and coercion gradually; that's how grooming works.

I'm not convinced. She couldn't risk getting pregnant and she'd have to be a virgin when she married. Antoine looks slightly uncomfortable, for some reason, but ploughs on. 'I don't know how to tell you this, Meg, you being an innocent country lass nowadays.' Uh? He's blushing. 'Non-penetrative forms of sex do exist.'

I'm confused. It's hard, I mean, *really* hard to embarrass Antoine, but he's been a bit funny for the last couple of days. First Uzi, now him. The world's gone mad.

He folds Wood into his new theory. The doctor arranges the whole sordid business, providing an additional service for the wealthy asylum donors and guaranteeing their future compliance, now he knows their dirty little secret. That way he ensures the future security of his asylum project and his research.

'Wood says he's loves her,' I say. 'Read the next part of his case notes. Both he and Lucy sound pretty innocent.'

Antoine thinks he loves his career more. Lucy's a sacrifice, in his mind, remember? Seeing my scepticism, he tries another tack. What would Ella do if Lucy confided all this in her?

'Confront the perpetrator.'

'Exactly. Ella ends up falling to her death from his roof terrace. Then Lucy dies mysteriously in a deserted chapel. We have a motive. We have means. Wood had opportunity and so did the other guys.'

Despite being fired up with enthusiasm and doubtless composing shock headlines in his mind, Antoine takes a look at Wood's latest case notes. I grab us a couple of beers from the fridge, then turn my attention back to my unwelcome trunk.

DR WOOD'S DIARY

26 MAY 1907

Lucy's cure is progressing. Her talking sessions and the electrotherapy have borne fruit and I have seen a marked improvement since she began the automatic writing. Her Hungarian Countess appears regularly with enigmatic messages from the other side. She seems concerned for Lucy's well-being, but she need not fear. Lucy becomes more vigorous with every session.

Her work with the children has helped her too, as well as benefitting them. I was most pleased with the play, which delighted our benefactors. It is a public testament to her rapid improvement under my care.

In today's talking therapy, Lucy told me her sleep is now deeper and more refreshing. If she does wake, she is only a little afraid. Having her friend there gives her courage, she said. There have been no more episodes of sleepwalking, according to Ella.

I asked her what would happen once she was married and Ella was no longer there. She blushed and said she expected that sometimes Mr Homeward would be there. His presence would make her feel safe.

'And when he is not?' I asked. 'Gentlemen may often keep to their own rooms, particularly once their wives are – forgive my indelicacy, but we must speak of it – are expecting a happy event, or are otherwise indisposed. Indeed, sometimes Mr Homeward's estate will take him to the country and he will not be with you for days or weeks.'

She tilted her head thoughtfully and considered this. 'Perhaps I may have Ella to live with me after I am married. Then I will never be lonely or afraid.'

At present I believe the friendship between these two ladies has a therapeutic effect on them both. Yet I have recently begun to think it could become unhealthily close, for Ella. Because of her tendency to inversion, I feel it will aid her recovery if Lucy's marriage weakens the ties of their friendship.

I suggested to Lucy that Ella would be returning to her family when she was better.

'I do not think so,' she replied. 'They are not a close family and Ella likes it here. She wants to stay in Europe.'

It is true that Miss Murray wishes to tour the Continent before returning, but she is not considering abandoning her American family, particularly her niece. I told Lucy her friend would want to see the little girl grow up. Her response surprised me.

'Ella will like my children better than Violet,' Lucy blurted out. She immediately put her hand to her mouth, in confusion. 'I apologise, I do not know what made me say that. Her little niece is dear to her, of course. It is only that I will miss Ella if she returns to her family.'

So Ella has succeeded in making Lucy emotionally dependent on her. As I know this will change once Lucy begins her new life, I have no immediate concerns. I asked how being apart from Ella will make her feel.

'Ella and I are like sisters, doctor. I should feel scared and lonely without her.'

'By then you will be a married woman. You will have Mr Homeward to protect and comfort you.'

'Alfred is a dear, kind man whom I respect and admire. But doctor—' she gave me a pleading look and continued, hesitantly. 'In truth, I am nervous about marriage. I am young and know so little of what it – *entails.*'

I reassured her that every young bride felt this way and, indeed, that any modest woman *should* feel so. There is no real issue with her readiness for marriage. They only tragedy is that she will not be my bride, she will be Homeward's.

I am not unaware of the bachelor life Homeward leads; I trust this will change with his marriage. He is lucky to be sharing his future with such a treasure and I hope he appreciates her worth. It is most certainly above rubies.

CHAPTER 24
INTERROGATING THE
ARCHIVE

A ntoine snorts. 'Above rubies. What a creep.'

I scan through some ancient gas bills I've extracted from the trunk, before throwing them onto the rubbish pile. 'Creep, maybe, but does he sound like a pimp? He's not happy about Homeward's loose morals, is he? And Lucy seems pretty innocent too.'

'Huh,' says Antoine. He goes back to his laptop and starts searching for any misdemeanours Wood and his 'accomplices' have successfully hidden from Sam, while I turn back to the trunk.

It's certainly a beautiful object. There's a touch of William Morris, about it, with its cedarwood top and sides, inlaid with ornate flower and leaf patterns in different coloured woods. Yet I've never liked the thing, even before it chained me to a past I want to forget. For my mother it was almost a religious artefact: a shrine to her father. An artist and craftsman, she said, not like the Harpy, who neglected them both. Then abandoned them.

Kathleen used to sit in front of the trunk like I'm doing

now. She'd take out objects from her past and sigh over them, ignoring life as it unfolded without her, in the present. Her most precious relic was a little powder blue box containing a lock of Michael's hair and his first bootees. There hadn't been a pink box with mine in, because I'd had the temerity to live.

Kathleen's other favourite item was a frothy concoction of white lace and tulle, shrouded in tissue paper. Her wedding dress. In occasional better moods, she'd take it out and hold it up to herself in front of the mirror.

'It would still fit me,' she'd say and I'd wince. The pathos was painful; it would have hung from her skeletal shoulders. In the mirror, the shiny white flounces cruelly emphasised Kathleen's grey skin and sunken eyes.

'I always hoped you'd wear it someday.' Next to her wraith-like reflection, I looked like a healthy lumberjack. 'Maybe it could be taken out?'

'It's lovely.' I'd say. 'How about cheese on toast for your tea, Kathleen? You'd like that.'

When she died I gave the dress to the RSPCA shop, along with her wardrobe of smart seventies and eighties frocks. I'll swear I saw bits of them the other day in a local pop-up shop, upcycled into witty retro outfits for twenty-somethings.

All that's left in the trunk now, apart from the snoring cat, are the piles of paper I found heaped up at the bottom of Kathleen's wardrobe, or stuffed into drawers. The residue, once I'd cleared her flat. The remainder. A mixture of rubbish and stuff I might want some day, like photos, letters and official paperwork. I didn't have the energy to deal with it twenty years ago. So I imprisoned it all in the trunk to make sure none of it escaped into my life.

I pull out a handful of paper from under Mulder, who wakes, looks deeply wounded and jumps out to lie on the papers I've already removed. I scratch his fluffy throat, before sticking my head back into the trunk. It smells of dust and unwelcome memories. I grab another fistful of papers.

I'm sorting it into two piles, utter rubbish and possibly not. The utter rubbish is easy to spot: old till receipts, bills, take-away flyers and free newspapers, from over twenty years ago. The possibly nots I barely glance at. Mainly they form a bed for Mulder, who rolls onto his back and stretches out into a star shape as he sleeps; I slip more bedding material under him.

By the time I get to the bottom of my beer bottle I've amassed a sack full of rubbish for recycling. It feels hugely satisfying.

Antoine looks up from his laptop. 'You don't hang around.'

'That's the easy bit. The difficult stuff's going to be in there.' I nod towards the small stack underneath my furry assistant.

'Want a hand? I'm getting nowhere trying to dig up dirt on these Edwardian worthies and—'

He's interrupted by the doorbell.

'Let's have our pizza,' he says. 'Before we delve into your own dark past.'

OPENING THE DOOR, I come face to face with Letitia in a moped helmet. How is she old enough to be delivering pizza? Still, better than the Saturday job I had at her age.

'Meg? You never said you *lived* in the old madhouse.' Letitia swivels her helmet to look round at the hallway. 'Creepy, innit?'

Antoine comes to see what's going on so I introduce them. 'Nice job you did on the Spiritual Machinists,' he says.

She takes off her helmet. 'You two found out who killed those girls yet?'

'Still on it, scoop,' he grins.

'Bet they're still roaming this murder house.' Letitia looks pointedly over our shoulders into my flat.

'You don't believe in demons,' I remind her.

'Ghosts is different. 'Specially crazy ones. I'm outa this place.'

Back in the flat Antoine lays the table, muttering about damage to his property values.

'Oh come on, a ghost adds thirty K,' I tell him. 'The spirits are actually combating your Brexit deflation. Plus, the De Morgans hanging out here must be almost worth a blue plaque.'

He brightens, suggests that Harriet bringing Trotsky to see the play ought to add value as well. We don't know Harriet's Russian revolutionary was actually Trotsky, but I don't bother pointing that out. I really like the idea of a young Leon watching Lucy's 'urchins' perform *Peter Pan*. I hope he appreciated it.

Antoine takes the box of vegetariana from me and puts it on the table. I switch on a lamp and get yet another minor shock. I wince and plug in Terry's surge protectors, which arrived unexpectedly this morning. Unexpectedly, because I got a message saying they were out of stock. That'll be Terry gifting them to me, diamond that he is.

I reach for a slice of pizza and Antoine tells me to sit down and eat like a civilised person. He's turning into his mum.

'Better than turning into my dad,' he says. 'Anyway, I didn't slap your hand, so I'm not.'

I grin. 'Wonder if I'm turning into my dad. Apart from the still being alive bit. He must have been well-organised too, to cope with my mum.'

'Was she always flaky?'

I pause with a pizza slice halfway to my mouth. Remember Kathleen dancing around, singing. More happy flaky before

Michael died, I tell him. Ditsy. Cautiously, because you have to be cautious about other people's crazy dead parents, he asks me if she ever saw a shrink. I remember the GP's bottles of tranquilisers, blister packs of antidepressants. I shrug. 'People didn't talk about that sort of stuff in those days, did they? It was an embarrassing secret.'

'Yeah, nowadays you'd have to join a support group for young mental health carers. Message them about your feelings on a daily basis.'

'Every age brings its new horrors,' I say.

AFTER WE'VE EATEN, Antoine gently evicts Mulder from his 'possibly not rubbish' bed, then picks up a tatty photo album and flicks through it. I sit next to him on the floor as he stops at a black-and-white picture of a bohemian couple, newly married.

'Kathleen's parents. Gerry and Liz,' I tell him.

She's a rangy sort of girl, dressed in a loose sweater and slacks. He's the source of my mother's Irish good looks and my unruly mop of hair. They radiate happiness and confidence.

'You look like your grandmother.'

'Kathleen called her the Harpy.' Antoine gives me a questioning look, so I'm obliged to explain. 'She said my grandad was a sensitive man; my grandma had no sympathy for him and no patience with either of them. Too strict, too keen on rules. Kathleen's father pretty much brought her up. Her mum was more interested in her work. Schoolteacher.'

The pair of teenage beatniks in the photo have their arms around each other. She looks adoringly at her new husband. The sensitive man.

Below their picture is another of them, taken a few years later with their daughter. She's an exquisite child who makes them both fade into the background. Then pages more of Kathleen, in her ballet clothes, on an outing, at Christmas. She really is an astonishingly beautiful girl, her big eyes framed with long dark lashes in her heart shaped face. She has poise, always at ease, her head tilted to the camera. As a teenager, she's never spotty or awkward. She just transforms into an elegant young woman, with glossy black hair and a bewitching smile.

'The camera loved your ma,' Antoine says.

I shrug. 'It was her bread and butter. You've seen her portfolio.'

Everyone who ever visited our flat saw her portfolio. It had pride of place on the battered coffee table.

He turns over some pages. 'Look. Baby Meghan.'

A family group. Me and Michael are about two. My father grins cheerfully out at the camera and Michael, a boyish version of my mum, laughs and waves his arms around. Kathleen smiles down at him, enchanted. I stare murderously at the cabbage patch doll I'm holding.

'Mom's got one of me and you at nursery at that age. You look happy in that.'

I was always happier at school. Because I'm bad, so bad. I don't remember Michael at nursery. According to Claudette, we had different friends, sunny, loveable, Michael and weird little me. I probably took the opportunity to get out of his shadow. As a twin you're born into love and intimacy with your mirror baby, but also into competition. It defines you. You are what they're not. And when they're gone, what are you, exactly? The shadow reappeared when Michael died. It was bigger and darker; it swallowed everything. There was no way out of it then.

I take the album from him, close it, put it aside. It can go in my attic, with my mother's portfolio. I pick up the next thing on the pile, an old postcard from Breda, having a lovely time on the Galway coast.

We find my parents' marriage certificate and Michael's birth and death certificates, scattered throughout the detritus of ancient Christmas cards and social security paperwork.

'Not much to live on,' Antoine remarks, passing me a benefit letter. 'Even then.'

There had been other money paid into Kathleen's account every month, I tell him. Kathleen sometimes said it was a widow's pension, sometimes that it was royalties from her work and sometimes that it was from her rich aunt, who lived abroad. I never knew what to believe. So we didn't get that much from the state, apart from housing benefit, but we scraped by. Then there was compensation money, from the company Dad had worked for when he died. Cash, that had been, turned up every month. The only post Kathleen ever opened.

'I suppose construction's a cash economy,' Antoine says. 'Especially back then.'

'Thing is, I never knew how official any of it was, or whether it would just disappear one day. There was no paper trail. Mum's benefit entitlement kept getting stopped because she was forever missing appointments and they kept threatening her with employment training schemes. You can imagine. So I had to work, once I got old enough. In case it all dried up.'

'I never realised.' He looks a bit stricken. 'I thought you just wanted better trainers.'

'Well, that too,' I say.

CHAPTER 25

TAKING CARE OF BUSINESS

I t's definitely helping to have Antoine here as I go through these unwelcome reminders of the past. Still tough going, but better than I expected. We bin the cards and financial stuff, put the certificates with the album. Satisfyingly, there's just a small heap of unopened post left. We get ourselves another beer and dig in.

Most of the older post is on top of the pile. There's stuff from thirty-five years ago, after my father died. Addressed to our old house in Dalston. Some paperwork involving a ten-grand mortgage against the house, with a shark company. Repayments at a ridiculously high interest rate. A series of unopened bills that started six months later, for mortgage payments, utilities and poll tax. Until the point where Breda took over the running of mum's finances: after the house was repossessed.

'You must be gutted about that,' says Antoine. 'It was a tiny mortgage.'

I shrug. It was just a house.

'But it'd be worth over a million now,' he persists.

Londoners.

You can't regret your mother's inability to cope, I tell him. She had a hard time, she did her best. It could have been worse. She could have landed me with a nightmare stepfather, or we could have ended up on the streets. And once I was old enough, it was easy for me to take over the household admin from Breda.

He nods, thoughtfully, then grins. 'Bet we don't find any unopened bills for your old business. No paper trail there.'

'Ho ho. You know I haven't done anything like that since I was an undergraduate? Benedict never knew and never should. Once I got a bursary for my postgraduate study plus some teaching work, I didn't need it any more.'

He holds up his hands. 'Not judging, here.'

I know he isn't. He sometimes came with me to the clubs, raves and warehouse parties where I worked. Not his scene exactly, he never did drugs, but there were always plenty of posh girls there. He'd wander round, chatting with loved-up strangers in his usual outgoing way, though he got fed up with being monitored, and sometimes searched, by plain-clothes coppers. They didn't monitor me. Because I didn't look like a dealer to them.

Don't get me wrong, it wasn't *Topboy*, or anything like it. I dealt pills to clubbers when I went out at weekends. That was it. Didn't deal at school, sourced safe product and stuck to my niche market. Just ecstasy. Didn't step on anyone else's toes, whatever the demand. I kept it small and carefully organised, stayed straight at work and never got caught.

I'm not proud of how I made a living. I've never kidded myself about the bad shit that happens further up the supply chain. But I needed a job I could scale up if our income disappeared, and scale down as exams loomed. I'd never have got into St Cadog's if I'd been stacking shelves twenty hours a week for the minimum wage. I took a calculated risk and worked the festivals that last summer after A levels, so I could support myself once I got to university. Which was lucky, because once Kathleen died I was totally on my own.

'Your dad always knew, didn't he?' I ask. 'About what I did?'

'Yeah, think so. His connections. He was pleased for me, having a mate with an illegal side hustle, used to say "that girl's got her head screwed on". Made me more like one of the family.'

'Not everything Terry does is illegal.'

Antoine shrugs. 'He's so dodgy he just makes it seem that way. Here.' He passes me some unopened greetings cards. 'These are addressed to you as well as your mum.'

A couple of Christmas cards from the possibly open-handed Aunt Rose. Postmarked Connecticut. Antoine's curious about who she is.

'Kathleen's great-aunt, I think. Lots of Irish people went to live in the US, didn't they? Here—' I unearth the album from the small 'keep' pile and flick through until I find the picture of Kathleen, in her modelling days, with Aunt Rose.

Rose is a woman of around seventy, in twinset and pearls, sporting a carefully coiffed Margaret Thatcher hairstyle. Kathleen's looking fabulous in shoulder-padded chic. They're posing on Waterloo Bridge with the Eye-less Southbank behind them. Out on a summer evening, like normal people. Who took the photo? Kathleen's father? Mine?

'Hard to believe she's a member of your family,' Antoine stares at the photo, fascinated. 'She looks so—'

'Respectable?'

'Strait-laced. Looks a bit like you, though.'

'If I dressed as a blue-rinsed New England matron? Good to know.'

'So, she's the rich aunt who helped support your mum?'

I told him it was probably one of Kathleen's romantic fantasies. She said she'd been close to Aunt Rose, but I don't remember ever meeting her.

'Still. Your own family's Aunt Ernestine.' Antoine picks some more greetings cards off the pile. 'Here's another Connecticut one, sent to your old Dalston house. August 1984. Addressed to you, this time.'

Greetings on my fourth birthday, in Aunt Rose's firm, flowing hand. My real aunt.

Antoine wants to know why I never got it.

'First birthday without Michael. Kathleen was in bits. We probably didn't celebrate it much.' The first time my birthday meant loss instead of joy. A date to mourn the person I wasn't. We find my fifth birthday card from Aunt Rose. It has a princess on it.

'Later on I started to get them. When me and Breda took over the post, after we moved up to the Poe.'

'You didn't get this one.' He hands me another unopened card, addressed to me at the Dalston house.

I peer at the smudged postmark. Purfleet, 1985. Purfleet? Breda or one of her sisters visiting friends, maybe? I open the envelope. The card inside has a pink teddy-bear on it and a gold number five. Something falls out. An old five pound note.

I pick it up, marvelling at how big and papery it is. Currency of a forgotten past. Then I read the card.

The world begins to tilt, everything slows down and I go cold.

'What?' asks Antoine. 'Meg, are you ok?'

I pass him the card.

He reads out loud. 'Happy Birthday Meggie, love Dad.'

DR WOOD'S DIARY

27 MAY 1907

I am pleased to record that Ella's progress is excellent. Today I broached the subject of her return home, once she is discharged.

'I intend to travel in Europe, first,' she told me. 'My sister might allow Violet to spend some time with me in France. We miss each other so much and it will be educational for her.'

I think it unlikely that her family will commit the child to Ella's care, given her recent history. Yet it was interesting to observe that her plans did not appear to include Lucy. I wondered if my concern about the strength of her feelings for Lucy was misplaced. I asked her if she would not miss her friend once she is married.

For a second her countenance displayed great unhappiness at this prospect, but she hid it almost immediately. 'Indeed, I shall. Perhaps she might join us in Europe.'

So that is her plan. I must take care that Homeward does not allow Lucy to stay with Ella in France, once they are both released. Being alone together in a country with loose moral codes might encourage their friendship to take an unhealthy turn indeed.

ELLA'S JOURNAL
MAY 28, 1907

There have been two alarming events recently. Both are highly
unwelcome, but I have weathered them with a degree of
strength and equilibrium I did not possess six months ago.

The first incident concerns Florrie. For the past few weeks
some of the more rational children have been allowed to come
to church with us. Lucy, Miss Englethorpe and I shepherd
them (a promotion from sheep to sheepdogs) and they enjoy
their outing immensely. None have thus far misbehaved, until
two days ago.

On Sunday, we all stood conversing outside the church
after the service. The children were standing together quietly,
as usual, when Florrie looked up with an expression of fear on
her face, then, with no warning, took flight down Cazenove
Road.

Nell gave chase, but my Florrie is fleet of foot. It seemed
she would get away, until Mr Chamberlain tore himself away
from Lucy and ran after her, overtaking Nell. He caught up
with Florrie and held the screaming and kicking child down,

until Nell and the other attendant, Vera, reached them. They pinioned her cruelly, marching her back to the asylum post-haste.

It is such a disappointing episode and so unlike Florrie. She is normally a self-possessed child. Dr Wood has been pleased with her progress and she did so well in the play last week. Florrie was subdued in drill today, perhaps because she is tired from all the chores Matron gave her as punishment for her misdeed. When I asked her about what happened, she was reluctant to talk. Eventually she told me this:

'I wished to be free, Miss. Everything was closing in on me and I had to escape before the demons got hold of me. It's the demons inside of me, Matron says, make me so wilful. Is it my fault, miss? Am I to blame?' She tugged the hair at her temples as if that would release her demons.

All this has troubled me, as I am fond of the child and thought she, too, was quite recovered. I have never seen any evidence of instability in her. Does it mean that we may all relapse, I wonder?

The second disturbing incident occurred today. Lucy came to me in tears, too upset to tell me the cause of her unhappiness. I soothed her and eventually she became sufficiently calm to confide in me.

She, too, has had a poisonous letter, no doubt sent by the same evil man who wrote to me two months ago. If she does not pay her blackmailer, he will tell Alfred about us. About our unnatural acts and perverted passion, according to this letter.

My first thought was to let him tell Alfred. Then Lucy might be free to be with me.

The poor girl was so distraught I could not say that to her. She confessed that she had not the money to pay and felt desperate. I imagine her dressmaker and the extras for her play have taken up all her month's allowance. Not to mention my beautiful birthday gift. I dried her tears and told her not to worry. She must leave me to deal with him and think of it no more.

I resent this man's effrontery. Why should he feel able to make money out of two people, merely because they love one another? I believe our love is a gift from God. I am not ashamed of it and hope that one day Lucy, too, will take pride in it.

That day has not yet arrived. I paid the sum required.

CHAPTER 26

RETRIEVER

I sip the hot sweet tea Antoine gives me. Another foodstuff from books. His fictional tea helps bring me back to reality. Still shaky and bewildered, I return to the pile of post.

There are more cards. I get Antoine to open them all.

My sixth, seventh and eighth birthdays, plus Christmas cards to me and Kathleen. All from my dad. I sit on the floor, surrounded by pink glittery cartoons and obsolete currency. 'He was alive? Four years after he was supposed to be dead? He was just – in Purfleet?'

Only the careful tact people use around the bereaved (or the unbereaved) stops Antoine saying that many would choose death. I can see it in his face.

'So that monthly cash?' he says. 'Child support?'

My mind does inelegant backflips. Unsatisfactory memories rearrange themselves into clearer patterns. Breda complaining that my father's godless family took over his funeral and didn't invite any of them. As far as I knew, he had no immediate family.

Antoine's hand hovers over his laptop. He looked at me in question.

I nod.

While he taps his keyboard I remember my mother resisting the entreaties of Father Dom and Breda to have a mass said for my dad. Didn't she want to shorten his time in purgatory?

No. Because he wasn't in purgatory, he was in Purfleet.

What next? Am I going to find Michael alive somewhere, a grown man? I re-read his death certificate, just to make sure. It still says meningitis. Three years old. Father notified death.

I sip my literary tea.

It's easier and harder than I thought, finding my father. Easier for Antoine to locate him, despite the common name. John Morgan. He's out there on the web, large as life and still living. Own website for his business, JM Electrical, with a photo of him and everything. Reviews on trusted trader, 4.5 stars.

Then there's his Facebook presence. Pictures of him with his wife, Donna, his two grown-up sons and his baby granddaughter, all there on public display. He's even got a golden retriever.

He's carried on having a whole life, when for me he's been in his grave for thirty-five years.

So, yeah. Harder as well as easier.

I shake my head. 'All that time, Kathleen lied. To everyone. Maybe she convinced herself, she hardly knew what the truth was sometimes.' I pick up a passing cat for comfort. Hide my face in Scully's furry warmth.

'It was selfish and cruel.' Antoine strokes Scully's neck. 'What your mum did.'

'She was ill.'

'You were four. And you'd already lost your twin brother. You needed your dad and he wanted to be there for you.'

'Four birthday cards and then he gave up? He didn't try that hard.'

Antoine points out my dad might have phoned, written, even come round, but my mum wouldn't have let him see me. He carried on sending money, after all.

'He ditched us less than a year after Michael died.'

'Your parents split up after they lost their son. Puts pressure on people, something that hard. He never left *you*.'

Scully's purring revs up to superloud. I can feel the vibrations down my arms as I cling onto her like a life raft.

I look at the happy Facebook family on Antoine's laptop, the cheerful old bloke and his comfortable wife, relaxing at a barbie in the garden of their semi. With the bloody dog.

The trouble with the dead is that they become legends. They occupy another zone of being, away from the mundane and the trivial. If your father dies in a building site accident when you're four, you invent a new, heroic father. He stays young and handsome, he even becomes cool. He doesn't become an ordinary bloke with Brexiteer friends who call him Jonno. I'm grateful he helped us financially, but honestly? I can't even think about making contact.

I know that for him I'd only be an unwelcome puzzle. A disappointment. Like my childhood self was for Kathleen. He won't want reminding about the bad old days, either; he's clearly happy in his new life.

Maybe if I'd opened the trunk years ago, it would have been different. It's too late now; the Purfleet ship has sailed.

I put down the cat and move my birthday cards to the recycling pile.

ELLA'S JOURNAL

MAY 29, 1907

8am

I am in a dejected frame of mind. I begin to wonder if my plight is a consequence of what I did, six long years ago. Am I being punished by God by being separated from the woman I love? Every moment that passes brings us closer to Lucy's wedding day. It is now less than a month away and I can hardly bear to think about it. Every time we speak of it, she tells me I must come and live with her once I am well. Alfred is happy with her plan; he does not wish Lucy to be lonely when he is absent.

I cannot do this. It would be agony to sit at his dinner table night after night, making conversation with my host and his wife. It would be worse to think of them together, when I am alone in my bed.

I cannot share her like this. It is too much to ask. I will not be a sub-plot in the drama of their marriage.

Yesterday I tried to bring matters to a head. When she told me she loved me perhaps she had not meant it, I said to her.

At least, not as I did. She protested that she loved me beyond anything, but our situation was difficult. We needed to be careful. We had our own reputations to consider and those of our families.

I told her that is not sufficient reason to marry a man she does not love. She hinted that her family finances are precarious. Alfred's people are wealthy, so I assume she must make the marriage for her own financial security.

I assured her I had money enough for the two of us. We could go away to Paris and set up home together. There are places there, even in society, where women like us are accepted. I have read of it and met American ladies who have travelled there.

'Ella, you are so generous and it is such a romantic idea,' she said. 'Yet once we are free from this asylum and I am comfortable, respectable Mrs Alfred Homeward, we can be together always and the world will not shun us. Particularly when I become Lady Godmansworth. We will enjoy our conventional life in London and can travel as we wish. We would not be happy as part of some shadowy, immoral Parisian set. We are good Christian women, Englishwomen.'

'We might have to adjust to a different way of living in Paris, but our lives would not be a sham,' I told her. 'No one would think anything of two ladies sharing a house; we could appear perfectly conventional, if we wished. We could even have our families to stay. I should love us to have little Violet spend time with us, learning French and exploring the city.'

I thought of the three of us walking hand in hand beside the Seine, with Violet in the middle. The future I imagined that day in the park, when I watched our reflections in the river. Not the future where our love is a shameful, hidden thing, but the one where we live without pretence. The other one. It is a future I want so much that it causes me pain.

She protested that we would not have our own children if we lived that way. Whereas in her scheme, we could bring Lucy's children up together. Would that not be delightful?

'They would be your children, Lucy. Yours and Mr Homeward's.'

'Alfred would not be interested in the little ones, he would rather be hunting or shooting. They will be ours.'

I do not know how we can resolve this. Sometimes I wonder what would happen if I told Homeward about us. Dr Wood, I'm sure, knows I am not attracted to men. I cannot hide that from an alienist. But Lucy's fiancé is not the sort to comprehend that two women may love each other the way a man and a woman do. He has not the imagination.

9pm

My mind went over all this so much that when I had my talking cure with Dr Wood today I finally confessed to him what happened that night in California.

It was a relief. He was kind and said I have no reason to feel guilt. Yet how can I not, if this is why I am undeserving of love?

I did not tell him about myself and Lucy. At best, he would stop me sleeping in her room.

After my session I felt a little more optimistic and began to believe I may persuade Lucy to come to Europe. She is not as conventional as she would have everyone believe. I told her there were many lady artists in Paris and that photography is seen as an art form there. She was most interested.

'You do have a gift, my dear,' I said. 'Even Mrs De Morgan praises your photographs. Imagine how your work would improve with other talented photographers to inspire you.

Think how many Parisian artists would wish to paint you, as Mrs De Morgan has done. You would be a muse, as well as an artist in your own right.'

I could see she was attracted by the idea. But then the light went out of her eyes and she shook her head.

'My father needs this alliance for his business. A title in the family will change his fortunes.'

'And you must sacrifice your life for your father's business?'

She winced at this and tears filled her eyes.

'My sweet Lucy.' I took her hand. 'So many people want so much from you.'

'I know it is bad of me.' Her voice choked, as tears began to flow, 'I should be strong, but sometimes I feel crushed by the weight of their need.'

'Hush now.' I put my arm around her. 'I want nothing but your happiness. I will protect you from them all.'

CHAPTER 27

INTO THEIR SOULS WITH HER CAMERA

I call Benedict with my weird news. 'What a tremendous shock for you, my dear,' he says. 'Perhaps you'll feel differently about making contact with your father once you've recovered a little.'

Or perhaps I won't.

'You must feel rather cheated of a relationship with him.'

Mainly I feel stupid, I tell him. I knew what Kathleen was like, but I never thought to check. I'm a genealogist and a trained researcher. I'm used to families having secrets and telling lies; I *always* check the source material.

'You really must not take any blame on your shoulders. Your mother was, at best, negligent of your emotional welfare.'

'She wasn't well.'

'Indeed, she may not have been ill-intentioned, but she was unable to give you the care you needed. It does rather sound as if she privileged her own inability to deal with rejection above your need to have a loving relationship with your father.'

'You mean if she couldn't have him, I wasn't going to?'

'Depressed people cannot always help being ungenerous in their behaviour.'

And that is why Benedict is so bloody great. He's always on my side, right or wrong. Like Antoine. They wouldn't ditch me a few months after my brother died. Who needs Jonno?

Mind you, as I tell Benedict, Antoine thinks not contacting my father is another example of my snobbery. Trying to erase my working-class origins. 'He says I'm behaving like Pip in *Great Expectations*.'

Antoine doesn't understand that I've taken the tools education gave me and created a whole, rational self, living in an ordered space of sanity, away from the madness, loss and chaos of my mother's world. I've created an ordered world for myself but not a normal one. Not like my father's normal world. The solutions we've found for evading the past are different. Meeting would throw that into relief and force us to focus on the darkness we've escaped from. It would be damaging to us both. Neither of us need to be dragged back and down.

'These things can be so hard to predict,' Benedict says. 'Your father might be delighted to see you.'

I change the subject. 'Listen Benedict, have you read the latest instalments of Ella's journal.'

'Awfully exciting, isn't it, though appalling that Lucy was being blackmailed. I do wish they'd been able to run away together. Perhaps they tried.'

'Yes, but Lucy was the photographer. Lucy.'

'It certainly brings a dimension to her that I hadn't quite appreciated.'

For Benedict, everything I'm unearthing is a literary text. For me they were real women. Lucy had talent, I tell him. She was perceptive. Ella loved her for a reason, not just because she was pretty.

'Yet Dr Wood doesn't seem to think of her that way,' he

muses. 'Incidentally, I've not had time to read it yet, but I've discovered another article by him. I'll send it over.'

THE OTHERS, including Letitia, who I'm keeping in the loop about anything critical, have their own views about Ella's latest revelations.

Letitia: She could see people, that girl. See into their souls with her camera.

Uzi: Lucy was a gifted artist.

Betty: I wonder who owns the copyright of Lucy's photos? I have to use them in my book.

Antoine: If she was so broke where did she get the money from for all the photography equipment? It was expensive back then.

Rowan: Taking pictures allows her to look at others. Instead of being looked at. Understandable.

And it is.
Until we find the pictures that aren't so understandable.

PSYCHIATRIC REVIEW

1908

Excerpt from Journal Article, *The House of Mirrors*, by Dr C. Wood

The patient is a 28-year-old woman whom I shall call Edith. She is of good family and is physically healthy. Originally from Britain, she has spent the last twenty years in America, where her family are now settled.

Edith has for some years experienced a strong sense of persecution, seeing conspiracies all around her. This leads to agitation and anger and can result in violent episodes which she cannot later remember. She displays recklessness and irritation. At times she cannot concentrate and is so restless it is difficult for her to remain still. Before she began treatment her agitation sometimes spiralled to such a point that she became insensible, which, again, she could not remember later. At times, whilst under my care, Edith has required sedation when her emotions become too violent. During our treatment it has emerged that she has regular dreams of persecution and imprisonment. At first, she could not remember these and denied having dreams at all.

Edith is an intelligent, well-educated young woman. Although she has the comportment and training of a lady, her manner is unusually frank and direct. She has a tendency to be blunt in her contributions to conversation and to contradict people in an argumentative manner. She says she abhors hypocrisy and speaks her mind. I have pointed out that the social wheels are kept oiled by a little diplomacy, and that ladies are often adept in these matters. Her response is that she will not defer to opinions that are ignorant and wrong in order to prevent the social machinery from creaking. Such statements give a good flavour of her personality. I should add that she can be a likeable individual with a refreshing outlook, if one overlooks her gruff manner.

Edith's Christian faith is solid, but I have observed that this is not always a source of strength to her. She has tended to view her illness as a punishment from God, not as suffering caused by traumatic events.

In the main, I have treated her with talking therapy. I have also prescribed daily swimming and walking exercise, to calm her excess energies.

In our early talking sessions, we explored her feelings about her family. She appears to have little attachment to her mother, whom she sees as a woman concerned only with superficial matters. Her mother dislikes Edith's forthright ideas and finds her friends alarmingly modern, Edith believes. She has a stronger bond with her father and acted as his assistant before she became ill. His work in law and local governance appeals to her rather masculine way of thinking. When her mental health deteriorated, she feels her father began to overlook her, writing her off as another silly, emotional female.

Her greatest family attachment is to her niece, the daughter of her older sister. She appears to give this five-year-old child, whom I will call Virginia, all the love and affection she feels she did not receive from her own mother.

The dreamwork has been critical in this analysis. My patient has a recurring dream of being trapped in a large house full of mirrors. She senses a malign presence in the dream house and flees through the building away from this unknown person, whom she never actually sees. She feels an urgent need to escape from the building, both to get away from this danger and in order to save someone else. Yet every time she thinks she has found a door, it turns out to be another of the huge mirrors. She bangs on the windows, but no one outside acknowledges her distress, or tries to free her from her prison.

In exploring her dreams, we have talked much of her feelings for the other person in the house and for the individual she has to rescue. She was able to excavate the emotions she felt for these two people, but not their identities. Finally, we had a breakthrough. She told me that the last time she had this dream, she had seen her pursuer.

She was tired of running from them, so she stopped, turned around and stood her ground. At first the person walking towards her down the corridor was someone she had known, before his death, six years previously. He was the son of one of her father's associates. In the dream she had feelings of loathing and hatred towards him. As this man drew nearer, he changed and became, in turn her father, mother, sister and brother-in-law. They all had hateful, hostile expressions on their faces. All were furiously angry with her. The figure then became every face Edith knew in society. It became the world. A world that wanted to destroy her.

Yet she stood her ground. As the furious monster of a

human being got near enough to touch her, it stood and stared at Edith, with violence in its eyes. Then, gradually, it shrunk until it was the size of a little child. It became less angry and rather melancholy. It turned into Virginia. Virginia looked up at her, with sadness and hurt in her eyes and said, 'Aunt Edith, why did you let them do this to me?'

At that point, Edith had realised the identity of the person she must save. It was little Virginia. She took the girl's hand and they walked together through one of the enormous looking-glasses.

We talked of the dream and I asked her about the young man. She did not wish to talk about him.

'That is the very reason why I must ask you about this person,' I said.

She paused. 'I have been told I must not speak of him.'

'It is a family secret you have been asked to guard?'

She nodded and I realised that we were nearing the root of her neurosis.

Edith was silent for a while when I told her this. A secret carried for years is a heavy burden. Yet she wished to live a life outside the pain of that remembrance. Indeed, she wished to escape through the mirror, as she had in her dream. She told me the following.

Six years previously, when she was in her final year at college, Edith was home for the holidays and attended a New Year's Eve party, hosted by her father's friend. All her family and most of local society attended. Their house was hot and claustrophobic and she left the main room to walk in the garden with a friend. Edith has a tendency to inversion, and this lady was someone for whom she felt a strong affection. They argued over something trifling and the friend returned to the house.

Edith stayed in the garden, upset and angry. As she paced

around in an attempt to calm herself, the son of the house appeared. She thought him a dull young man, whose only conversation was of sport, and had never paid him much attention. On this night he had drunk too much and was overly familiar. She tried to repel him but he would not go. He came closer and grabbed her arms, then began to kiss her. Edith is physically strong and was able to push the man away, but this appeared to excite him and he redoubled his efforts.

'I will not go into the details,' she said. 'This man pushed me onto the ground and forced himself upon me. It happened quickly and I was unable to stop him. Whilst he was – carrying out this act, I was able to pull a pin out of my hair and stab him in the neck. He drew back then and knelt there, holding his neck and squealing and sobbing like a child. I rose, straightened my garments as well as I was able and went into the house.'

She had told no one about the incident, feeling too disgusted and ashamed. Later she heard the young man had sickened and died. He contracted poisoning of the blood, as a result of a small wound in his neck, she had been told.

'I killed him,' she told me. 'I did not mean to, but when I stabbed him with my hairpin that is what happened. I became a murderer. That is why God has punished me.'

Her sense of guilt over his death was not the reason she had told her family of the incident, however. Three months later, when she was back at her college, she realised she was with child. She returned home.

Her mother refused to believe her. She thought Edith was using the dead man as a convenient scapegoat to cover her own misdemeanours. Edith had sullied herself and let down the family, she told her.

Edith's father was at first sympathetic to her and angry with her violator. Yet he had quickly let himself be swayed by her mother and came to believe her version of events. If he had, instead, chosen to believe Edith's account, he would have been obliged to cut off relations with her attacker's father, thus making an enemy of his influential ally. What's more, he would have brought an illegitimate grandchild into his household. These actions would have been ruinous for his political ambitions.

Consequently, she was packed off with her married sister to relatives in New England, where her daughter was born. Virginia was raised as her sister's child, but Edith resisted any attempt by her sister to adopt her formally. She loved her daughter and intended to reclaim her one day, she told me.

Edith's psychological problems began during her pregnancy. Although she saw gradual improvement over the following years, a sudden severe relapse, brought on by witnessing a catastrophic earthquake and its aftermath, prompted her family to seek my help.

Since the patient first spoke of her family secret, we have explored the matter many times. The unacknowledged trauma has created a complex emotional pattern. We have worked on the guilt she feels about her attacker's death and this has somewhat alleviated her paranoid delusions. For example, she no longer sees me as a sinister laboratory scientist, conducting questionable experiments on her. Beginning to acknowledge her repressed sense of shame and vulnerability has also decreased her anxiety and aggression.

Her love for her daughter is not untinged by the taint of the child's origins, although she steadfastly refuses to recognise this. She has expressed a desire to bring her daughter to Europe to live with her, once she leaves the asylum. I have asked her if that would be in the best interests of the child, who now has loving parents and a stable home. Would it not be a great wrench to be torn from this? Furthermore, if Virginia were to become her acknowledged daughter, would not the circumstances of her conception have a disastrous effect on her relationship with the girl?

'She is my daughter, Dr Wood, and I will decide what is best for her. And for me.'

DR WOOD'S DIARY
5 JUNE 1907

Just as I have made a breakthrough with Ella, I am presented with a setback. At our automatic writing session last night, Countess Zana spoke through Lucy as usual. This time, her message was for Ella. The relevant part of the transcript is below.

Countess Zana: It is a message from a little girl. She wishes to speak to her aunt Bella.

Lucy: There is someone here called Ella. Is that the name?

Countess Zana: Yes. Aunt Ella. She says that it is beautiful here and she is happy. Aunt Ella is not to worry about her.

Lucy: How long has she been with you, Countess?

Countess Zana: She has only just passed over to the vale of light and beauty.

Lucy: What is her name?

Countess Zana: She is called Violeta.

When Harriet read out the transcript, Ella became extremely agitated. She demanded to see it, snatching the paper from Harriet. As she read it, she began to shake, then, letting it fall from her hands, she collapsed on the chaise longue, weeping violently and tearing at her hair. I was obliged to intervene and sedate her. She is now sleeping.

Knowing how attached Ella is to Violet, I sent a telegram to her father, telling him Ella was concerned that the child might be unwell. A reply came promptly. Violet was healthy and happy. By coincidence, Mr Murray's London solicitor wished to call on me at my earliest convenience regarding some legal paperwork.

It is frustrating that the connection conjured by our Tele-pathic Transfer Engine has set my patient back, when she was recovering so well. Clearly the dead, as well as the living, can be unreliable.

Today's visit from Murray's solicitor has also caused me some concerns.

Mr Hawkins is not the type of dry, dusty legal gentleman we are used to of old, but a brisk young man, smartly dressed. Quite the new mode of lawyer. I would expect nothing less from a gentleman as modern and forward-looking as Zachariah Murray.

Once Mr Hawkins had settled himself in my study, he came straight to the point. He told me his visit was a delicate matter: the parentage of Violet. It would surprise me to know, he informed me, that Violet's real mother was not Ella's sister, Mrs Standhope, but Ella herself.

I gave no sign that Ella had already disclosed this secret to me.

Mr Hawkins produced a sheaf of papers from his briefcase. The whole family wished to put this arrangement on a more formal legal footing. To this end his American counterpart had drawn up a legal document, which the family had signed.

'You wish Miss Murray to sign these papers, also?' I asked him.

'That is the desire of her whole family,' he replied.

I told him Miss Murray had recently told me she wishes to raise her daughter herself.

'Dr Wood, in your medical opinion, is Miss Murray fit to bring up a child? Apart from the damage to her reputation, would not the social ostracism caused by such a situation further threaten her fragile mental state? I need not add that her family would be unable to recognise her, should this ill-advised route obtain.'

I considered his questions carefully. My concern is always for my patients first and foremost. Ella has experienced trauma that has marked her body as well as her mind. It has also marked her future. Even if she were well enough to be a mother, the child's proximity would be a daily reminder of that violent event. Add that to social isolation and withdrawal of parental love and support, and I cannot see Ella being able to maintain any steps to recovery she makes here, once she is back in the world.

'In that case,' Mr Hawkins said, 'I do not require her signature. Only yours.'

I thought hard about his request. Maternal love can be a powerful force and I was aware that Ella would not want this formal adoption to go ahead. Yet the desires of the troubled mind often work against the interests of its possessor and I believed this to be the best path for her. I must act at all times for the good of my patients and provide the reasoning they lack.

I also realised, from the tenor of Mr Hawkins approach, that if I did not acquiesce, Mr Murray would remove Ella from my care and place her in an institution where the superintendent was less scrupulous about ethical considerations. Such a man would be prepared to agree to anything the family wanted. There are, sadly, many such institutions.

With some misgivings, I signed the papers.

ELLA'S JOURNAL
JUNE 10, 1907

How long it took me to trust Dr Wood, when I first came here. Now I regret ever believing in him. I told him my secret and he betrayed my trust. He has conspired with my family to separate me from my child.

It is hard to push my mind to think of these words and translate them into code. Hard, too, to write upon this page. My mind and body are slowed and confused by his drugs. Yet I must make a record of what they have done to me.

Some days ago, I do not know how many, I awoke to find myself back in my room. Feeble sunlight filtered through the curtains. I felt bleary and confused, as though I had slept for a very long time. Immediately upon waking, I experienced a great and terrible weight bearing down upon me, crushing my spirits. I groped around in my mind for the source of this oppression. Gradually, then with sickening clarity, I began to recall it.

Violet, my Violet, was dead. My God had been a vengeful

God and had taken her from me. This, not separation from Lucy, was my punishment for taking a life.

No, I thought. My little girl. You cannot have died. I will not let you go. I must have cried out, then, for Nell's face swam into focus.

She warned me to calm down, or she would have to fetch the doctor.

I did not and so she did.

Dr Wood's face loomed above me smiling grotesquely. Countess Zana was not always correct, he told me. Was that not good news? I tried to sit up, but the world started spinning and I was obliged to sink down again.

'Violet?' My voice came out hoarse and cracked.

He had me sit up, slowly. Gave me water to drink.

Violet was alive, he told me. As my muddled brain took this in, a sense of joyful warmth bloomed within me. Had I felt strong enough I would have embraced him. Yet still I was anxious.

Was she in danger? I asked him.

He told me Violet was safer than ever, having been taken fully into the loving care of my family. I still felt nothing but relief, not understanding the implication of his words. I tried to brush away the tears that coursed down my cheeks, my movements clumsy and ill-coordinated.

Dr Wood went to say that my family would look after her now, giving her all that she needed. There would no longer be a stain on her parentage and I was free to live my own life. I was slow, my brain befuddled by the drugs, and at first I did not understand what he was saying. He repeated himself and eventually it sunk into my sluggish understanding.

'Fanny has adopted Violet?' I croaked. 'How can this be?'

It was the best thing for her future and for mine, he assured me.

'I do not consent to this!' I found my voice and he flinched at the sound. Perhaps I was shouting. I did not care.

He told me I did not understand. I could not give, nor withhold, consent. My family must act both for me and in the best interests of 'the child'.

I shouted out and tried to scramble out of bed, but Nell and another attendant stopped me.

'You do not see this now,' he said, as they held me down, 'because your reason is affected. In the future you will understand that this is the wisest course of action.'

'Never!' I cried. Then came the sting of an injection and another gap of time drifted away.

I woke this afternoon and no one was here. I was glad to be alone. I pushed my drugged mind to remember all that had happened. The horror that Violet might have died, the joy that she had not. The blank sense of betrayal and dark chasm of loss when I realised they had taken her away from me.

Last week I had a daughter and now they have stolen her. She will never live with me nor call me mother. Violet has not died, it is true; but part of me has.

I will never recover from this.

CHAPTER 28

AN UNEXPECTED
GRANDMOTHER

Poor bloody Ella, no wonder she had mental health problems. What horrors she went through. The rape, finding herself pregnant, then being blamed for it all by her family; feeling that she was responsible for the death of her attacker; having to give up her child when she was too vulnerable to resist.

What a catalogue of abuse. How furious, desolate and betrayed she must have felt.

I run birth certificate searches in the New England states for Violet Murray, September, 1901. Find her in Connecticut. Mother, Emmanuella Hope Murray, gentlewoman. Father, unknown.

Amateur family historians are a curse. Has Betty never even thought to get a copy of her mother's birth certificate? How sloppy is that? I didn't ask her, though, did I? I've been negligent there; I'm the professional, after all.

I kick off an adoption search, which will take a while. In the meantime, I run a marriage search for Violet Standhope and find one for 1927, when she married Victor Gardiner.

I tell Antoine it's official. Ella is Betty's grandmother, not her great-aunt. Can I do another simple sketch, he asks, because it's all very well for me, but everyone else gets confused about this family tree business. I scribble one out and stick it up on the shared area.

Zachariah = Claire
Martins
                    |
          ┌─────────────┐
William = Fanny   Ella
Standhope |
                      Violet = Victor
                        | Gardiner
                      Betty

IT'S 9AM IN CALIFORNIA, so I message Betty. Has she read my latest uploads? Her answer comes back straight away.

Betty: Oh Meg! My grandmother. It all seems so obvious now.

I suggest a video call.

Betty's sitting on her terrace in the sunshine. 'Mom's birth certificate wasn't among her papers when she died. She must have destroyed it, out of shame. To think I never bothered to get a copy, because I knew her birth date and the names of her parents.'

I indicate that she isn't the first family historian to mistakenly take her parents' word on trust.

'It explains so much about my mother,' Betty continues. 'She had a horror of anything unconventional. I know she was a different generation and values change, but the fifties were a decade that fitted her perfectly; she was totally committed to being a conservative hausfrau. So different to Ella. She never liked me asking questions about her family or the past. Now I know why.'

I ask her if the revelation sheds light on any other aspects of her family.

'Well, despite being Democrats, my family have quite traditional values. So the terrible way they treated Ella back then, it's not surprising. I'm a maverick like her, so I'm proud she was my grandmother and honoured to be writing her history.'

I'M sure all this must have some bearing on Ella's death. But how and why? I go back to deciphering her journal, looking for clues.

ELLA'S JOURNAL
JUNE 12, 1907

So, I have lost Violet. What unspeakable pain it causes me to write this, but write it I must. I need to face what they have done.

I am vastly diminished by my loss. I feel a complete emptiness.

Once I realised Dr Wood must have been complicit in the theft of my daughter, I charged him with it. He asked me what I thought might have happened had he not acquiesced to my family's wishes. Would they not have moved me to an institution where they could bend the superintendent to their will?

My family may well have behaved as he suggests, and then I would not only be separated from Violet but from Lucy too. Dr Wood wants me to tell him how I feel about his actions but I am loath to tell him of my anger and pain.

I can never trust him again.

Perhaps God is punishing me because I killed Violet's father. Or perhaps He is testing my love for my child? For I am not one to sit around moping and am already forming a plan to get Violet back. I shall become quite well, so that no one can ever again say I am unfit to be a mother. I will then employ lawyers to annul the adoption, which was carried out without my consent, when I was not in a position to oppose it.

All of this may take some time, but I am prepared to be patient. When Violet is a little older, I shall write and tell her that I am her real mama and that I am making plans for her to join me. I will be living in Paris, or perhaps Rome, by that time. Lucy is beginning to entertain the idea of us going to Europe together. She thinks she may be able to do it after she is married, at least for a period. I still hope to persuade her that she should come with me instead of going ahead with the wedding.

One day Violet will join us and the three of us will walk along the Seine together, in the spring sunshine. Or we will throw coins in the Trevi fountain and make wishes. What will I have to wish for, by then?

All my dreams will have come true.

HACKNEY COMET

26 NOVEMBER 2019

An Edwardian Murder Mystery

Two young women died mysteriously in Stoke Newington, on
the same day, over 100 years ago. Although both deaths were
recorded as accidental at the time, new evidence suggests
otherwise. Stoke Newington has its own Edwardian murder
mystery.

Ella Murray and Lucy Northaway became friends when
they were inmates at Abney Asylum, on Manor Road. Ella fell
from the roof terrace of the asylum on the evening of 20 June
1907 and died on impact. Lucy had been discharged on the
morning of that day. By the evening, she had plummeted to her
death from the gallery of Abney Park burial chapel.

Both women were in their twenties and came from wealthy
families. Both are buried in Abney Park Cemetery. They
became close friends and, later, lovers, when they were incarcerated in the asylum by their families. Here they were treated
by the unconventional psychoanalyst, Dr Charles Wood.
Although many of Wood's methods of curing mental illness

327

were years in advance of their time, he also used a technique called spirit writing as part of Lucy's therapy. He held seances where he claimed Lucy became possessed by the ghost of a Hungarian Countess. This caused her to write spirit messages from 'the other side'. These sessions used a steampunk-style electrical invention, the 'Telepathic Transfer Engine' which was invented by Wood's friend, Professor Gunther Von Helson.

Dr Wood and Professor Von Helson were part of a group called the 'Spiritual Machinists'. They believed that new technologies, like the Engine, would enable them to contact the dead. The Machinists all attended the radical non-conformist Church of United Souls in Upper Clapton (now Bethesda Chapel).

Lucy was being treated for 'hysteria'. She believed herself to be the victim of a vampire attack, much like her namesake in Bram Stoker's *Dracula*, which had been published ten years earlier. A beautiful, charming young woman, she was painted by the famous pre-Raphaelite artist Evelyn De Morgan in her greatest work, 'The House of the Spirits'. Lucy was also a talented photographer.

Lucy was about to marry another of Wood's friends, the Hon. Alfred Homeward, when she died, yet Wood's own case notes suggest he was strongly attracted to Lucy himself. A few months after Lucy's death, Homeward married a chorus girl, Gertie Stubbs, who was expecting his child.

Ella was a gay American suffragist, from a prominent family of Californian philanthropists. In common with the rest of his profession at the time, Dr Wood believed that Ella's sexual orientation could be 'cured'. Ella was being treated for trauma following a rape, which had resulted in pregnancy. Her suffering increased when her family separated her from her daughter.

This murder mystery came to light recently when Hackney-born genealogist Dr Meghan Morgan cracked the code to Ella's asylum journal and discovered the romantic relationship between the two women. They were passionately in love and shared a room at the asylum. Dr Morgan learned that Ella planned to travel to Paris on her release and wanted Lucy to join her. Did someone try to stop them?

Other prominent local people on the board of the asylum were manufacturer Barnabus Grimthorpe, construction magnates William Finleigh and Ezekial Chamberlain, and suffragette and philanthropist Harriet Kerr. One of the male board members had been implicated in a murder some years before these young women's deaths and another had been accused of rape.

Staff at *The Comet* have built on Dr Morgan's work by delving into the newspaper archives, to discover more about the suspicious nature of the deaths. Hackney student, Letitia Lewis, has also contributed important background information about the Spiritual Machinists, uncovered as part of her GCSE local history research project.

Could any of the people involved with the asylum be implicated in the tragic deaths of these two young women? Dr Morgan and *The Comet* continue to investigate the secrets of Abney Asylum.

Can you help?

The Comet calls on anyone whose ancestors were connected with Abney Asylum in 1907. Can you tell us anything, however small, that might shed light on this mystery?

CHAPTER 29

LOCATING DEMONS

I t's 4am and I wake with all of the awful stuff about the asylum going through my mind. Ella and her lost child, who became Betty's strait-laced mum. Ella and Lucy's doomed relationship. Their terrible, untimely deaths and the possibility of a murderer at the asylum.

Ella's beginning to sound delusional in her last journal entry. Was she more unbalanced than we've realised? Can we actually trust her account? Or does she just seem deranged because we know that none of her plans ever came to pass.

All the other people who wanted so much from Lucy parade through my head. Dr Wood, her fiancé, her parents, Harriet, Von Helson, Evelyn De Morgan. The children. Did that wear her down so much that when someone – maybe Grimthorpe, Finleigh or Chamberlain, or even Wood – tried to exploit her sexually, she felt unable to repel them?

Then there's Ella, trying to shield Lucy from everything. Did she find out she hadn't succeeded in protecting her from sexual predation? How had she reacted? Had she marched up to the offender and demanded to have it out with him there and then? Had she threatened to tell her friend Harriet? Or to alert Alfred or Lady Barnum to what was going on?

If anything was.

Also, the last entry in Ella's journal is for the 19th June and she died on the 20th. I've translated some of the final paragraph and it mentions a second book that she planned to use as a journal. What if she started it? We won't have the end of the story.

I've sent Betty off to search her attic and get her family to look everywhere; we need that second book. We have to know.

Tossing and turning in bed, I realise I'm obsessing about the dramas of 1907 partly so I don't have to think about my own family's weirdness. My mother letting me believe my father's dead, when he's actually living in suburban bliss with Donna and the golden retriever. Does he even know Kathleen's dead? Did they ever get divorced? Then there's my half-brothers, or step-brothers, whatever they are. Do they know about me? My dad's new family probably resent my existence. They'd resent me more if I turn up, over-educated and under-socialised, brushing the dust of the tomb off my coat, as I crash their jolly barbecue like a messenger from a middle-class Hades.

Another image that's been running through my dreams, as if I don't have enough weirdness to deal with, is Uzi's picture of me. Insofar as it *is* a picture of me. Uzi warned me she didn't do realism and I've been pretty much expecting to emerge as an unrecognisable character in a horror movie.

Which would have been okay.

What she actually presented, when she unveiled her work to me and Antoine last night, was something far more disturbing.

The figure that's central to the picture does look like me. Well, me channelling Boudica. Head thrown back, she gazes directly at the viewer, a challenge in her eyes. Under her foot she crushes the supine figure of a weeping angel, collaged in from a photo of Lucy's grave. She seems to be drowning the angel of grief in a stream of water. Or are they its tears?

There's a lot of other stuff going on in the picture. Uzi's used the old asylum portraits and her photos of the cemetery to weave together little tableaux. Ella's there, her stance echoing mine, but her foot resting on the Abney Park Cemetery stone lion, as though she's a game hunter. Underneath scrolling letters say 'out of cruelty came forth riches'. Wood's shown leaning forward over a pile of children's bodies; Von Helson's hands strangle something that might be a stone dove; and Harriet's book rests on a bent and burdened marble figure. Throughout the picture, Uzi's trademark nightmarish backdrop of vines, creepers and unwholesome flowers spread their tendrils. The asylum children's faces peer out forlornly, hungrily, from the foliage. Water drips from the leaves, looking at times like blood.

Horrifying though it is, I can see it's a powerful artwork. I tell Uzi so.

'You look incredible,' Antoine says, in a funny, absent voice.

It might be a flattering portrait, but in truth I'd like to escape from the picture. Instead it's haunted me all night. Along with everything else.

I try reminding myself I'll be free to go home in a week or two when I've completed Monarch's stuff. I can finish Betty's work from there, where I'll be less affected by it all than I am in this spooky place. My own family drama might feel less acute once I leave London too. Yet, annoyingly, I feel a faint stab of regret at the idea of leaving, underneath the overwhelming sense of relief.

Finally giving up hope of getting back to sleep, I get up, drink coffee, start work early. Spend all morning on the archive, getting a lot of tedious stuff done, which will keep Monarch happy and get me home earlier.

I find nothing relevant to Ella and Lucy until the afternoon, when I come across the packet of photos. More pictures of the young actors from the Peter Pan play. I now see that they were taken in the schoolroom Ella says they used as a dressing room. At first, the pictures seem charming and rather haunting. You can see that the world's been a harsh place for these kids. It's in their eyes.

Then towards the bottom of the packet I find three photos that are a bit weird. The fancy dress of the fairies gets more scanty, and the way the kids are posed for the camera, looking vulnerable, sometimes flirtatious, showing off a bit, sometimes scared? It just feels odd. They remind me of the infamous Charles Dodgson photo Antoine brought up when we visited the De Morgan Centre. I know the view that his picture implicated Dodgson has been discounted, because, as Benedict pointed out, that was how children were often depicted in the mid nineteenth century.

But these asylum photos were taken fifty years later.

Taking pictures of the photos and sending them to the others feels distasteful (and borderline illegal) so I message Uzi and Antoine. I've got something suspicious to show them when they come to reclaim their cats, I tell them.

Antoine looks at the pictures with disgust, Uzi with the focussed attention she uses for art objects. She even puts Mulder down while she looks at them.

'Why would Lucy take pictures like this?' Antoine puzzles.

'You think they're hers too?' I ask.

'That intensity and informality, it is her signature,' Uzi says. 'The humour, also, in some of the cast photos.'

'Am I being a philistine, Uzi?' I ask. 'Or are these ones as dodgy as I think they are?'

'They are uncomfortable,' she admits, reluctantly.

'Unsavoury,' says Antoine.

'Do you think maybe – she wasn't given a choice?' I ask.

'She was coerced,' says Antoine. 'By Grimthorpe. With Wood's blessing. Although the other worthies could have been in on it.'

'Eww.' I look at the pictures again. Imagine Grimthorpe directing Lucy and the child, off camera. What a foul idea. I think about Florrie and the demons she tried to run away from, that day at church. Maybe the demons weren't in her head at all. Maybe they were in the congregation.

Like Letitia said, it's people who give girls problems, not demons.

'The photos were taken in Wood's asylum,' Uzi says. 'They are here with all the other archive material. Wood authorised them.'

As they rise to go, picking up their respective cats, Antoine's phone goes. He hauls his Scully up under his chin, where she bats his face winsomely with her paws.

'Right mate. Send it through and go and talk to her ASAP.'

Ending his call, he grins at the two of us.

'Perfect timing,' he says. 'Someone's come forward with information. His grandmother was in the asylum and tried to expose Wood. He's emailed Sam a cutting about it. Result.'

HERTS ADVERTISER

18 AUGUST 1939

Immorality and exploitation in a London insane asylum

Allegations have come to light of immoral and sinister activities in a London lunatic asylum, thirty years ago.

Annie Moran, 42, a widowed maid of all work in a respectable Hertfordshire vicarage, told the *Advertiser* her story. As a child, Mrs Moran was incarcerated in Abney Asylum, Stoke Newington. While there, she claims she was forced into immoral acts with several gentlemen.

'Terrible things, those men did to me. I will not call them gentlemen as they did not act like gentlemen, for all their money and fancy airs,' Mrs Moran told our reporter.

She said other girls, and sometimes boys, were subjected to similar outrages.

'We was given sweets and pennies if we didn't cry. My friend, Florrie, escaped one night, for she could take no more of it. She found work in the service of a good Christian family. Florrie got me a place with the family, which is how I was able to leave there.'

Mrs Moran declined to name her violators, fearing, she said, that this would put her, or her children, in danger.

Dr Charles Wood, 65, superintendent of the asylum, told the paper that lunatics often had infantile fantasies of this nature.

'My record of success in curing such individuals speaks for itself,' he said.

Mrs Moran's employer, the wife of the Reverend Stephen Sizewell, encouraged her maid to speak out.

'The police must be alerted to this outrage,' the doughty matron told our reporter. 'We shall not be silenced; I will persuade Annie of this. Such immorality and exploitation cannot go unpunished in the face of God or man.'

CHAPTER 30

SILENCED WITNESS

Within minutes Betty responds to the article.

Betty: Annie and Florrie! And those other poor children, how horrible.

It really is. Annie and Florrie have become real people to me; it torments me to think what they and the others went through, locked up here and abused like that.

Betty: She said gentlemen. Grimthorpe? Homeward? I so hope they didn't attack Ella, too, after all she'd been through.

Me: Homeward seems more interested in adult women.

Benedict: We don't yet know whom Annie is accusing. Did Mrs Sizewell contact the police?

Antoine: No report of it. War was declared a few weeks later.

Annie and the Sizewells were both silenced by a Luftwaffe bomb in 1940.

Rowan: Are there any more witness accounts of abuse at the asylum?

Antoine: Not that we've found

Uzi: Lucy was going to expose them. That is why they killed her

Me: Let's see what's in Ella's last entry before we jump to any conclusions.

ELLA'S JOURNAL
JUNE 19, 1907

I hardly dare to write these words: my dream has come true. Lucy has agreed to come away with me instead of marrying Mr Homeward

She is doing this in her own fashion. She does not wish to tell Alfred and his aunt, let alone her family, because she thinks her parents and Lady Barnum would pressurise her into the marriage. So she is pretending to go along with their plans for the wedding.

This behaviour is not to my taste; I would prefer a more direct and honest approach. Homeward's only crime is to love Lucy and he does not deserve to be humiliated in this way. More importantly, I do not wish her to be separated from her family, however poorly they have treated her, and I fear this will happen if she deceives them. Yet as I do not want her family, or Mr Homeward's, to prevent our escape, I shall go along with Lucy's scheme.

I have told her the truth about Violet and she was not at all surprised. Lucy says she could tell I was Violet's mother, from the way I spoke of her; it was a mother's love I showed, not an aunt's. How well she understands me. She was so gentle and sympathetic about the suffering I have endured and so sweet about my daughter. We will make a loving home for Violet, if I should ever win custody, she told me.

Of course, there are no 'ifs' about the matter. I *shall* reclaim Violet and we will all live together in Paris. What a happy home that will be! I pray for this future every day.

The wedding is planned for a week hence. Lucy will be released tomorrow, to spend time with her family before the event. However, unbeknown to Dr Wood and Mr Homeward, she has told her mother she will be staying with Lady Barnum.

In reality, she will be with me. In Paris.

Tomorrow afternoon I will excuse myself from my bathing therapy, complaining of a headache. I must to lie down until dinner time, I will tell them. In reality I will escape to meet Lucy in Abney Park. For the past few days I have been surreptitiously chiselling out toe holds in the mortar of our boundary wall, so that I may easily climb over into the cemetery.

We will then take a cab to her hotel, where she will have some of my things packed up in her cases. In the privacy of her room, she will disguise us both for the journey, as the police may be on the lookout for me by this time. I will be an escaped lunatic. It is possible that in the search for me, her absence will also be discovered.

We leave for France by train, early tomorrow evening. Despite the constant pain I feel over Violet's (temporary) adoption, I am excited by this prospect. I am to escape to another land and a new life with the one I love. How can I not be joyful? We will have the future together I saw reflected in the water, that day in Paradise Park. The other one.

I am sad I will not see Harriet again and cannot even bid her farewell. She has become such a good friend in the time I have spent here. I have enjoyed our wide-ranging talks and she tells me how much she values my company. I remain grateful for the many interesting books she has lent me, while I have been incarcerated. I think I may write to her, but cannot give an address to receive a reply. Lucy says I must not, but I believe she is a little jealous of my friendship with Harriet. She is so sweet to want me all to herself.

At any rate, much as I hate to deceive Harriet, she cannot know that, today, Lucy will conjure the spirit of Countess Zana for the final time. I have no stomach to attend, after the horror of my last session. I only hope the experience does not tire Lucy and make her doubt her resolution.

Well, I have certainly been a good patient and carried out my alienist's instructions. I have filled all of this little book with my lady's journaling and am obliged to start another. I have a blank one ready. It is with pleasure that I look at the empty pages and think of the exciting events I shall set down there. I will no longer need to use my code, when I write of our escape and our life together on the Continent.

Perhaps this diary has not been exactly run-of-the-mill journalising, as there has been nothing about fashionable clothing or society dinners. There has been much about love and romance, but as that has all centred around a lady, I believe my journal to be a little uncommon. Yet perhaps not as uncommon as the world may think.

DR WOOD'S DIARY

20 JUNE 1907

Lucy left us this morning, to travel to her family in Manchester, where she will stay until her wedding. She is now well enough to resume a normal life, with my support. Even the marks on her neck have grown fainter, of late.

Once she is married and settled, I will attend her on a weekly basis, to ensure the continuation of her improved health. She will need my help for some time to come and I will be delighted to provide it. On a personal as well as a professional basis, I admit. Had things been otherwise, she might have become the angel of my asylum on a permanent basis.

It was not to be. Homeward is a good man at heart and will look after her. She likes and respects him, even if she does not love him. As, I believe, she loves me. Homeward offers her a place in society, wealth and, in time, a title. All I have to offer her is my genius, which is of little value on the marriage market. History may judge its worth differently, but that is scant consolation at this moment. Yet I am resigned to our sad situation and must hope that our future talking sessions do not cause either of us too much pain.

Although I know her early departure from here is better for us both, at present I am profoundly melancholic. I cannot eat or settle to anything and feel a marked sense of loss and dread. Yet Lucy's return to health is a triumph for me. It proves that the combination of my talking cure, the electro-therapy, and our revolutionary Spiritual Machine, can work together to cure a patient who is profoundly ailing. I am writing her case up as a paper, which I believe will create a significant impression on the world of psychoanalysis. Lucy will help make my reputation.

She is greatly missed by others in the asylum. When I joined the ladies for lunch today I noted that Ella was distracted all through the meal, being unable to eat or hold a normal conversation. I had little appetite myself, and Miss Englethorpe, too, was subdued although characteristically she made an effort to converse.

Ella asked to be excused from her bathing therapy and retired to her room for the afternoon, to rest her head. The loss of her friend has hit her harder than I expected.

I looked in on her shortly after tea. She was not resting, but pacing about her room, her costume somewhat dishevelled. I suspected she has been out in the grounds without permission, indulging in her childish pastime of tree-climbing, but today was not the day to quiz her about this. When I spoke with her, however, I perceived her mood had changed. She was no longer obsessing about the absence of her friend; instead, she appeared shocked and blank. She must be processing her loss.

I suggested she set down her feelings in her private journal. She acquiesced and I returned ten minutes later to find her writing furiously. I believe this to be positive sign. She is beginning to acknowledge her pain and work through this separation from her beloved friend.

CHAPTER 31

BITTERSWEET

'I'm glad Lucy agreed to their elopement in the end,' I say. 'It sounded earlier like Ella was just fooling herself.'

'Bittersweet victory, given that they both got offed the next day,' Antoine replies.

We're having a Scooby Gang Saturday brunch in the Cat. Lots to talk about.

'Perhaps Ella was fooling herself,' says Uzi. 'We only have her word for this.' She's looking paler and more worn than ever. Rowan and Antoine tell me she just snaps about the importance of her work if they say anything. So they don't.

'That may be true,' Benedict says. He's up for one of his weekend symposiums, staying with me, this time. 'Yet I'd like to believe her, myself. It's such a shame we don't have her second journal.'

Antoine agrees but says that we more or less know what happened with Lucy and Ella now. 'Ella hadn't been climbing trees, like Wood said, she'd been climbing the wall into the cemetery to meet Lucy and run off with her. One of the child abusers saw them together in the chapel. Maybe Lucy warned the man to go away, said she'd tell the world about him, otherwise. So he killed Lucy but Ella escaped back to the asylum, not knowing what it was all about, but devastated at what she'd witnessed and at losing the woman she loved. Then another of the abusers arranged to meet her that evening in the roof garden and shoved her over the edge of the parapet.'

'Ella wouldn't have just stood by while someone attacked Lucy,' I object.

'Maybe Lucy was already dead by the time Ella got there,' Rowan puts our coffees down on the rickety table.

'Then why would they need to kill Ella?' Antoine asks.

'She saw him, but too late to save Lucy?' suggests Benedict.

It seems like we'll never understand exactly what happened that day. We won't know who killed Lucy in the chapel. Who pushed Ella from the roof terrace to her death. Antoine and Uzi think Wood, who then fabricated his own diary entry to cover his tracks. They think he's implicated in the child abuse and she was going to expose him. Betty is adamant it was Homeward, acting in a jealous rage; perhaps their deaths were nothing to do with the child abuse? Benedict and Rowan are more inclined towards the businessmen, given that Grimthorpe is a known abuser and Finleigh may have killed before.

I don't know who or what to believe.

Wood says he saw Ella writing in her journal in the afternoon, but she must have used her new book. It was her first and final entry. The one where she recorded what she'd seen in the cemetery chapel that afternoon. Betty's been able to find no trace of it. I suppose the murderer might have destroyed it if he knew about it. Or else it just got lost in the Murray family attic.

It's horrible that their relationship was cut short when they were nearly free to live their own lives. It feels like their story really needs to be told; they need justice.

I wonder if the children ever got justice. Unlikely – there are no reports of it. I dug out the photos of Annie and Florrie after I read Annie's interview. Looked into the dreamy face of little Tinker Bell; re-consider the calm but resigned expression of Wendy Darling, and remember the demons she was trying to escape. Maybe if we'd managed to fully unravel Lucy and Ella's story, that would have helped us find out who was exploiting them too; and all the other lost boys and girls.

But our trail's gone cold.

I INVITE everyone round to dinner tomorrow (takeaway, obviously), before heading back to my flat. Then I spend the afternoon on the Monarch work, to put off the thing I *really* don't want to do.

Now I've found out as much as I can about Betty's grandma, I need to finish clearing out my own family chest of secrets. Let's face it, there can't be any bombshells bigger than the one I've already dealt with. I'm tired of feeling so frazzled and destabilised by all this. Being round here, having to remember things I'd rather forget. Having the dead come to life.

I badly need to rest.

Still, I'll be home soon. I can relax, put it all behind me. Just need to finish excavating the detritus in this trunk. I'll pour myself a glass of wine and get down to it. I can finish this today.

That will make me feel better.

CHAPTER 32

A LETTER FROM THE DEAD

When I finally force myself to sit down in front of the chest, it's heartening to see that there's only a small pile of post left inside. Twenty-year-old stuff from the few months after I went to university.

I open and discard a few pieces of junk mail and church circulars. Find an unopened letter from me, back when I first started at St Cadog's. Kathleen wouldn't answer the phone, so it was the only way I could make contact. Opening it, I find that the letter's sympathetic concern for Kathleen's well-being can't conceal my gushing teenage enthusiasm for my new life at St Cadog's. It's obvious I've found a place where I can become myself. A home.

Good job she didn't read it, really.

After the first letter I sensibly sent postcards instead. I found those in the living room when I'd returned that first Christmas. Not that I took much notice of them at the time.

At first, I thought Kathleen was asleep when I arrived home, exhausted, after an eight-hour journey, including the five-hour delay when the train broke down at Bristol. Her bedroom door was open, but it was way past midnight, and I was about to tiptoe off to my old room. Until I saw the empty pill bottle, lying theatrically on its side, next to the bed.

An ambulance came quickly, and the medics did what they could, but she was almost dead when we got to the hospital. So the inquest verdict was accidental death, not suicide. If the train hadn't been delayed and I'd got her to hospital earlier, she'd have lived.

A cry for help, the coroner said.

My not-aunts told me I mustn't blame myself. Thirty-eight was a difficult age for a woman like my poor mother, the Lord bless her soul. She wouldn't have wanted me to take this terrible tragedy onto my young shoulders.

Freed from the stigma of mortal sin, we had the pleasure of a funeral mass, seasoned with equal amounts of denial and shame, at Our Lady of the Sorrows. The smell of incense still makes me gag. After we'd trekked to Wanstead for the crema- tion, we had the joy of sherry and sandwiches back at the church hall, so devout busybodies could say, 'Wales, now that's a fair way, why do the young ones have to stray so far? Did you not want to be nearer your ma?' And so Father Dom could tell me what a good woman my mother had been, despite her tragic life, and how the Lord would have mercy upon her soul. Which struck me as theologically inaccurate, but I didn't argue.

I BRACE myself and pick up the next item from the pile of unwanted memories. A short, unopened, letter from my undead father, enquiring if Kathleen had re-considered his divorce proposition. He was prepared to do right by her, he said, if they could come to some agreement. He was sure she'd moved on after all this time and it was high time he and Donna tied the knot; they owed it to their boys.

It's dated a few weeks before she died. I consider the implications and find sharing a burden of guilt doesn't make it any lighter. He must have found out about her 'accidental' death, eventually, if he pursued the divorce; I wonder if anyone told him not to take this terrible tragedy onto his shoulders?

Some more mailshots and other detritus, then the next item of any significance is a sturdy cardboard envelope, with a Connecticut postmark. Real Aunt Rose was still going twenty years ago. Must have been knocking ninety by then.

The package contains a thin notebook and a letter.

Dear Kathleen

I haven't heard from you for many a year, but I hope this finds you and your family well.

I've spent the last week doing a mortality clear-out of my documents. When you get to my age, it's important to be practical. I don't want to leave my children with a great pile of paperwork.

In particular, I don't want them to see this notebook, which, by rights, should be yours. It was the property of my unmarried aunt, who died young. It's an old family scandal that she had a daughter, who was adopted by my mother and brought up as my sister. My adopted sister is long dead and my relations with her daughter, Liz, have been less than cordial since she abandoned her own child in London, when she returned to America. Her deserted child is, of course, you. You are the rightful owner of your great grandmother's journal.

It is written in some kind of code, which I do not understand and have no mind to decipher. I'm an old woman and I have no wish to learn more about Aunt Emmanuella's dubious life. You may want to find out more, or if I know you, you may not. Your mother, I know, would ferret out any skeletons in the family closet and announce them to all the world. You are not like her at all and I trust in your discretion.

Love and best wishes
Aunt Rose

What? I think. *What? This is mad.*

I check the notebook. It is, indeed, the second of Ella Murray's diaries, in her usual code. Half a dozen pages are covered in her neat hand; the rest is blank.

I sit back and tried to make sense of this absurdist of absurd coincidences. I look again at the letter. Rose called Kathleen's mother Liz. Liz was Violet's daughter. Liz, short for Elizabeth.

Betty.

The only possible explanation is that it's no coincidence. Betty's known all along that she's my grandmother. That's why she employed me to find out how my great-great-great-aunt Ella died.

Only it turns out Ella's my great-great-grandmother.

Just when you think you've got away from your family, it turns out you've spent the last few months in their employment.

Stalking them.

The dead you've been breathing life into turn out to be your dead. Their stories implicate you. They turn around and they look at you.

I take another slug of wine, sit back on my heels and try to digest it all.

What the Hell is Betty playing at? Betty the Harpy. Did she think I'd refuse to work for her if I knew who she was? Is she playing a game? Is this part of the hereditary lying, like my mother telling me my dad's dead?

It's midnight and I'm reeling from what I've just found. Shocked and blank, like Wood says Ella was. It's too much to take in. I pick up my phone and fire off a text to Betty, saying that I've found the second of Ella's diaries in my mother's possessions. Asking her when she was going to mention she was my grandmother.

I regret it the moment it's sent. Unprofessional. Even if my family are all lying nutters, I shouldn't sink to their level. Her reply comes back immediately.

Betty: Please don't be angry Meg. I'm getting on a plane right away and coming over. I'll explain when I see you.

I stare at it and shake my head. I've never had the impression that Betty was the little old lady type, but she must be in her late seventies, should she be going around jumping on planes like this? Am I meant to feel guilty? It's late, I've had too much wine and I can't take any more. First John Morgan and his bloody normal bloody life. Now Grandma Betty, the Harpy, who abandoned her depressed husband and troubled daughter, then secretly wormed her way into my world, got herself in a text group with my friends and made me spend the last three months researching my own family history. A history of certified insanity.

I'm not going to decipher my great-great-grandmother's journal tonight, that's for certain. My sympathy for Ella's cooled a little. Maybe Uzi's right, maybe Ella was fabricating reality in her journal.

Just like her descendants.

I'm not in a hurry to find out which of our suspects killed her any more. They've all been dead nearly a hundred years. Betty can go and deface the culprit's grave any time she likes, once I've de-coded the journal.

As long as she doesn't expect me to join in the family fun.

CHAPTER 33

TEMPTED BY FIRE

I t's gone midnight but I know Antoine's out with his journalist friends. I prevaricate, then text him. He calls a second later.

'I'll come straight back.'

I'm on my way to bed, I tell him, no need to wreck his night or wake Benedict, who's already asleep in the spare room. Just thought he'd want to know.

He comes back anyway. Makes me tea. Tells me this is nuts and I really don't deserve any of it. But maybe Betty's not evil and crazy, just misguided?

I ask if he'll text the others for me. Then I scribble out a quick sketch of Betty's tree for him to upload, on the basis that it will be therapeutic to get it out of my head and onto the page.

Ella
|
Violet = Victor
| Gardiner
Gerry = Betty
Brady |
|
Kathleen = John Morgan
|
Michael   Meg

It isn't.

NEXT MORNING BENEDICT brings me coffee before he leaves for his symposium.

'What a terrible shock for you, my dear,' he says. 'Would you like me to stay?'

But I have to face Betty alone. She's probably not dangerous. Physically. Although who knows, with my family?

She's turning up this afternoon. I've just got time to decipher the damn journal before she gets here. Or I could take a match to it. Might be the best solution, nothing good ever comes from delving into *my* family archive.

I flick through it. There are two entries, both on the last day of Ella's life. Eventually my need for answers overcomes my resentment; I reluctantly start to decipher my own personal book of the dead.

CHAPTER 34

GRANDMA'S HANDS

I've read it now. Ella's journal. Not an easy read. I know everything; it's much worse than we thought.

THE INTERCOM GOES and I brace myself. Buzz Betty in through the front gate.

She's come straight from the airport, wheeling her smart little carry-on case. In the dim lighting at the front of the building, I can just about recognise her, now, as the newly-wed beatnik from Kathleen's family album. Tall, spare, loose-limbed. She's also as intense in the flesh as she was in our video calls, and somehow more concentrated. Her trademark confidence has dissolved into visible tension.

I am *not* going to be tricked into feeling sorry for her.

I avoid her hungry eye contact, grab the suitcase and step back to avoid any possibility of an embrace as I usher her to the front door. She looks up at the gloomy building, squares her shoulders and walks through the great oak doors, which

359

open for us in their eerie way. She moves like a much younger woman; I think of Ella, and how she struggled to find outlets for her energy.

Once in the flat, I notice the dragonfly brooch on the lapel of her well-cut jacket, as I take her coat.

'Lucy's birthday gift.' She touches the delicate art nouveau piece gently. 'Now I know it shows that Ella was loved, it means so much more to me.'

I stare at the beautiful object, appalled. It's flown from a horror movie into my living room. Turning away, I pour us some wine. It's only five o'clock but we're going to need it.

She goes over to look at the trunk. 'That's one of Gerry's, isn't it?'

I nod and she puts her hand on it reverently, as if it were a coffin at a funeral. Then she turns away, accepts the drink.

Do I look like Betty, I wonder, as I place myself opposite her on the other sofa? Maybe in the set of her shoulders, the length of limb. As Breda pointed out, I inherited that unfeminine ranginess that skipped a generation in pixie-like Kathleen. I think of Ella's strong, statuesque figure in the photo. Lucy's photo.

'I don't know where to start.' Betty looks uncomfortable, perched on the little sofa, clutching her glass like a life raft.

'Why didn't you tell me?' It comes out harsher than I intended.

She says she assumed I'd work it out. That a genealogist would know her own family tree. Then once she realised I had no idea, it seemed easier to keep quiet. Kathleen wouldn't have given her a good press.

'She said you were a Harpy.'

She raises her hands, palms up. Strong hands, expressive. My hands. She tells me Kathleen wanted no contact with her after she left. Betty's letters to her were returned unopened and Kathleen refused to speak to her when Betty called. Gerry accepted the maintenance cheques Betty sent him and signed the paperwork when she made the house over to him and Kathleen. Her daughter wouldn't take a cent from her directly.

'I was notified by the police when Gerry died – we never got divorced – and I came back for her. I kidded myself that she might come with me to San Francisco. Instead, she refused to acknowledge me, even at the funeral.'

Kathleen hadn't told me any of this. Not the bit about her mother financing them, or giving them the house, or that she came back to get her, only to be rebuffed.

'Kathleen remained on good terms with my Aunt Rosemary, who'd visited with us at the house in Dalston,' Betty continues. 'Rosemary spent time with her again after Gerry died, when she was on holiday in England.'

Mysterious Aunt Rose. Rosemary, Violet's adopted sister.

'I guess Rosemary wasn't my aunt, was she, biologically?' Betty asks. 'She was, what? My cousin?'

'First cousin, once removed,' I reply, absently. Rose was another not-aunt after all.

I retrieve Kathleen's photo album from the trunk and find the picture of her and Aunt Rose on the Southbank.

'That captures her well.' Betty puts her glass down on the side table. I take a seat next to her and we look down together at conventional Cousin Rose in her twinset and pearls. She tells me that although Rosemary disapproved of her, she warmed to her beautiful, hyper-feminine daughter. So after Gerry died, Rosemary was prepared to launder Betty's monthly allowance to Kathleen through her own bank account, as Kathleen wouldn't have accepted anything directly from Betty.

I digest the fact that Betty carried on supporting my mother after my grandad died and after Kathleen got married. Supported me, in fact.

'Did you know about us?' I ask. 'All the time?'

Betty rubs her temple with long bony fingers. Witches hands. My hands.

Rosemary had refused to reveal much, she tells me. Betty had abandoned her daughter and her punishment was to be kept in ignorance. Rosemary never told her that Kathleen married and had children. She didn't even tell her about Kathleen's death, but in all fairness, Rosemary's own health was poor by then and she herself died a few weeks later. Betty hired someone to track Kathleen down after Rosemary's death. It was an easy job for them to find out the terrible news.

'My only child, dead, at thirty-eight. Another suicide, reading between the lines. First Gerry, then her. What had I done to them? I retreated from that chapter of my life, concentrated on my work. You can imagine my shock when I started researching my family history and discovered Kathleen had married and had children. I had a living granddaughter. I contacted you because I wanted to ... make amends. To explain. I know no one can forgive me, I can't even forgive myself.'

'What happened?' I ask. 'Between you and Kathleen?'

'Oh, Meg. I'll have to go back to the beginning for it to make sense.' She swallows a mouthful of wine. Puts down the glass, carefully. Takes a deep breath.

She tells me that my grandfather, Gerry, had been a charming, handsome Irishman and Kathleen had worshipped him. So had Betty, for a quite a while. Gerry was in California, when she first met him, visiting relatives. It was love at first sight and they got married, secretly, within weeks of meeting.

I show her the picture of the teenage beatniks in the album. She smiles ruefully. She was only eighteen, she tells me. She didn't have much sense. Her family were furious, a carpenter wasn't their idea of an ideal son-in-law, but the marriage was a done deed. They couldn't interfere.

Betty went off back to London with her new husband and had Kathleen soon after. It was 1959 and this was Betty's big rebellion against her mother and the whole claustrophobic 1950s American horror show. Europe sounded like freedom to her. As it did to Ella.

Reality was sobering at first. She ended up as a teenage housewife, in London, where she didn't know a soul. Betty didn't take to domesticity. Gerry was out at work all day and she was alone with the baby. That wasn't easy and it soon became clear that Gerry had his own problems. Sometimes he was tremendous fun, full of enthusiastic plans and at other times he was withdrawn, quiet and lethargic. Bipolar, probably, we'd say now. No one thought about things like that back then.

Gerry was always wonderful with baby Kathleen, a natural parent. His mood swings made it hard for him to hold down a job, so after a while they agreed he'd mind Kathleen while Betty got her teaching certificate. She worked at a secondary school in Homerton, a tough job that she loved. Gerry did his craftwork, which was becoming fashionable and was able to sell his pieces. It was much better for his mental health than the pressures of construction site work.

Betty had some money of her own, left to her by Fanny. In reality, it probably came originally from Ella, Betty now thought. She used some of her capital to buy the Dalston house for a couple of thousand dollars. The rest produced a small income that helped them get by. For years they were happy enough, in their unconventional, hippyish way. She developed a technique of encouraging Gerry when he was down and calming him when he was up. She talked to their GP and together they got Gerry to accept medication, which also helped, although the diagnosis was always a bit vague. She and

Gerry loved each other and it would probably have been okay, if it hadn't been for the difficulties with their daughter.

Kathleen adored her father but her relationship with her mother was strained. From an early age she demanded things like frilly, impractical dresses and hated Betty when she wouldn't let her have them. Gerry doted on his beautiful little girl and indulged her every whim.

They got offers of child-modelling work all the time. Kathleen was delighted and Gerry thought they should take them, but Betty didn't want the child to become obsessed with her own appearance. It was unhealthy, she thought. Education and personality mattered more. Kathleen bitterly resented her mother's intervention.

It was the same with everything. Kathleen would go running to Gerry whenever Betty thwarted her in any way. He'd give in, which led to tensions between them.

Kathleen always loved having boys pay her attention. When she was just twelve or thirteen, she'd defy Betty, dress up and sneak out to meet boys – men – of seventeen or eighteen. She never had any female friends; she didn't have time for other girls.

'I know I wasn't the best mother in the world, but I tried. I kept trying. I still have no idea where I went wrong. I could get the respect of a roomful of teenagers at work, even help them to learn, against the odds, but I couldn't do a thing with my own daughter. I took her to child psychologists, but she turned the charm on with them and behaved as if I was the unreasonable one.'

Apart from drama classes, Kathleen had no interest in school and constantly truanted. She was convinced she was going to be a top model; she'd be on her way already, if her mother wasn't holding her back. Kathleen left school the day she was sixteen and started to work in modelling, against

THE HAUNTING OF ABNEY HEIGHTS

Betty's wishes. Gerry signed the contract and went on to become her chauffeur, chaperone and manager.

'As a teenager, Kathleen started accusing me of being unsympathetic to Gerry when he was in a down phase and of limiting him when he was up. It was a wilful misreading of my technique for keeping his moods level, which had worked for years. Kathleen began to convince Gerry that I was working against him; she encouraged him to stop taking his medication. It all led to terrible arguments.'

In the end it drove them apart completely. By the time she was seventeen, Kathleen's strategy of encouraging Gerry's manic phases had made his condition much worse. For his part, he'd helped turn her into a little doll who lived for male attention.

The situation made Betty desperately unhappy; she'd dread the weekends and find reasons to stay late at work. That summer, at the end of term, she went back to the US for a few weeks, to clear her head. While she was away, Gerry and Kathleen wrote and told her it was better she didn't return. They were happier without her. Betty called them, tried to talk it through. Gerry was clear he didn't want her to come back and Kathleen refused any direct contact with her.

What could she do if they didn't want her? Except make sure they had a roof over their heads and some financial support? She left them to it.

'A year later Gerry hanged himself in his workshop. The only time Kathleen spoke to me after that was to tell me Gerry's death was my fault. Which,' Betty picks up her re-filled glass, 'is true, in part. I failed. As a wife, as a mother.'

I look at the woman next to me, leaning forward now, tense with guilt and anxiety, despite her exhaustion.

'She could usually find someone else to blame,' I say.

Betty looks tremendously relieved. She sits back on the sofa. 'Guess she didn't change, huh?'

I shake my head.

'Were you – close?' she asks.

I give a mirthless laugh. 'She didn't even like me.'

Betty puts her hand on mine. It feels cool and dry. 'Join the club, Meg,' she says.

ELLA'S JOURNAL
JUNE 20, 1907

I am in such distress and confusion, I cannot say. Today was to be the happiest, most exciting day of my life. Yet now I do not know what to think. I am forcing myself to sit down and write this before they call me to luncheon. I hope it will help me collect myself, so that I may get through today with some a composure.

I have discovered there are secret forces at work in this asylum. Evil forces, of which I knew nothing. Somehow they hold the woman I love in their clutches.

Yesterday we finalised every detail of our plan. Lucy would leave the asylum in the late morning and secure a hotel room near the railway station. After luncheon I would meet her and we would travel together to her hotel. No one would notice my absence until dinnertime and by then we would already be on the boat to France.

This morning Lucy was completing her final packing. It is no job for a lady, but she did not trust it to Annie, who was too distraught at her departure to be of much use. When I went in to offer my help, just half an hour ago, there was little left to do. Lucy was putting her papers in a portmanteau and I picked up a fat envelope of photographs that had fallen under the bed.

She must not leave her exquisite pictures behind, I told her. Photographs were spilling out of the packet. I admire her portraits so much, so I slipped the top one out of the envelope.

Lucy looked up from her task and her eyes filled with panic. 'No. Those are private.'

I had never before heard her speak sharply. I took a step back from her, in surprise, as she leaned forward and made a grab for the pictures. I looked down at the image in my hand and shock jolted through me, like an electric current. My hands began to shake and the other photographs in the packet fell out onto the carpet with a rustle of falling leaves.

I stared at the picture. I could not believe what I saw.

It showed a gentleman visitor to the asylum with one of the child inmates. I do not want to write their names. I will say them in the rightful place when this horror is made public. The child was unclothed and the act that the man was perpetrating on her is something I cannot set down here. It is too foul, too unspeakable.

I looked down at the loose photographs which formed a dark pool at my feet. Different men, different girls and boys.

Different horrors.

'What is this?' I could hardly get the words out.

'It is not as it appears, my love.'

I winced when she mentioned our love in the presence of such filth. She noticed.

'I was given no choice,' she said. Quietly, sadly.

'They forced you to take these terrible images?'

She looked like a frightened little girl herself, nodding, slowly, her big scared eyes fixed on me. How could this be, I asked her. Why could she not refuse? Or tell Dr Wood and Matron? She shook her head. I had a shock of realisation. Could Wood and Matron Siskins be involved with this evil? She must go to the police, I insisted. There was no other way to protect the children. These men would continue their visits to the asylum once we left.

'But, my darling, then we could not go away together,' she said piteously.

We could not leave things this way, I told her.

'Trust me my love,' she said. 'I have a plan. I can make these men stop because I have kept these pictures. They do not realise I have them, they think me stupid. I must go now, but when we meet in the chapel later, I will explain everything.'

CHAPTER 35

NASTY LITTLE SECRETS

'Those poor children.' Betty says. 'To think their abuse was so systematic that it was recorded. And in this building!' She shivers and looks round at my flat.

Everyone's over at mine this evening to hear the last of Ella's entries. They aren't something anyone should read alone. I wish I hadn't.

I'm perched uncomfortably on a dining chair, between the two sofas. Mind you, nothing about this evening's going to be bloody comfortable, so who cares about a numb bum? Antoine's to my left with Uzi and Rowan on the long sofa. Benedict and Betty are on the little sofa, to my right, with Mulder and Scully colonising their laps.

I made sure everyone ate before I started on Ella's journal. It wasn't going to improve anyone's appetite. Luckily the pizza wasn't delivered by Letitia this time. What would I have told her if she'd asked me who killed the two women?

'We were right,' Antoine says. 'One of the child abusing

bastards must have caught up with Ella and Lucy later. And Wood was in on it, I knew it. But there is more, right, Meg?'

I nod. The next part of Ella's account was written in the early evening.

'Are you feeling quite well, my dear,' Benedict asks Uzi, who's looking far from well after hearing Ella's account.

'It is horrible,' she mutters. Rowan pours a glass of water and hands it to her.

'Do we need a break?' I ask. 'Or shall I go on?'

We all look at Uzi.

'We do not know,' she says, 'that this is true.'

'But why would Ella lie?' I ask.

'She has no motive,' Betty adds.

Uzi looks from me to Betty. 'It is natural that you both think that. She is your relative.'

'We *have* seen some slightly dodgy photos that Lucy took, mind,' Rowan says. 'So it kind of follows that there might be worse.'

'Shall we hear what Lucy says about it?' Antoine's impatient, as ever.

'What Ella claims that Lucy says,' Uzi insists.

I re-open my laptop and continue.

ELLA'S JOURNAL

JUNE 20, 1907

5pm

I am trying to organise it in my head. How it all came to this. I
cannot think clearly. I have done a terrible, unforgivable thing
and God will not forgive me. Not this time.

If I endeavour to set the facts out in a line, maybe it will
make sense to me. If I tell exactly what happened, in every
detail, if I recall what was said and how I felt, maybe my
thoughts will be clearer; although nothing will ever make it
right, or good.

It has all gone bad.

I have gone bad.

After Lucy left, I did not know where to put myself. My
mind revolved around those hideous images. How and why had
those men made my sweet, gentle Lucy a witness to such
cruelty and debauchery? Let alone a recorder of it?

Perhaps, I thought, they had some dark hold over Lucy?
There was no other way they could have forced her to take

those vile pictures. Had they merely threatened her, surely she would have come to me? She must have kept the photographs to protect herself from these fiends and to get justice for the poor children. I would help her. We would send the photographs to the police and then we could carry on with our plans to be together. That was the best solution.

This is how my mind ran on. How stupid I was.

People I had trusted had turned out to be monsters, that much I knew. They were monsters who had ensnared Lucy in their depravity. From the scant clothing the children sometimes wore in the photographs, it was clear many of them had been taken on the evening of the play. Dr Wood and Matron Siskins had been busy with visitors that night. Had these dreadful men taken advantage of this? Or were Wood and Siskins implicated? Were they in the pockets of these men?

So many questions churned through my head. I told myself I would learn more later and we would bring these men to justice. Then, terrible as this episode had been for Lucy and the children, it would be behind them. My mind reeled when I thought that during the months I had known her, my angel had been forced to watch horrors being visited upon the children she loved. Her little Annie. My Florrie. It cannot have been just the once, there were too many pictures. How had she coped? Why had she not confided in me?

Lunch was a miserable affair; I could not eat. Wood was solicitous about my (genuine) headache, but I tried to avoid catching his eye. He ate little himself; could that be because he suspected Lucy had left with photographs that could indirectly incriminate him, I wondered. My mistrust of him was now amplified by the possibility that he might be consciously corrupt. I kept my eyes down and attempted to look composed, despite the way my mind whirled.

After lunch I excused myself and came to my room. I changed into practical walking clothes, concealing my important papers and journals in the capacious pockets. It felt good to act, rather than sit and be tortured by my thoughts. I slipped carefully out of the side door to the grounds, without seeing anyone. The friendly touch of light summer rain cooled my aching head and kept everyone indoors.

I strode towards the cemetery wall, past the cedar trees. Behind the trees I was safe, shielded from sight. The wall is over eight feet high at this point, but my toe holds, combined with the luxuriant ivy which cloaks it, enabled me to climb its slippery height with relative ease. Scaling the wall reminded me of the great trees I used to climb at home, to the horror of my mother and sister. I recalled how I showed Violet how to climb up with me, last year, when Fanny's back was turned. When she is older, I thought, as I dropped down into the damp bushes of the cemetery, we shall climb the trees in France, while Lucy stands at the foot, laughing and applauding us.

That will never happen now.

Once over, I straightened my clothing as best I could and made my way along the paths to the chapel. I know the way well, from our walks. Indeed, we took our last one there only yesterday.

Yesterday. It seems like an eternity. Everything was different then.

Everything before this afternoon feels like a story in a book I once read. A beautiful story. But at its heart, just fiction.

I arrived at the chapel and entered the shadowy interior, with its pools of coloured light. The nave was cold and empty. I paused a moment, taking in the iron fleur-de-lis ornamentation on the back row of the pews, which always made me think of France and our future life together. This would still happen,

I told myself, as I looked upwards at the staircase, spiralling its way up into the gloom. My twisted path to answers and, I still believed, to freedom.

I ran up the stairs to the internal balcony. Lucy stood there, one hand on the rail. Her face, lit by the coloured light of the window was turned towards me, wreathed in smiles. Her beauty illuminated the gloom more than the florid window.

'My darling, I feared you would not come,' she said.

Her sweetness calmed my fears. I embraced her and held her close. I could extricate her from this evil web, I thought. I believed, then, that my guidance would support her and together we could bring about justice.

Gently, I asked her about the photographs. Why could she not at least send them to the police? What had those monsters said or done to make her fear them so?

'I—' she looked down, as if ashamed. 'I need these pictures. They are my security.'

I stroked her hair and told her she was safe with me now. I was her security and would not let them harm her. She said she was not rich like me, so, puzzled, I assured her that my money was her money.

'And if you tire of me? My family will not have me back. I must have something; I can make these men pay for what they have done.'

I was so appalled, when I finally understood her meaning, that I could not speak. She was angry at them, I reasoned. They had harmed her by making her watch that horror. She wanted revenge, for the children. Yet someone so good and pure must not sully herself with blackmail.

'They *should* pay for what they did,' she insisted.

A terrible thought occurred to me. Had they already given her money?

'Not enough,' she said. 'I shall make them pay and pay. I shall bleed them.'

I was confused. My angel, a blackmailer? None of it made sense. Yet her intention was clear. The chill of the chapel crept into me then, remembering that I, too, had been blackmailed.

'You wrote me that letter?' I felt I would never be warm again. 'About Violet?'

She looked penitent. She had not known me well then and stopped when she began to care for me, she told me. My heart yearned and I tried to believe her. Then she added, 'You were never like the others.'

The others. Now I was colder than the dead, buried outside.

'Everyone has secrets they will pay to have kept,' she continued, with growing confidence. 'Countess Zana told me all about them. William Finleigh. My "honourable" fiancé. Some of them I worked out for myself. Even your friend Harriet and saintly Dr Wood have something to hide.'

'Was Dr Wood involved in this depravity? Was that how it came about?'

She laughed. She actually laughed. 'Not he, he is much too pure. His weakness is that he was in love with me. He would have been compromised if the board found that out. His purity makes him so naïve that, as those vile men are so liberal with their patronage, he trusts them to have the run of the place. I saw what they were straight away. All three of them. Pompous little William Finleigh is the worst, his sins are legion. The Countess told me all about the stains on his soul. Smarmy Ezekial Chamberlain, and disgusting old Barnabus Grimthorpe follow where he leads. The revolting creatures sniffed around my classroom and theatre group like dogs on heat. They wanted to be left alone with the children, but I wouldn't let that happen.'

She paused. I clung onto some hope She had tried to protect the children from them. She had tried to do what was right.

Lucy smiled. 'Well, I would leave the room for just long enough to come back and catch them in the act, so I could make them operate on my terms.'

I did not understand.

'Can you not see, Ella? Then everyone could have what they needed. The children had money, treats and less interference than if I were not there. They had the comfort of my presence. The men had their photographs to take away, to drool over and paw themselves over in secret. And I?' She smoothed down the front of her gown. 'I was able to survive.'

Still I did not fully comprehend. Survive? Had they threatened her life?

'My father's business is failing.' Her voice was harsh, impatient. I had never before heard it so. 'I have not had an allowance since I have been at the asylum. I have had to make my own way.'

My heart stopped as I finally let go of hope.

'You did all this for gowns and gloves?'

Her face hardened. Her lips drew back from teeth. 'You have not been poor,' she hissed. 'You have no idea. I had never before needed to struggle with patched clothing and leaking boots. It was humiliating. All the time I was expected to keep up the exterior of a lady and make a good match to save the family fortunes. Have you any idea how impossible that is with no money? Lady Barnum would have rejected me out of hand if I had turned up to tea dressed like a beggar.'

I tried to make sense of what she was saying. 'But ... the children. They loved you.'

She sighed, impatiently. 'They would have loved anyone who paid them attention and gave them treats. I lessened their

THE HAUNTING OF ABNEY HEIGHTS

ordeals and made sure they were recompensed. They have all been through much worse, where they come from, and got nothing for it. It is the way of the world, Ella. Powerful creatures feed on smaller, weaker ones. If you do not want to be prey, you must protect yourself.'

I could not take it in. She had never been fond of the children? What were they to her, a means of making money?

She laughed. Not her usual musical tones but a coarse cackle. 'Oh Ella. You have no idea. I did not dislike them, but children will be parasitic, too, if you let them. They want your time, your attention, your love. They have so many needs and give nothing back; they just suck life from you. Their presence intrudes into proper, true love between adults. That is why you are better off without Violet.'

How could she even speak of my love for Violet in this context? How could she imagine that losing her caused me anything but pain?

'Yet now you are no longer her mother, you are free to travel to Paris with me.'

It is true that if I were still Violet's legal guardian, our plans would have been different. I would have needed to wait until my release before I could make a life with her and Lucy. Slowly I began to realise. Lucy was jealous. She had never wanted to share me with Violet.

'I wanted you to be free to be yourself. Violet would have caused you heartbreak. She would have resented being taken away from Fanny. It is better for everyone the way I have arranged it.'

Then I realised. My automatic writing message from Violet? That was nothing to do with Countess Zana. That was Lucy.

She had arranged it.

That was the point at which I fully appreciated what Lucy

was and what she had done. Until then I had half-heard, half-understood. Much as the suffering of the children caused me anguish, I had tried to believe what she was saying. She had been suddenly poor and desperate, she had curtailed the men's foul activities. But once I realised she had purposefully lied about Violet's death, all that changed. She had known I would collapse with horror if I thought Violet dead. She had calculated that this further evidence of weakness would give my family the chance to take my daughter from me, permanently.

This she did because she did not wish to share me.

I knew her then to be selfish and cold hearted. Monstrous. Her sweetness was a cover, a trap to ensnare people. I had thought of Lucy as fairy-like, but in truth she was a dragonfly. Entrancing and captivating, but in reality a carnivorous predator. She was not just a blackmailer, she was a procurer of children to feed men's base desires. This she did for money.

Now my heart beat so furiously it pounded in my head and all the coldness I had felt vanished from me. I was a woman of fire. I grasped her by the arms and looked down at her face. That angelic face.

Yet angelic no more. Her beautiful features were transformed into something hard and vicious.

'You are a monster,' I cried.

She threw back her head and laughed that hideous new laugh. 'A monster whom you love.'

I shook her and screamed at this thing that used to be Lucy. She struggled to get away from me, her fingers tearing at my hands. I was stronger and retained my grip. She cursed, terrible words that I would never have thought to hear from those delicate lips, and then bent her neck down and sunk her teeth into my wrist. Blood flowed.

In that instant I realised that not only had I lost Violet

because of her, but now I had lost the Lucy I'd loved. In her place was this snarling, biting demon.

The fight went out of me with this realisation; as the blood flooded down my wrist, I loosened my grip. She carried on pulling, with all her might, to get away from me. Her momentum took her backwards and with loud and terrible scream, she overbalanced. Before I could catch her, she pitched backwards over the railing.

Many things passed through my mind in that second, as I looked at the absence where Lucy had been. It is not a long fall, I thought. Twelve feet or so. She may not be harmed. I have fallen that far as a child, climbing trees, and she is an adult woman.

I looked over the balcony edge. She lay still, on her back.

As I reached the bottom of the staircase I found Lucy slumped, half lying, half standing at the back of the nave. She had fallen onto the iron ornamentation on the back row of the pews and it had pierced the left-hand side of her chest. Her heart. The spike of a fleur-de-lis stuck up through her dove-coloured jacket. A dark red stain crept out around it, like something alive.

In death, her face again looked angelic, her cornflower eyes open in surprise.

I drew back in horror at what I had done. For the second time in my life, I was a murderer. Dr Wood has helped me to recover from my guilt at killing someone I hated; now I have killed someone I loved. Lucy committed evil deeds, but I am worse, now.

God will not forgive me.

Despite her terrible sins, I wanted to kiss her white cheek, touch her little hand, tell her I had loved her. But I was too unclean. Even the fallen Lucy was too pure for me to touch.

How I returned to the asylum I do not recall. It is a blank in my mind. My first memory of being back here was when I was in the parlour standing in front of that infernal machine. The Telepathic Transfer Engine. The device that enabled Lucy to separate me from Violet, when she invented a message from her spirit guide. Even when she had genuine messages from the spirits, she had used her gift to manipulate others.

I opened the evil box and stared down at the fragile glass tubes and delicate brass pistons. I placed a cushion on the Engine's workings, before picking up a heavy marble table lamp; I did not want to be disturbed. Holding the lamp over my head with both arms I smashed it down on the cushion with all my strength. Again and again I attacked the evil Engine. My blows were powerful, but their sound was muffled. Finally, panting with exertion I replaced the lamp and cushion. I closed the lid on the destroyed remnants of Von Helson's terrible machine.

Now I sit here in my room and record all this horror and destruction in my lady's journal. I will also record my one good act. I put all the money I have to hand in an envelope. I scribbled a note to go with it. Then I slipped downstairs to the laundry and managed to intercept Florrie, without any adults seeing me. I thrust the envelope into her hand, whispering that she must open it in secret. I hope it enables her to escape, one way or another.

All that is left is to carry out the only course of action open to me. I cannot live like this, without Violet, without the Lucy I loved and with myself, knowing what I have done. I have brought this horror on myself because of my stupidity and poor judgement. How could I have not seen what she was? How could I have made such a terrible error in trusting her and giving my heart unstintingly? I have been a fool.

My stupidity has made me a murderer and this time the fault lies squarely with me.

I know where Dr Wood keeps the key to the roof terrace. That is a long drop, not like falling out of a tree. It is just. It is what I deserve.

My path is clear.

CHAPTER 36

REVELATION

Everyone's silent after I finish reading Ella's last entry. Even Antoine and Betty.

One of the lamps on the side table starts to flicker. I lean over to switch it off and get a small shock for my pains. Despite the circuit breakers.

I hear a low hiss from my right. Scully has jumped onto the arm of Benedict's sofa next to me, arching her back and baring cruel white fangs. Topaz eyes opened wide, her fierce gaze is fixed on the sofa in front of her. Her fur's standing on end and her tail's turned from a black feather to an upright bottle-brush. I stroke her, trying to calm her down, but she ignores me and carries on staring ahead of her, every muscle tense.

'It was Lucy,' says Antoine. 'All along. She was our metaphorical vampire.'

'Lucy had marks on her neck,' Uzi, sitting next to him, murmurs. 'She looked a little dazed.'

'Self-inflicted?' Betty suggests.

'Maybe not consciously so,' Benedict says. 'She was mentally ill, apart from the sociopathic tendencies.'

'Not surprising with her upbringing,' Rowan adds. 'Not that I'm making excuses for her.'

'So, the puncture wounds on Ella's wrist really were a vampire bite,' Betty says.

The other light starts to flicker and, sighing, I get up to deal with it. Antoine turns the first one back on. It works fine now.

'Ouch!' I get a stronger shock from the second light. The first light starts blinking again.

'What's happening with these electrics?' asks Betty. 'And what's eating the cats?' Mulder, always a little slower off the mark, is now copying his sister on the other arm of the sofa, next to Betty. They've transformed into furious beasts, ears flattened, hissing angrily at the space in front of them. Or ... at their beloved Uzi?

In the strange tattoo of light and dark, we hear a voice, low and sweet. 'I wanted you to be free,' it says. We all looked at Uzi, whose mouth the words issued from. Though it isn't her voice. 'I wanted you to be free.' Shrill now and louder.

She stands up, wild eyed in the flickering light. Mulder and Scully start howling, wild banshee-like screams.

This is madness. I move to turn on the overhead lights, create some normality.

'No,' shouts Betty, just as I put my hand to the switch.

In that brief instant, do I hear another 'no' echoing from somewhere far away? It seems that way. A strong, authoritative woman's voice.

What happens next is pain in my hand, travelling through my body. A sense that I'm moving backwards, crashing into things. Then nothing.

BETTY'S ACCOUNT

DECEMBER 1, 2019

I have a creepy feeling about that old asylum, when the cab drops me outside of it on Sunday night. When I visited earlier in the day I was so focussed on meeting my granddaughter that the building was just background. This evening I feel concerned for her, living in that place.

She's a great girl. Independent, intelligent, a bit eccentric. Everything I would have liked my daughter to be and everything I failed to encourage in her.

Maybe we just grow up in opposition to our mothers.

What a relief it is to find someone who understands. All these years people have judged me but Meg just gets it all without my having to explain. I hate to think how it was for her, growing up with Kathleen. I wish I'd been there for her.

So, here I am in this eerie place, having dinner with my granddaughter and her friends. The location is unsettling but the people are congenial. I feel like I already knew them from the text group. Her old schoolfriend Antoine is just like I expected, bright guy, full of energy and enthusiasm. I can see he's fond of Meg. His young roommate Uzi is a little odd, but her partner, Rowan, tries to keep her grounded. Great to meet Meg's old college professor, Benedict, too, what a lovely man.

We're all in a state of shock when Meg finishes reading out the horrifying final diary entry. To think that Lucy committed those unspeakable crimes. To think that her death was no one's fault, just a tragic accident. It's so sad that Ella blamed herself and took her own life. Sad to think that children carried on suffering at the hands of those evil men.

There's a lot more to say about Ella and Lucy and what happened all those years ago, but that's for later. For my book. Right now I'm focussing on my living relative.

The moment Meg stops reading, the lamps in her flat start acting up. So do the cats, who were previously adorable fluff-balls. They go wild. The big grey one, who's been purring on my lap, leaps up and starts hissing menacingly through bared fangs. He's staring at Uzi.

In the flickering light, we hear a voice crying, 'I wanted you to be free.' It seems to come from little Uzi, yet somehow that doesn't fit.

I knew whose voice it really is.

I always thought that the hairs on the back of your neck standing up was a figure of speech. Turns out it really happens, to humans, not just to cats. When I hear that voice shouting, 'I wanted you to be free,' the back of my neck prickles and I know something evil is in the room with us.

The cats set up a blood-freezing howling, their great eyes still fixed on Uzi. Or on what's speaking through Uzi.

Meg gets up to switch on the overhead lights. Something tells me that's going to be dangerous; I jump up and shout out to her to stop.

A second too late.

As soon as she touches the switch there's a cracking sound and a flash. The light stays off. In the staccato lamplight I watch with horror as Meg shoots several feet backwards and lands on the floor in the corner. As she falls she knocks over the side table and the two lamps on it crash onto the fur rug underneath. The bulb of the electric lamp smashes and its exposed filament starts sparking; the unlit kerosene lamp also breaks with a pungent smell of oil. Before any of us register what's had happening, the oil-soaked rug catches fire. A sheet of flame rises up between Meg and the rest of us.

The others leap to their feet. Antoine's calling out her name and frantically trying beat out the flames with a blanket. Benedict grabs a jug of water from the coffee table and throws on the flames. Neither have much effect.

Terrified, the cats head for the kitchen area, as far away as possible from the fire, continuing their unearthly howling as they crouch, shivering, on the worktops.

I'm desperate to help Meg. My own granddaughter. But I can tell there's no way through that wall of fire; the path to rescue her lies elsewhere.

I don't know what makes me move to the flat door, or why I want to open it. I know it's the wrong thing to do when there's a fire. I feel impelled, as if something's telling me it's the right course of action to save Meg. Little Uzi gets there before me. She stands in front of the door, her eyes blazing in the firelight.

'They give nothing back,' she screams up at me. 'Nothing.'

The voice that comes out of her mouth isn't hers at all.

She reaches up and pushes me viciously in the chest and her hand catches my dragonfly pin. It comes undone and digs hard into the base of my neck. It hurts like heck and I can feel blood flowing from the wound. A lot of blood. I put my hand up to stem the flow.

'Uzi,' cries Rowan, bounding over to us. 'Stop it, come back to us.'

Rowan tries to grab hold of her arms, but, without her eyes leaving my face, she lashes out with lightning speed and punches Rowan in the solar plexus. Rowan would make two of Uzi, but caught unawares, goes down like a ninepin.

Uzi glares at me triumphantly. Over the unearthly howling of the cats, I hear Antoine and Benedict, behind me, shouting to Meg as they try to beat out the flames. There's no answer, just the hissing sound of the water they're throwing on the fire.

Blood's gushing down my neck, soaking my clothes and making me weak and dizzy. I can't let it deflect me. I may be an old woman, but I'm Ella's granddaughter and I'm no pushover. With the last of my strength I shove Uzi aside, hard and fast. Taken by surprise she loses her balance and falls backwards over Gerry's old trunk. Pulling the door open, I step to one side.

'Clear out of the way,' I shout at the others. 'Get to the side.'

'No,' screams Uzi, from where she still lies, crouched on the floor. 'I wanted you to be free.' Her face looks crazed in the flickering firelight.

There's a rushing sound from the corridor outside, accompanied by a forceful voice. 'My path is clear.'

Uzi struggles to her feet and throws herself at the door to close it. With lightning speed Rowan leaps toward her in what looks to me like a football tackle (rugby, I later learn), pinning her to the ground. The door stays open and the rushing sound gets louder. I'm feeling weaker, now, and I'm only just able to register the strong smell of chlorine, as the water pours in through the doorway, towards the flames.

Explosions of darkness dance before my eyes, I feel myself falling and everything goes black.

CHAPTER 37

A DIFFERENT LIGHT

I open my eyes to the bright overhead lights of a hospital ward. There's a smell of disinfectant and anxiety.

Someone is holding my hand.

A face. Antoine's face. Tired and strained.

'What? Where?' I mumble.

He squeezes my hand. 'You're safe now, Mogs,' he says.

DR WOOD'S DIARY

27 JUNE 1907

11am

Another dreadful event has occurred. It has plunged me into the deepest gloom.

Not a week after Ella's fatal accident, comes the terrible news of Lucy's death. Her poor body was found yesterday in Abney Park chapel, where she had fallen from the balcony.

She was to be married in just a few days' time.

How can this have happened? Lucy's accident appears to have occurred on the day she left my care. The day Ella died. It breaks my heart to know that she lay there all alone for those five long days. So near. I had believed I was discharging her into the care of her family, where she would stay until her marriage. Homeward had the same understanding. Her family, however, thought she was staying with Lady Barnum.

Today the police discovered that on leaving here, Lucy took a cab to an hotel. Here she booked a room for one night. Later, another cab driver then brought her to the gates of Abney Park, where he was told to wait for her return.

After that, no one knows what happened, or why she would travel back here to visit the cemetery. The police view it as an accident and as the coroner is likely to take the same view, there will be no further investigation.

It is conceivable that a young lady about to be married might stay in London for a night. She might wish to order her trousseau. Yet, to do so alone is improper for a woman and Lucy was always so careful of her behaviour.

I am struggling to come to terms with this terrible loss. In truth I am desolate. I can neither eat nor sleep and worked all through the night.

Work is my only solace now.

Ella's death was a blow, to me personally, as well as to my asylum and its reputation. She was an uncommon woman, and I liked and respected her candid personality. She worked hard at her recovery and I still do not understand how she came to die in such a way.

Lucy's death opens a new dimension of horror and grief. I now realise how much I looked forward to treating her in the future, despite her new status as Homeward's wife. How I envied Homeward his prize, a scant a few days ago. Now he must be a broken man. He has my sincere pity; we will mourn together.

Can it be a coincidence that Lucy and Ella both fell to their deaths on the same day? At or near my asylum? Surely it cannot have been a suicide pact? Melancholia was not part of the symptom pattern for either patient. They were both enthusiastic about the lives that lay ahead of them. Therefore it occurs to me that foul play should not be discounted.

Could someone have arranged to meet first Lucy, then Ella and murdered them both, in the same terrible manner? Yet I cannot think who would do this, or why.

4pm

Von Helson has uncovered something most unsettling. We are obliged to consider whether this is connected with Lucy's tragic death.

Our Telepathic Transfer Engine has been sabotaged. When Von Helson opened it today, for the first time since our last spirit writing session, he found that someone had taken a hammer to the workings and broken it up beyond repair. My dear friend himself is broken by this, as well as by the death of his sweet young medium.

We do not know when this damage occurred, only that it happened since the last time we used the Engine, a week ago. The day before Lucy and Ella died.

We must face the possibility that the Engine may have been a factor in Lucy's death. A less than friendly spirit may have entered her in our last session, the night before she left us. She was so permeable and open to ghostly invasion. It may have possessed her and caused her to do damage to herself.

Could it be that Lucy, possessed by some dread spirit, also destroyed the machine? It would not normally be within her capacity, but demons and madness lend strength to the frailest form.

I cannot raise any of these doubts with the police as I do not wish to have my staff, Von Helson or myself suspected, and I certainly do not want my asylum brought into disrepute. The minister of our church and the chair of the League for Psychic Studies have already contacted me. They have questions I shall have to answer about a possible connection between our work as Spiritual Machinists and these tragic deaths. I fear they may want to investigate our use of the Telepathic Transfer Engine.

Even if there is no connection between the Engine and these tragedies, I will have to discontinue this line of research.

I must preserve the good name of my asylum above everything.

CHAPTER 38

TRIPPING OUT

'For a while I was confused,' Uzi says. 'I cannot remember too much about it.'

It's a week since our night of fire and flood. Uzi collapsed and was admitted to hospital with me. She'd been through some kind of breakdown, the medics thought. Working too hard. They prescribed rest, a concept she's struggling with. Rowan's taken time off to help her with it.

Grandma Betty was hospitalised too. She lost a lot of blood from her neck wound and then hit her head when she passed out. No joke at her age; she could have died saving my life. She's back on her feet now and as forceful as ever, bossing me around. I guess I'll learn to put up with that.

Antoine was treated for the burns he got trying to reach me. What a hero. Neither of us are likely to be permanently scarred, partly because of the way Benedict was chucking water around, apparently.

Apart from poor Uzi, who's actually been through more than any of us, it seems like everyone tried to save my life. Even the cats tried to tell us something was wrong.

Once everyone thought me and Uzi were ready to talk about it all, they organised a meal at the Cat, after hours. Claudette and Terry were invited too.

'I have to admit,' I say, 'I don't understand why we didn't all get fried when the water came in. Like the prom scene in Carrie?'

Benedict chuckles. 'Literature teaches us much, but you have to understand it in context. That was the 1970's. Now electricity trips out – shuts down, that is – in the presence of water.'

Sometimes the breadth of Benedict's knowledge amazes me. I wouldn't have thought he even knew that tripping out was a thing. I'm sensing the benefit of David's practical expertise here.

'I almost killed you, Meg,' Uzi is sombre with the horror of what happened. 'I was like Carrie.'

'It wasn't you.' Rowan puts a hand on Uzi's shoulder. 'It was something working through you.'

'Possession,' says Betty. 'By Lucy's evil spirit.'

'Seriously?' Antoine looks sceptical.

'Can you think of another way to explain it?' Betty asks. 'Any of it?'

'We know the fire was down to a problem with the electrics, the investigation proved that,' Antoine says. 'Meg's surge protector made it worse, they think. That's why the lamp caught fire.'

'Wasn't one of mine,' Terry says. 'Sold out weeks before, they did. As the boys in blue will tell you.'

It remains a mystery where my dodgy surge protectors came from. Terry's records have been raked through by the police. They tried to work out whether my order had been hijacked by someone malign, but there was no evidence of that. We hadn't told the police that we thought Uzi had sent it when she'd been unhinged. How she knew where to get faulty electrical equipment was anyone's guess.

Uzi turns to me. 'I have no memory of sending those things to you, but I knew you had ordered them.'

We reassure Uzi that she's blameless. Whatever happened to her wasn't her fault, we tell her, she suffered a lot and we're glad she's recovering. We'd also realised that it must have been Uzi who'd wiped all the records from the shared drive a few weeks back, but we haven't mentioned that to her.

Uzi's still anxious that her talent might evaporate along with the return of normality; she produced some of her best work in her crazed state. We carefully don't mention that, either. She's looking better now, she's obviously sleeping and she's slowed down a bit.

'You've got to admit that the pool water putting out the fire can't be explained by natural causes,' Betty says to Antoine.

'Something structural went wrong,' Antoine says. 'A valve broke, the pool-filling sensor malfunctioned and the whole thing overflowed. That's what the report says. Freak accident.'

'Doesn't explain what actually caused the break and the malfunction,' Betty says. 'Or why it would happen just in time to save Meg. Big coincidence.'

Claudette leans towards her son. 'Sometimes great unhappiness or passion doesn't go away. Sometimes it sits, dormant, then comes alive when the time is right. For good or evil.'

Antoine just shakes his head. 'Monarch does everything on the cheap, so the building has construction flaws. Uzi's been working hard and had a breakdown that made her imagine she was possessed by Lucy.'

'Lucy was in direct contact with Uzi,' Rowan protests. 'Sending her messages. We've seen some of them.'

'Please,' Antoine scoffs. 'How would that even work?'

'Maybe through the Engine,' Betty says. 'Ella and Wood noticed Lucy was fascinated by electricity and by the Engine. She knew she could use it for her own ends. If she could affect the power in the building, maybe she could find her way into electronic devices.'

'Inscribe herself onto the Internet,' Benedict muses. 'Haunt the airwaves. H. G. Wells would certainly approve.'

Antoine looks exasperated. 'Look, I love the idea of the steampunk Engine as much as anyone; but this is reality, not fiction. Anyone could have sent those texts.'

'Lucy literally used phrases from Uzi's texts in the automatic writing,' Rowan insists. 'Plus she used what Uzi told her to blackmail Finleigh and Homeward. She was the Hungarian Countess Zana. Short for Ursana. Transylvania was part of Hungary in 1907.'

'Coincidence,' Antoine says.

'What about the old-fashioned phrases Uzi started using, then?' Rowan asks.

Antoine remains unconvinced. 'Costume drama. Blame the BBC.'

'I was not sure what was happening at the time,' Uzi says. 'She called herself FairyGirl and admired the artwork I posted. We got chatting. I thought she was my friend, she understood me so well.'

'She took everyone in that way,' Betty says. 'They were all smitten with her, even her psychoanalyst.'

'We became so close that I felt her with me all of the time,' Uzi continues. 'Now I know none of it was real and she was using me. To find out things so she could blackmail people and harm you.' She looked at me. 'Violet's descendant. She hated Violet, she was jealous of her. She wanted Ella all to herself. She made me hurt you, also, Betty, when you were protecting Meg.'

Betty puts her hand up to her neck. 'Ella's dragonfly brooch disappeared in the flood.'

'*That* is a mercy,' Claudette says.

Betty nods. 'It was always a cursed object.'

'So why didn't Lucy try to electrocute or immolate you?' Antoine asks Betty. 'Violet's daughter?'

'I was only there a few hours,' Betty says. 'I don't think she was as aware of me until I stood up to her. It was as though she was in the building. She became part of the fabric; so did Ella. As if they'd always been there, dormant, but Meg coming to stay brought them to life, like Claudette says: Lucy to harm her and Ella to protect her.'

'You're seriously telling me the building's haunted?'

'Your cats felt it too,' Betty says. 'Remember what they were like that night?'

'It is not haunted now,' Uzi says. 'They are gone.'

Antoine casts his eyes to heaven.

'Don't you ever feel that the past leaves traces of itself on buildings?' Rowan asks him. 'Like a memory?'

'Only in our heads,' Antoine says. 'Our own memories. And in the architecture and design. That's all.'

'It doesn't explain why such strange things happen in places like Abney Heights,' Rowan says. 'It's as if they're borderlands between one world and another. Sensitive people, like Uzi, are more likely to be affected by it.'

'Much as I'd love a haunted house exclusive, it sounds like you've all been ODing on the Horror Channel.'

'Don't knock it, son.' Terry says. 'Flourishing market nowadays, dark tourism. You could turn this to your advantage.'

Antoine groans. 'Come on, Meg, help me out here. Tell me you know you were saved by your grandmother, not your great-great-grandmother?'

'I spend my time chasing ghosts, Antoine,' I say. 'I don't expect to find them.'

EPILOGUE

1 JANUARY 2020

I'm back home in my tumbledown cottage now, trying to leave it all behind me. Pulling all this together has helped me learn something: once you've opened the archive it will never close again. You have to live with your dead.

And, hey, some aspects of that are good. I've gained a grandmother, a woman I really like, though naturally she drives me up the wall. She came back to Abney Heights for Christmas. Antoine cooked and I poured the drinks. Claudette, Terry, Benedict and David joined us. Rowan and Uzi video-called us from Romania and even Letitia swung by on Boxing Day. I've never had a big family Christmas like that before; it's a lot better than people make out.

I'm anxious about Grandma Betty. She's seventy-eight this year and I'm going to lose her, aren't I? In five years, statistically. So I shouldn't get too attached. Antoine says 'Christ, Meg, just make the most of her while she's still here; anyway, Betty'll live till she's a hundred.' Naturally he's not missed the opportunity to claim my life's turned out to be a Dickens novel after all. Only it's *Oliver Twist*, not *Great Expectations*.

I've made peace with Breda and the rest. They're good-hearted people, really, just different to me. They were genuinely concerned when I was in hospital. Breda even brought grapes. So I did a pre-Christmas visit to Southend after all and it was actually alright. Easier with Antoine there for moral support, of course, but then a lot of things are.

I'm even trying to pluck up the courage to contact my father. Betty was horrified when I told her what Kathleen did. She says he was married to her, so he'll understand more than I give him credit for. Especially as he left. He might actually be pleased to see me, have I thought of that?

I've come to terms with my grandad's trunk, too and brought it home with me. It doesn't have the same power any more, now I've gutted it of its secrets. It's just beautiful and sad.

So, plenty of good stuff's come out of it all. There's still a load of bad crap lodged in my head, though. That's not disappearing anytime soon; the nightmares are still vivid. It's like everything that's happened in the last few months has taken me apart and put me back together again, but the parts don't fit properly yet.

As for the others, well Rowan and Uzi swung by, when they came to Wales to celebrate the Winter Solstice, with Rowan's hippy friends. Benedict was delighted to see them, he and Rowan really get on; I suppose they've both got that spiritual thing going on, in different ways. Uzi's a lot better now, more relaxed than I've ever known her. She's started working again and her talent's still there, strong as ever. Stronger, even, so that's a relief. The two of them stayed with Rowan's folks and then went to Uzi's dad in Brasov for Christmas itself, so seems like they're more of a thing now.

Though what do I know about relationships?

Antoine's been to stay. A few weekends. He's here now, in

fact, but still asleep. He brought Mulder and Scully with him this time. Says they can board with me for a while, seeing as they've become my familiars. They seem to love it here. My witch's cottage makes Antoine laugh, but he likes it really. Well, he does keep tidying up and stuff, but I guess I'll get used to that.

Antoine's taken on Letitia to do some Saturday work for the paper. Local research. The articles about Lucy and Ella caused so much interest he's going to run more pieces on local history. Not just Victorian and Edwardian, but the fifties and sixties too. Maybe even as recent as the eighties, which seems like ancient history to Letitia, but five minutes ago to me. Antoine says long-term locals are interested because they want to feel that their past matters, and new Hackney dwellers want their area to have a colourful history. We all like to think that our buildings, streets and communities have a fascinating past. Letitia, herself, is on a mission. All this history, it's about real people, she says. People whose lives weren't always easy but who were interesting and did things that mattered. If she doesn't give them a voice, who will?

BENEDICT AND ROWAN both feel we should forgive Lucy. They say the childhood trauma she went through determined her fate; she was a victim before she became a vampire. Her world was so confined, and her choices so limited, it warped who she became. How can we possibly imagine what it was like for her? She really did love Ella deeply, if jealously, so we should have the generosity of spirit to forgive her for the terrible things she did.

Betty says Lucy was a sociopath who enabled paedophiles to exploit children. A massively convincing one too. No one suspected her in her own time, apart, perhaps, from Homeward, when he talked about her being corrupted. If she *had* got away with it, what sort of partner would someone like that have made for Ella?

Antoine pretty much agrees with her; says that Lucy was prepared to collude with horrendous cruelty and that nothing she did benefitted anyone but herself. She used everyone around her. Including Uzi, Betty observes. And Uzi is definitely not minded to let it go, no one haunts her and gets away with it.

I don't want to hold a grudge against the dead, and I know Lucy didn't become manipulative and evil by choice. Yet however damaged she was by her childhood, however harsh the world was for a gay Edwardian woman, she occupied a position of relative privilege and could have made different choices. Unlike Florrie and the others. So it's hard for me to forgive her; maybe my spirit's not generous enough. I'm not as good a person as Benedict or Rowan.

Lucy's gone now, Uzi says. Totally gone, not a glimmer or an undercurrent to be seen or felt. She doesn't feel so gone when I wake up from the nightmares, but that will pass. I know it will.

Naturally, Ella's still around. I still read my transcripts of her journal and think about her. How she wanted to escape to the freedom of Europe and how horribly her plan was destroyed. It seems more poignant in the last few weeks, since Europe escaped from us.

All the other dead darlings haven't gone away either. They still turn up in my troubling dreams. Florrie, Annie, all the little fairies and the lost boys. What happened to them? Did they ever understand what Lucy did? Were those men able to carry on their abuse, after Lucy left? Were the children's lives completely blighted by it, or did they survive to find some happiness? They crowd my sleep, jostling to tell me their stories.

Once the dead get their claws into you, there's no getting away. Ask Letitia.

BECAUSE ELLA never made it to Europe, Betty's hatched a plan she thinks will be therapeutic. We're all going there on Ella's behalf. I'm certainly hoping it will exorcise something inside me, make me feel I've done right by my great-great-grand-mother. Help me move on, past the nightmares, get some stability back.

Betty's booked a place just outside Paris for a week over Easter, then a villa by the Italian lakes. How fab is that? How generous? Ella's paying for it, Betty says, so to do her justice we need to enjoy it properly.

There's loads of space and everyone's invited, for however long they want to stay. We're all travelling there on the Eurostar together, in a modern, eco-friendly enactment of the journey Ella never made. Antoine's coming for the whole time and working remotely, like me. Uzi's looking forward to the Louvre and the Italian lakes, David to the grand continental gardens and Claudette to the French cuisine. Terry will be doing post-Brexit deals, Rowan will be making connections with the European eco-pagans and Benedict intends to spend the time reading and promenading, much like Ella.

We all know we enjoy a level of liberty Ella could only dream about. It's been a hard winter so we're looking forward to celebrating her memory in our spring escape; and no spectre of past evil can return to stop *us*.

A NOTE FROM THE AUTHOR

Hi there! You've reached the end of this book so I hope that means you enjoyed it. Thankyou for spending time in the world I've created to share with you.

If you enjoyed your time there, I'd love you to leave a review on Amazon or Goodreads. Reader reviews are hugely important to authors, as they're the best way for other readers to hear about our books.

Massive thanks if you take time to leave a review!

ALSO BY CAT THOMAS

SYNTHETIC

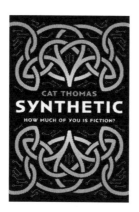

In 2071 Lona has two problems

Ancient Celtic tales are coming to life...

...and the Faith Police are framing her for murder.

Yet how much of it is real?

As Lona and her band of misfits struggle to find the killer, life begins to unravel. Virtual reality games invade their world; ghostly stories stalk them. To save her sanity and her life, Lona has to confront her troubled past; her friends have their own secrets to face.

In a world of religion and surveillance they must tread carefully in their quest to solve the crime, and prevent more mayhem.

Can they solve the mystery of the tales before something monstrous destroys them all?

Synthetic weaves a captivating blend of contemporary fantasy and cyberpunk, laced with dazzling dark humour.

ACKNOWLEDGMENTS

Stoke Newington's beautiful 'dissenters' cemetery', Abney Park, helped to inspire this story. Much appreciation to all the lovely people who work so hard to look after it, fund it and keep it open to the public. https://abneypark.org/

The De Morgan Centre is also a real place, although by 2019 it had moved from London to a new home at Cannon Hall in Barnsley. *The House of the Spirits* is entirely fictional but you can see plenty of other gorgeous works if you visit the collection. https://www.demorgan.org.uk/

Many thanks to my patient, clear-sighted and thorough editors, Scott Pack and Eleanor Abraham. Thanks also to everyone who read my previous work and whose interest and enthusiasm encouraged me during the long, long process of writing this book.

Most of all, thanks to Paul for his understanding, patience and support.

BIBLIOGRAPHY

Below are some of the texts which helped me imagine a technological past that never happened. Books about local history gave me a context and works on women, spiritualism and technology helped me to think about the many meanings of automatic writing.

In addition to the works below, extensive reading on women, psychoanalysis and mental health issues, past and present, helped me frame the context for some of the characters in the novel, and consider how they might be perceived by others.

Furthermore, the work of novelists such as H. G. Wells, E. M. Forster and Henry James gave me a sense of the social, intellectual and cultural world inhabited by some of my 1907 characters.

The De Morgan Centre *William and Evelyn De Morgan*. London: The De Morgan Centre.

Fara, P. (2002) *An entertainment for angels*. Cambridge: Icon Books.

Fara, P. (2005) *Fatal attraction*. Cambridge: Icon Books.

Geller, J. L. and Harris, M. (1994) *Women of the asylum*. New York: Doubleday

Hayles, N. K. (2005) *My mother was a computer: digital subjects and literary texts*. Chicago: University of Chicago Press.

Heffer, S. (2017) *The age of decadence: Britain 1880 to 1914*. London: Random House.

Holland, E. (2014) *Edwardian England: a guide to everyday life, 1900-1914*. London: Plum Bun.

Kittler, F. A. (1986) *Gramophone, film, typewriter*. Translated by Geoffrey Winthrop-Young and Michael Wutz. Stanford: Stanford University Press, 1999.

Kittler, F. A. (1997) *Literature, media information systems: essays*. Amsterdam: OPA.

Owen, A. (1989) *The darkened room*. University of Chicago Press: Chicago.

Rutherford, S. (2008) *The Victorian asylum*. Oxford: Shire

Smith, G. (1995) *Stoke Newington*. Stroud: History Press.

Smith, G. (2013) *Hackney: from Stamford Hill to Shoreditch*. Stroud: History Press.

Tromp, M. (2006) *Altered States*. New York: University of New York Press.

Thurschwell, P. (2001) *Literature, technology and magical thinking, 1880 –1920*. Cambridge: Cambridge University Press.

Watson, I. (2006) *Hackney and Stoke Newington past*. London: Historical Publications.

ABOUT THE AUTHOR

Cat Thomas writes spooky sci-fi, ghost stories and other twisted fiction. Her debut novel, *Synthetic*, was published in 2019.

Originally from South Wales, Cat lives in East London, UK.

You can keep up with her books and stories, and access exclusive pre-release materials and giveaways at: http://www.catthomas.org

You can also find Cat on Facebook at https://www.facebook.com/twistedfiction101, where she'd love to meet you.

A CIP catalogue record for this title is available from the British Library

ISBN 978-1-9160251-5-8

Gwillion Press

Cover design by Sarah Whittaker

.

Printed in Great Britain
by Amazon

12471653R00246